TO: DAVID

Happy READING!

Bye Jennie

12/29/2009

The Lost Spellweaver

Elfdreams of Parallan I

Ǿ ∞ Ǿ

Albträume

Benjamin Towe

authorHOUSE®

AuthorHouse™
1663 Liberty Drive
Bloomington, IN 47403
www.authorhouse.com
Phone: 1-800-839-8640

First published by AuthorHouse 9/28/2009

ISBN: 978-1-4490-2541-0 (e)
ISBN: 978-1-4490-2539-7 (sc)
ISBN: 978-1-4490-2540-3 (hc)

Library of Congress Control Number: 2009909288

Printed in the United States of America
Bloomington, Indiana

This book is printed on acid-free paper.

The thread of life...
Fates...
The Spinner spun the precious thread of life over her distaff.
The Allotter measured the length of the narrow thread with
a mysterious red rod. The Unturning, the inevitable for those
mortal, chose the manner of the individual's death and cut the
thin thread with her dreaded shears.

Wisps...
Threads...
Threads of Magick...
Threads of fate...
Threads of time...
Threads connecting worlds ...
Dreams connecting worlds ...
Dreams of Magick...
The Magick of Dreams...
Magick connecting dreams...
Magick connecting worlds...
Dream raiders...
Elf pressure...
Albtraum...
Albträume, elf dreams, nightmares...
Dreams...

TABLE OF CONTENTS

Ancient Parallan

Northern Warrens

Aulgmoor

Drith

River Ovnash

Gap Keep

Mirror Mountain

Foothills of Bone

Mirror Lake

Wild Woods

Green Vale

Meadowsweet

Red Meadow

Alms Glen

Lost Sons

Propinquity of Alms Glen

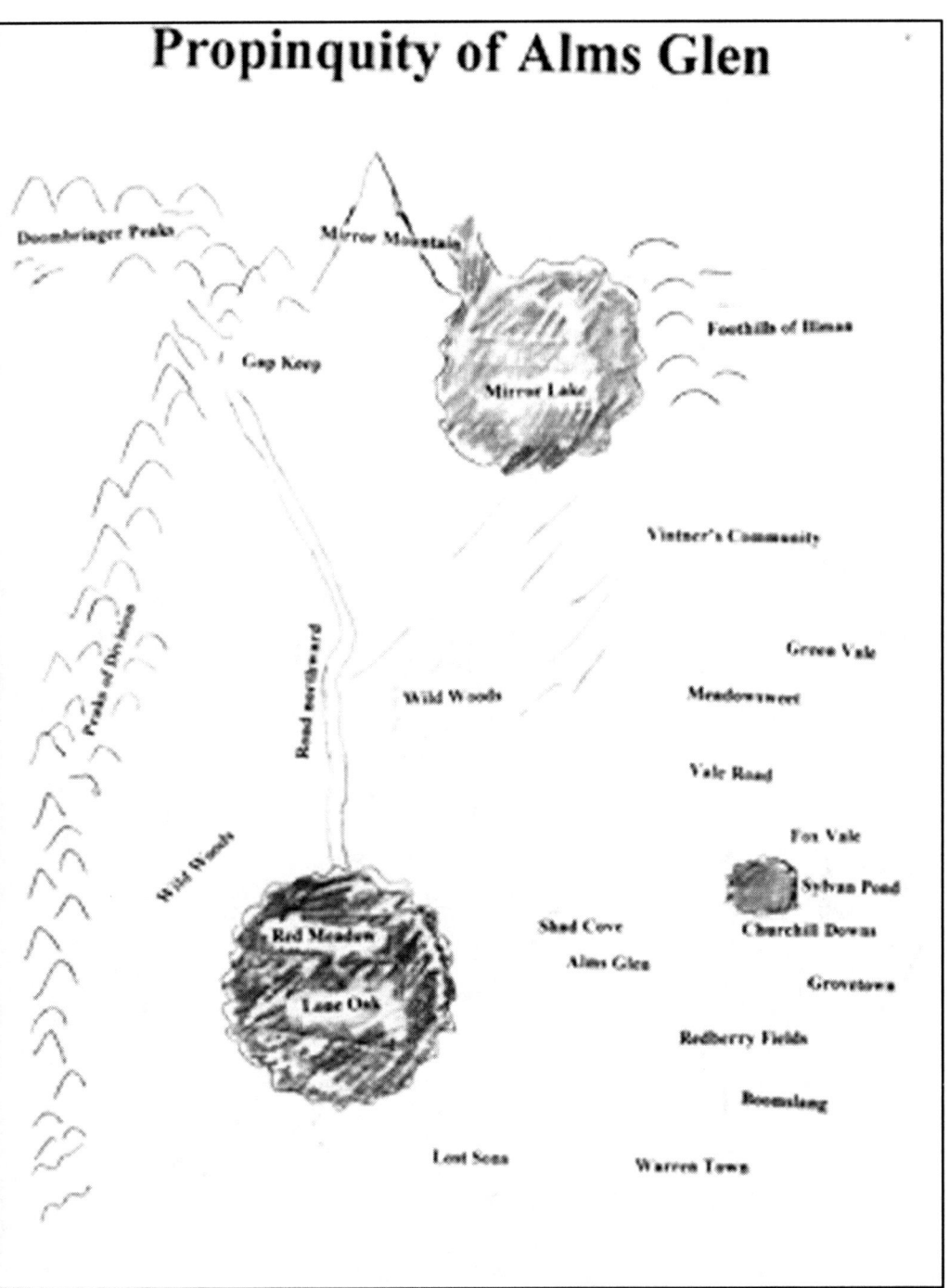

PROLOGUE

In the *far distant future...*

Heroes of Donothor vanquished the Red Mountain Giants and their allies in the Iron Mountains War. Odd green elfish beings allied with the giants, used strange wands, wielded wondrous weapons, and created weird and wonderful mysterious potions.

Three hundred years before the Iron Mountains War, disappearances and enchantments plagued Kanath and Tindal, the towns of the south in Donothor. Word reached the leaders of Donothor that a red-haired enchantress fomented the mischief, and they dispatched Ranger patrols from the citadel Lyndyn, the largest city of the land of Donothor and the center of government of the kingdom. The Rangers investigated but never found the perpetrator.

The episodes ended as mysteriously as they began.

Truth be known, the young Sorceress Chalar victimized a handsome young thief and received an unexpected gift from the tryst. The red-haired vixen realized she was with child, returned to her home Ylysis, and confided to Rymona, the kind Dark Elfish handmaiden who attended her mother Alluna.

"It's best we not trouble your father Morlecainen with these tidings," the handmaiden warned. "He laboriously searches for your mother Alluna. Instead, I'll lead you to Black Dragon's Horn under the ruse of studying the ways of the Dark Elves. King Cellexa of the Dark Elves will welcome you."

Knowing her father Morlecainen obsessed with the return of his life-mate, Chalar agreed and traveled to the Dark Elves' stronghold under the pretext of studying the ways of her maternal grandfather King Cellexa. Businda, her mother's twin sister, looked after the young Sorceress and kept Chalar's secret. Dark Elfish handmaidens cared for Chalar during her confinement and used their midwifery skills to bring little Ravenna into the world of Donothor. The beautiful child Ravenna had predominately elfish features, but her blazing red hair, unequaled powers of Magick, and remarkable slight of hand quickly differentiated Ravenna from other Dark Elfish toddlers.

The child's mother Chalar returned home to Ylysis. Evil dreams seduced and ultimately consumed Chalar.

Wisps...
Threads...
Threads of Magick...
Threads of fate...
Threads of time...
Threads connecting worlds ...
Dreams connecting worlds ...
Dreams of Magick...
The Magick of Dreams...
Magick connecting dreams...
Magick connecting worlds...
Dream raiders...
Elf pressure...
Albtraum...
Albträume, elf dreams, nightmares...
Dreams...

Businda raised Ravenna, who flourished under her aunt's love and affection. No one had the audacity to ask the child's lineage. Though Dark Elfish blood flowed through her veins, it was the blood of her maternal grandfather Morlecainen's people that endowed Ravenna with longevity.

Businda gave the child the family name Nocerre. The child's mother Chalar had etched the name on a parchment along with the phrase "charming and better looking than most."

Called the Sorcerer of the Lachinor, Morlecainen ultimately found and saved his life-mate Alluna from the clutches of the vengeful black dragon lord Xollos. Celebrating his greatest personal victory, the Sorcerer of the Lachinor returned to Ylysis, resumed his crusade for power, and embroiled the lands of the dwarves, gray elves, the Lachinor, and ultimately all of Donothor in great conflict. Many Dark Elves shared the fate of the Sorcerer of the Lachinor and fell, including Lexx the only son and chosen heir of Cellexa.

Heartbroken, King Cellexa floundered in his later years, and the leadership of the Dark Elves fell upon the stronger of his twin daughters Businda.

After succeeding her father, the queen of the Dark Elves returned to the policies of isolation and secrecy that had been characteristic of the reclusive swamp folk for so many generations. Under Businda's rule, the Dark Elves flourished, as did the small child.

Ravenna took to the wood, befriended the small creatures, and quickly revealed her talents, including the Magick of her mother Chalar and grandfather Morlecainen. The child also possessed her mysterious father's slight of hand. Capable of sneaking silently as a toddler, the child oft times evaded the watchful eyes of her caregivers.

One warm afternoon Queen Businda noted that her niece was missing and fumed, "Where is that child?"

"She is likely in the wood, my queen. She seeks the flowers and critters. Having learned more Magick, Ravenna adds bright colors to drab colored things. I saw a dead log given all the colors of the rainbow. She colors snakes yellow and makes the reptiles sing so they cannot surprise the mice and birds. Watching her is evermore challenging," the matron answered.

Businda walked dauntlessly into the wood and retrieved the child.

When Ravenna matured, the young sorceress expressed the strong desire to find out her lineage. The wise queen worried for the youngster's safety, but Queen Businda did not oppose her headstrong niece. Ravenna supplemented her command of Magick with a quick hand and an aptitude with the bow and sword. The bowyers of Black Dragon's Horn fashioned a self-bow beyond compare for the princess. Fletchers used feathers of the rare platinum cockerel as fletchings for her arrows. Though the Queen of the Dark Elves truthfully wanted to help Ravenna, Businda didn't know the identity of the child's father. The extent of the queen's knowledge was that "he wandered north" and bore the name "Nocerre."

So Ravenna Nocerre followed a trail that was twenty years old. Citing that her appearance mimicked the sorceress of old, elderly tavern patrons in Tindal and Kanath feared her approach. Noting the old codgers' fears, Ravenna carefully kept her command of Magick secret and safe. Little by little she picked up bits and pieces of information. Old patrons remembered a quick-fingered thief named Tigarn and a young red haired vixen. Stories from old victims of enchanting spells led Ravenna to the Fane of the Setting Sun where she had audience with the high priestess Knarra. The young elf wandered the lands without learning any more of the thief called Tigarn Nocerre.

Ravenna ultimately traveled to Lyndyn, became a valued member of the Rangers of Donothor, proved her valor repeatedly, and returned safely from many missions. Generations of Rangers served with her, aged, and went on to their forefathers, but Ravenna maintained her youth and vigor. In reality her longevity, red tresses, and skills of Magick derived from the same source.

Ravenna served loyally in the Iron Mountains War.

A hundred years after the war, reports again surfaced of the odd green elfish folk. Fearing more trouble, Kallenhahn Aivendar the King of Donothor dispatched Ravenna to investigate. Now Captain of the Rangers of Donothor, Ravenna followed clues into the dungeons of Red Mountain and disappeared.

Wisps...
Threads...
Threads of Magick...
Threads of fate...
Threads of time...
Threads connecting worlds ...
Dreams connecting worlds ...
Dreams of Magick...
The Magick of Dreams...
Magick connecting dreams...
Magick connecting worlds...
Dream raiders...
Elf pressure...
Albtraum...
Albträume, elf dreams, nightmares...

Centuries later...

The Wandmaker stood alone and stared at the slowing rotating central stone. The spherical six-foot diameter boulder dominated the chamber of the gray stones, where many generations of Wandmakers had practiced their rare craft. Eighty-eight identical smaller stones revolved around the massive gray stone. The fourscore and eight smaller stones moved at precisely the same speed in counterclockwise orbits in the same plane. Each small stone was 1/88th the size of the large central stone. Some indistinguishable gray rocks shared orbital paths. Nearest the central stone, one small stone revolved in an orbit with twice the diameter of the central stone. Another single stone coursed through an orbit of thrice the diameter of the big stone. Next two stones circled in an orbit four times the diameter of the central stone. The pair maintained the same speed and kept a constant separation. Then three stones coursed through an orbit five times the diameter of the big rock. Then five stones circled at an orbit of six diameters. Eight stones circled at seven diameters. Thirteen flew around the inner stone at eight diameters. Twenty-one circled at nine diameters.

Finally thirty-four circled at ten diameters. Thus the outermost of the small stones circled at a constant speed in an orbit of thirty feet radius. Individual stones maintained a constant distance from the central stone and those that shared its orbit. The furthest stones were twenty-seven feet away from the central stone. The big stone maintained a position precisely in the center of the chamber. It sat above the floor so that its center was thirty-four feet above the floor. This allowed the little stones to maintain their orbits without striking the floor.

The eighty-nine stones bore identical symbols.

$$\acute{\text{Ø}} \propto \acute{\text{Ø}}$$

The symbols weren't engraved. They were more part of the stones. The Wandmaker Cringal noted the runes on the stones emitted their customary grayness. Cringal had worked in the chamber of the stones for many seasons. The eighty-nine stones had never changed.

Until now…

The Central Gray Stone ominously left its central location and eerily wobbled downward and approached the lone figure in the chamber. The small stones froze in position. The symbols and grayness faded from the little stones. The Central Stone's grayness also faded as it neared. Though faint, the symbols remained.

Instinct told the Wandmaker to flee, but he felt his feet were fixed to the floor. Cringal could not run away. Chills coursed down his spine. The chamber became hot, and then cold, and the Magickman labored to breathe. The six-foot diameter sphere stopped precisely three feet from his face. The faint symbols disappeared and an image formed in the usually smooth gray surface of the slowly rotating sphere. Though he wanted to close his eyes, Cringal could not turn his gaze from the horrific face that filled the surface of the sphere.

A fell voice rose from the image and permeated the air, "The time has come today. You must repay the debt of your forebears. You're indebted for the first wand. The fading of the central stone and activation of this dweomer mean I am vanquished. If we are having this conversation, the implausible has happened. If I have diminished, you will diminish. Your people will suffer and eventually perish. You can restore the Magick of the sphere and the greatness of your people. You must take the treasured Central Stone to the surface world when the gray sun draws nearest. The gray light will restore its power… and your power to create. You cannot restore *me*, but you can continue my *line*! Carry my seed to the light of the gray sun Andreas!"

Why did this befall him?

This night Criss Cringal despised the title Wandmaker and regretted having the power to create the wands carried by the Vydaelians.

The image in the sphere changed…to the face of the Wandmaker Noelle who preceded him. With each passing belabored heartbeat, the current Wandmaker saw the image change to reveal another face of earlier Wandmakers.

All-in-all ninety-nine generations of Wandmakers had preceded Criss Cringal. Ninety-nine images passed before Cringal's eyes. He had just seen their faces and looked upon the history of Vydaelia. Many like Criss Cringal had merely done their jobs.

Drenched with sweat, Criss Cringal awakened from the dream. The Wandmaker realized he remained in the sanctuary of his warm bed. He leapt from his divan, slipped on his yellow robe, and rushed to his workroom, the chamber that contained the stones. As always the gray central sphere radiated the strong gray lights. The eighty-eight smaller stones obediently circled the central rock. Just as his predecessors had done, Cringal slumped onto the workbench.

Bereft of sleep, he would rest no more this night. From this time forward, dreams troubled Criss Cringal.

For the ninety-ninth time, the Master of the Dreamraiders had delivered his message. For the 99th time, it was just a dream.

Long age, the first Wandmaker had stared into the sphere and saw only the reflection of his anguished face.

The first Wandmaker…

Wisps…
Threads…
Threads of Magick…
Threads of fate…
Threads of time…
Threads connecting worlds …
Dreams connecting worlds …
Dreams of Magick…
The Magick of Dreams…
Magick connecting dreams…
Magick connecting worlds…
Dream raiders…
Elf pressure…

Albtraum…
Albträume, elf dreams, nightmares…

Ages before the times of Ravenna Nocerre, the 1st Wandmaker, the 98th Wandmaker Noelle, and the 99th Wandmaker Criss Cringal…
In an ancient world of three suns…

Alfkors

Alfkors...the elf cross protected against malevolent elves.
Elves?
Dreamraiders?

CHAPTER 1
Gifts of Andreas to the People of the Forest

The Teacher Edkim breathed deeply and basked in the thick gray light. The wandering sun Andreas emitted the gray light, drew near the land, and now filled the usually amber skies. Edkim had been the spiritual leader of the Drelves for twenty-four years and at this moment witnessed his first Approximation of the wandering gray sun Andreas. Would Andreas this time grant his ilk the gift of a Spellweaver? The ultra rare purveyors of Magick were born only during these extraordinary times. Now the Teacher waited outside the stately red oak that was the home of life-mates Carinne and Glinne. Skilled Drelvish midwives attended Carinne, who was laden with child and confined. The Teacher waited and hoped.

Three very different suns gave light to Parallan, the world of the Drelves. Total darkness never covered the land. The little yellow sun Meries traversed the sky in sixteen hours. When Meries drew high in the sky, the little star bathed the World of the Three Suns with amber light, warmed the world, and gave imparted beautiful yellow and orange hues to the skies of Parallan. Rather than a round bright spot, the dark sun Orpheus was akin to a large dark unmoving spiraling defect in the sky. Giant Orpheus gave little light and controlled the movement of Meries. Andreas, the Gray Wanderer, appeared in the sky irregularly. Oft times Andreas came into view as a gray speck on the horizon. From time to time the wanderer left the skies altogether. Every now and then the gray sun wobbled a bit closer to the World of the Three Suns.

Eight-hour periods of waxing and waning amber light made up one cycle of Meries. The little yellow sun never left the horizon, but every sixty cycles Meries slunk down in the amber sky and lingered at its zenith for a time of fifteen cycles, or 240 hours. These nadirs of Meries's light were called dark periods. During the dark period the scant light that reached the World of the Three Suns derived mostly from great Orpheus with variable contribution from the Gray Wanderer. Thus the times of greatest light were called light periods, the lesser light were amber periods, and the cyclic extended periods of least illumination were called dark periods.

Some peoples used the arbitrary term "day" to describe one eight hour cycle of bright light and the term "night" to describe the eight hour amber periods. The terms day and night had little meaning during the 240 hour-long time of decreased illumination of the dark period. Most folk simply used the term dark period. But the time from the beginning of one dark period to the beginning of the next was consistently the equivalent of 75 cycles of Meries, or 1200 hours.

On the odd occasion the Gray Wanderer drew near Parallan. The Approximations of Andreas gave wondrous gifts to the fauna, flora, and folk of Parallan. During these totally unpredictable Approximations, the Gray Wanderer filled the sky, bathed the land with its deep gray light, and augmented the forces of Magick in the world.

Many peoples of Parallan celebrated the significant rituals of their given ilk during the dark periods. For instance the Drelves harvested the tubers of the enhancing plant only during the dark period. Vital to the Drelves, the enhancing plant's tubers matured in eight dark periods. Thus, a season of the harvest encompassed eight dark periods, and equaled the time of 600 cycles of Meries; 480 cycles of light and amber periods and the equivalent of 120 cycles of relative darkness. Drelves called the time between harvests a "season of the harvest" or a "year."

Drelves usually matured in fifteen to thirty *years* and chose life-mates when they found love. If blessed by good health and bountiful harvests of the disease fighting enhancing root, the forest folk lived to see hundreds of harvests. Teachers oft lived longer, and the ultra rare Spellweavers had uncommonly long lives.

Crossing a wandering monster or a voracious plant ended many lives prematurely in the World of the Three Suns. The Drelves were an uncommonly careful people and lost few of their numbers in such ways. The Drelves remained within the central forests of Parallan and never infringed on the territories of others. All the same, the forest folk's ancestral enemies the Drolls and Kiennites brought war to the forest people. Encountering a Droll's axe, Kiennite's bow, or shaman's spell shortened one's life very quickly.

"Teacher, it is time," Glinne's familiar voice called.

Edkim entered the great tree. Grayness bathed the small group gathered in the friendly confines of the great red oak. Typical of Approximations of the Gray Sun Andreas, the giant gray ball hovered near the World of the Three Suns and blocked out the light of Meries and the black giant sun Orpheus. Amber gave way to gray. Ordinary gave way to Magick.

The Teacher Edkim had presided at the ceremony of lifetime commitment that united the young Drelves Carinne and Glinne several harvesting seasons earlier. Now he was present at Carinne's time of confinement. Blessed with natural beauty, Drelvish females were more lovely and radiant when they were with child.

The light of the gray sun had concentrated on the great tree where the young couple resided. In times past, the dense cone of gray light had indicated the most blessed of occurrences for the Drelves, the birth of a Spellweaver.

The grayness of the Approximation of Andreas produced the darkest times on the lands, but also awakened forces of Magick.

You saw just about everything.

For the most part, little amusements occurred, but the gray light of Andreas transformed the World of the Three Suns and heightened Magick. Songbirds changed their tunes. Hummingbirds knew the words and sang phrases. Rocks radiated auras. Elephants flew. Other than the times of Approximations, Magick was limited to the varied spells of Drelvish Spellweavers and the lesser dweomers of shamans of the goblin-like Kiennites.

Spellweavers were always born during the times of Approximation, but the birth of a Spellweaver was the exception instead of the rule. Most Approximations passed without the birth of a Spellweaver. On the other hand, every Kiennish offspring born during the time of the gray light had the limited powers of a shaman.

Young for a Teacher, Edkim had seen a hundred harvests of the enhancing root. Drelves typically described longevity in terms of harvests of the precious plant's tubers. The tubers matured in eight dark periods. Some Teachers lived their entire lives without witnessing a single time of the gray light. Ten generations of Teachers might pass between births of Spellweavers.

Was this was one of those rare times?

Newborn Drelves were called sprouts. The exceptional midwifery skills of the Drelve matrons brought sprouts into the World of the Three Suns. Two new voices rang through the long *hollowed* and now *hallowed* base of the great red oak home of Glinne and Carinne. Witnesses beheld the gray light concentrating on the two sprouts.

Auras danced upon every item within the dwelling, and all within sensed a great wave on the usually tranquil sea of Magick. Though most Drelves were unable to cast spells, Magick touched the forest people, and they usually detected its presence.

Carinne and Glinne had anticipated one child and chosen the name Gaelyss. Each looked at the other with bewilderment. The appearance of the gray light, the arrival of Edkim, three midwives, and a contingent of elders of Alms Glen had made the long awaited arrival of their first born even more of an affair to remember. Now two babes arrived. The second son was given the name Yannuvia.

Both sprouts were robust and healthy. Edkim joined the elders and the gathered community in the common area of Alms Glen.

The Teacher began, "The long wait is over. We are given Spellweavers."

"You…you said *Spellweavers*. What…?" the elder Blanchard queried.

"Yes. Spellweavers. Carinne and Glinne have two sons. The gray light is strong upon both. Two copies of the ancient spell book appeared," Edkim, replied.

"Two copies…two copies of *the Gifts of Andreas to the People of the Forest*! Has this ever happened?" the elder continued.

"Neither in the recorded annals nor the tales we tell by the fires. The most recent copy of the ancient spell book replicates when a new Spellweaver is born. The three Teachers, who preceded me, never saw the book's replication. We have been so long without the embellishment of Magick. The gifts from the Wanderer are called Gaelyss and Yannuvia. The sprouts are very healthy," Edkim replied.

"Then we will accept them as gifts of the Gray Wanderer. The family needs rest. Everyone should return to his tree for a rest period. We must prepare a festival of celebration. Teacher, please prepare the enhancing root for the festivities. This is indeed a day for our people to remember and cherish," Blanchard said triumphantly.

The elder then led the group back to their trees.

Edkim tarried and looked toward the great red oak. Brilliant flashes of silver intermingled with the deep gray light, which danced around the massive trunk of the tree.

The Teacher sighed and thought, "All my life I've wanted the opportunity to receive and teach a Spellweaver. What a boon this can be for my people! Two Spellweavers! But am I capable of teaching them? How does one teach someone who has so much more potential power and ability? How?"

Drelvish rangers carried word of the event far and wide. All Drelvedom celebrated the births of the Spellweavers.

Edkim quickly realized Gaelyss and Yannuvia were gifted and possessed power of Magick. The sprouts grew into nymphs. Nymphs were Drelves who had lived through two to five seasons of the harvest. Nymph hood described this time of life. From nymphs, Drelvish children grew into Drelvlings. Drelvling described young Drelves between five and thirteen years old. Neophyte described a Drelvling or adult Drelve who had not actually harvested the tubers from the roots of the enhancing plant. *Chosen* was a term reserved for thirteen-year-old Drelves selected to accompany the Teacher to the hamlet of Meadowsweet and the treasured Green Vale to harvest the enhancing root tubers. Most referred to the tubers taken from the roots of the enhancing plant simply as *enhancing root*. While sprouts and nymphs, all Drelvish spawn stayed in close contact with their mothers and fathers. Gradually as Drelvlings grew into older childhood, the young forest folk spent more time with the Teacher and less with their parents.

Spellweavers differed.

Learning about all aspects of Drelvedom was paramount to the ultra rare Spellweavers. The parents of young Spellweavers parted with their children more quickly.

As soon as Gaelyss and Yannuvia were weaned, walked, and entered nymph hood, the twins spent more time with the Teacher than Drelvlings of the same age. When the twins began to spend more time with the Teacher and elders, Carinne and Glinne returned to their very important roles.

The Spellweavers' mother Carinne, an exceptional purveyor of balms and potions, worked with her peers and taught her trade to Drelvlings. She led an annual trek to a very secure fertile region of the Drelvish lands, a place called Sylvan Pond. An accomplished archer, the ranger Glinne worked with the renowned Drelvish bowyer BJ Aires and served in the defenses of Alms Glen.

Gaelyss and Yannuvia grew into Drelvlings during the time of relative peace. Even as nymphs, the brothers engaged in playful competition. Gaelyss changed flower petals to red, and Yannuvia changed them to violet. Gaelyss made grass grow; Yannuvia shortened the stems. Gaelyss stuck strictly to rules and the middle of the road; Yannuvia experimented and strayed as far to the side as he could without straying off the path. Both learned quickly and performed all tasks asked of them. The Teacher Edkim supervised play and learning, and the older Drelves secured the area around Alms Glen.

At the beginning of the twins seventh year, the Teacher Edkim called them to the Old Orange Spruce.

"It is time," the Teacher began.

Edkim reached into his ever-present rucksack and removed a text. He then removed another. The identical books bore runes written in the Old Drelvish language of the annals. Both books were titled *The Gifts of Andreas to the People of the Forest*. The Teacher placed one book in Gaelyss's hands and the second in Yannuvia's hands. When he placed the books in the Spellweavers' hands the book's leathery covers changed. Odd additional runes appeared on the covers of the tomes. Gaelyss and Yannuvia stared at the books they held.

The Gifts of Andreas to the People of the Forest
ΛΑΡΛΣ
A&Ω

"What? What does it say, Teacher?" Gaelyss asked.

"Please, Teacher, what do the phrases mean?" Yannuvia added.

"I haven't seen such writing. But then again I've never seen copies of our precious tome in the hands of Spellweavers. I've held a copy of the tome since I became Teacher. It's to be presented to Spellweavers as soon as they can use it. In your cases, two copies have appeared. I find no instances of twin Spellweavers in our histories, though there have been times of multiple Spellweavers. Don't *you* understand the runes?" Edkim asked.

Finding it odd that the Teacher didn't have an answer, Gaelyss replied, "No, Teacher. I don't know what it means. Will you teach me the spells of the tome?"

Yannuvia added, "I don't understand the writings, Teacher."

"I am not a Spellweaver. I cannot interpret the tome. I'm afraid you're on your own, my young friend. I can only assist you in the general knowledge of our ilk and the World of the Three Suns. You must study the tomes. Each will become a legacy of its Spellweaver. From this moment your spell books are unique. Beyond what I've told you, I can only say study the text thoroughly," Edkim, answered.

The youths took the Teacher at his word. Aided by *the Gifts of Andreas to the People of the Forests*, the young Spellweavers learned spells such as Entangle and Plant Growth. The spells reinforced the protection the everred forests gave Alms Glen.

Like Teachers before him, Edkim encouraged strength through study and training and safety by isolation from enemies in the sanctuary of the forest. Thick unforgiving dense forests surrounded Alms Glen to the northeast, south, and east (if a compass were available). These primeval forests gave natural protection to the Drelves. Walkabout bushes, orange Triffids, pyrocanthas, and Tree Herders roamed these forests and preyed on Drolls, Kiennites, and unwary Drelves.

A broad meadow of brilliant red permagrass separated the forest around Alm's Glen from the wild game infested forest to what would be the west and northwest. Only one tree, the ancient Lone Oak, lived among the red grass and lent its name to the meadow. Unique to the Lone Oak Meadow, the red permagrass remained the same from season to season. The height of the blades never changed. Nature or Magick replaced individual destroyed blades. Streams and rivers cut through the wild woods. One such stream flowed from Mirror Lake northeast of Alms Glen, and created the legendary Alluring Falls, and emptied into the underground realms of the deep caverns beneath the Peaks of Division and the Doombringer Peaks. Most rivers and streams continued to the great western and eastern seas. All manner of beasts filled the inhospitable areas.

The smooth red meadow provided a clear view to the Drelvish sentries stationed in the trees at the periphery of the Alm's Glen forest. Many generations of Drelves had sat in their perches watching for their enemies, the Drolls and Kiennites or a rampaging beast such as a flying wyvern emerging from the wild forest.

The great Lone Oak was old, but not in comparison to the age of the world. Unlike the masterful red oaks, which often were homes to Drelves, tree sprites, wood nymphs, huldra, dryads, hamadryads, silkies, wood trolls, and a myriad of other fanciful beings, the Lone Oak was only a masterful tree. Even during the time of Magick, the Approximation of the Gray Sun, the lofty tree could not uproot and move about like the tree herders, red triffids, and walkabout bushes. Situated precisely in the center of the red meadow, the Lone Oak was a revered landmark. The solitary tree was easily visible from all areas of the wide meadow. The circular meadow of the Lone Oak had a circumference equal to 6765 Yardley paces.

Enos Yardley was a Drelve who had the uncanny ability to take a step of unvarying length. Of course, this was true only during the Approximations of Andreas. During one such Approximation, the Drelve Yardley stepped out the circumference of the meadow. One of Yardley's paces was exactly equal to 36 inchworms placed end to end. The inchworms were common to many worlds. Their length was arbitrarily called an *inch*. One of Yardley's paces was arbitrarily called a *yard*. Someone had the idea to call 1597 of his paces a *mile*. Unlike Magick, Nature allowed measurement.

The great Lone Oak had leaves of yellow, orange, red, and violet color. The tree's height was 89 yards. The circumference of its trunk was 89 yards. The tree had 89 branches with 89 leaves on each branch. The Lone Oak had always been this size. Legends held the great tree simply appeared during an ancient Approximation of the Gray Sun. Supposedly the leaves of the great tree bore Magick. Likewise picking the leaves cursed the harvester. Folklore told of many other consequences of violating the hallowed icon. As a result the folk of the World of the Three Suns respected and left the great tree unbothered. If one found a leaf on the ground, lore held it was free for the taking and gave the power to restore life. But no one had ever found a leaf lying on the ground and tested the folklore. These were stories told to induce children to sleep. Some scholarly types reasoned the old tree was just that, an old tree. Many trees in the Drelves' forest had unchanging dimensions. Many trees replaced their leaves as they fell. The seasons did not change is this part of the world. Everything under the amber skies remained red, orange, and yellow. Trees walked, talked, ate, slept, laughed, and cried.

The ancient enemies of the Drelves, the Drolls and Kiennites occasionally loosely allied and made forays of aggression into the forest. For generations, the well-placed bowshots of the Drelve archers, the natural defenses of the forest, and the enemies' fear of Spellweavers' Magick had kept the Drolls and Kiennites at bay. Stories of Drelves' Spellweavers bred Elfdreams, or nightmares for Drolls and Kiennites. The Lone Oak Meadow provided a buffer for the Drelve defenders. Even in the dark period, it was impossible for their enemies to approach the edge of the Alm's Glen forest unnoticed. Large red oaks, thick underbrush, and orange triffids composed the edge of the Alm's Glen forest. The ambulatory rather small triffids were beneficial tree herders who groomed the forest and attended their brethren. Triffids seldom grew taller then the height of three Drelves, about five Yardley paces. Rarely other tree herders wandered into the area and served a tour of guarding the forest.

Two tree herders called the area around the Lone Oak home. Drelves treasured the friendship of the venerable Old Yellow and the younger Loyce Vanoy. Old Yellow bore only yellow leaves. Tree herders normally didn't give up their names, but Loyce foolishly engaged in a game of chance with a crafty old Drelve named Clarke Maceda, lost the gamble, and gave up his name.

The denizens of the woods aided the Drelve defenders. Unfortunately any Drelve that chose to leave the sanctuary of the Alms Glen forest exposed himself to the openness of the red meadow and the dangers of the wild woods across the way. Drelves rarely undertook tasks such as Enos Yardley's pacing the perimeter of the meadow unless bathed by the gray light of an Approximation, supported by numbers, or accompanied by a Spellweaver.

Now the puerile Spellweavers assisted in the defenses by casting defensive spells such as Auras, Protection from Normal Missiles, Ensnare, Plant Growth, Entangle, Animal Friendship, Fairie Fire, Purify Water, and Speak with Animals. As neophytes, Spellweavers were limited to low level Magick. Also, the abilities of Spellweavers varied; that is, some were more gifted than others. Both Gaelyss and Yannuvia were clearly gifted and developed the unusual ability to cast the powerful Wall of Thorns Spell.

In the annals or written histories of Drelvedom, an ancient writer surmised that throughout worlds of Magick, level defined the power of a given spell and also referred to the relative power of a spell caster, such as a first level wizard casting a first level spell or a twentieth level wizard casting a seventh level spell. Of course a twentieth level sorcerer could cast a first level spell if he so desired. All Drelve Spellweavers cast first level spells. Some never advanced beyond this capability. This was an arbitrary definition, a matter of semantics. It was, after all, Magick. *At this point in time* no Drelve had ever been to another world, so it was also supposition.

Likewise, the annals supposed creatures such as wyverns, Baxcats, lee cats, Leicats, griffons, griffins, griphins, gryphons, hamadryads, humming birds, pi rannas, leprechauns, Manticores, medusas, dragons of various colors, nagas, troglodytes, Pegasi of various colors, satyrs, dryads, Minotaurs, pixies, sasquatch, trolls, wyrms, wyverns, sirens, huldra, chimeras, sphinxes, banshee, boogie men, bogeymen, brownies, centaurs, hippogriffs, Dobies, Efreet, fauns, fawns, foans, sprites, adherers, shape changers, doppelgangers, and other fanciful ilk evolved similarly under the influence of Magick.

Again it was supposition.

The annals remarked that ordinary folk like Drelves, Kiennites, Drolls, ogres, giants, and perhaps even Menders were unique to the World of the Three Suns. These were things academicians discussed by their fires and in their studies. Common folk spent too much time working and scratching out an existence to consider such things. People considered such things when the Gray Sun drew near and Magick flourished.

As the wise elder Blanchard had said, "It would be difficult to imagine a world without Magick."

But for the Teacher Edkim, Blanchard was the smartest Drelve in the forest, at least in the thinking of Yannuvia. Elder of the largest hamlet in Drelvedom Alms Glen, Blanchard had defied his parents and elders and explored much of the known world far beyond the central forests the Drelves called home. His eyes had beheld the Kiennites' stronghold Aulgmoor high in the Doombringer Mountains to what would be to the north, the wild woods across the wide Lone Oak meadow to the west, the impassible mountains and the wide plain below the Ornash River to the south, Mirror Lake and Mirror Mountain before the Peaks of Division in the center of the lands and roughly northeast of Alms Glen, and the lands and great forests beyond the largest hamlet in Drelvedom to the east.

For seven seasons of the enhancing plant, the puerile Spellweavers grew into Drelvlings in relative peace. Because the constant threat of random attacks by Drolls, Kiennites, or wandering monsters, experienced Drelve sentries called rangers, young Drelves gaining experience, and the tree herders Loyce Vanoy and Old Yellow kept vigil at the fringe of the forest.

Such duty was considered an honor. Young Drelves were not allowed to be at the edge of the wood until their tenth season. The elders felt it too dangerous.

Yannuvia and Gaelyss entered into friendly competition and honed their skills. The battles between the brothers generated no ill will, just friendly rivalry.

CHAPTER 2
Early Friendships

At an early age, Yannuvia befriended a she-Drelve named Kirrie, who was a season younger. Truth be known, Yannuvia shared more time with Kirrie than he did with his brother Gaelyss. Four other exceptional Drelvlings shared the birth season with Yannuvia and Gaelyss. Not Spellweavers, Meryt, Bryce, Zack, and Debery were thus a season older than Kirrie and often accompanied Gaelyss, Yannuvia, and Kirrie on formal schooling activities and informal tomfoolery as well.

Along with the Spellweavers, the four were chosen as neophytes. The older males resisted Kirrie's accompanying them at first, but Yannuvia spoke up for the season younger she-Drelve. Gaelyss spent more time alone, but sided with the four close friends Meryt, Bryce, Debery, and Zack more often than not. Yannuvia remained Kirrie's staunch advocate. Yannuvia could not convince his brother and four close friends to include the season younger male Drelvlings Zachary and Taylor in their affairs. Zack particularly disdained the accompaniment of his cousin Zachary. Yannuvia assumed it was the similarity of their names. It was really more of the second grade and first grade thing in school children of other lands. Being a season younger, Kirrie, Zachary, and Taylor would not go to Meadowsweet and the Green Vale with Yannuvia, Gaelyss, and the others. Only the most promising Drelvlings of each season became *Chosen* and made the trip with the Teacher to harvest the enhancing plant tubers from the Green Vale.

It was a mixed honor, for the trip was dangerous.

Gaelyss and Kirrie became steadfast friends. Oft times the two youngsters explored together and fomented children's mischief. Having heard the adults speak of the beauty and mastery of the Lone Oak, the pair formulated a plan to see the great tree firsthand.

"Won't we get into trouble, Yannuvia?" Kirrie asked plaintively.

"We won't, as long as we don't get caught. I found a big piece of Invisimoss and some gray berries in the Teacher's basket. He used them to lecture to the older class. Vioss and Bystar told me of them," Yannuvia answered.

"Vioss and Bystar are so much older. They will be going to Meadowsweet and the Green Vale this season, will they not? They always get us in trouble.

The Teacher Edkim will be angry. What if we lose the items? Invisimoss is hard to find," Kirrie murmured.

"We'll put it back. He'll never know. We'll only use two of the gray berries. Besides, I know where some grow," Yannuvia replied.

"Yuck! The gray berries are disgusting. Do we have to use them?" Kirrie continued.

Yannuvia replied, "The strong scent of the gray berries disguises our scent, and the invisimoss enables us to walk undetected to the fringe of the forest. Don't you want to see the Lone Oak?"

"Yes, of course I do. It's just…won't it be dangerous?" she implored.

"I'll look after you," Yannuvia promised.

Kirrie acquiesced. Yannuvia took the gray berries, popped the skin on each of the thumbnail sized fruits, and rubbed the juice on Kirrie and then himself. The smell overwhelmed their senses initially. The young Spellweaver then threw the sheet of invisimoss over his shoulder, placed his arm around Kirrie, and held her close.

"I can still see you," Kirrie exclaimed.

"Of course you can. You're inside the moss," Yannuvia explained.

"Oh. The moss does feel good. It's soft and warm," Kirrie said as she snuggled closer to Yannuvia.

The Drelvlings sneaked along the pathway. The light period continued. They avoided passing near Drelves they saw working at various tasks. Folk they passed turned up their noses and sniffed the air. Gray berries gave the scent of a skulunk passing a distance away. Skulunks were not Magick. They just smelled bad. Kirrie's legs grew tired after they walked a ways, so Yannuvia stopped at the base of a large everyellow tree. The pair rested and munched on some delicious trail mix. The lingering odor of the gray berries depressed their appetites a bit, but the trail mix still was good. After a respite they continued onward.

"Quick, get off the trail. Someone's coming!" Yannuvia whispered. The little Drelves slunk to the side of the path and sat beneath a bramble bush.

A Drelvish ranger walked near them, stopped for a moment, sniffed, and looked all around. Alas! It was Rumsie! He was the most astute of all the Drelvish rangers! Kirrie gasped when he looked right toward them, but after a moment the Sergeant Major of the sentries of Alms Glen shook his head briefly and proceeded along the way.

As he walked away the Drelvlings noted Sergeant Major Rumsie murmured, "A Baxcat or skulunk must be nearby."

Relieved they had not been discovered, the Spellweaver and his companion stood and continued on their way.

Kirrie whispered nervously, "Do we really smell as bad as a Baxcat? My father says the little cats hunt in tandem with a larger cat called a Leicat. The little Baxcat disguises their scents and irritates prey's eyes with its foul smelling spray and the big Leicat does the dirty work. Or is it the other way around? Do you think any such beats tarry nearby?"

"No. I thought Leicats were the ones that smelled bad. At any rate, if they were near, they'd flee us. We smell too bad to eat," Yannuvia replied.

By the end of the light period they reached the edge of the forest. Massive everreds served as watch points for the Drelvish sentries. Edging through the underbrush, Yannuvia and Kirrie gazed out onto the magnificent expanse of red grass called the red meadow.

The stately Lone Oak sat squarely in the middle of the red meadow. The tree stood the height of 89 paces of Enos Yardley. Its height was 3.14 times greater than its diameter. The great tree had 89 evenly distributed branches with likewise uniformly dispersed yellow, orange, red, and violet leaves on each bough. Generations of Drelves reported the Lone Oak never changed.

"Legend says the leaves of the great tree bear Magick, but more legends tell of horrific consequences of picking the leaves. If one finds a leaf on the ground, lore says it's free for the taking and gives the power to restore life. But no one has ever found a leaf lying on the ground, so the folklore has never been tested. I see no leaves on the ground, but the tree is so far away. It would be nice to have a looking glass. Do you have a "toot and see scroll" Kirrie?"

"No, but I want one. I've asked for one as a gift," the she-Drelve answered.

"Don't we all. The Lone Oak's surely as beautiful as we've been told," Yannuvia answered.

Invisimoss shielded them from the keen eyes of the sentries, and the gray berries disguised their essence form the guards' keen noses. Inspired by the sight of the massive tree in the center of the meadow surrounded by the expanse of brilliant red grass, Yannuvia started to sing a jingle he had written for his little friend. The Drelvlings' plan worked well until young Yannuvia started singing.

The sentries were not deaf.

The guards heard the little Spellweaver's off key notes and found the youths. An austere older Drelve named Clarke led them back to Alms Glen and the Teacher. Both accepted their punishment, a period of cleaning mud from the fine footwear of the rangers after the next storm. The adventure and sharing the punishment only strengthened Kirrie and Yannuvia's friendship.

Walking back with Sergeant Major Rumsie to the everred trees at the edge of the forest to resume his watch, old Clarke fumed, "Risky behavior! The little blighters should be spanked!"

Sergeant Major Rumsie replied, "Yes, they do. So did I."

"You did such, Rumsie!" Clarke exclaimed.

"Of course I did. That piece of invisimoss has been around a long time. The Teachers leave it in sight purposefully. I saw the Lone Oak when I was seven, and I cleaned boots for a period," Rumsie confessed.

"I'll be darned, so did I," Clarke laughed.

The Drelve defenders returned to the red meadow.

CHAPTER 3
Old Yellow

Rain...

The Drelves enjoyed every drop that fell from the golden clouds that filled the amber skies of the World of the Three Suns. Life giving waters revitalized the forests. Rain also brought mud, and mud stuck to the boots of the rangers or sentries that guarded Drelvedom and Alms Glen.

Mud meant Yannuvia and Kirrie had a date with a hundred pair of muddy boots. Taking her hand, Yannuvia led Kirrie past the taunts of his brother Gaelyss and their four friends Meryt, Zack, Debery, and Bryce. Soon they reached the simple tent where the sentries had left their footwear. The Teacher Edkim sat on a stump.

"Hello, Spellweaver. Hello, Kirrie. Are you ready to serve your punishment?" the Teacher asked.

"Yes, Teacher," the pair answered in unison.

"You know you must clean each shoe individually. The footwear is important to our guards. The material must be clean in order for the sentries to climb stealthily, silently, safely, and without harming our friends the red oaks and everreds that allow us to use them as perches to survey the field. The role of cleaning the shoes is an important one. In fact, it's a task that I usually perform alone," Edkim said.

"You clean the shoes Teacher! Are *you* being punished?" Kirrie asked with amazement.

"No, child. It's an important duty that I do willingly. I am going to share this duty with you this cycle of Meries," Edkim said.

"It should be our task to clean the boots, Teacher. You should go sit by the stream and smoke your briar pipe. We will clean every boot," Yannuvia promised.

"I'll help you. By the way, what have you learned?" the Teacher asked.

"We should follow the rules and do what the elders say. The rules are for our own good. That will keep us save," Kirrie answered.

"And you, Spellweaver?" Edkim continued.

"I learned you should take every precaution not to get caught, Teacher. I've learned Invisibility does not impart Silence. Gray berries smell bad, but they work. By the end of this day, I'll know how to clean boots," Yannuvia cleverly replied.

"Good answers. Let's clean some boots," the Teacher said enthusiastically.

While the rain pattered on the canvass about them, the threesome worked and soon had cleaned every boot.

As the amber period started, Kirrie and Yannuvia bade the Teacher adieu and headed back to the common area. The rain had stopped.

"Let's go to the stream. Perhaps a water sprite will be there and give us a surprise," Yannuvia suggested excitedly.

"Do you want to clean more boots? We should get home. With our luck it's more likely a tree sprite will drop an acorn on our heads. That hurts so much," Kirrie interjected.

"I have trail mix. It's a while until the rest time starts. Let's go," he beseeched.

"Why do I let you talk me into these things?" Kirrie moaned but took his hand, and they headed for the stream near the common area.

Both looked about for the friendly water sprite, but she was away. At least there had been no surprises from above. The Drelvlings sat by the brook and started to munch on the trail mix.

Suddenly Yannuvia realized they were not alone.

A voice entered their minds, "Little Spellweaver, are your hands tired from the boot cleaning?"

Following a loud splash, two large tree roots dangled by them in the babbling waters.

"A tree herder! How did you get here?" Yannuvia asked.

"I wanted to meet the youngsters who sought the experience of seeing the Lone Oak. I tend the Lone Oak, among other things," the voice answered.

A massive old tree with uprooted roots sat by them. Well, not actually sat, but dangled its thirsty roots in the refreshing waters. The tree herder had only yellow leaves, though they were all manner of hues of yellow. Its truck had such a wide breadth that two adult Drelves would have difficulty reaching around the circumference. Kirrie glanced upward and noted the tree herder was about seven Yardley paces high, or 21 feet in other measurements.

"I know you! You are Old Yellow! I've heard the Teacher and Rumsie talk of you! You are amongst our greatest allies. How'd you get to the stream? The path is too narrow. How'd you pull up your roots?" Yannuvia rattled.

"Questions, little one. Too many questions! I do what tree herders do. Old Yellow is not my name, but it's a moniker I accept. Lots of worse things one could be called," the tree herder's voice echoed into their minds.

"What is your name?" Kirrie asked.

"Kirrie, tree herders won't tell you their names. How did you get here?" Yannuvia added.

"The same way I get to my trees. You don't think I'd be able to drag these roots very fast, do you?" the tree herder answer.

"How are you talking to us? I don't exactly hear your words. It's more like the wind rustles through your leaves and helps us understand you," Kirrie continued.

"That's right," the tree herder answered in the same manner.

"You didn't answer my question!" Kirrie continued, somewhat miffed.

"That's right," Old Yellow persisted.

"We're not getting anywhere," Kirrie grumbled.

"Would you like to get somewhere?" Old Yellow asked.

"What do you mean?" Yannuvia inquired.

"I've got chores to do. It's time to tend the Lone Oak. Would you like to go with me?" the voice queried.

"We've been in enough trouble, tree herder. We can't get caught on the red meadow. Besides, it'd take a long time to get to the red meadow, and I'm tired," Kirrie answered.

"Won't take but a second. Just jump on my lower branches. You only saw the great tree from nigh a thousand yards. You want to touch the old tree, don't you? It's good luck," Old Yellow suggested temptingly.

"I'd sure like to see the Lone Oak up close," Yannuvia added.

"You're getting us from the frying pan into the fire, Yannuvia. But I can't let you go alone," Kirrie interjected pseudo-bravely.

Yannuvia and Kirrie climbed onto the lower branches of the tree herder. Old Yellow murmured something and in a flash they arrived by the Lone Oak.

"Whoa! How'd we get to the red meadow? We're right by the great tree. It's…it's beautiful," Yannuvia marveled.

"Tree herder's Magick," Old Yellow muttered.

The light of the amber period faded and the dark period began. In the dusky light, the trees on the fringe of the red meadow were indistinct.

"The rangers have looking glasses. Won't they see us?" Kirrie asked.

"The sentries expect to see me tending the Lone Oak. I do this every dark period. See the leaves on the ground. I must gather them and treat them respectfully. Go to the far side of the great tree. They won't be able to see you from the trees. Touch the bark. My old friend won't mind," the old fair tree herder said.

The great Lone Oak had leaves of yellow, orange, red, and violet color. The tree's bark was like soft leather. Soft breezes rustled through the big leaves. A sense of tranquility came over the little Drelves as they watched Old Yellow tenderly care for the massive tree. The youths marveled at the dexterity of Old Yellow's massive limbs. The tree herder gently picked up each fallen leaf and molded the Lone Oak's leaves into his branches where they disappeared. After a few moments the shepherd finished his work.

"It's a lovely place, isn't it? This meadow has seen so much conflict. Birds and winged beasts drop seeds onto the red meadow. Animals dig up the grass. Energetic farmers tried to plant seeds many seasons ago. It's always been the Lone Oak and the red grass. That's all. Jump aboard kids, I'll have you back at your homes in a flash," Old Yellow chimed.

Reluctantly Yannuvia and Kirrie left the great icon and climbed onto the tree herder's lower branches. True to his word, Old Yellow muttered something in tree herder tongue and the threesome were back at Alms Glen. Old Yellow's sudden appearance startled the Drelves in the common area, and Kirrie and Yannuvia used the opportunity to slip back to their home trees.

The experience of seeing the Lone Oak and traveling with the tree herder was one of the grandest times had by the adventuresome duo.

The best of times Kirrie and Yannuvia included that spent with their friends, two older Drelvlings named Vioss and Bystar. Vioss and Bystar took the youths under their wing and allowed the young Spellweaver and the little she-Drelve to experience the thrills of exploring the forest with them. Older Drelvlings were allowed to explore the areas around Alms Glen. But any forays beyond the local area were to occur only in the company of adult. Drelvlings had much to learn. The most important tasks included the trips to Meadowsweet and the Green Vale to learn the harvesting of the enhancing root. Only the Chosen, the most promising of each season of the harvest's group of Drelvlings, accompanied the Teacher during their thirteenth season, but all Drelves ultimately got to participate in the enhancing root preparation. All Drelvlings had to learn the ways of the forests. Drelves only hunted the fruits of the forests. They limited their intake to fish and eggs, if bountiful. This meant trips beyond the friendly confines of Alms Glen. Usually at about ten years' age, youths began to accompany adults. Vioss and Bystar sneaked Kirrie and Yannuvia into cloaks

"We're going to get in trouble again," Kirrie lamented.

"No, I cleared it with my father Banderas. Besides, in these cloaks they can't recognize you. Just keep quiet and keep out of the way, and you'll learn lots of good things," Vioss answered.

Vioss and Bystar brought them to the fringe of the forest to meet the Drelvish rangers who were leading the expedition into the deeper woods.

A ways into the woods the older Drelve Dienas discovered the youths when Yannuvia used an Entangle Spell to thwart an attempt by a walkabout bush to trip Dienas.

"He's a Spellweaver, Banderas, what were you thinking? We've brought a Spellweaver this far into the woods! If Rumsie doesn't have our hides, the Teacher Edkim or the elder Blanchard will," Dienas chagrinned.

"He has to learn, Dienas. We can't shelter him. He just saved us from a lot of heartache courtesy of that confounded walkabout bush. We'd have had to spend hours getting you out of its tentacles. His brother Gaelyss won't leave the teacher's side and won't take his nose out of a Spell Book. My son Vioss told me young Yannuvia wanted to get closer to the forest. I'm sorry if I got us in hot water," Banderas answered.

"Well, he did save me from the walkabout. But not a word of this to the elders or the Teacher. We'll end our sortie and head back before the amber period ends. By the way, thanks, Yannuvia. I feel the Teacher and the elders are a bit too cautious," Dienas replied.

The early lives of the young Drelvlings progressed in orderly and predictable manner.

Then…

CHAPTER 4
Yannuvia's First Dream

Gaelyss and Yannuvia completed a day of vigorous instruction with some playful Magick. The Teacher Edkim had returned from Meadowsweet with the precious enhancing root. After attaining the age of 13 seasons, the Chosen Drelvlings received the honor of accompanying the Teacher to Meadowsweet and then on the Green Vale, the only place in the central forests of the world where plants were green and the Enhancing Root flourished. Though not all Drelves participated in the harvest, learning of the properties of the plant was a rite of passage for all young Drelves. The journey was not without danger for the trip began at the end of the red meadow and led the travelers along the fringes of the protective red orange forests, where they might fall victim to foraging parties of Drolls and Kiennites.

All of Alms Glen celebrated the successful harvest with a great feast. Only the guards posted in the trees at the Lone Oak meadow's edge had to wait their turn to celebrate. They left their posts only when relieved. Merriment continued well into the dark period when little Meries sank to near the horizon. Finally the youths were ushered off to their comfortable bedding within the red oak trees. Yannuvia snuggled into the soft dry moss, which covered the large inner root of the tree, which as usual molded to fit his growing frame. He relished the softness and warmth of the deep red moss. Nature's gentle nurse, sleep, soon found the young Spellweaver.

His mind retraced the events of his recent cycles of Meries, which the elders called days. He dreamed of the beautiful meadows around Alms Glen and the flora and fauna common there. The pleasant images faded to red. A flash of brilliant redness superseded the soft red glow.

Wisps...

Threads...

Threads of Magick...

Threads of fate...

Threads of time...

Threads connecting worlds ...

Dreams connecting worlds ...

Dreams of Magick...

The Magick of Dreams...

Magick connecting dreams...

Magick connecting worlds...
Dream raiders...
Elf pressure...
Albtraum...
Albträume, elf dreams, nightmares...
Dreams...

Then the face of a beautiful feminine person appeared in the young Spellweaver's dream. Yannuvia had only looked upon Drelvish females. This person was not Drelvish. The very tall and alluring feminine individual had creamy skin, soft blue eyes, and coal black hair that fell gracefully down her back and chest. Wearing a blazing red dress, the female walked gracefully back and forth across a field of clover as she spoke. The odd *green* clover had purplish flowers. Yannuvia had never seen green clover; all the clover in the forests of the World of the Three Suns was orange and red. Blue flower petals showered around the beautiful female. Had he dreamt in color before this time? Where did the unusual plants grow?

"You *are* the one. Your power is unlimited. We can help you fulfill your potential. You can have everything. That includes me. Seek the treasures of the forest. Come to me. Don't you desire me?" the figure softly murmured.

Yannuvia stirred uncomfortably.

His dreaming mind asked, "What do you mean? No person can own another. My love and commitment is to the forest and my people. I don't seek self-enhancement. I don't understand 'desire.'"

Speaking in a dream...
Interacting with one's dream...
Hearing one's dreams and responding...
Speaking and hearing one's dreams respond...

Yannuvia hadn't experienced such previously. Was it stranger than seeing an elephant fly during an Approximation of the Gray Sun or more unusual than watching a Spellweaver perform Magick?

"You are too young. You will come to know of what I speak. Come into the forest, Yannuvia. Come to me," the figure purred in a pleasant voice as she spoke to the sleeping youth.

Blueness slowly surrounded her blithe form. A brilliant flash of blue light followed and she then disappeared from the youth's subconscious.

Yannuvia slept fitfully the rest of the night and awakened after the rest period with a headache. He left the tree and looked into the clearing where his mother Carinne and several other female Drelves prepared the first meal after the rest period. His friend Kirrie worked with their mothers. He studied them. The Drelvish females were outwardly pretty. But it was their dispositions and demeanor that made them so pleasant. Kirrie flashed her ever-present smile toward him. Yannuvia always felt his people were the loveliest folk in the forest, but then again as far as he knew the Drelves were the only folk in the forest. He based his opinions on his readings, the teachings of Edkim the Teacher, and the stories told by the elder Blanchard and others.

Blanchard, Edkim, his fundamental knowledge of Magick, and the experiences of his simple life in the beautiful forests around Alms Glen afforded the Spellweaver no tools to interpret the visions from his sleep. His young mind could not understand the dream. He had only known the gentle affection of his mother. Yannuvia found it difficult to get the face from the dream out of his thoughts.

What did she mean?

Where was *she*?

Who was *she*?

He had more questions than answers. Should he ask Edkim the Teacher? Would the Teacher think him foolish?

Dreams…

Albtraum…

Hearing one's dreams and responding…

Speaking and hearing one's dreams respond…

Yannuvia loved exploring the woods more than his brother Gaelyss, who preferred the lessons of the annals, math, and the spell books passed down from earlier generations. Yannuvia often slipped away and made short forays into the forests where he made many friends among the trees and animals. Sometimes Kirrie accompanied him. When he was lucky, the older Drelvlings Vioss and Bystar went along and taught him about some of the more exotic plants. Ultimately, the lessons of the Teacher would get around to these plants, but Yannuvia didn't want to wait until he was eleven or twelve to gain knowledge he could have now.

The Teacher Edkim and his parents Carinne and Glinne chastised him for his indiscretions. Try as he might Yannuvia looked into trees all around the common area of Alms Glen but never found the image from his dream. The young Spellweaver felt at ease and one with the forest. Learning of damage fomented by the wanton axes of the Drolls chagrinned him.

Though the Drelves were adept at concealing themselves from the Drolls, occasionally casualties occurred.

The eighth year of the twin Spellweavers saw tragedy. The teacher Edkim led the Chosen and others to Meadowsweet and Green Vale to harvest the enhancing root. Seven Drelvlings accompanied the older Drelves. On the way to Meadowsweet the party narrowly avoided a group of Drolls who had penetrated the forest. Several accurate bowshots form the archers dissuaded the Drolls and the group proceeded along the way to Meadowsweet.

After a bountiful harvest, Edkim led the party back to Alms Glen. On the return journey the group was ambushed by another group of Drolls who were accompanied by Kiennites. The Kiennites numbered an illusionist among their ranks and the devious spell caster had made the large Drolls appear as orange triffids. The trap worked on the fatigued Drelves. The scouts came within striking distance of the enemies before they recognized the ambush and lost the advantage of their accurate longbows. Three veterans named Emerson, Blake, and Palmer and two neophytes, Vioss and Remy, fell to the great axes wielded by the Drolls. Another neophyte Bystar fell to a Magick Missile spell from the Kiennite spell caster. Edkim entered the fray and slew the Kiennite spell caster with a shuriken. The Drelves managed to escape without further losses.

At Alms Glen, the elders called the community together, and the Drelvish folk mourned their lost kindred. Yannuvia was particularly touched by the deaths of the neophytes Vioss and Bystar. The neophyte Remy was from the hamlet Boomslang, named for the colorful snakes that hanged from the trees and created loud thunderous sounds by snapping their long tails. Young Yannuvia had befriended the older Drelvlings and had accompanied them on many excursions into the woodlands.

"I must avenge my son Vioss," Banderas screamed.

The older Drelve Dienas agreed with his friend Banderas, saying, "We can't allow the Drolls and Kiennites to attack and slay our people wantonly."

Many Drelves zealously sought action against the Drolls.

After much heated debate, the elders overrode the objections of Yannuvia's father Glinne and others and chose to refrain from counterattacking the Droll's villages near the Drelve forest.

The decision created a rift among the forest people. Dienas, Banderas, Yiuryna, and others asked the elders' permission to leave Alms Glen and establish a new community south of the Lone Oak meadow. Blanchard granted their request, and the disgruntled Drelves uprooted and created the independent community Lost Sons, in memory of the neophytes killed by the Drolls and Kiennites. The autonomous village would send representatives to Green Vale at the time of the harvest, share in the enhancing root, and send rangers and archers to contribute to the common defense of the area.

Yannuvia also felt frustration at the elders' refusal to avenge the deaths of the Drelvish guards and neophytes. Instead the Drelves of Alms

Glen strengthened the natural defenses in the area where the attack had occurred. They enlisted the aid of the orange triffids and stretched vines and roots between cooperative plants and trees. The young Spellweavers Gaelyss and Yannuvia cast Entangle and Plant Growth Spells in many areas. This Magick enhanced the natural barriers. Yannuvia often sneaked away and visited his old friends at Lost Sons. He enabled their defenses with Entangle and Plant Growth Spells. The young Spellweaver told no one of his excursions, but his brother Gaelyss sensed the effects of the spells. Gaelyss neither confronted Yannuvia nor reported the activity.

Following a few dark periods, Drelvish archers posted in the tall everred trees noted the approach of a group of Drolls. The burly enemies charged the woods. Some fell after Drelvish arrows struck them. The thickened underbrush turned the others away. The wolf-faced hobgoblin-sized Drolls soon returned with three goblin-like Kiennites. The Kiennites produced bows and fired arrows into the underbrush. The arrows hit their targets and burst into flame. The underbrush burned, but the Magick cast by Gaelyss and Yannuvia resisted the flames. Then the Kiennites extended their pale gnarly digits and cast Flame Spells, but the Magick vines again resisted the flames. Accurate Drelvish archers released arrows and ended the lives of two Kiennites, and the other enemies tucked tail and ran.

From the everred trees, the old Drelvish Clarke Maceda commented, "Odd. I've walked the World of the Three Suns for 1100 seasons of the harvest and I've never seen Kiennites fire flame arrows. The Spellweavers' Magick made the arrows ineffective, but twas still a foreboding sight."

"Lucky we have Spellweavers," the veteran Beaux added.

Drolls returned twice with large timbers soaked with tar and set them ablaze, but the Magick vines resisted the flames on both occasions. The Drolls tired of the venture, fled, and fomented trouble elsewhere. The Drelves remained vigilant. Several dark periods passed and the large wolf-faced enemies did not return.

For several dark periods the young Spellweaver Yannuvia brooded in his red oak tree or in the thickened underbrush of the forest near Alms Glen. Finally Edkim the Teacher approached the youth and spoke with him at length. The teacher's wisdom and encouragement helped the youth deal with the loss of his friends. Yannuvia reluctantly joined his brother Gaelyss in studying spell books and learning the ways of the Drelves. Little Kirrie often accompanied them in the lessons. Though she enjoyed the company of both, it was clear she was partial to Yannuvia.

The remainder of the year passed uneventfully and Edkim led a very successful party to harvest the enhancing root.

CHAPTER 5
Yannuvia's Second Elfdream

Wisps…
Threads…
Threads of Magick…
Threads of fate…
Threads of time…
Threads connecting worlds …
Dreams connecting worlds …
Dreams of Magick…
The Magick of Dreams…
Magick connecting dreams…
Magick connecting worlds…
Dream raiders…
Elf pressure…
Albtraum…
Albträume, elf dreams, nightmares…
Dreams…

She appeared in Yannuvia's dreams again during his ninth season.

The young Drelvling had finished a particularly busy light period and sank into the soft down of the mossy bed within his red oak tree. The bedding had never felt so good and sleep came quickly. His mind retraced the events of recent days. After revisiting, the flora, fauna, and beautiful meadows around Alms Glen, his slumbering mind saw warm redness and then the face of the beautiful female he had seen only in this now recurring dream. With only the wondrously beautiful Drelvish females as a comparison, Yannuvia found her beauty different but equivalent. Again the appealing matron had soft velvety light skin and azure eyes. The female stood beneath a great oak tree with odd green leaves. This night the dream raider chose a deep blue shiny gown. Her hair was as black as the fur of a noir skat. The noir skat was a reclusive creature that roamed in the subterranean caverns and ventured into the fringes of the forest. In a world without darkness the noir skat's coloration placed it at a disadvantage. The beast's innate ability of displacement negated that disadvantage. Some called the noir skat a displacer beast. Edkim told of the fierceness of the feline in his lectures.

Why was Yannuvia thinking about a predator like the noir skat when he looked upon such beauty?

"You are older now. Have you considered my words? You witnessed the power that Magick can give you! You have seen the ravage of your people and witnessed the devastation of your beloved forest. Through the power of Magick, you can avenge them and stop this carnage. Also, you can caress me. Aren't you interested?" she cooed in a pleasant voice.

It was a dream, after all.

Or was it? So odd...

Hearing one's dreams and responding...

Speaking and hearing one's dreams respond...

Before he *answered*, the voice appeared again, "Do you prefer this?"

She waved her hands sinuously and changed to a gray dress. Her hair became deep green. The unusual green hair color appeared natural on the shoulders of the female. The grayness of the dress mimicked the pleasant light of Andreas.

In his elfdream, Yannuvia stood in a field of green clover and basked in the warm light of a single sun with an alien blue sky overhead. He resisted speaking. He then felt hot.

"My patience growsssss thin! But I will carry on! You will sssseek me out one day! You will find me. When you do, you will like what you find. Power ...power, young one, will beckon to you. None can resssssisssst itssss call. You will tire of the wrongssss your people endure. You will asssssk my Massssster' ssss aid," the she-person warbled.

Her voice changed from melodic to stern as she finished her brief lecture. The longer the beautiful female spoke, the more pronounced her lisp became. Blueness surrounded the fetching feminine figure. She bussed her perfect lips, blew a kiss toward Yannuvia, and slowly faded from the dream.

The young Spellweaver awakened in a pool of sweat. Similar to his tears, the Spellweaver's sweat was sparkling, iridescent, and multicolored. Drelves and particularly Spellweavers rarely perspired. Though he found the image in his dreams pleasing to look upon and enjoyed her pleasant voice, aging two seasons had not given Yannuvia any more insight into the meaning of the dreams, and the kiss she sent toward him did not temper the sharpness of her harsh words. The youngster shook off the effects of the dream, munched on some warm booderries and milk tree cream, and dressed for a day of study and exploration. He left the comfortable red oak designated to him by the Teacher. Yannuvia missed his mother's enticing breakfasts and to be honest her morning hugs, but the Teacher determined it best for the twins to live on their own. The premise was they'd concentrate better on their studies. Yannuvia joined his brother Gaelyss and the twins continued their studies.

Yannuvia yearned for free time to explore the forests, and his mind often returned to his lost friends. If he gained more powers he could help his people stand against the larger Drolls and sneaky Kiennites. He examined every red tree and orange bush. The walkabout bushes were always a challenge. When the elusive plants sensed an examiner nearby, they uprooted and walked about. Displacer plants were tricky also. The actual plant was either a pace to the left, right, front, or rear of where it appeared to be, and its auburn thorns were quite hostile. Peashooters fired projectiles from their stems that stung intruders. But most of the flora was friendly. The contrary plants served the purpose of educating the unwary of the intricacies of the forests. The orange triffids helped the youths in their horticultural studies.

Yannuvia saw beauty in all plants, including the cantankerous varieties.

CHAPTER 6
Moochie the Droll

The big Droll preferred the name Moochie, though it was not the name his mother Minnie had given him. She called him Kevin. He was a member of the Korcran Clan. Moochie's father Mickey had taken the group from obscurity to one of the more powerful clans in the Peaks of Division. Early in his life, Moochie took up the typical Spartan life of his folk. Because the cub, as Drolls sometimes referred to their youth, had a knack for sneaking snacks and goodies intended for others he picked up the moniker Kevin the Moocher. Being called Minnie's moocher got the youth piping mad. He preferred *Moochie*. Bigger and stronger than most young Drolls, he made his peers pay for teasing him.

After taking a drubbing at Moochie's hands, a defeated opponent named Reggie moaned, "If he wants to be called Moochie, so be it!"

Drolls were muscular and powerful. Long flowing manes dominated their physique. Some might refer to them as wolf men, but other than their wolf-like faces, the ruggedly handsome folk had nothing in common with the canines. Ubiquitous throughout the world of the three suns, wolves roamed the Doombringer Mountains. Like wolves Drolls were somewhat nomadic, but more powerful clans established territoriality in prosperous and rich areas.

Alliances with the gnarly Kiennites advanced Drollen clans. Moochie's father Mickey made several trips to Aulgmoor, the center of the Kiennites' domain. Aulgmoor housed the most prominent Kiennites. Less powerful than Moochie's folk, the gnarly Kiennites had rare spell capabilities and complemented the powerful Drolls well. The alliances served to keep the two folk dominant in most of the area of central Parallan, as some called the World of the Three Suns. The Ornash River basin, Doombringer Mountains, and the Peaks of Division occupied much of the central region and were prime hunting ground. Many wild fruits, vegetables, and berries grew in the plains and on the hillocks. Drolls and Kiennites allowed some ilk to live and grow crops in their territories, but pity the interlopers if the landlords grew hungry or impatient. The richest lands in the entire world were the central forests, inhabited by the Drelves. Both Drolls and Kiennites coveted theses lands, but the main thing spurring them was the resistance of the forest people to subservience. Most Drollen commanders sought to get the better of other peoples. Some just liked to fight.

Moochie liked to impose his will on others.

Moochie was fond of fighting.

His father Mickey spent most of his time in Aulgmoor and the Gap Keep, an ancient fortress manned by the Kiennites in the Peaks of Division and left Moochie in charge of the clan's forces. An older Droll named Bluthgar assisted young Moochie, and a younger Droll named Dolenz came to the Korcrans' realm with a traveling minstrel show. Younger Dolenz exhibited skills in dealing with the temperamental firehorses. Dolenz, Moochie, and Bluthgar became great friends. Young Moochie gained a reputation for ruthlessness, but also cunning and determination. Kiennites sought his services. One of the greatest opportunities for a Drollen commander and his forces was serving in the area of the central forests. There was a better chance to get into a fight, and a greater chance of gathering booty. With each passing dark period, Kiennites feared the Drelves more and clamored for action against the forest dwellers. Drelves numbered among them persons called Spellweavers. According to the zealots, Spellweavers grew more powerful with each passing dark period. Drollen and Kiennish lore told of a green area of untold wealth and resources located deep within the everred central forests where the Drelves lived. Also, the area allegedly contained the source of the Drelves' powers. It would certainly be a blue bee in a Drollen commander's bonnet to capture a Drelvish Spellweaver or find a means to enter the central area of the Drelves' lands.

Moochie hoped for such an opportunity.

The loudest voice in Aulgmoor came from the Kiennite shaman Lord Melphat. Melphat was the eldest son of Dydracks, the old leader of the Aulgmoor warren. Warren was a term the Kiennites used to refer to their organized communities.

Word had come to the Doombringer range of increased activity far to what would be south if one held a device called a compass. The Impassible Range was a group of mountains that bordered the extreme region of the great plain below the Ornash River and beyond the central forests of the Drelves. A narrow band of mountains and foothills sat before the great mountains.

In times past, Drolls and Kiennites had allied to fight many wars against giants, ogres, and hobgoblins that inhabited the Impassible Mountains. Called the alliance of the Doombringers, the Drolls and Kiennites prevailed in these ancient battles. The giants' numbers had dwindled to the point there had been no threat. Rumor held the giants retreated to the depths of the subterranean caverns and cowered therein.

Now stories reached Aulgmoor of new threats to the domain of the Drolls and Kiennites. Odd folk had been seen in the plain beyond the Ornash. Merchants, minstrels, and vagabonds reported strange findings, such as murdered giants, bewildered ogres, and signs of Magick. Vendors from the Emerald Isle in the Great Western Sea brought rarities like red ale and pipeweed to the leaders of Aulgmoor and demanded payment. The leaders of Aulgmoor required items such as precious stones, hides, and raw materials to pay the seagoing merchants.

The events to the south concerned Melphat. The Kiennite also bore great enmity for the Drelves. Melphat proposed a scouting journey to investigate the goings on in the south, but the Kiennish warren leaders felt there was little risk. The arch-shaman Melphat approached the Drollen clans for support. Mickey Korcran told Lord Melphat of his son Moochie. The young commander Moochie caught Melphat's eye, and the Kiennish noble came to the Korcran clan's lands to speak with Minnie's Moochie.

Lord Melphat's plan appealed to Moochie, who agreed that the Drelves became more powerful with time and goings on in the south threatened his ilk. He actually hoped they did. Moochie preferred fighting to just hanging around. After a very productive meeting with Lord Melphat, Moochie sent four of his most trusted warriors Phastin, Addipex, Tenate, and Gruth with the shaman.

Moochie went to his lean-to and sat down on the noir skat hide, which provided cover for his austere bed. The massive Droll popped the cork from a bottle of mead, tipped the bottle, and drank deeply. The Kiennites could keep their expensive red ale. Moochie preferred the simpler things. His mind remained focused on actions at Aulgmoor. At least Lord Melphat was trying to take action. Melphat's younger brother Saligia was more militaristic and interested in the power struggle within the Kiennish social structure. Melphat, like Moochie, was a guy of action. Moochie smiled wryly as he considered the import of his fire brigade to the Kiennites' plans. Both Melphat and Saligia appreciated the value of the firehorses. The Korcrans had assembled a hundred of the extraordinary steeds.

Would they find and capture others? Without the stone, doing so will be difficult. Moochie recalled the gray stone, a family heirloom that had disappeared from his father's locked chest. The lock remained fastened but the stone had been taken without the key and without discharging the warding glyph placed on the chest by Kiennish shamans long ago. Who took the gray rock? Could the artifact be replaced? For that matter, how did the first stone come into the Korcrans' possession? Thinking about the thievery of the artifact wouldn't help Moochie Korcran find sleep!

Taking a few deep breaths, the big Droll settled down and watched the embers fade in his fire. Thankful for the efforts of the blue bees that made the honey and the gnomish brew masters who produced the beverage, he enjoyed the warm feeling from the dark blue mead.

He *needed* a fight.

His skills dulled.

The powerful beast closed his eyes.

Drolls dreamed of battles in the woods, chasing down hoodoo hares, bungling in the jungle, tripping the heavy fantastic (a burly forest bear), eating bountiful feasts, drinking good mead, and sharing time with beautiful Drollen females, she-Drolls to some. Moochie tried to keep thoughts of Kiennish and Drelvish women from his mind. He considered them unattractive, though the Kiennish females from Thabell were intriguing. The odd giantess and ogress he had seen were a different matter. He found them very attractive. Briefly, Moochie though of the feminine creature he, and all Drolls, most despised, the Cheethra. Cat-like Cheethras had well-proportioned curvaceous bodies, heads and manes of a great cat, and venomous fangs. Why hadn't he seen a male Cheethra? The thought of fighting a Cheethra invigorated the Droll. Then the warmth of the mead calmed Moochie.

Soon he slept.

The Droll's mind wandered to a warm light period on Roper Mountain. He ran in the reeds with his favorite pet Asta. Asta was a red dawg. Moochie and Asta shared the light period with the beautiful raven haired she-Droll Hannah. Hannah Dakota had every characteristic that made a female attractive. Her wolf face was perfect. Her teeth were perfect canines. Her smile and growl were mesmerizing. The young she-Droll Hannah ran with Moochie and Asta. Next he dreamt of his great victory against his chief adversary for leadership of the Korcran clan, his cousin Mitchell. The Droll's dreams recounted experiences of capturing the elusive firehorses. His mentor Bluthgar and young Dolenz accompanied him. Catching firehorses. Drinking mead and ale. Kicking butt. One pleasant dream followed another. He envisioned his childhood friend Reduc, who now served as Moochie's personal guard and stood at this moment outside the Commander's tent. Then...

Wisps...

Threads...

Threads of Magick...

Threads of fate...

Threads of time...

Threads connecting worlds ...

Dreams connecting worlds …
Dreams of Magick…
The Magick of Dreams…
Magick connecting dreams…
Magick connecting worlds…
Dream raiders…
Elf pressure…
Albtraum…
Albträume, elf dreams, nightmares…
Dreams…

The images Moochie enjoyed faded to redness. A flash of brilliant red followed. Moochie tensed in his sleep. A face entered his dream. Horrific and vaguely female, the creature had fiery red eyes, unsightly wings, and long muscular arms ending in long curved talons, which were covered in dark ichors. The strangely attractive creature pursed her lips, blew the sleeping Droll a kiss, and simply hissed, "Pleasant dreams, big boy! How do you like these?"

The she-beast revealed long curvaceous legs.

"Who…what are you? Why do you invade my sleep?" Moochie asked.

Hearing one's dreams and responding…

Speaking and hearing one's dreams respond…

"My, you're a handsome one!" the voice clamored.

"Why am I talking to you when I am sleeping? You are a Drelvish Spellweaver, aren't you? I'm doomed! Though I cannot challenge you, I call you a coward! Face me when I can fight!" Moochie responded defiantly.

"Calm down! Calm down! Calm down, you son-of-a *****! I'll kick your *** anytime, anywhere! But that's not my purpose in being in your dreams. Is this picture easier for your simple mind?" the she-beast asked vehemently.

She changed to the precise image of young Hannah Dakota. Every detail was accurate all the way to the individual strands of her thick hair.

As he slept Moochie perspired heavily and moaned plaintively. The hardened warrior was accustomed to physical but not mental torment. It was new to him.

"You insult my mother and defile the memory of my life's love. You know she fell to a wyvern shortly after the images that were in my mind. My warriors are my life now. If you seek to influence me, find a way to advance their efforts," his sleeping mind replied.

"You opine over your lost love. Pure ***** heat, that's all she felt for you. Suffer as much as you will, wolf-beast!" she uttered disdainfully.

"Face me and say such things!" Moochie growled.

"You tempt me, wolf-beast. I'll give you this. At least you have some fight in you. And you *are* absolutely beautiful, at least to my eye. I'm enjoying this task. Our paths will not meet in battle, but I'll do as you want and help your warriors. You'll find my gift when you awaken," the image growled in Hannah's voice.

Blueness surrounded her muscular form. She faded away. A flash of brilliant blue light followed. Moochie the Droll wandered deeper into sleep.

In awhile a voice called to him. He jumped from his slumber to find loyal Reduc shaking his shoulder. Reduc had stood guard by the Commander's pergola.

"Commander! Wake up! Your father summons you," Reduc said urgently.

"Was anyone outside the tent, Reduc? Did you hear anything?" Moochie asked.

"Do you still sleep, my friend and Commander? The night remained quiet. I was outside your tent the whole of the amber period. A lovely morning greets us," Reduc answered.

"I'm awake! Tell my father I'll join him soon," Moochie growled. Reduc saluted, turned, and left Moochie alone. The big Droll winced. He first noted the headache that had greeted him.

Too much mead!

Not enough fighting!

Terrible dreams!

So real!

It was then he noted the quiver with six deep red arrows lying with his longbow.

CHAPTER 7
The Dream Raiders

A flash of red light heralded the feminine Dream raider's arrival in the austere rocky cavern. Her blithe form stood on a red stone.

The Master of the Dream Raider's evil presence dominated the grotto and filled the area with red and mauve auras. The fiend held a bejeweled chalice in one of his many macabre appendages.

"Do you like this pretty item?" the Demonlord asked.

"Yessss, Massssster," the she-demon replied.

The feminine Dream Raider preferred the moniker Deceiver. She always gave answers the Demonlord wanted to hear. He was, after all, male. The she-demon knew exactly…she knew what males wanted to see and hear. Akin to Succubae, she was just more…deceitful.

"This little cup is going to be of assistance. I've spent a fortnight refining the bowl. The greedy ones won't be able to resist its beckoning," the Demonlord crowed.

Twelve inches tall with a base six inches in diameter and stem six inches long, the bowl held little more than a cup of liquid. Multi-colored auras of Magick surrounded the deep maroon chalice, which gave off intermittent bursts of deep purple light. Flowing runes covered the bowl, pristine stones of all colors lined the rim, and other precious stones, any one of which was priceless, decorated the cup. Many phials containing green, lavender, clear, orange, red, yellow and black liquids filled the shelves of a peculiar six-foot high, four-foot wide red wood cabinet, which sat by the grotesque Fire Demonlord.

The attractive but shadowy she-demon sighed and said, "It'ssss beautiful, Massssster!"

"Yes, it is stunning. Sit by my fire and I'll tell you of its creation, my pretty," the Demonlord commanded.

The Deceiver smiled coyly and sauntered to his side.

The hulking fire demon began, "I used maroon ore from the depths of the Gray Abyss to create the chalice. I compressed the ore into a molten mass, smoothed the sizzling metal into a rounded base, and shaped the vessel to my liking. I formed a third arm to hold the cup whilst I worked. My talons created a rounded base, thick stem, and deep bowl. Whilst the metal was malleable, I pressed one of the gray stones into the soft metal. I always enjoy the gray light. It's as refreshing as a breath of sulfurous fumes. Watch this."

The massive Demonlord changed to a mauve mist. The mist encircled the artifact, which hovered in mid air where the demon's hand had held it. The mist playfully assumed the forms of a red dragon, gorgon, and then a six-headed pyrohydra. The Master of Dream Raiders, the Fire Demonlord answered to the name Uyrg. His vileness then assumed his favorite and usual form.

"Massssster..." the she-demon muttered appreciatively.

"Did you enjoy the images? I infused the cup with my essence, my power. I engraved the metals with symbols of the Abyss, the cursed pentagram, and the pathetic trefoil. I despoiled the figure of the trefoil. Finally, I engraved the cup with an upward triangle," the Demonlord hissed.

"The pentagram is cursssssed! I encountered it engraved on treessss. Why an upward triangle, Masssster?" she queried.

"Oh, my pretty. You must travel more. You should travel to the blue world...never mind. Not yet. It's still too primitive. Not enough Magick. The pathetic ones refer to the downward pointing triangle as 'the chalice.' Water! It flows downward, my beauty. The downward triangle symbolizes heaven, the grace of heaven, and the womb. The figure is one of their most ancient symbols of feminine divinities. I hate femininity and motherhood. *Uh...not you, though*! Observe the beautiful gemstones. Amongst the most rare of the worlds I've entered, they catch the eyes of the greedy and weak-minded. This little cup has helped me defile and ruin all things gentle, good, kind, and above all feminine. All things, that is, my lovely, but you," the Demonlord puffed.

"Am I ssssspecial, Massssster?" she cooed.

"Of course," the Dream Master lied. "But you must work on your lisp."

"I'll try. It'sssss Jusssst natural for me, *Master*. Master! I did it!" she jubilantly declared.

"Yes, my special *girl*! Don't *overdo* it!" the Demonlord said icily.

His demeanor changed.

The she-demon sensed his frustration, labored to control her lisp, and asked timidly in her most seductive voice, "I'm sorry I displeased you, Master."

"Not to worry. Sit by me, my pretty. I've just got things on my mind," the Master requested.

"I'm sure you'll figure everything out, Master," the Deceiver hissed. She managed a wry celebratory smile for overcoming her hissing.

"It's one of my *projects*. I underestimated the power of the cursed world. Magick is pandemic! Not to matter, I consider it a bit more of a challenge.

I can't pinpoint my target in Koorlost. The fool has gone missing. While he's away, I'm going forward with my plans. Even *I* don't always understand Magick," the Demonlord muttered with uncharacteristic humility.

"It vexessss you, doesssssn't it, Massssster?" She quizzed timidly.

He fumed silently for a moment then continued, "****! Cursed Staves! ****! You did it again! Watch the lisp!"

"Sorry, Master!" the winsome she-Demon quipped.

"I'm not really angry with you. It's the ******, *confounded staves!* Although we've been on this sorry rock they call a world for eleven years, I don't really know how many staves exist. I've also found a Light Sorcerer named Gwindor who bears one. He's rummaging around in the woods looking for...I don't know what he seeks. I've invaded his dreams, but the ****** staff protects him. He travels with a transmorphed dragon, the same type we captured last year. This Light Sorcerer created a Ninth Level dweomer, very strong protective Magick that will be difficult to overcome. If the fool Boton manages to get himself killed whilst off on some dimwitted foray, Gwindor becomes our greatest adversary. Though he is young, Gwindor is no paltry, puny, 'wet behind the ears' sorcerer. He is good, very good, and challenges us. My foes might just have a chance. One must always plan. I shan't underestimate my enemies."

"You will make them bow before you, Massssster," she said emphatically, but with a bit of a lisp.

"Thank you for your reassurance. These foolish Light and Dark Sorcerers seek rapaciously the power to go between worlds in an instant, the power of Translocation. This ability is innate to our kind. So long as there is a thread of Magick between worlds, we traverse without time passing beyond the number of heartbeats we feel. Time will always vary for *them* when they go between worlds; it may be later, earlier, slower, faster.

"E equals em cee squared, indeed! Magick is not Nature! It's Magick! Perhaps there is a Nature to Magick as there is Magick in Nature. Time will always vary for those to whom the power is not innate. True, with shypoke eggshells and rare tomes, they might travel without error in their own world, but beyond that it's not to be constant. Shypokes are now extinct. To my knowledge, the little wyrmkins were native only to the world of sorcerers and a place called Texas. To be or not to be!" the Demonlord muttered and stroked his hardened red chin with several talons.

"Oh, Massssster, you speak beautifully, but in riddles. Time? Texas? Wyrmkins? Two bees not being two bees! Your words are beyond me," she said. Mesmerized, the Deceiver tried as best she could to hide the lisp.

"Time is a difficult concept, my pretty. Forget about the bees! Texas is a place you don't mess with! Wyrmkins are little dragons. Be careful if you encounter a little gray one. Gray dragons are deceptively powerful, resistant to charming and beguiling, and purveyors of powerful illusory Magick. Think about the elves. When fools watch elves dance, they since the passage of a few hours when years may actually pass. Just do as I say, and use the red and blue stones I created. Influencing dreams will eventually bear fruit. It works for elves," the Dream Master commented.

"You are so smart, Master. Symbols block the elves. Elves are confined to a single world. I hope I can one day manipulate dreams as well as you do," the she-Demon cooed and gently pulled a talon across his thickened red brow.

"Thank you, my lovely! Your words are heartening. The other morons I have on my team are not so reassuring. Mighty Arachnis has not arrived. How go your efforts in the *home* world?" the Demonlord queried.

"The thread between this world and the other grows stronger. My travel likewise grows easier. Master, why do you call that odd world the home world?" she awkwardly asked.

"Twas where I came to be," the Demonlord answered succinctly and did not elaborate.

Realizing he was to say no more in this matter, she took a deep breath, and timidly reported, "Two, Master. Two of the forest people touch the shores of the sea of Magick. One seldom leaves the side of his mother and talks only of what I'd call *Light* Magick. The other treks into the forest and seeks new adventures. He feels anger at the loss of his friends. But he *issss*… uh, sorry, Master. He *is* a young fool. I enter his dreams just as you suggest. I make my image as alluring as I know how to do, but he does not respond. I guess he *issss* a fool, or else too young."

The Demonlord smirked and replied, "If he resists *you*, he is a fool, even if young. You have done what I asked. The seed is planted. I knew there were two. I only need one. The other is of no import. Did the gnarly ones make use of the flame arrows you gave them?"

A warm, no hot, blush radiated from her enthralling form and filled the grotto with deep red hues.

"I suppose. They are not very, sssssmart, Master. Their attackssss fell short. Only a few of the forest ilk fell," the she-demon answered and regained a bit of her composure.

"Watch the hissing! The gnarly ones call themselves Kiennites. To me they're glorified goblins. The arrows were simply flame arrows. I only added a fire spell. I only wanted to get the forest folk's attention. Seeing their enemies shooting fire at them probably accomplished this. Truth be told, the Kiennites are weak in Magick, even in the gray light. But they'll serve my purpose, just as you do, my pretty. Now, I think you should return to your efforts. Did you distribute the red arrows, those I made from the Tuscon feathers?" the Dream Master asked.

"I don't enjoy telling the truth. I gave six red arrows to the wolf-faced captain. He is stronger and prettier," she reported.

"Best be telling *me* the truth, pretty thing! Don't become infatuated with the Droll. His days are likely numbered. I trust your abilities. Do you have the stone?" the Demonlord asked.

The she-demon retrieved a round gray stone. The spherical rock stood out in the redness of the grotto and emitted bursts of gray light as she grasped it.

"Yessss, Muh-Master. Isn't this just a rock?" she stammered, trying to speak crisply.

The Demonlord released the chalice. The artifact floated by him. He extended an appendage and slowly moved his pronated hand to and fro. The she-demon saw a flash of gray light, and a second stone appeared in the Demonlord's hand.

"Hardly. It's quite the exceptional rock. Take this also," he commanded.

She timidly took the stone from the Demonlord. Arcs of deep gray energy flashed between the stones she held in her hands. Grayness bathed her.

The Demonlord continued, "Return to the *home* world. Proceed as I have commanded. Utilize the indigenous folk. You'll find denizens of the world of the gray light easily swayed. Use the stones; avoid the forest people during the Approximation of the Gray Sun, should that occur. Not even I can predict such times. *Remember, for those lacking the innate power of Translocation, time is not constant between worlds connected by Magick.* But you can expect to find similar creatures have evolved in such worlds. Be wary. Rarely powerful sorcerers live among the forest people. Use the stones. Invade their dreams. Do what you do...what we do. Then return here. I'll have other tasks for you."

"Are the Drelvish spell casters Light Sorcerers or Dark Sorcerers?" the womanly creature asked.

"Just sorcerers. They mainly dabble in dweomers that accentuate Nature," Uyrg commented.

"Master, why do you choose such insignificant spell casters?" the she-Demon asked.

"Don't underestimate Magick! Magick at times confounds even me. Use your skills. I know you will do well," the Demonlord added comfortably.

"Yes, Master," she answered.

The Deceiver turned, walked away from the Dream Master toward the edge of the grotto, stepped onto a blue stone, and disappeared in a flash of blue light.

CHAPTER 8
A Difficult Choice

Three seasons of the harvest, 24 dark periods, passed.

Thrice the Drelves harvested the precious enhancing root uneventfully. Minor skirmishes occurred along the fringes of the forest, but the Drolls and Kiennites avoided conflicts with the Drelves in the friendly confines of the forests in the central landmass around Alms Glen. Kirrie comforted Yannuvia when he reminisced about the times spent with Vioss and Bystar. Yannuvia stood almost a foot taller than most of his ilk. His muscular frame towered at least five feet tall. His integument was typical, pleasant shades of amber and orange. By the campfire, his long locks were the typical silver-gray of youth. The Drelve's hair and skin changed to blend into the forest. Like all his kind, Yannuvia blended well into the red and orange flora of the central forests. When bathed by the amber light of the three suns, the Drelves' coloration camouflaged them in the tall red grasses on the Lone Oak Meadow. Gaelyss spent time with Meryt, Bryce, Zack, and Debery, but sneaked away to study spell books whenever he could.

The Approximations of Andreas were totally unpredictable. It was then the gray sun filled the sky, bathed the land with its deep gray light, and augmented the forces of Magick in the world. No Approximations had occurred since the births of Yannuvia and Gaelyss.

Many Drelves urged Edkim the Teacher, Blanchard, and other elders to carry the fight to the enemies, but the Teacher and elders recalled earlier military failures and continued the policies of isolation, avoidance, and defense. Yannuvia remembered the loss of his friends Vioss and Bystar. As a Spellweaver, he was included in the community meetings. Ordinarily Drelvlings were not included until their thirteenth year. But Spellweavers were so rare that the youths were included in all the community activities.

Gaelyss kept near the teacher Edkim, old Blanchard, and the elders. Yearning to hear more of their stories, Yannuvia spent more time old Clarke Maceda, Sergeant Major Rumsie, the bowyer BJ Aires, the scouts and archers, and Dienas Banderas and Yiuryna of Lost Sons. He practiced with the bow and became rather proficient with the weapon. Activities in Alms Glen increased as the time of the harvest approached.

The gray wanderer Andreas flirted with an Approximation. Sometimes the nomadic sun approached only to retreat again rather than drawing near the land. These toggles also occurred unpredictably. The annals and the elder Drelves told of great harvests when the sun was near. Though old, Blanchard had never seen a harvest under the gray light of an Approximation. When the twin Spellweavers were born, the Approximation occurred before the tubers were mature. Edkim and the elders found it hard to contain their excitement regarding not one but two Spellweavers reaching the age of thirteen years and accompanying the Teacher on the harvest. Plans proceeded orderly and the Teacher called the community together in the common area of Alms Glen.

Yannuvia struggled to remain interested in the business affairs of the meeting. When the council adjourned he took a brief walk with Kirrie in the beloved woods around Alms Glen. The amber period was beginning and another dark period was nigh. Meries settled near the horizon between the trees, but the young Drelves knew the small sun would soon slingshot back into the horizon and bring its brightest light. Small animals skittered about and birds filled the air with song. Kirrie bade him good-bye and went to her home. The young Spellweaver took a deep breath and walked to his red oak home. Walking through the tree's bark was always refreshing. Yannuvia never tired of the feeling. His skin tingled as he entered the comfortable bedchamber.

Would this be the night *she* returned to his dreams? He had with subtleness asked some older Drelves about dreams, but they had shed no light on the dream's significance.

Anticipation of the upcoming harvest and the trip to Meadowsweet and Green Vale made sleeping difficult, but Yannuvia eventually fell asleep.

Soon…

Wisps…

Threads…

Threads of Magick…

Threads of fate…

Threads of time…

Threads connecting worlds …

Dreams connecting worlds …

Dreams of Magick…

The Magick of Dreams…

Magick connecting dreams…

Magick connecting worlds…

Dream raiders…

Elf pressure…

Albtraum…

Albträume, elf dreams, nightmares…

Dreams…

Redness surrounded him. Then the young Spellweaver stood in the field of green clover. His dreaming eyes scanned the field. She was nowhere to be seen. Then in the distance a figure appeared and walked seductively toward him. Frozen in the dream, his mind watched her approach. Clingingly, an orange dress wrapped about her pale skin. Her flowing auburn hair moved gently as she walked.

The female reached him and said, "You have reached the age of thirteen seasons of the harvest. Your spells are stronger. I've watched you in the woods. You have much potential."

Yannuvia was able to speak, "Why do you torment me and not my brother?"

"Torment? Am I that unpleasing to look upon? I'll change for you," she answered. She moved her hands slowly and darkened her hair to a ruby red. Her garment changed to a glistening silver dress.

"No! You're…you are pleasing. I…I just don't…" the youth stammered.

The field of clover changed to a dense wood. The blue sky changed to the familiar amber skies of the World of the Three Suns. The dream had taken Yannuvia to *his* world. He heard the roar of water and felt mist upon his face. It was so very real! He heard her soft voice.

"Follow the sound to the Alluring Falls," she cooed.

"I don't know the Alluring Falls? They are not within our forest," the youth objected.

"That's where you must go," the voice insisted.

Then Yannuvia sensed his feet were moving along a grassy then stone path. The roar of water intensified. He knew he was approaching a waterfall. Then he stood on the ledge and peered behind the rushing water and saw the continuation of a thin rocky ledge behind the waterfall. There was barely enough room for a single person to walk along the ledge. Getting wet was a given. The passage behind the waterfall was thirty Yardley paces long. The water felt surprisingly warm as it spilled back against him. The dream was so real. He was driven to step upon the ledge. The ledge was only about the width of three of his small feet and furthermore was slippery due to a covering of algae. The falls dropped a total of a hundred feet with a direct drop of ninety feet immediately below him. The water crashed upon large rocks below.

"Jump! It will be pleasant," urged a soothing voice, which differed from that of his svelte companion.

He found his foot slipping toward the edge.

"You might fly! Think how that would impress your friends. You will make new friends," the voice suggestion.

The voice grew into a chorus and was even more alluring. Unable to resist, Yannuvia took the single fateful step needed to leave the narrow path and fall over the fall. His eyes saw the rapidly approaching boulders at the bottom of the falls.

Death!

"No!" he screamed and bolted up in his comfortable bed.

Soaked with sweat, the young Spellweaver felt his heart pounding in his chest. He jumped from the covers and stood on the plush naturally mossy-carpeted floor of his tree home.

Dream!

No...

Wisps...

No...

Threads of life...

She *stood* beside him. He was taller than most Drelves but still not as tall as she. The female from his dreams gently took his sweating hand and squeezed slightly. She gently bent toward him and placed her soft lips against his quivering cheek. Yannuvia felt wisps of her long hair brushing against his face and interlocking with his long silver-gray hair. He smelled the sweetness of her breath and a pleasant flora essence, not unlike the pleasant smells of his mother. The young Drelve pinched his left thigh. The pain told him this was not a dream. She teased his hair with her long supple fingers.

"Who? How?" he stammered.

"Sshhh. Lie down and rest. You've much to do. Take this stone. Let no one know you have it. It'll protect you, but only if you *alone* how of its existence," the stunning female murmured.

She extended her hand and placed a spherical gray stone in his left hand. Initially a perfect sphere, the gray rock transformed to fit the contour of the youth's left hand. When he switched it to his right hand, the stone softened, warmed, changed to its enantiomer, and fit his grip perfectly. The rock weighed very little and actually felt lukewarm in his palm. Intense warm gray light filled the room. Yannuvia reflexively but only briefly closed his eyes. When he opened them, he saw a flash of blue light, and she was gone. Clutching the gray stone, Yannuvia sat on the edge of his bed, breathed deeply, and looked around the room. The only changes were the presence of the gray stone, his frayed emotions, and tangles in his hair...*elflocks.*

Yannuvia went to the hidden entryway to his tree home, passed through, and looked into the common area in the center of Alms Glen. In the low light of the dark period Yannuvia saw little activity. Specifically, he saw no evidence of the interloper. He returned to his bed, but did not find sleep again this rest period. He clutched the gray stone. The rock melded with his tense digits and comforted him.

As soon as he heard activity outside, Yannuvia climbed out of bed, laboriously and painfully combed the tangles from his long thick hair, left his tree, and joined his fellow Drelvlings. His brother Gaelyss dominated the conversation. The young female Kirrie placed herself as near Yannuvia as she could. Gaelyss could talk of little else but the upcoming trip to Meadowsweet and Green Vale to harvest the enhancing plant. Yannuvia nearly burst to tell the others of the stone and his encounters with the female, but her words continued to reverberate in his mind. *Tell no one!* The stone felt warm within his raiment and emitted pulses of energy when the young Spellweaver *thought* of speaking of it. After their meal the youths went about their separate tasks. Yannuvia sought out the Teacher Edkim.

Edkim busily prepared for the upcoming trip.

"Teacher, may I ask you something?" Yannuvia began.

"I have many tasks to perform, young Spellweaver, as do you. Our journey begins in just two cycles of Meries. What troubles you?" Edkim asked.

"I…I'm not troubled, Teacher," Yannuvia answered.

"But you are, young one. I know you well. Please state your thoughts," the Teacher responded.

"Please tell me of the Alluring Falls. Where are they?" Yannuvia queried.

"Why do you inquire of the enchanted falls? Where did you learn of them?" Edkim asked.

"One of the older…" Yannuvia began.

"None of the Drelvlings know of the falls. It's a secret kept among Teachers and Spellweavers, but only when Spellweavers have made the journey to Green Vale and matured. The area is too dangerous. Many have ventured there, but few return. You must never go to this area. Nonetheless, I'll tell you of the falls. We avoid the area. They are located nigh three days march beyond the forest edge. One must travel northward through the wild woods, then travel eastward and south of Mirror Lake, move northward at the lake's eastern shore, edge along the dangerous Foothills of Illman, and follow the river to reach the enchanted falls. There are many legends about the Alluring Falls. Most frequently, lore blames malicious sirens for tragedies that occur at the falls. Passersby can't resist the enticing suggestions made by the sirens. The sirens' songs are said to torture the naked ears. Some say a young and beautiful witch was thrown over the falls generations ago and she pronounced a curse on the area with her dying breaths. Magick pronounced in its caster's death throes is said to be particularly potent, even more so than spells cast in the light of an Approximation of the Gray Wanderer Andreas. But others say the spirits of all who perish at the Alluring Falls remain eternally, long for companionship, and entice each passerby to leap and join their eternal unrest. Others say mischievous water sprites underestimate the danger of the falls and unintentionally lure unsuspecting passersby to their doom. Some creatures don't comprehend the significance of death and therefore are not aware of the gravity of their deeds. And there are those who say the passerby's mind plays tricks on him. If one expects something to happen, it oft times does. Suffice it to say, it's an area that we, and you particularly, must avoid," the Teacher ended emphatically.

Yannuvia stood quietly.

"Does that answer your question?" Edkim asked. "If so, both of us must get back to our preparations."

"Thank you, Teacher. I'll be on my way," Yannuvia answered politely.

The young Drelve noted Edkim was visibly upset by his questions and left the Teacher to his multitude of tasks. Avoiding the clamor of his fellow neophytes, Yannuvia made his way to the edge of the forest. Looking above, he saw the disc of Andreas appeared a bit more prominent. The elders had pondered whether an Approximation might be near at the council meeting, but at this point the wandering sun was merely a bit closer than the last period. In just two more cycles of Meries, Edkim would lead the neophytes, including the twin Spellweavers, on the pilgrimage to Meadowsweet.

With difficulty, Yannuvia resisted the urge to set out toward the Alluring Falls. He completed his tasks, including grudgingly reading from the copy of the ancient spell book, which the Teacher Edkim had given him in his seventh season. Gaelyss had a similar book. Whenever a new Spellweaver was born, the Teacher provided the new sorcerer with a copy of the ancient text, which was entrusted to the care of the Teacher and titled *The Gifts of Andreas to the People of the Forest*. When a Spellweaver was born during an Approximation of Andreas, Magick duplicated the Drelves' spell book. Copies appeared for both Gaelyss and Yannuvia. Each Spellweaver's priceless spell book recorded his life experiences and new spells he learned. This made each spell book unique. Legend held the Spellweavers learned new enchantments when the gray sun drew near. Magick engrained new spells in the Spellweaver's mind. The recipients recorded new dweomers in the ancient spell book. Once a Spellweaver mastered and entered a new spell in the tome, the spell remained forever etched on the tome's pages. Not all Spellweavers mastered difficult dweomers. Magick was finicky. At the time of a Spellweaver's death, his spell book became part of the legacy of the Drelves. Teachers archived the old spell books, but only passed the spell book of the most recent Spellweaver to new Spellweavers. The Teachers never understood the Magick. Teachers were not Spellweavers. However, the secret of the ancient tome's duplication eluded even the greatest Spellweavers.

The Teachers taught all Drelvlings the legend of the spell book during their earliest lessons. Like Magick, the legendary spell book was part of Drelvish life.

The excitement of the upcoming harvest and his first trip to Green Vale energized Yannuvia. The young Spellweaver's mind recalled early childhood lessons about the spell book, Meadowsweet, Green Vale, and the enhancing plant.

Magick was like a great sea. Individual spells caused either tiny ripples or great waves. The level of the Magick and the power of the spell caster determined the size of the wave. In worlds of Magick spells were classified by their *level*, oft times between one and nine.

The most important facet of spell casting was the innate ability of the spell caster. Most spells required verbal, somatic, and material components. The spell caster must unerringly mutter the verbal or spoken component, painstakingly perform the somatic gestures, and utilize the proper material components. Verbal components might be protracted orations or a single phrase; gestures might be intricate or as simple as pointing; material components might be unique, readily attainable, or rarely unnecessary. Gathering some materials might take several lifetimes.

It was Magick.

The conversation with Edkim peaked Yannuvia's interest. While Gaelyss and others spent the entire period readying for the upcoming journey, Yannuvia retreated to his tree, studied his spell book, and inexplicably readily understood the subject matter. In the quiet of his tree home, the youth took the gray stone from its hiding place. Yannuvia touched the spherical gray stone, and again the gray rock transformed to fit the contour of the youth's left hand. The Spellweaver shifted the dreary rock from one hand to the other and marveled at the suppleness and malleability of the stone. Its temperature varied, but the stone never took on the lifeless feel of the pretty pebbles he found in streams.

The Spellweaver made several movements with his hands and muttered phrases of old Drelvish language. As he spoke them, the phrases he uttered appeared on the vellum and recorded the incantation in his spell book. When the youth gripped the gray stone, the Silence Spell took effect. When the young Spellweaver removed his hand from the stone, he ended the Magick. Yannuvia generated the Silence Spell without using any material components. He only pronounced the command and grasped the stone.

After he finished the spell, Yannuvia still held the gray rock and noted dampness. A small quantity of reddish syrupy liquid appeared on the stone. Alarmed, he quickly checked for wounds on his hand but found none. The liquid felt more like the twinberry syrup his mother placed on his breakfast cakes. The thin red syrup soaked into the bread and imparted a pleasant taste. At times, Drelves drank the twinberry juice as a beverage. Forgetting the pleasant taste of twinberries, Yannuvia tentatively rubbed a bit of the red liquid between his thumb and forefinger and raised the fingers to his nose. Though every instinct told him not to taste the liquid, curiosity won out. He gingerly touched the liquid to the tip of his tongue and tasted the liquid. He found the taste slightly bitter but pleasant. He felt warm, flushed, and developed a slight headache. Oddly a sense of direction appeared in his young mind. Edkim had told him general directions to the Alluring Falls. The stone's ichors somehow bestowed Yannuvia with the detailed route to the Alluring Falls.

The Spellweaver's slight headache abated and the gray stone now felt cool in his hand. He saw no more of the red liquid. Fatigue overcame the youth and he lay down on his comfortable bed and slept.

Dreams came. His mind visualized the descriptions he'd heard of Green Vale. He saw Kirrie's face, his mother Carinne, and then Vioss and Bystar. Redness replaced the images.

Wisps…

Threads…

Threads of Magick…

Threads of fate…

Threads of time…

Threads connecting worlds …

Dreams connecting worlds …

Dreams of Magick…

The Magick of Dreams…

Magick connecting dreams…

Magick connecting worlds…

Dream raiders…

Elf pressure…

Albtraum…

Albträume, elf dreams, nightmares…

Dreams…

Following a flash of red light…

Again, he walked along the pathway toward the Alluring Falls. He felt the spray of water. A soothing voice said to him, "Remember what you have learned. Remember the power of the stone."

In the dream, Yannuvia touched the stone and recited the incantation of the Silence Spell. In his dream silence surrounded the young Spellweaver. He edged his way carefully along the passage behind the waterfall and discovered a hidden portal. He felt gentle tugs on his raiment and sensed wispy images amongst the sprays, but heard no voices. He edged his way through the secret door behind the waterfall and entered a chamber.

A table sat in the center of a stone cavern. A small chest sat on the table. A faint yellow light illuminated the room, but the source of the illumination was not apparent. In the far recess of the room on the side opposite the entryway, he saw two stones on the floor of the stone grotto. One was made of a blue tile, and the other was red.

His left hand left the stone and ended the silence spell. He heard the soft voice again, "Find these treasures. These are for you alone."

The images faded from his mind and he dreamed of the twinberry syrup coated breakfast cakes. He awakened refreshed and pondered, "Why didn't I see the blue light?"

"I'm here, silly," the beguiling feminine voice teased.

Within the confines of his little tree, Yannuvia was not alone.

She sat cross-legged on the floor and stared up at him. She wore an emerald green dress and boots made of a tan material. A simple black ribbon held back her long hair. Her lips parted and cooed, "I enjoy watching you sleep. Are you rested?"

"Who are you? How do you bypass the Magick of my tree? Why are you…" he quickly asked?

"You are chosen. I watch you because it pleases me to do so. Are you ready to seek what awaits you?" she answered.

"I must trek with the Teacher to Green Vale. The trip requires several cycles of Meries to complete. I'm a Spellweaver. My people expect me to follow the Teacher and harvest the enhancing plant. I can't go traipsing off to some waterfall! I've responsibilities!" he argued.

"You should follow *your* path. Yours is a different road. Take a chance on me," she suggested seductively.

"The Teacher says the Alluring Falls are cursed. They are dangerous!" Yannuvia replied.

"That's the conventional wisdom of your people. That's what the Teacher wants you to know, to feel. Why do you think this area is forbidden? Why do most of your people never learn of the area? Has the Teacher ever presented you with a gift such as the gray stone?" she countered.

"I've received guidance, nurturing, and protection from the Teacher and the elders. I don't always agree with the decisions of the council, but I follow their advice," Yannuvia staunchly replied.

"You are a Spellweaver. But you are only one of two. Gaelyss can accompany the Teacher to Meadowsweet. Generations have passed since your people had the gift of Magick. They have always had the herbs and roots of the forest. You have the chance to give your people something they have never had. Limitless Magick…through you! Like the gray sun was always present! Yes, I know the power of the gray sun. Have the Teachers ever spoken of the gray stones, such as the one you hold? You've seen a fraction of their power. You've seen what one stone can do. Imagine the power of multiple stones. What if I told you the grotto behind the falls holds another? You should act while you can. Did I not warn you of the danger of the falls? Did I not avail you with a means to protect yourself? Heed my advice. Seek the power hidden behind the falls, young Spellweaver," the female urged.

Yannuvia sensed urgency in her voice.

"Tell me what I must do," Yannuvia reluctantly replied.

She continued, "When you are behind the waterfall, you will find your entry barred. Eight gemstones will appear to you. They will reveal to you their order. You should touch them only in the order they suggest. Touch the first precious stone only once; touch the second gemstone only once; touch the third gemstone twice; touch the fourth gemstone thrice; touch the fifth jewel five times; touch the sixth precious stone eight times; touch the seventh gemstone thirteen times, touch the final jewel twenty-one times. You must do this precisely as I say. This mechanism is available to only you. There could be greater rewards, if you know what I mean?"

She stared seductively into his young eyes. Yannuvia sensed the need to do anything, or everything, she asked. At this moment, had he been standing at the verge of the Alluring Falls, he would have gladly walked over the rim of the falls had she asked.

She bent down and gently kissed his left cheek. Her delightful pheromones overwhelmed the young Drelve. He had seen only thirteen seasons of the harvest, and facing the female's charisma, his youth betrayed him.

"Consider my words, Yannuvia of the forest. Consider…me," she cooed seductively.

At this moment the flash of blue light filled the tree and she disappeared.

To follow the Teacher to Green Vale, as he knew he should, or seek the treasures allegedly hidden behind the forbidden falls…

The young Spellweaver made his first difficult choice.

CHAPTER 9
Journey's Beginning

Yannuvia's mind was set. There would be other seasons to travel to Green Vale. All his life he had eagerly anticipated his first trip to gather the enhancing root. Now he had chosen to forego the trip. Yannuvia realized the rite of passage was prerequisite to his assuming positions of leadership and maturity among his people. Even as a Spellweaver, participating in the harvest was essential. His brother Gaelyss would surpass him in the knowledge of the enhancing root that added potency of the Drelves' potions, unguents, and elixirs. On the other hand Yannuvia hoped to attain unique knowledge and artifacts before accessible to his people, move Magick forward, and make the Drelves less vulnerable to the marauding attacks of the Drolls and Kiennites.

The mysterious matron of his dreams made her way into his everred tree home and left the stone. She had not elaborated on the origin or nature of the device. She alleged treasures were hidden in a grotto behind the Alluring Falls and revealed to him their location. The Teacher Edkim had told him legends about the waterfall. Yannuvia found no maps leading to its location. Edkim had given him only a general idea. Now the gray stone had *somehow* given Yannuvia the waterfall's location.

The young Spellweaver told his friends neither of his dreams nor the gray stone and kept the stone hidden in his tree. When he should have been resting, Yannuvia had studied the complex rock for many amber periods, consulted the libraries of vellum in the Teacher's tree, and read *the Gifts of Andreas to the People of the Forest*. He discovered no information about the unusual stone. The rock emitted more gray light whenever the gray sun was higher in the sky.

Yannuvia had envisioned falling to his death at the suggestion of the voices of the falls. The visitor to his dreams warned him of the dangers of the falls and presented him with the gray stone and the secret of silence to evade the waterfall's enchantment. Why would she lie about the treasures?

There was nothing for it!

Yannuvia gathered supplies, made ready, and slipped through the common area. The Drelvling knew the propinquity of Alms Glen well. Every tree was a landmark as well as his friend. Navigating to the fringes of the red meadow and the local fauna posed no problems. Soon Yannuvia reached the edge of the Lone Oak meadow. Ironically now he had to sneak past the Drelvish ranger outposts and he wanted no delays.

Drelves had powers of observation secondary to none.

Scent…

No problem…

The scent of another Drelve would not alarm the sentries.

Visibility…

Drolls and Kiennites lacked the Drelves' ability to blend into the forest. Even the most alert sentry would have difficulty sensing one of his own blending in the forest and sneaking past. Why should a Drelve want to sneak past the guards and slither across the red meadow into the dangerous wild woods across the way? The sentries weren't watching for people leaving the forest!

Sound was another matter. The keen hearing of the Drelvish sentries detected the snapping of the smallest red pine needle. Yannuvia learned an important lesson when he serenaded Kirrie six seasons ago and alerted the sentries. The observant sentries caught the Drelvlings outside their approved bounds. Cleaning boots made one more careful. The memory warmed Yannuvia. If the sentries caught him, Yannuvia felt he could allay their concerns. Spellweavers required materials for their spells. The area at the fringe of the meadow was a good place to find such materials. The Spellweaver wanted to test the effectiveness of the Silence Stone. As he neared the fringe of the forest, the young Spellweaver clutched the gray stone and muttered arcane phrases. A blanket of silence fell over him and an area about three paces in all directions around him.

The Drelve intermingled with the reds, oranges, and yellows of the flora of the forest and inched past the scouts. He saw his father's friend Kitt perched in the lower branches of a red elm. The Spellweaver easily slipped past and into the scrub beyond the forest. He followed the forest edge around the red meadow, entered the wild woods, and trekked northward toward Mirror Mountain.

Yannuvia was now in unfamiliar territory.

The plants in the forest changed. The friendly red oaks, red elms, and the helpful tree herders no longer surrounded him. Odd creatures skittered past. Surrounded by his circle of silence, he knew predators could not hear his approach, but on the other hand he could not hear their hunting calls. His remarkable hearing and keen sense of smell kept him on even footing with any beast in the forest. The Silence created another dilemma for the young Spellweaver. He could not cast his limited spells. After much debate, he eased his grip on the gray stone, ended the Silence, and actually welcomed the sounds of the forest. Though unfamiliar with his surroundings, he was still in a forest and more or less at home. He paused, munched on some trail mix made by his mother, and plotted his course.

Yannuvia looked to the sky and saw Meries retreating toward its zenith. The amber period was beginning.

Was Andreas nearer?

Was the gray sun flirting with an Approximation? More than likely he witnessed one of the unpredictable sun's toggles toward the World of the Three Suns. Back at Alms Glen, the Teacher would be preparing the pilgrims to begin the trek to Meadowsweet on the morrow. Just one day remained before the beginning of the dark period. Yannuvia knew the Teacher, his parents, and the scouts would soon be scouring the woods for him. The neophyte Spellweaver paused only a moment and reflected. Again he felt he made the right decision, and turned eastward and walked along the southernmost shore of the large Mirror Lake. Mirror Mountain's reflection dominated the clear waters.

Yannuvia heard the growl of a noir skat and scurried up a weeping willow. The very nourishing purplish tears of the weeping willow quenched his thirst. Tempted, the Drelve pulled the gray stone from his raiment but found none of the red liquid. Then he remembered the headache. The point was moot, for there was no red liquid on the stone.

Yannuvia moved deftly through the underbrush. He reached the eastern shore of Mirror Lake and saw the Foothills of Illman directly ahead. The Drelvling turned northward and paralleled the lake. As with all Drelves, the forest was his element and seemed to clear a path for him. He walked through the entire light period, pausing only for brief respites, nourishment, and refreshing drinks from the streams. His dream had given him a generally accurate idea of the area, but the Spellweaver acknowledged he was, for the moment, lost.

Yannuvia stopped, listened intently, and heard a distant rumble in the distance. Did the sound indicate he neared the Alluring Falls?

The young Drelve had journeyed far into the yellow-red forests. Few Drelves entered this area, because the elders and Teachers discouraged travel to the wild woods. Yannuvia risked discovery by roving bands of Drolls, Kiennites, and other ilk. The Spellweaver squinted his eyes in the dimming light. Meries neared its low point. This was the last cycle of the little yellow sun before the dark period. The gray sun Andreas was... nearer.

Andreas...

Sometimes only a speck on the horizon...

Sometimes never seen at all...

Sometimes almost filling the sky and blotting out the light of Meries with its own gray auras...

Yannuvia liked the times when the gray wandering sun appeared. He felt stronger during the sun's toggles toward the world. The Teacher spoke of the rare Approximations and said Spellweavers learned new spells without the need of reading books! The last Approximation had occurred his birth year.

Having never witnessed an Approximation of Andreas, Yannuvia knew little about the movements of the gray sun and even less about Magick. But the brown-haired elders knew little more of the odd sun's movements. Drelves lacked facial hair and the grayness and red-orange tint faded to brown as they aged.

Learning spells without study...

Come to think of it...the gray stone had given him the Silence Spell.

The roar of the falls grew louder. But he heard more.

Nearby...

A babbling brook...

Voices...

Laughter...

CHAPTER 10
Missing

Edkim had slept little during the rest period and eagerly awaited the end of the amber period. Edkim had been Teacher of the Drelves now for thirty-seven harvests. His tenure had seen the attack six seasons earlier when six Drelves, including the neophytes Remy, Vioss, and Bystar had been killed. This was the 13th season of the twin Spellweavers Yannuvia and Gaelyss. Many generations had passed since a Spellweaver had accompanied the party to Meadowsweet and Green Vale to harvest the enhancing root. Now two reached their thirteenth season, and the responsibility to oversee the trip fell upon Edkim. Insuring the maximal potency of the enhancing root required harvesting the mature tubers during the eighth dark period of their growth, and Edkim knew the time was nigh. The trek to Meadowsweet must begin after the next amber period. From Meadowsweet the group would make the journey to Green Vale and complete the vital mission. Edkim had this light period to make the final arrangements in Alms Glen. Then there would be one more effort to rest during the following amber period after which he must gather his charges and begin the journey.

One eight hour day and one eight hour night and all must be ready.

The young Spellweavers had progressed well in their studies. Gaelyss had outpaced his brother in the formal studies and followed a straight and narrow path. Yannuvia had been the more adventuresome of the brothers and required more supervision and guidance. Of late the youngster had been even more aloof and quiet during their discussions. Other Drelvlings had spoken to the Spellweaver only to have their words fall on seemingly deaf ears. Others reported Yannuvia's absence from games and training.

Edkim and the elders cautioned all Drelvlings against going beyond the confines of Alms Glen, but the Teacher feared Yannuvia ignored the warnings.

The Teacher had made his individual preparations. He gathered items from his residence, the Old Orange Spruce, the traditional home of the Teachers. He went about the trees and assured the others were making ready. Rumsie was in charge of security on the journey. Sergeant Major Rumsie was a veteran archer and knew the path to Meadowsweet well. The Teacher had chosen a group of scouts and archers to accompany the group. In addition to the twin Spellweavers, four other neophytes would make the journey. The same rite of passage was occurring in all Drelve settlements, but the group from Alms Glen made up the largest contingent.

Edkim found Gaelyss ready and waiting. The young Spellweaver impatiently thumbed through his well-worn spell book and nodded his eagerness. The Teacher then went to the red oak where Yannuvia resided. The great tree offered no resistance to the Teacher's entry. To the Teacher's dismay, Yannuvia was not home. A quite check of the community confirmed Edkim's fears that the young Spellweaver had left Alms Glen. The distraught Teacher rushed through the forest, checked the known favorite places of the young missing Spellweaver, proceeded to the edge of the forest, and looked out onto the meadow of the Lone Oak. The great tree stood as a silent sentry. Edkim didn't find young Yannuvia. The guards on duty had neither heard nor seen anyone including the youth.

Edkim quickly called a council meeting.

"I cannot locate Yannuvia," the Teacher said dejectedly.

"He is not in the village or the surrounding forest," Balewyn, the senior archer added.

"He must be found. The trip to Meadowsweet cannot be delayed. The root must be harvested during the dark period. We cannot delay," the elder Debby insisted.

"I'm aware of that, but I can't leave without the Spellweaver," Edkim insisted.

"You can and must proceed, Teacher. The Spellweaver Gaelyss will accompany you. We will send parties to search for Yannuvia, but we cannot compromise the security of the harvesting group and the safety of Gaelyss. The most veteran scouts and archers will have to support the mission. We cannot leave those remaining in Alms Glen undefended. We must continue surveillance of the most critical areas of the forest. Young Yannuvia has been told many times to stay within the confines of the area around the compound. He knew the importance of the harvest. There is nothing more critical to our people. Our very survival depends on the successful harvest. Yannuvia knew these things," the elder continued.

"He's not been himself of late. Something has been on his mind," Edkim said in the young Spellweaver's defense.

"My brother needs a keeper," Gaelyss blurted. "I cannot believe he has jeopardized the harvest!"

"He has not jeopardized the harvest, young Gaelyss. His presence is not essential. We've had several generations of harvesting the root without the presence of a Spellweaver. The harvesting of the precious enhancing root is a prelude to becoming a mature member of the Drelve community. Missing the harvest is Yannuvia's loss. He will accompany the Teacher next season.

We cannot delay. Edkim, you will proceed at the beginning of the bright light. I suggest the party members get some rest," Debby continued.

"Will you give your permission, elder, and allow me to search for my son," Glinne asked.

"My dear Glinne, how can I do that? Our people need you. Young Yannuvia has advantages of Magick against the creatures of the forest. He's been told to avoid the Drolls and Kiennites. Perhaps Yannuvia will return before the morrow and join the party. We must proceed with the harvest. I will say no more," the elder concluded.

Everyone knew the elder's word was final and accepted her decision. The meeting ended. Dejectedly Edkim returned to the Old Orange Spruce and made his final preparations.

CHAPTER 11
The Bowyer's Elfdream

Drelvish bowyers dried wood from yellow yew trees for three full seasons of the harvest. Fletchers created hand made arrows from the many woods of the forest. Fletchings were made of many feathers. The bowyers shaped the wood into sections over another two seasons. Gently removing the bark from the back of the wood, they used a single piece of wood, creating a self-bow. The inner heartwood resisted compression and the outer sapwood performed better in tension. This combined in a single piece of wood to form a natural laminate effect. The bowyer then applied a concoction of wax, resin, and fine tallow to make the wood water resistant. Most bowstrings were made of hemp, flax, or silk. Drelvish bowyers harvested the silk of the purple glowworms during the dark period and used this to make the bowstrings. Silk taken when the gray sun drew near amplified the power of the bow. Most longbows had a range of about 200 yards. The best bows might have a range of 360 yards. Silk gathered during an Approximation might double the range.

BJ Aires, the bowyer and fletcher of Edkim's generation, was the greatest Drelvish bowyer since the time of Byrum Goodale. The mark *BJ* signified the current bowyer's efforts. Also an exceptional fletcher, BJ enjoyed his work and produced the fine bows and arrows the Drelvish folk used to defend their realm. BJ's unique technique produced the finest arrows. His arrows gave another 100 yards of accuracy and distance. Many years of hard work nurtured BJ's exceptional talent. He strived to get better with each bow, arrow, or quiver he created. Oldsters like Blanchard compared BJ Aires in the same breath to Byrum Goodale.

Byrum Goodale was one of BJ Aires's forebears. Bowyers engraved their mark or insignia on the back of the bow. BG signified Byrum's work. Laboring several hundred seasons ago, Byrum Goodale created exceptional devices. Byrum preferred the self-bow. Old Blanchard's grandfather had walked the lands of the World of the Three Suns as a contemporary of the great bowyer BG.

Bows bearing the mark *BG* were now quite rare, as even the finest weaponry ultimately succumbed to time and usage. Though he had a great yearning to do so, BJ had actually never held one of the great ancient bowyer's works. Over time BG's creations were lost to the Drelves. Stories told that one of the last surviving BG longbows fell into the hands of Drolls many years ago during an ill-fated journey to Meadowsweet.

On the morrow, the Teacher Edkim anticipated leaving for Meadowsweet with the remaining Spellweaver Gaelyss, four neophytes named Zack, Debery, Meryt, and Bryce as per tradition in their thirteenth season, and the veterans Rumsie, Beaux, and Klunkus. BJ Aires shared the excitement felt by all Drelvedom. A Spellweaver participated in the harvest of the enhancing root for the first time in many generations. Unfortunately, he shared the concern of his fellows for young Yannuvia. BJ Aires had helped in the last minute searches for the lost Spellweaver. Unfortunately he had no more luck than Glinne, Edkim, Rumsie, or any of the others.

Although Drelves were not hunters and indeed disdained meat, the forest folk were oft times forced to defend their realm against marauding beasts from the wild woods across the red meadow beyond the Lone Oak. Much like the role of Teacher, the bowyer trade was passed along from generation to generation, but not necessarily along family lines and very unlike the rare Spellweavers who were born during the Approximations of the wandering Gray Sun Andreas.

BJ sighed. The time of the Approximation was nigh, the length of the gray sun's visit was unpredictable, and every moment of the gray light was precious. The light of the gray wanderer Andreas magnified the bowyer's efforts, just as it did those of all Drelves and most creatures of the World of the Three Suns. BJ knew he would need all his energies to work as long and hard as he could whilst the Gray Wanderer was near. Now was his time to rest. Fatigue overcame the bowyer, and BJ reclined on the red oak bench in his simple workshop. The tired craftsman stretched, sunk into the soft fibers of the red oak, and closed his eyes.

Soon he slept.

Fond memories of young Yannuvia entered his mind. From his fifth season the little Spellweaver spent time with the bowyer and marveled at BJ's creations. The other twin Gaelyss never shared Yannuvia's enthusiasm for the bowyer's work, but a little she-Drelve named Kirrie often accompanied Yannuvia. Yannuvia and Kirrie's images faded. BJ's subconscious turned to his life mate Camille and his little daughter Caroline. Thoughts of his trips to the Green Vale entered his mind. The Thirttene Friends on the odd occasion allowed the bowyer access to pieces of their branches so that he could use them in his wares. The very pleasant memories faded...

Wisps...

Threads…
Threads of Magick…
Threads of fate…
Threads of time…
Threads connecting worlds …
Dreams connecting worlds …
Dreams of Magick…
The Magick of Dreams…
Magick connecting dreams…
Magick connecting worlds…
Dream raiders…
Elf pressure…
Albtraum…
Albträume, elf dreams, nightmares…
Dreams…

Redness surrounded the bowyer in his dream. In dreamland the bowyer journeyed to a chilly workroom in an austere shop. An old chap with a familiar face worked at the bench. BJ had seen sketchings depicting the great bowyer Byrum Goodale in the journals and schoolbooks the Teacher had used. In his dream, did he now look upon the great bowyer of old?

"Resting, are you?" the old Drelve asked.

"I was…I am… Are you…?" the sleeping BJ managed to muttered.

"I am whomever you want me to be. It's your dream. Yes, then, I'm Byrum Goodale. As a bowyer of the forest, you should appreciate these materials," the old voice warbled.

Speaking in a dream to the greatest bowyer in Drelvedom's history…
Interacting with one's dream…
Hearing one's dreams and responding…
Speaking and hearing one's dreams respond…

On the work bench hazy images appeared. BJ saw four shafts of fine blue wood of equal length, four beautiful scintillating feathers, and four fine arrowheads.

"What do I look upon, old one?" BJ murmured.

"Ah, you won't see these anywhere or *anytime* soon, bowyer. Blue wood…beyond rare…the bluewood trees are no more. The blue wood's heartwood makes the strongest and longest lasting implements. Phoenix feathers…have you seen a phoenix! For that matter, have you seen a Tuscon? Neither is a common sight. The arrowheads are titanium alloy. I don't expect you to know of titanium. No arrow will fly faster, further, or more accurately than one constructed of these materials that merge Nature and Magick," the old Drelve's image said.

BJ didn't understand how one speaks to another in a dream, but he replied, "Do you speak of elf-arrows? Elf-shot? Elf-bolts? Lore of my trade tells of exceptional bolts. Our enemies the Kiennites fired arrows that burst into flame. But I know nothing of blue wood. The Teachers read to us of mythical birds such as the phoenix. Titanium...alloy...these words mean nothing to me."

"Elvessss are credited with too much..." the figure grumbled.

"Elves are *mythical*. I don't know these materials," BJ protested.

"Oh, but you could learn of such things, craftsman. If you possessed such rarities and assembled them in the gray light of the wandering sun, they might help your young Spellweavers. Such materials cannot be replaced. Use them judiciously," the old Drelve's image countered.

"How would you know of our young *Spellweaver*? History tells us our people were without a Spellweaver during your tenure. That's another reason you were...uh, *are* so valuable to the folk of the forest," BJ answered.

"But *you* know of your *Spellweavers*. The twin brothers...it's your dream! And you are sharing it with me," the wavering old voice labored. The elderly Drelve's image shimmered. His brown hair changed to the silver of youth.

"Still, I'd rather you not talk of the Spellweavers," BJ continued.

"Fair enough! I've shown you the best of my wares. Now let your eyes enjoy some pleasantry," the image suggested.

The vision in the dream changed. BJ saw his life-mate Camille in the simple but beautiful dress she wore during their ceremony of lifetime commitment. The bowyer watched the images quietly.

"Quite pretty! Are you enjoying your dream?" the voice continued.

The tone of the voice changed. Though the craftsman saw the image of his beloved spouse, he heard an unfamiliar, raspy, yet seductive voice.

Uncomfortably seductive and alluring...

BJ stirred uneasily.

"Do you prefer this visage?" the now feminine voice asked.

The image changed to the face of a beautiful matron. Though in his travels BJ had seen many females of ilks other than Drelves, he did not recognize the ilk before him. He considered the Drelves, particularly his Camille, the loveliest denizens of the forests. But this tall, very alluring female had creamy skin, soft blue eyes, and a pleasant voice as she spoke to the sleeping bowyer. She wore a blazing red dress. Coal black hair fell gracefully down her back and chest.

"Who are you?" BJ asked.

"Relax. Breathe deeply! Allow me to entertain you. No one works harder for his folk than you, bowyer. Allow yourself a respite. Gaze upon me," the sultry voice suggested.

She changed.

The female now wore a flaming red warrior's tunic. Her hair changed to deep red. A warrior's bandana and headband complemented her garb and enhanced her appearance. She carried a long bow, a self-bow BJ reasoned. She extended the weapon and revealed the logo *BG*. The female warrior sauntered toward BJ Aires. She walked across a field of green clover, greener than anything the bowyer had beheld save the greenness of the Green Vale. She reached him, extended her left arm, and softly stroked his left cheek. She drew her lips near as if to kiss him. Though dreaming the Drelve smelled the sweetness of her breath.

"No!" BJ muttered.

"Why not allow yourself the pleasure of my company?" she cooed.

"No!" BJ shouted.

"Ingrate! No one refusssssessss me!" the voice reacted angrily.

She changed yet again.

A different face now entered BJ's dream. Horrific and vaguely female, the creature had fiery red eyes, unsightly wings, and long muscular arms ending in long curved talons, which were covered in dark ichors. Still the creature was strangely attractive. She pursed her lips, blew the sleeping Drelve a kiss, and simply hissed, "Pleasant dreams, big boy! How do you like these?"

The she-beast revealed long curvaceous legs.

"Get away from me!" BJ insisted.

The female smiled wryly and stepped back.

"You have a pawn's role to play, bowyer. I'll leave you to your foolish simple dreams. But remember the words you've heard in these dreams. Everybody's got to serve somebody! You can't serve but one Spellweaver, bowyer. Remember who had interest in you and the forest. Consider who will best lead your people. And remember bowyer, I'll see you in your dreams," the image said laughing.

Blueness surrounded her and she then faded.

BJ Aires bolted up, drenched in sweat and relieved to find he was alone in his work area. Perplexed by his hunger, the bowyer wiped his brow and looked about the workroom. Gray light filtered through the open window. BJ leapt from the red oak bench and ran to the window. Andreas was drawing near but had not reached full Approximation. He had wasted little of the precious gray light.

The time…

How long had he slept?

Something glinted on his red hard wood table.

Four arrow sized shafts of blue wood…

Four fine feathers, whose colors changed by the moment…

Four deep gray extremely sharp arrowheads…

"Titanium alloy, I suppose. The stuff of dreams…the stuff of elf-bolts," the bowyer muttered.

CHAPTER 12
Water Sprites

Yannuvia edged forward, dropped to the ground, crawled along the friendly forest floor, reached through the underbrush at the rivulet's edge, and peaked into the area. At the moment his keen hearing was more valuable than *Silence*. He kept the stone ready.

Three little unquestionably feminine creatures with pointed ears creatures played in the stream.

Were they water sprites?

Should he avoid them?

The Teacher Edkim had said the little creatures could be unpredictable and temperamental. The young Spellweaver generally avoided creatures with which he was unfamiliar. But his situation compelled him to investigate. Many unfriendly creatures inhabited these woods.

Like goblins, hobgoblins, and Kiennites, water sprites had pointed ears. Elves, Drelves, and Drolls lacked pointed ears. Drolls had big ears. As far as Yannuvia knew, goblins, hobgoblins, and elves did not inhabit the World of the Three Suns. In fact, the Teacher said elves were mythical.

Yannuvia had never seen water sprites. He listened intently.

Illarie jumped from the thick red grass on the bank of the slowly flowing brook, launched her two-foot long body into a perfect arch, and split the water gently. Disturbing the water of the stream as minimally as possible was the water sprite's goal and the point of the game.

"Good one!" laughed Condee as she watched from the lowest branch of the great red oak that shaded the brook from the amber light of the little yellow sun Meries.

"I can do better!" Ellspeth boasted.

She flipped her fiery red hair over her dainty shoulders, gracefully leapt into the air, and dove flawlessly. Her tiny frame created no disturbance as she entered the peaceful brook.

"Yeah!" Condee shouted gleefully.

She extended her little light blue hands. Playful sparks of many colors sprayed harmlessly into the air around the blue-haired sprite.

"No fair! No fair!" Illarie protested. "She used Magick! I detected the 'part water' spell. You cheated!"

Ellspeth joined Condee in joyous laughter. Illarie pouted. Small plumes of white smoke spewed from orange-haired Illarie's pointed ears.

Yannuvia felt uncomfortable in this area of the forest. He knew little of the wild woods, having only stared at its borders across the wide red meadow of the Lone Oak through his looking glass. According to his Teacher and the elders, everyone, including the powerful Drolls, worried that this part of the forests was enchanted and avoided the area.

The Teacher, elders, Drolls, and everyone were correct. This part of the forest *was* enchanted.

The young Drelve had heard stories of water sprites. During his last excursion into the area, his father Glinne had found evidence of the little creatures, but had not seen them. Yannuvia wanted to learn more of them. He gripped the gray stone bequeathed him by his mystery guest. He whispered and used little energy in casting the Silence Spell upon his soft boots. The Spellweaver used the juice of the ever-present red basil berries to disguise his scent. Red basil berries were a great boon of the forest. The little fruits were fragrant, tasty, loaded with nutrients, and also imparted a very powerful fragrance which covered the essence of most creatures. The pleasant fragrance hid him from the noses of most enemies. The bushes bearing the fragrant berries flourished throughout the woods and the denizens of the forest expected the aroma of their fruits.

The pleasantness of the red basil contrasted with the malodorous gray berries.

The ubiquity of Red basil contrasted sharply with the rarity of Blackthorn.

The prized Blackthorn stood out among the largely red and orange foliage of the central forests. Rumors held the large shrubs or small trees were more prevalent in the mountain areas. The common name was derived from the dark bark and skin, and from the thorns or spines that it bore. White flowers covered the Blackthorn in early growing season in the mountains. Sailors of the great western sea reported the Emerald Isle had four distinct seasons. The Teachers deemed this unscientific, unnatural, and unlikely. But the stories held that in its native regions the blackthorn was often the first flowering tree. Blackthorn bore a fruit called the sloe, or slaes by some peoples, similar to a small damson or plum, suitable for preserves, but too tart to eat unless deeply frozen in the ice or snow of the highest peaks. A potent potable called sloe gin was made from the fruits. Blackthorn was valuable as hedging and a cover for birds.

A straight blackthorn stem was valued and traditionally made into a walking stick called a Shillelagh. A Shillelagh was a wooden club or cudgel, typically made from a stout knotty stick with a large knob on the end. Edkim the Teacher carried a Shillelagh, which had been passed down through generations of Teachers. The Teacher spoke of a legendary place called the Emerald Isle, where the blackthorn grew commonly. No Drelve had ever visited such a place, and the island was supposedly located somewhere across the great Western Sea. Legend held the plants on the emerald isle were mostly *green!* The Drelves only knew green plants in the Green Vale, and the Drelves knew more of the forests of the World of the Three Suns than any other ilk.

But this was legend and stories. Other stories held the blackthorn cudgel carried by the Teachers fell from the sky during an Approximation of the Gray Wanderer Andreas. Like most his brethren, Yannuvia felt this was more near the truth than a far-fetched story of green plants growing on an island where there were four seasons and times of darkness.

Recalling the Teacher's lesson helped Yannuvia pass the time as he watched the activities in the brook. Yannuvia's concentration turned back to the water sprites…

Among the interesting little creatures, the young Drelve had seen only what appeared to be feminine creatures. No males…

At his height of five feet, the Drelve towered over the two-foot tall creatures. The sprites had long shiny blue, orange, or red tresses. They had pointed little ears, deep green eyes, curvaceous pleasing bodies, smooth shiny pale blue skin, and lyrical voices. Their skin took on the deep blue-green color of the pure waters of the stream whenever they dived into the brook and made them virtually undetectable in the waters. (Only the most discerning gaze detected them!)

Certainly named appropriately, the water sprites were about the same size as tree sprites that inhabited the forests in many areas but particularly in the forests of the mountain ranges to the north.

Yannuvia hoped water sprites differed from tree sprites. Exhibiting a mean streak, tree sprites delighted in dropping acorns and stones onto unwary travelers below and aligned with more malevolent creatures. The beloved Teacher Edkim thoroughly described tree sprites in the oft times boring lessons that Yannuvia and other young Drelves had endured.

These benign little woodland beings seemed to only resemble the tree sprites in stature. The water sprites did nothing that appeared to inflict harm on the world around them. Yannuvia had *seen* them cast only playful Magick like Faerie Fire, Aura, Plant and Water Spells. He wanted to *hear* them. Yannuvia relaxed his grip on the Silence Stone and ended the silence.

The three sprites were so…pretty.

He knelt down, watched, and listened.

Illarie, Condee, and Ellspeth continued to play in the water. Suddenly Illarie raised her right hand and placed two delicate blue fingers to her perfectly formed pale orange lips.

"Sshhh! Do you hear something?" Illarie asked.

Her comrades interrupted their games and listened. Soon three pairs of dark green eyes stared directly at Yannuvia. He was discovered. The Drelve anticipated three Charm Spells.

Instead the blue-haired Condee asked, "Are you a troll? Are you a Droll? Are you going to eat us?"

Yannuvia did not speak.

Orange-haired Illarie then said, "Maybe he's mute. Maybe he doesn't speak our tongue. He looks big and dumb! Let's change him to a slug!"

Was she bluffing?

Transformation was difficult Magick!

Yannuvia could not do that sort of spell! *No* Spellweaver had cast such a dweomer! *The Gifts of Andreas to the People of the Forest* contained no such dweomer! The water sprite's words burned his ears.

Yannuvia stood and said, "I'm bigger than you, but I'm not dumb! Top this!"

The young Spellweaver snapped his right thumb and third finger and created a blue smoke ring. The smoke ring wafted away from him, moved toward Illarie, and harmlessly surrounded the sprite. The ring shimmered briefly and then burst into sparkles of Faerie Fire that briefly filled the air around the befuddled sprite.

Illarie pouted.

Ellspeth kept a small blue index finger pointed at the Drelve and said, "I've never seen trolls, Drolls, or giants, but my Mother Nature told me trolls were ugly, Drolls were strong, and giants were very big! He's not ugly enough to be a troll. Maybe he's a Droll. Mother told me that giants walk the forest. He's got to be at least five feet tall! I didn't think giants would be *that* big!"

Condee drew her petite bow, placed a dart within it, drew the bowstring taut and said, "If you try to hurt us, I'm going to shoot you!"

Yannuvia extended his arms to his side and pleaded, "My bow is upon my back. My sword is sheathed. If I had wanted, I could have hit you with an attack spell. You wouldn't have known what hit you!"

Twang!

Condee lost her grip on the bowstring and released the small projectile, which struck Yannuvia in the left thigh. No bigger than a dart, Condee's bolt barely broke the Drelve's skin.

"Oops!" the sprite chagrinned.

"Ouch!" Yannuvia groaned.

"I'm sorry! I didn't really mean to shoot you!" Condee clamored.

"You little bugger! I'm going to…no…I'm not…I guess…gosh! You *are* pretty. Your hair is so…so blue! May I stroke your tresses? On the other hand, may I kiss you?" Yannuvia rambled and walked toward the blue-tressed sprite.

"You dummy! You know the dart will enamor whomever it strikes. Didn't you listen to the cherub Cupid's warnings?" Illarie complained.

"Do you have any antidote?" Ellspeth asked.

Condee stammered, "Yes. The cherub gave me something called repulsion. It's back at the…"

"Stop! Don't tell him where we live!" Illarie cautioned.

Yannuvia stumbled into the brook and started to sing. His voice was melodious but the words didn't make sense. He approached Condee.

"The big guy is getting closer!" she screamed.

"Shoot him again!" Illarie ordered.

Condee fired a second bolt from her bow and struck Yannuvia in the opposite thigh. Ellspeth drew her bow and pulled a bolt from her quiver.

The bewitched and bewildered Spellweaver reached for Condee but the sprite was too quick and ducked out of the way. The love struck Drelve fell face first into the stream. The water was only three feet deep where he fell, and he quickly got back to his feet and started to pursue Condee. The water sprites clamored to the side of the stream. Ellspeth drew her bowstring taut, but Condee stopped her.

"How do you know the poison won't kill him?" the blue-haired sprite asked.

"I don't! What do you care? If all three of us shoot him, maybe he'll chase after all of us. Have you got any better ideas?" Ellspeth asked.

"No!" Illarie agreed and fired one of her little darts into Yannuvia's thigh.

Ellspeth also shot the Drelve.

"One little, two little, three little…what are you, anyway?" Yannuvia crooned inharmoniously. Unmusically the Spellweaver continued uttering gibberish. He sang, "Your red hair is beautiful. Your orange hair is beautiful. Your blue hair is beautiful. All of you are beautiful. Your speech is like that of singing birds. May I kiss every one of you?"

Four little darts in his thighs caused the young Drelve little pain, but the poisonous darts slowed his movement. Befuddled, he stopped in the middle of the stream.

The three sprites huddled briefly, moved away from the stream, and followed a pathway in the woods. With his head spinning a bit Yannuvia shook off his confusion and chased them down the trail. The sound of the roaring waterfall grew louder. Ahead the three little females went to a loosely organized collection of underbrush. One after the other the three slipped into the undergrowth. Yannuvia ran haphazardly toward the brushwood. The trees began to spin around him. Yannuvia lost his balance, fell to the ground, and skinned his knees. The Drelve's eyelids became heavy and he fell asleep. The last thing he remembered was three tiny voices and three tiny ropes of incredible strength looping around him.

"He's too big to bring inside!" Illarie cried.

"Magick will shrink him. He'll fit! We've disabled him. We can't just…" Condee's voice faded.

The three sprites struggled and dragged the unconscious Drelve through the entryway to their abode. Yannuvia fell unceremoniously to the stone floor. Three little bodies fell upon him and rubbed a gooey ointment onto the small wounds on his thighs.

Yannuvia opened his eyes. He'd heard mature Drelves talk of drinking too much fermented red basil juice and awakening on the morrow with a humdinger of a headache.

Yannuvia allowed he shared such a headache.

The Drelve found himself in a dry well-illuminated room. The young Spellweaver stood with difficulty, backed to the mossy wall behind him, and scanned the chamber. Something moved above him! Illuminating glowworms covered the irregular ceiling and gave light to the chamber. He no longer heard the roar of the waterfall. In fact the only sounds were his sighs, the skittering of the glowworms, and the barely audible breathing of the three sprites. The three water sprites cowered about ten paces away near the opposite wall.

Not ten Yardley paces… ten little paces! Yannuvia stood two feet tall! He was only as tall as the sprites! Given this frame of reference, the chamber was twenty feet wide, fifteen feet long and three feet high!

Evidently Magick shielded the vestibule leading into the grotto and reduced those entering to sprite-sized.

Though not as profound as the stillness created by the gray stone's Magick, an awkward minute of silence passed. Yannuvia certainly wasn't proud of the results of his first battle. Three pint-sized females had bested him!

The Spellweaver was thankful no others witnessed the battle.

Illarie stammered, "We didn't mean to hurt you. You surprised us. What are you?"

Yannuvia answered, "That's a fair question for me to ask you?"

Condee answered, "We are friends of the water and the woods. What would a *giant* know about such things?"

The Spellweaver protested and said, "I'm not a giant! I'm a little taller than most of my friends, but I'm not that *big*. And now, I'm no taller than you! What is this trickery? How do you know Magick?"

"How does anyone *know* Magick?" Ellspeth countered.

"Good point," Yannuvia acknowledged.

"Are you a sorcerer?" Illarie asked.

Suddenly Yannuvia realized that he might be telling the little creatures too much. Then he considered that they could have certainly slain him had they desired and indeed probably saved him from becoming dinner to some marauding predator. But then again, they had put him in that circumstance with their little darts! Going over the falls, as he did in his dream, might have been a better fate.

"Yes. I am a Spellweaver. I am also a friend of the forest," the Drelve answered.

"Then you are our friend as well," Illarie conceded.

"I'm still in love with your blue-haired friend," the Spellweaver teased.

Blue-tressed Condee jumped back but then realized that the Drelve laughed as he spoke.

"You may call us by our names. I'm Ellspeth Doole. Your blue-haired friend is Condee Rytte. Our friend is Illarie Quinton. And show some respect. We are likely older than you!" Ellspeth demanded.

"I'm sorry. I'm Yannuvia of the Drelves. I hail from Alms Glen. I'm glad to know you, even under these circumstances. I'm also quite interested in the barb with which you shot me. And the unguent you applied to me! Just how long was I out?" he replied.

"A while. On rare occasions our winged friend the cherub comes to the forest and brings us gifts such as the bows and darts. We'd never used them before today. They were supposed to make you sympathetic to us. The cherub never told us they created such strong emotions. The arrows are tipped with Passion Nectar. The unguent is something he called Repulsion. We don't know how to make them," Illarie confessed.

"Tell me more of this Cherub," Yannuvia asked.

"He is...you don't need to know more of him right now. We have heard of the Drelves of Alms Glen and Meadowsweet. Kiennites befoul our woods. They enter seeking blackthorn for its slaes. Their shamans seek also rare herbs and destroy indiscriminately. Magick does not favor them, but they have some arcane powers. They can create illusion. We tarry near their campfires and hear their stories of your people. If you are their enemies, we infer you are likely our friend. But we shan't be reckless. Our enemies' enemies aren't necessarily our friends. I...we don't quite trust you yet," Ellspeth declared.

"I see your pointed ears. I mean I see your point. I suppose you are right. I'm hungry. What do you have to eat?" the young explorer inquired.

"We have some slaes. Are you familiar with them?" Illarie responded.

"I've read and been taught of the fruit of the Blackthorn. Is there Blackthorn near this place? I thought it wouldn't cycle in areas where the everred trees grow," Yannuvia asked.

"Blackthorn doesn't grow in the wild woods, as you call our homeland. We're told it's common on the Emerald Isle?" Condee replied.

"Then there *is* an Emerald Isle," Yannuvia said.

"Yes. We aren't sure where it is located, but Cupid tells us green trees are native to the Emerald Isle and go through cycles of growth. It's reached only by flight or boat. The cherub brings us things from the green land," Ellspeth answered.

"You mention this guy, the cherub, again. He sounds evermore interesting. What do you give him?" Yannuvia inquired.

All three blushed, but Illarie answered, "He appreciates our company and spells. You should not assume we would..."

"Easy. Easy. I'm not insulting your integrity or accusing you of moral turpitude. I'll try some slaes. Are they also called sloe berries?" Yannuvia said, hoping to get back to the subject of food.

"Yes. We'll get you some. Rest," Illarie said.

The three sprites left the young Drelve alone.

The young Spellweaver sat in the austerely furnished chamber. Small chests lined the far wall. Sprites would need only a small storage area for their small and scanty clothes. Soon the females returned with several dark blue fruits and other fruits of the forest. The famished Drelve recognized blue apples, orange bananas, and red grapes. He shared nourishment with the sprites.

The four talked until the amber period ended. The water sprites advised Yannuvia avoid the Alluring Falls. Reluctantly they gave him detailed directions to the waterfall. Yannuvia knew it was time to resume his quest.

The immature Spellweaver pondered many things. Where were the Teacher, his brother Gaelyss, and the party to Meadowsweet at this moment? Were his people worried, or worse yet, angry?

When he really didn't understand why he pursued the substance of a dream, how could Yannuvia expect others to do so? '

The water sprites gave the Drelve more slaes and other fruits, and Yannuvia bade them farewell and squeezed through the opening to their den. Once outside he was again five feet tall.

The amber period had ended and, the World of the Three Suns had entered the prolonged dark period. But the land was darker. Grayness dimmed the subtle amber light. When Yannuvia looked to the sky, he saw Andreas filled much of the sky. The Gray Sun drew nearer by the moment.

The young Drelve witnessed his first Approximation of the Gray Sun. Would it be his last?

CHAPTER 13
Behind the Alluring Falls

His tryst into the deep forest to the forbidden area around the Alluring Falls now led Yannuvia beyond the home of the water sprites. His journey had been far longer than any the young Spellweaver had undertaken previously. As he trekked forward Yannuvia pondered the number of steps his fellow Drelves would take to reach Meadowsweet and Green Vale.

The deafening roar of the water told him the journey finally neared its end. The Spellweaver saw a pathway behind the falls and excitedly started toward the opening. Then he remembered the warnings of his dream and grasped the gray stone. Just as he heard the first word spoken by an enthralling whispering voice, Yannuvia completed the phrases activating the Silence Spell, and absolute quiet abruptly surrounded him. The young Drelve edged onto the narrow footpath, splashed his way behind the falls, and discovered a slightly wider area behind the fall. The narrow precarious pathway continued to the opposite side of the falls. After inspecting the damp rock wall behind the falls, Yannuvia's deft fingers silently and gingerly explored the wall of stone. Initially he found only cold wet stone.

Had the matron of his dreams lied about the grotto behind the falls?

Undaunted, the Drelve continued to investigate the area carefully but withdrew his hand when he received a slight shock. The face of the rock wall changed and a secret door appeared. Probing warily, he found no opening mechanism. As the Drelve watched a large engraving appeared and then dominated the door.

Now beyond the images in his dream, Yannuvia shuddered. The Drelve stared at the figure of a monster. The eight legged, eight eyed (two large red and six small black eyes), bloated creature sported a barbed tail similar to a fully-grown wyvern. Huge warty lumps covered the beast's body, its gaping maw bared huge fangs, and its modified first appendages mimicked claws.

Water sprayed the young Spellweaver from behind and chilled him. Yannuvia found the silence created by his Magick unnerving, but he yet feared the enchantment of the waterfall and remained reluctant to release his right hand's grip on the gray rock within his raiment. Though he had discovered the door Yannuvia saw no mechanism to open the portal, and he didn't know where the portal lead. His lovely matronly visitor had told him to seek the treasures behind the waterfall and touch eight stones. The creature's eyes drew his attention. The young Drelve checked closely. The figure's eyes were gemstones...precious stones. Exquisite black opals formed six eyes, and two larger brilliant red stones shaped the remaining eyeballs. Light emanated from the red stones.

Abruptly, one of the black opal eyes rotated and rose from the face of the rock. Something beckoned the Spellweaver to touch the little black stone. Yannuvia remembered *the feminine Dream raider's* words.

"You should touch them in an orderly fashion. Touch the first stone only once; touch the second stone only once; touch the third stone twice; touch the fourth stone thrice; touch the fifth stone five times; touch the sixth stone eight times; touch the seventh stone thirteen times, touch the final stone twenty-one times."

The young Drelve gingerly extended his left index finger, touched the little black stone once, and felt the briefest of shocks. Gray light flashed from the opal. The dark gemstone returned to its position among the six black eyes.

"Not so bad," the Spellweaver thought *silently*.

A different opal rose into the air above the engraving. Yannuvia shrugged and touched the little red basil berry-sized gem a single time. Again he felt the sharp twinge of discomfort. The opal descended to the surface of the engraving. Almost obediently, a third eye rose from the surface and floated eerily before the rock wall. The Drelve touched the black opal twice and felt two little shocks. The opal returned to its position. Another black eye's separation from the wall followed. Yannuvia touched this fourth stone three times, received three shocks, and watched the lovely opal return to its spot on the rock wall. The fifth eye rose from the wall, hovered before the Spellweaver, delivered a little shock in response to his five touches, and then returned to the figure's horrific face. The remaining black opal rose, and Yannuvia touched the gem eight times and received as many little jolts. The opal then returned to its designated position. The first red eye then separated from the wall. Brilliant red light flashed before his eyes. Yannuvia methodically touched the stone thirteen times, although he received a tiny shock each time he tapped the red diamond.

"What am I doing?" he thought silently.

Then the final eye rose from the surface of the engraving. Yannuvia squinted from the brilliant red light and touched the slowly rotating stone. The first time he touched the rock the gem felt icy cold. Words and phrases appeared in his mind. He touched the stone a second time and felt great heat. More phrases appeared in his consciousness. He touched the stone again and again until he had touched it a total of twenty-one times. A different sense moved through him each time he touched the rock. Bitter taste, sweet smell, sharp pain, brief blindness, but mostly hot and cold feelings ripped through the young Spellweaver. Each time Yannuvia touched the red gemstone, another phrase appeared in his mind.

A spell…?

Did the phrases represent an incantation?

After he touched the red stone twenty-one times, the crimson jewel obediently returned to its position. The entire caricature of the monster shimmered briefly.

Did the wall move?

For a moment, Yannuvia feared the monster was coming to life. Instead, the engraving faded from the wall. The stone behind the waterfall separated, created an opening, and exposed eerie red light beyond the portal. Had silence not bathed him, Yannuvia sensed the grating of the rock would have overwhelmed the rush of the waterfall.

There was nothing left for it.

Yannuvia stepped through the opening and into the grotto behind the waterfall. Still wary of the legends of the Alluring Falls, he maintained his grip on the gray stone to keep the Silence Spell active and inched into the room. An eerie red glow filled the area, but the Spellweaver could not see the extent of the cavern. The uncommonly cold and uncomfortably dark grotto challenged his sensitive eyes.

Was he alone?

Suddenly he felt the foreboding sensation of being watched! Yannuvia turned quickly, saw no one, but noted the opening to the cavern slammed *silently* shut! He ran to the wall but found only solid rock. The portal had vanished. The Drelve turned and stared into the dark recesses of the barren cavern. Now feeling disadvantaged by the silence, Yannuvia released his grip on the gray stone and broke the spell.

To his surprise, the grotto was quiet. He heard not a peep from the nearby waterfall!

The Drelve drew his short sword. Though not the strongest student of books, Yannuvia was accomplished with weapons. Moments seemed like entire cycles of Meries. Slowly red light diffused throughout the cavern, and the temperature of the grotto increased. Beads of violet sweat dropped from the young Spellweaver's brow. The first bead splashed to the stone floor and burst into a myriad of colors. Yannuvia kept his keen vision and hearing on high alert.

A flash of intense red light filled the cavern and enabled the Drelve to see the dimensions of the massive cavern. The irregular ceiling was the height of six Drelves. The cavern extended eighty-nine paces to the far wall and thirty-four paces to both sides of the Spellweaver. The distance to the irregular ceiling varied from twenty-one to thirty-four feet. A hulking form appeared in the center of the grotto.

The hideous being had eight legs and eight eyes. Its two larger eyeballs were red and six smaller eyeballs were black. The bloated beast was twelve feet tall and sported a barbed tail that dwarfed that of a fully-grown wyvern. Huge warty lumps covered the creature's body and its gaping maw bared huge fangs. Two appendages were modified to form claws. Far more ugly than its likeness on the cavern entryway, the creature stared directly at the Drelve.

Having no spells to battle such a beast, Yannuvia sighed and reckoned his short life was at an end. Drelvish Spellweavers mainly used defensive spells and Magick that enhanced their natural surroundings. The beast could easily use its fangs and talons to mince the Drelve.

Undaunted, the young Spellweaver extended his sword and shouted, "If you mean to eat me, get on with it!"

Standing on a red stone, the hulking beast ignored the Drelve, moved off the red tile, reached a foreleg downward, picked up the flattened red stone, placed it *somewhere*, and dropped a deep blue flattened tile on the cavern floor. Yannuvia took a step backward, sheathed his short sword, and pulled his finely made bow and quiver.

When the beast did not react, Yannuvia pressed his apparent advantage and fired an arrow toward the beast's left red eye. With blazing quickness the monster deflected the projectile with its foreleg and then glowered at Yannuvia.

Thinking he may as well try, Yannuvia directed his left hand toward the beast, muttered a few old Drelvish phrases, and fired a Magick Missile toward the creature. The unerring spell struck the behemoth but caused no noticeable harm. The beast growled ominously but did nothing.

Yannuvia broke into a run, sped around the cavern away from beast, ran his fingers along the wall, but unfortunately found no exits. Realizing it was the furthest point from the monster, he went back to his original location and panted. The beast manipulated its forelegs and produced a small table. It then placed a chest made of blue wood upon the table. The creature muttered a short incantation that augmented the light in the grotto and then peered at Yannuvia.

Alas!

The creature was a spell caster!

Given this knowledge, Yannuvia grasped the gray stone, muttered the incantation to reactivate the Silence Spell, and directed the area of silence toward the beast. The dweomer failed and an area of silence developed about ten paces to the left of the beast. Yannuvia learned that Magick cast upon an unwilling recipient didn't always work. The effectiveness depended on many factors. The ancient spell book, *the Gifts of Andreas to the People of the Forest*, contained several dissertations involving spell casting. One lesson talked of a difficult concept called Magick Resistance. Take home lesson…spells didn't always work.

Yannuvia drew his sword, ran toward the beast, and shouted, "I'll not die without a fight!"

The creature paid little mind to the advancing Drelve. When Yannuvia reached the beast, the monster held the Drelve back with an extended foreleg. Yannuvia thrust the short sword several times to no avail. Frustrated, he withdrew. Looking around the grotto desperately, he saw the flattened blue stone resting a few paces to the right of the beast.

Using the innate Spellweavers' power of Detection of Magick, Yannuvia sensed a powerful aura about the flattened blue stone. What was its purpose? Given the beast had produced the stone, it was likely to be of little benefit to the Drelve. For an awkward moment, Yannuvia's eyes fixed on the creature's red eyes.

The beast disdainfully returned the young Spellweaver's gaze and said in Drelvish tongue, "It took you long enough to get here. You are not of much account, young sorcerer. I don't see what the Master sees in you, but I'll present his gifts as he directed."

The beast spoke the tongue of the forest people affluently, but his guttural voice lacked the usual lyrical Drelvish tones.

The Drelve blushed angrily and shouted, "No one is my Master. Who are you? What are you? What do you want? Again, if you mean to eat me, get on with it!"

The beast sighed, growled something about getting the worst assignments, and said, "I am Arachnis. I'm not a *what*! I would like some respect, but otherwise I want nothing. I'm here to give you the Master's gifts, ingrate! Don't you realize you've already received a boon?"

Yannuvia attempted to step backward but realized he was pressed against the rock wall. The Spellweaver breathed deeply, and tried to clear his mind. Facing an eight-legged, eight-eyed creature made concentration difficult. Still the Drelve tried.

Wait!

The phrases!

The phrases that appeared in his mind when he touched the stones that gave him entry to the cavern *were* an incantation! He muttered aloud,

"I don't understand. It's a spell. It's…it's a fire spell. The spell books of my forefathers have no such Magick. How?"

"It's Magick, fool. It's a gift. Be appreciative. All you must do to enact the spell is possess this stone," the creature called Arachnis answered.

Arachnis placed a gray stone on the little bluewood table and continued, "This is a fire stone. Normally a fire spell requires sulfur and the power of… never mind. You wouldn't understand."

For all intents and purposes the little gray rock was identical to the stone the female dream raider had given Yannuvia. Realizing the beast could kill him at any time, Yannuvia sheathed his short sword and said nothing.

"So far you haven't shown me ****, young Spellweaver. Why do you come to this grotto, Yannuvia of the Drelves? What do you seek?" the beast asked sardonically.

"Magick. I seek Magick. I seek Magick for the betterment and defense of my people," the Drelve answered.

"Aye. You seek Magick. But you seek Magick *not* for the betterment of your people but *for* yourself. *She* got to you, didn't she? *Her* smile beguiles you, doesn't it? What else do you seek, Yannuvia of the forest, a bit of the forbidden fruit? Eh?" Arachnis continued sarcastically.

"What do you mean? Fruit is not forbidden. The fruit bearing trees gladly share their fruits with those who respect them. However, one should not be wasteful," the Drelve naively and quizzically answered.

The hulking beast lifted the little bluewood chest and muttered, "You *are* a fool. I can't believe I'm here messing with you when I could be…never mind. There's nothing for it. Pay attention, young shaman. The treasures within the chest are gifts of my Master. He is a kindred spirit and friend of the forest. But he fears the vile Drolls, Kiennites, and other ilk will again ravage the woods. He wants you to have these items."

The demon transformed his forepaws into small delicate hands with seven digits and manipulated an ornate latch on the little chest.

"You said *other* ilk. What peoples threaten the forest beside the cruel Drolls and Kiennites?" the Drelve asked.

"Your world has many peoples. One will come to great prominence. But you have within your grasp the means to further your people," the beast responded.

"The Teacher tells me there are few gifts with no strings attached. What do you want of me?" the youth queried.

"These gifts and their mastery require only time …and service. For now the only commitment you make is to grant my Master a future audience. That's all," the demon said reassuringly.

The creature's words lacked sincerity, and the tiny seven-fingered hands only furthered the beast's demonic appearance. Obviously perturbed by the little Spellweaver's questions, Arachnis touched the latch on the chest. Following a lyrical chime, the latch sprang and the little doors opened. As the doors opened, the chest levitated in front of the demon. Table legs eerily descended from the floating chest to the floor of the cavern and transformed the chest to a table. Auras of Magick flashed from the transformed chest. The demon removed several items from the inner compartment and placed them on top of the table.

Arachnis placed a chalice upon the little table. The ornate cup was twelve inches tall with a base was six inches in diameter and stem six inches long. Its bowl held little more than half an average tankard of ale. A faint mauve glow surrounded the chalice. A large upward pointing triangle dominated the bowl. Flowing runes covered most of the bowl of the deep red cup. Pristine stones of all colors lined the rim of the cup. Precious stones adorned the sides of the cup. Similar gems made up the eyes of the demon's image on the cavern entryway,

Unnerving sounds and dark lights pulsed from the device. Echoes and auras filled the chamber.

The demon placed the red tile on the floor of the cavern, raised his left hand, and muttered an incantation. Following a flash of red light, a cabinet appeared on the red tile. The demon moved his grotesque foreleg slowly back and forth. The cabinet moved away from the red tile to the demon's left. The bluewood doors of the cabinet slowly swung outward. Taller than a Drelve and wider than a mooler, the cabinet contained many little crystal phials containing green, lavender, clear, orange, red, yellow, and black potions.

Following another flash of red light, a figure appeared on the red tile. The young Spellweaver recognized and nigh welcomed the alluring female from his dreams. Appearing as she did the first time he dreamt of her, the tall alluring matron had creamy skin, soft blue eyes, and coal black hair that fell gracefully down her back and chest. She wore a glowing scarlet outfit.

The svelte female walked gracefully to the cabinet, looked back toward Yannuvia, smiled, and seductively said, "I'm glad you are with us. We have lots of pretty things for you."

"You are beautiful, but Arachnis is not visually pleasing! I'm drawn to the beautiful chalice!" the young Spellweaver muttered. He sighed, stepped forward, and stared at the flowing runes on the chalice.

"You look upon the Cup of Dark Knowledge, the Chalice of Mystery. The pretty little cup creates powerful Magick. Do you think it's as pretty as I am?" the female asked suggestively.

The massive eight-legged creature took a small phial from a pouch he clutched tightly with a foreleg. Using his tiny seven-fingered hands, the beast gently manipulated and removed the stopper from the phial. Carefully Arachnis poured the contents of the phial into the chalice. Dark as a lump of coal, the thick gooey liquid flowed like molasses. When the first drop touched the cup's bowl, a deep red glow briefly bathed the chalice. Then intense auras of Magick and faint humming sounds filled the room. The red light around the chalice changed from wine to amber to green. When the last drop of liquid spilled into the cup, black light emanated from the chalice and bathed Yannuvia. The Drelve felt chilled to the furthest depths of his being.

Using Comprehend Languages, an innate ability of Drelve Spellweavers, Yannuvia read the runes etched on the Chalice of Mystery.

"I give you my blood through which you will receive all you seek. You in turn give to me your all."

Troubled, young Yannuvia shuddered.

The beautiful female removed several phials from the cabinet and carried them to the table. She placed three phials filled with green liquid, two phials filled with lavender fluid, and single phials filled with uncolored, red, and yellow liquid on the table by the beautiful goblet.

The taller female stepped toward Yannuvia, bent downward, and gently kissed his left cheek.

Arachnis grunted disdainfully and placed a tome on the table. Yannuvia noted unfamiliar runes on the cover of the tome. The Spellweaver's Comprehend Languages ability failed him.

The woman noted Yannuvia's confusion and softly said, "Twill require a Read Magick Spell to decipher the runes. You will soon grasp the dweomer, little one. Just bear witness."

At this moment the crowded tabletop bore the bejeweled chalice, the arcane spell book, the gray firestone, and eight phials of liquid. The female produced a sparkling gem and held it before the Drelve's eyes.

"Peek through this fascinating stone," she teased.

Yannuvia squinted, looked through the stone, and saw auras of Magick emanating from all the items on the table.

The female continued, "It's a Gem of Seeing. Such rare gems reveal the presence of Magick."

"That's enough small talk," Arachnis growled. "Proceed. You can explain to the Master why we have tarried."

"Ssssshut up, Arachnisssss!" she hissed.

"Slipped up, didn't you? Hissing again. Beware the feminine types, young Spellweaver, they'll give you no respect," the demon guffawed.

The female's nostrils flared, and little puffs of red smoke slipped from her nose.

She regained her composure and said, "Relax. The Master favors you. Watch!"

"One potion makes you larger, one potion makes you small. The ones others may give you will do nothing at all," she sang lyrically.

Mesmerized, Yannuvia asked, "What is your name?"

"Do you like Alice?' she teased.

"Yes…I suppose," he replied quizzically.

"Then, my name is Alice," the female cooed agreeably.

Alice took the phial of clear colorless liquid, delicately removed its seal, and carefully poured the uncolored potion into the Chalice of Mystery. The liquid sizzled and the room filled with auras of Magick.

"Uncolored," she uttered.

Alice then unstopped the phial containing yellow potion and carefully poured its contents into the goblet. Immediately the cavern filled with aromas of many lands. Yannuvia smelled first the most pleasant fragrances of the forest and then the odor of gray berries and Leicats, the vilest odors he could recollect.

"Yellow," Alice snickered.

Next she unstopped the phial of red potion and decanted every drop into the cup. Visions of Yannuvia's most pleasant and fearful experiences appeared on the walls of the grotto. Of the pleasant images, there were many. He saw Kirrie, Old Yellow, the Lone Oak, his mother Carinne, the Teacher Edkim, and Banderas and Dienas of Lost Sons. The image of Banderas and Dienas faded, and the young Drelve saw an image of Drolls killing his friends Vioss and Bystar.

"Red," Alice murmured.

Finally the female took one of the three phials of green liquid, opened the vessel, and poured the liquid into the cup. Beautiful birdsong and lyrical voices filled the room. Screeching sounds like the wail of the wailer and the roar of the Baxcat followed.

"Green," Alice added.

She rolled the beautiful gem of seeing between the second and third fingers of her left hand. For the first time Yannuvia noted the length of her fingernails… talons.

Flashing a wry smile, *Alice* dropped the beautiful gem into the effervescing fluid in the cup.

"Uncolored, yellow, red, green, and one thing Magick," she commented platonically.

Yannuvia watched the chalice. Many colors flashed from the device. His two companions quietly watched the effervescing fluid.

Finally, Arachnis said, "Take the Fire Stone. It is the Master's gift."

Yannuvia hesitated.

"Don't be afraid. It'ssss for you," Alice added encouragingly. However, she slipped up and hissed a bit.

The massive Arachnis harrumphed.

Tentatively, Yannuvia extended his hand, and touched the gray stone, and felt a brief surge from the silence stone within his raiment. Quickly the Drelve withdrew his hand.

"It'ssss OK. Just don't allow them to touch," the female encouraged.

Arachnis harrumphed again.

On the table the firestone appeared spherical, about a foot in diameter, and indistinguishable from the silence stone. Yannuvia picked up the gray rock. When he touched the artifact, like the Silence Stone, the Fire Stone conformed to the dimensions of his hand and felt soft and warm. The young Spellweaver immediately sensed the uniqueness of the little gray rock. The incantation of the Fireball spell appeared clearly in his mind.

"It's yours. A gift of the Master," Arachnis said matter of factly.

"What is its origin? What is it called?" Yannuvia asked.

"Your people will have a name for such stones one day. My Master calls it a Xennic Stone, and I don't ask him why. Don't look a gift horse in the mouth," Arachnis grumbled.

"My people don't subjugate horses and make them beasts of burden. Drolls capture, break, and ride fearsome fire horses; Kiennites ride little stone ponies. Noble Kiennites ride saber-tooth mares. Why would one give a horse away? I've heard my father Glinne refer to Kiennites by certain parts of the horse's anatomy," the young Spellweaver wondered.

"Whatever are you saying?" the hulking Arachnis grumpily responded.

"I've heard my father say 'in the world there are more horse's rears than horses.' He always laughs when he says this," Yannuvia answered energetically.

"Shut up and listen. Remember, my Master reserves a future audience," Arachnis growled.

The Drelve pondered briefly the meaning of "a future audience." Yannuvia then gingerly placed the Fire Stone in the opposite side of his garment. Precisely like the Silence Stone, the second gray rock almost adhered to his skin as though it were a part of him. Until he willingly removed it, Yannuvia felt the artifact would remain where he placed it.

His hideous face broke into a wry grin and Arachnis said, "A sorcerer should be interested in the spell book. Are you not a sorcerer, *Spellweaver*?"

The ersatz Alice battled her hissing and muttered, "He *is* a sorcerer, Arachnis! Sssshut your mouth and allow him to think. He issss in a predicament. How'd you like to trade placessss...*places* with him?"

She extended her left hand and gently stroked Yannuvia's long hair.

"What manner of ilk are you?" Yannuvia challenged.

"We are not from this neck of the woods. We are friends of the forest and Magick. Like elves! Red elves! We want to be your friends," she answered encouragingly.

Startled, Yannuvia declared, "Elves? Elves are mythical. Lore says elves are malevolent and cause nightmares! Elfdreams! Shouldn't I fear you?"

"Relax. Young fool. We're not red elves. We're demons. Her name really isn't Alice. Why don't you look at the ****** book?" Arachnis growled.

"What is...what are demons? I know of no such folk. The spell book bears the same sort of lettering as the cup. I...I can't read this language," Yannuvia stammered.

The Spellweaver gave a partially truthful answer. Although he couldn't read the runes on the tome, his Comprehend Languages translated the writing on the chalice. Magick encrypted the runes on the spell book.

"Don't con us, sorcerer. *Everyone* can read the message on the Chalice of Mystery. That's the Master's intention," Arachnis growled.

The female *Alice* replied. "Look at the book. It won't harm you."

"Get on with it! If I wanted to eat you, I would have already done so!" Arachnis bellowed angrily.

Confronted by the big grumpy beast's anger, Yannuvia jumped back briefly. Then the Drelve gingerly touched the vellum. His thin fingers moved across the surface of the tome. The spell book's cover was velvety soft, and the raised runes were smooth to the touch. Flashes of light emanated from the nearby chalice. The runes on the tome and the chalice began to glow and produce beams of colored light. Appearing in the order of red, orange, yellow, green, blue, indigo, and violet, the beams danced around the grotto. When he looked toward the chalice, Yannuvia felt dread and uncertainty. But when he touched the tome, the young Spellweaver had an odd sense of power. The Drelve placed both hands around the book's binding and lifted the volume. The nigh weightless thick text shrank to fit comfortably in his hands. Feeling felt like the neophyte he was, the Spellweaver opened the spell book understood none of the intricate etchings written on its pages.

Perhaps if he had gone to the Green Vale at least once before he took on such a foolhardy mission…

Too late now…

"I…I can't read it," he confessed.

"Of course you cannot. It's written in the language of my Master. Your simple languages spell won't help you decipher the runes. You'll have to drink from the Cup of Dark Knowledge to understand these writings. The potent potable is prepared. Accept my Master's benevolent offer, Spellweaver. You'll become the greatest your ilk has known," the bloated Arachnis condescendingly proclaimed.

"I…I fear the cup. I don't understand…" Yannuvia timidly replied.

"You don't have to understand, runt. Just drink it! I'm tiring of you!" Arachnis bellowed.

"Arachnissss! Give him some time! He'ssss young," *Alice* protested.

"I'm not as generous as you are, Deceiver. My time is too valuable. Time's a wasting, kid," the frustrated benefactor muttered.

The eight-legged beast sauntered to the far side of the grotto. Purple fumes steamed from Arachnis's many apertures. The warts on his back jiggled back and forth as the massive beast moved about.

The matron shrugged, placed both hands on the Drelve's shoulders, bent forward, and kissed his trembling lips. Yannuvia didn't really now how to react. The soft warm touch of her lips was beyond pleasant, and he marveled at the sweetness of her breath. The young Spellweaver recalled the sensation of the four poisoned darts imbedded into his thighs by the water sprites. His head began to spin.

Yannuvia opined, "Am I *charmed*? Am I to suffer the fate of those who fell over the falls? For I have seen this place in a dream. I have seen my fall from the precipice beyond the falls. Alice, are *you* the siren of the falls? Are you a dryad? Are you huldra?"

His eyes beheld the beautiful female. Yannuvia had never seen a dryad. Had he *dreamt* of a dryad? His tortured mind recalled the Teacher's stories of mischievous and even malevolent forest spirits and the legends of the Alluring Falls.

Her soothing voice beckoned to him, "You seek Magick. But you are Magick. I can give you many things, Magick man?'

Her fingers continued to gently effleurage his back. Yannuvia stood mesmerized.

She bent forward and whispered into his ear, "I am not your bane. Do your ears hurt? Do you want to jump off the falls? I have bartered with the sirens for some time with you, my handsome friend. I should think you'd be grateful."

Yannuvia pinched his thigh. This was not a dream. Youth clouded his judgment.

The matron soothingly sang, "When are you going to make up your mind? When are you going to love *me* as much as I love you? When are you going to make up your mind? Cause things are going to change, so fast. All yours heroes have gone away."

The flustered youth meekly answered, "I've decided. I'll quaff the liquid from the cup."

Alice the Deceiver smiled, gently bussed his lips again, stepped away from him, and pointed toward the lovely chalice, which sat on the table. The fluid within the bowl of the cup gently effervesced. Arachnis took notice and moved slowly toward the table in the center of the grotto.

Nervously, Yannuvia extended his left hand and touched the cup. Expecting a shock or a painful transformation, he was relieved to only feel the coolness of the deep maroon metal. Slowly he raised the cup. The aroma of the fluid was very different.

Not unpleasant…

Different…

The Drelve sighed and tipped the cup. The first drops of the cup's contents touched his lips and then his tongue. He quickly drank the entire contents of the bowl.

"It is done," Arachnis said flatly. "I'll be gone."

The demon took the chalice from the table. He then placed a small fine leather bag down on the table and left the remaining potions.

Arachnis stepped onto the blue stone, muttered, "Whatever the Master desires," and disappeared in a flash of blue light.

Yannuvia glanced toward the stunning matron standing within an arm's length to his left. Each neuron sharpened within his brain. The complex fire spell now seemed simple. The young Spellweaver waited for something terrible to befall him, but a few moments time passed uneventfully. The female smiled but remained silent.

The opened spell book, the little leather bag, two phials filled with green liquid, and two phials filled with lavender fluid remained on the bluewood table. Yannuvia stared at the spell book intently.

"Everything is intended for you. These gifts will enhance your life. Indeed, they and I will give you life. The Master says your potential is unlimited. The potions may come in handy. The green one makes you smaller and the purple one reverses the effect. The Bag of Concealment is a great way to store things. However, the Master's spell book is the greatest boon. Not easy reading," the female sighed.

"No...but I'll try," Yannuvia answered.

The young Spellweaver glanced at the opened book and understood the meaning of the shimmering flowing runes.

"Fire spells. They are fire spells," Yannuvia observed.

The Drelve touched and stroked the binding of the tome. A ring of blue fire developed around the couple and the table. The diameter of the circle of blue fire was thirteen paces. He tentatively closed the book and looked at the runes on its cover.

"What does it say, *Sorcerer*?" she seductively asked.

"Don't you know?" he posed.

Glancing toward his comely companion, he saw an undeniable change in her coloration. Her skin briefly reddened, and the same fire that surrounded them burned in her eyes. Then she recouped her pleasant lovely appearance. Perhaps the nearby flames had merely created an illusion. Her lips regained their appeal.

"Oh, goodness, no. I'm a simple servant, not a sorcerer like you," she continued.

Yannuvia answered, "My studies have only just begun. My spells protect the forest and the Drelves, my people. I haven't even been to...I probably shouldn't tell you anything more. I can now read that this is a spell book of Dark Magick. Its title reads 'Death by Fire.'"

"Dark Magick? What makes Magick *dark?*" the matron inquired.

"It's just a term. My Teacher says the Kiennites cast destructive spells against my people. The Teacher calls these destructive spells Dark Magick. The Kiennites employ materials in their spells. I think the spells in this book only require the little rock in my raiment. That doesn't make sense," Yannuvia answered.

"Isn't Magick...just *Magick*?" Alice observed.

"I *wish* I'd had more time to..." Yannuvia started but the female quickly interrupted.

"Don't sssssay that word! Not here! Pleasssse," she stammered fearfully.

"Nobody can make a *wish* come true, not even during the time of the Approximation. It's documented in the annals of the forest," Yannuvia objected.

"Don't underestimate Magick, young Spellweaver. Yesterday, would you have believed possible what you have seen today?" she continued.

Yannuvia flipped through the pages in the volume. One by one, he read the spells. *Alice* turned away from him, walked through the intense blue flames, and returned to the cabinet from which she had obtained the phials. From therein she retrieved a decanter and two mugs. When she returned to Yannuvia's side, he noted the devices were made of the same red wood as the table. She poured a deep purple liquid from the decanter to the mugs and pushed one of the mugs across the small table in the center of the grotto toward Yannuvia.

"What is this?" he asked suspiciously.

"After all this, surely you must trust me. *Ever* have I enabled you! Had I not come to you in your dreams, you'd have never learned of these treasures! *Ever* have I guarded you? Had I not warned you, you would have fallen victim to the sirens. Had I not protected you, Arachnis would have eaten you and simply told the Master you had an accident. Surely you'll allow me the honor of toasting your success and newfound powers. But, not to worry. Though not a fruit of the forest, this is a bounty of Nature, the juice of the byneberries. They grow deep beneath the world's surface. You'll find the beverage refreshing. It'll make your studies easier," the svelte female implied.

"I think...I'll let you drink first," the young Spellweaver suggested.

"Silly youth. If I wanted you dead, I'd summon the sirens. I'd have given you to Arachnis. Simply in coming here, you've exhibited foolhardiness. Drink your beverage," the womanly figure scolded.

She tipped her mug to her moist lips and drank deeply. Yannuvia did not see her chew a small cluster of white berries before she drank the draught. Had he seen them, the Drelve would not have recognized mistletoe berries. Mistletoe did not grow in the World of the Three Suns. Where it was native, mistletoe grew near the top of trees.

She pulled down the mug and smiled.

The deep purple juice stained her lips.

Those perfectly shaped soft warm lips...

"Here. Have your first little taste," she snickered.

The temptress dipped her finger into his mug, put the bit of liquid to her lips, and then gently bussed his lips and transferred a bit of the purple juice.

Yannuvia blushed and licked his lips. The juice was very sweet. Was the sweetness due to the juice or his lovely companion? The Spellweaver tilted the mug and tentatively touched the thick purple liquid to his lips. The body of the beverage was as full and beautiful as that of the exquisite female that stood before him. He took a long deep drink...

Something wasn't right...

Dizziness...

Vertigo!

The room started to spin violently. The blue flames intensified. As he fell to the floor of the cavern, Yannuvia saw his feminine companion's complexion change to deep reddened skin. Azure flames filled her eyes. She supinated her blithe hands and revealed long harsh razor sharp talons.

She hissed, "My name issss not Alice."

Was this…the end?

Threads…
Threads of Magick…
Threads of fate…
Threads of time…
Threads connecting worlds …
Dreams connecting worlds …
Dreams of Magick…
The magic of Dreams…
Dream raiders…
Albtraum…
Albträume, elf dreams, nightmares…

Ø ∞ Ø

Yannuvia awakened cold, bothered, bewildered, and…and alone in the dark dank grotto. The cavern smelled musty… like old dust.

Other than a mild headache and a bit of stiffness in his joints, the Spellweaver felt none the worse for the wear. Drelves lacked facial hair. If Yannuvia had been able to see his long locks, he would have noted a hint of brown at the roots. Drelves did not gray. With age their fine hair changed from the fair reddish yellow-orange to brown. His hair seemed to have grown several inches. His nails seemed long.

Odd…

The spell book, two green potions, and two lavender potions sat on the table in front of him. The small brown bag rested on the table by the spell book. Perhaps it was made of the hide of some small animal. Yannuvia reached out his hand, worked the stiffness out of his fingers, felt, and lifted the little sack. The "Bag of Concealment" surprisingly had little weight. He peeked inside the bag and found other items, including very small squares of the odd blue and red stones he had seen the creature called Arachnis utilize.

Yannuvia placed potions in the bag. Mysteriously, the bag's weight and shape did not change. The spell book was larger than the opening to the bag. Nevertheless the Spellweaver touched the tome to the bag. The book reduced its size and entered the bag! Out of curiosity, the Drelve placed bag against the edge of the bluewood table. The table obediently entered the bag. The same thing happened when he touched the cabinet. Through Fairie Fire Spells, he illuminated the grotto. Yannuvia explored the grotto and unsuccessfully searched the solid walls for an exit. He thoroughly read the spell and clutched the firestone but found no spell to help him.

Then he remembered Arachnis departed the cavern via the blue stone.

He removed the blue stone. Before his eyes, the blue stone expanded to half his body's length on a side. The entire bag was about two hands in length. Removing the blue stone did not change the bag's weight.

There was nothing for it.

Yannuvia stepped on the blue stone.

CHAPTER 14
Watching

Tomayo stared across the fields of deep red grass. Another light period, the time of greatest light, was ending uneventfully. A Drelvish archer, Tomayo was amongst the best of his ilk. Without question the Drelve accepted the long stretches of thousands of heartbeats confined to the high branches of the everred trees at the fringes of the forest of Alms Glen. It was his duty to watch the field for signs of danger.

The great Lone Oak stood unmoving in the center of the red meadow. When he looked at the magnificent tree, Tomayo sensed the presence of an ally, another sentry. By the campfires, elderly Drelves detailed many legends of the great tree.

Did its leaves restore life?

Did picking its leaves curse one beyond life's end?

Why had no tree dweller called the great tree home?

Why did tree sprites, trolls, woodcutters, glow grubs, phannens, and dryads avoid the tree? Drelves respected more than feared the tree, but the Drelvish Teachers had also stressed the sanctity of the massive plant.

Only orange and red triffids and tree herders approached the tree, and they shed little light on the tree's origins. During Approximations of the Gray Sun Andreas, triffids uprooted, carefully dragged their exposed roots across the red grass to avoid disrupting the blades, slowly moved across the expanse of the meadow, and groomed the area around the base of the Lone Oak. If the Lone Oak changed, the difference was imperceptible. Its leaves ever fluttered in the gentle breezes.

Tomayo pondered the many stories. Like any dedicated Drelvish scout, the veteran maintained his vigilance and watched the wide expanse. With the aid of the little looking glass he carried, his keen vision saw every blade of grass and individual leaf on the trees of the wild forest 1597 Yardley paces away.

1597 yards, if one preferred…

Yards, as one of Enos Yardley's paces was called…

Arbitrary…

Tomayo head a faint rustle in the hedgerow behind him and detected a familiar scent. The presence of his familiar hand confirmed Rumsie's arrival and signaled Tomayo's shift neared its end. Drelves stealthily disguised their steps, scent, and appearance with the help of many aides within the forest. Rumsie didn't try to hide his approach from his comrade Tomayo. The Sergeant Major of the forest guard, Rumsie took hands on approach to the security of the forest around Alms Glen and took his turns watching the red meadow and supervising his subordinates.

"How goes the watch?" Rumsey asked.

"Quiet. Occasionally a mooler appears on the far side of the meadow. They are so large I can see them without the looking glass. I suppose the big purplish red bovines are slow learners. After all this time and so many tries, you'd think they'd learn the red grass is inedible. Still they try. I saw a wyvern flying near the distant mountains. It flew toward the Peaks of Division, but away from Mirror Mountain. First one I've seen in two dark periods' time. Otherwise, I saw no signs of Drolls or Kiennites this watch. In fact cycles of Meries have passed since Beaux saw the Drollen party along the woods at the edge of the wild forest. The light becomes grayer. I see Andreas over the edge of the distant Doombringers. Do you think this is the sign of an Approximation?" Tomayo reported.

"The Teacher Edkim thinks we might see the first since the births of the twin Spellweavers thirteen years ago. The wandering sun is unpredictable. Our people could use the effects of the gray light. It makes our enemies cower and strengthens us," Rumsey answered.

"The Drolls and Kiennites have not mounted an attack in several seasons. Is there some kind of truce, Rumsie?" Tomayo asked.

"Drolls and Kiennites don't understand the concept of truce and peace, Tomayo. There is always risk of attack. We suffered great casualties six seasons ago. I had hoped you might have word of the young Spellweaver Yannuvia. The time nears for us to depart to Meadowsweet and the Green Vale. The Teacher Edkim worries, and my friends Glinne and Carinne fear for their son. The elders and Edkim insist the harvest must proceed," Rumsie said with concern.

"Then the young Spellweaver has not returned. I'm sorry. I haven't seen him," Tomayo replied.

"As I feared, my friend. I have a favor to ask of you. Can you continue your vigil? Beaux, Klunkus, and I must accompany the Teacher and neophytes to Meadowsweet and protect the remaining Spellweaver Gaelyss. I ask you supervise the observation of the realm. You are my most experienced scout. Your skill with the bow is second to none. I worry about the recent sightings of the Drolls. Where there are a few, there may be many, and Kiennites likely accompany them," Rumsie asked.

"Sergeant Major Rumsie, I'll gladly stay at this post as long as you need me. But, I worry. With the rarity of Spellweavers and absence of young

Yannuvia, should we risk sending young Gaelyss to Meadowsweet and Green Vale? Shouldn't our lone remaining Spellweaver stay within his red oak at Alms Glen and not jeopardize his safety?" Tomayo replied.

"Gaelyss attains his thirteenth season of the harvest. According to the Teacher, Gaelyss's being a Spellweaver makes his going to Green Vale and learning to harvest the enhancing root all the more important. The Teacher thinks an Approximation nears. If that should happen whilst the root is harvested, the plants will have greater power. But you are right. Protecting the young Spellweaver is paramount. On the other hand, we cannot delay. We must harvest the enhancing root in the dark period, and that is nigh. Now I must return to Alm's Glen. We will depart for Meadowsweet on the morrow. Clarke Maceda is scouting the perimeter. When he finishes, he will allow you a brief respite. I…I thank you, my friend," Rumsie said.

"Go with good speed, Sergeant Major Rumsie. Clarke and I will maintain the watch. I hope the young Spellweavers reunite. Our people have been so long without the power of a Spellweaver. I have hopes of a safer world for my Drelvlings," Tomayo answered.

"As do I," Rumsie replied.

The Drelve adeptly descended the everred tree and disappeared into the underbrush.

Soon a weathered older Drelve ascended the tree and stood by Tomayo. Clarke had seen many seasons of the harvest but the older Drelve wryly refused to tell anyone his exact age. Though Tomayo thought Clarke was much too old to be defending the perimeter, the tired archer was glad to see the cantankerous veteran. The rigors of the watch took its toll. The dedicated Tomayo relished a brief rest.

"What is your report?" Tomayo asked.

"Drolls are near the perimeter. I smell them! The scent is strong. Though I saw none of the wolf-faced beasts, I'm convinced the enemies have ventured into our realm. We last saw them seven days ago. A mooler herd gathers in the valley beyond the Alluring Falls, and predators gather to take them. Unfortunately all this activity makes scouting difficult," old Clarke reported.

"Thank you for your help. Your experience is valuable," Tomayo said.

"My experience is more valuable than my legs, Tomayo. I feel every one of my eleven hundred and six seasons. Yep, you're the first of this generation who knows my age. I'll make no excuses. I'll do the best I can," Clarke replied.

"Who goes to Meadowsweet?" Tomayo asked.

The veteran munched on trail mix.

"Rumsie leads Beaux, Klunkus, the Teacher, young Gaelyss the Spellweaver, and four other neophytes named Meryt, Debery, Zack, and Bryce," old Clarke reported.

"Nine is a small number to gather the root," Tomayo observed.

"Tis all we can spare. The elders have employed anyone who can fire a bow to defend the forest," Clarke replied.

"That includes *young* ones like you," Tomayo joked.

"I volunteered for Lone Oak duty. Gazing upon the great tree energizes me and restores my youth," the older Drelve said.

"Has the great tree changed in your time, Clarke?" Tomayo asked.

"It hasn't changed since my great-great grandfather's time," the old one answered matter of factly.

"Has anyone ever taken the leaves?" Tomayo queried.

"I have only the knowledge of the annals, the campfire songs, and the Teachers, my young friend. Now I suggest you finish your lunch, allow these old eyes and bones to relieve you, and grab a bit of rest," Clarke suggested.

"Have you seen the bowyer, BJ Aires?" Tomayo asked.

"Not since we returned from searching for young Yannuvia, but the bowyer oft times loses track of time when he works," Clarke answered.

As a gesture of camaraderie, Tomayo placed his hand on the old Drelve's shoulder. The archer descended the tree, reached the trunk of the everred, pushed gently against the soft mossy red bark, and went through the tree's bark to the rest chamber within the friend of the Drelves. Drelves made their permanent homes in plush great red oaks. The austere inner chamber of the everred lacked the comforts of home but served well as a place to rest and recover one's energies.

Tomayo quickly slept.

High in the tree, Clarke gazed through the amber period's light across the field. The old Drelve joked of infirmity, but his eyes had not dimmed. He saw nigh as well as the much younger Tomayo. Clarke Maceda peered through a small looking glass and systematically scanned the edge of the distant wild forest beyond the Lone Oak. When he looked toward the extreme northern edge of the wild woods, the old Drelve saw subtle movement among the underbrush.

Perhaps a mooler...

Maybe a predator looking to make a meal of one of the big purplish red bovines...

No...Clarke saw...

One...

Two...

Three...

Four...

Four Drolls...

Four Drolls and a Kiennite...

Five camouflaged enemies slunk along the edge of the forest.

Clarke remained still. The Drelve knew the enemies lacked his keen vision and looking glass, but Drolls had uncanny sense of smell. He rubbed a fragrant red basil berry between his fingers allowed the juices to run between his digits. The five interlopers had not entered the red meadow. None of the peoples of the World of the Three Suns claimed dominion over the wild woods. In fact, everyone entering the wild woods faced danger. Drolls and Kiennites often roamed the rugged forests. Most beasts of the wild woods did not cross the red-grassed meadow. The red grass was inedible.

No prey...

No predators...

All intelligent creatures feared the legends of the Lone Oak.

The five foolhardy creatures were within their right to travel in the wild woods. But there was a thin dividing line, specifically 1597 yards, between foraging in the wilds and transgressing against the Drelves. Respecting the Drolls' keen hearing, Clarke watched the quintet closely and remained silent. Calling out to his comrades risked alerting the Drolls of his location. Drolls knew the Drelves watched the perimeter of the red meadow. The red meadow was the only access to the central forests around Alm's Glen. Carnivorous plants, walkabout bushes, and thick underbrush created the inhospitable boundary of the Alms Glen forest and effectively served like the outer curtain of a stone citadel.

The five figures moved along the edge of the wild wood. Suddenly one of the Drolls fell. Clarke's keen hearing detected screams of anger and fear. The three remaining Drolls and the Kiennite rushed into the wild woods and disappeared from his sight.

Clarke watched and waited.

CHAPTER 15
The Dryad

Amica restrained her laughter.

Her second stone hit one of the Drolls squarely on the head. Below her the three large wolf-faced scouts and their gnarly Kiennish companion peered above them for their tormentor. The dryad, or tree sprite matron as she was oft times called in the World of the Three Suns, first saw five marauders near the edge of the forest of tall everred trees she called home.

She enjoyed lingering near the fringes of the meadow of the great Lone Oak. The stately tree loomed alone in the distance, the only tree standing in the wide expanse of brilliant red grass that surrounded the round meadow. Once Amica had playfully walked the circumference of the hallowed meadow. Her small legs made the trip in 17,711 steps. Amica's pace was about a third as long as a typical Drelve. She was much faster in the treetops. Amica seldom ventured into the forest around the Drelves' stronghold, because the elders of Alm's Glen and Meadowsweet, the two major communities of the Drelves, did not welcome her mischief. Try as she might, the woodland sprite could not resist fomenting tomfoolery.

She surmised the four Drolls and single Kiennite were an advance party of a larger group. Obviously of some import, the Kiennite wore fine raiment and carried an ornamental scepter. Drolls and Kiennites often allied and antagonized the Drelves, the forest people who inhabited the forest beyond the red meadow. Their attempts to penetrate the dense forest where the Drelves lived usually met with little success.

Amica created the illusion that she was a Drelvish child in distress and drew the Drolls and Kiennites to her woods. Tree sprites and dryads had simple abilities of illusory Magick. More mature dryads had the ability to *charm*. Similar in stature to a Drelvling and speaking the Drelvish dialect fluently, Amica accomplished the illusion fairly easily. She topped it off with a couple of particularly pointed insults. A well-placed bolt from her tiny bow struck one of four Drolls in the scouting party. The byneberry poison in the bolt quickly put the big creature to sleep. His four comrades, the three remaining Drolls and the Kiennite, ran into the woods and chased the dryad. Delighted, Amica skittered up a tree and moved fluidly amongst the upper branches from tree to tree. The Drolls and Kiennite thrashed into the underbrush and chased after her. The Kiennite blindly fired a crossbow into the air, but the bolt came nowhere near the agile tree sprite.

Amica dropped a red oak acorn and shouted, "The sky is falling!"

The red oak acorn missed the Drolls and burst into a little puff of orange dust when it hit the ground. The dust irritated the skin and sensitive noses of the Drolls and the three sneezed uncontrollably.

"I'm going to tear you up completely!" the largest Droll shouted.

Amica laughed.

"Save your breath, Phastin. She'll have to come down sooner or later," the Kiennite said encouragingly to his bigger companion.

"Cast a spell upon her, Melphat. She's making fools of us all!" the frustrated Droll shouted back at his Kiennish companion. Phastin was the older brother of the Droll's promising Lieutenant Moochie.

"I have no spells that will fool the varmint. Dryads can see through Kiennish illusory Magick," Melphat answered.

"I don't have a clear shot at her. She's too **** fast!" Phastin roared as he fitfully moved his bow to and fro.

Amica followed by hurling a blue bees' nest toward the Drolls and Kiennite. The angry bees swarmed out of the hive, flew onto the beleaguered Drolls, and inflicted many painful stings. The Kiennite uttered a brief incantation and repelled the bees.

The Repel Insects Spell saved Melphat, but the indignant bees continued to sting the Drolls. Each sting raised a blue whelp on the Drolls. The three ran deeper into the forest.

Melphat chased after his comrades shouting, "Phastin, Addipex, Tenate! Stop! She's luring you deeper into the forest!"

The dryad hurled two stones and the second found its mark.

The wounded Droll growled expletives and said many bad things about the tree sprite matron and her mother. Amica fired another crossbow bolt, put another Droll to sleep, and reloaded her bow. Then red light surrounded the tree sprite matron and she saw a blur on the ground below her.

Another adversary attacked the Drolls with blinding speed and in a moment's time ripped the two standing burly heavily armed Drolls and their sleeping comrade apart.

The Kiennite Melphat shouted phrases and begin a spell, but a powerful blow killed him before he completed the incantation.

Terrified, Amica looked for the Kiennite and Drolls' attacker. The tree sprite matron squeezed back against the red oak and tried to hide behind the branches and leaves.

To no avail…

"Hold sssstill, you little vixen," a female voice hissed.

Hard razor sharp talons surrounded the tree sprite's skinny neck and pinned Amica to the red oak.

The dryad shuddered.

"Don't try anything, prisssssy. I need ssssomeone with your talentssss, but you are replaceable. What issss your name?" the attacker demanded.

"Uh...Amica...Amica Carmisino. That's my name. Ask me again, I'll tell you the same!" the captured tree sprite insisted.

"Don't teasssse me! That issss a good name. I might usssse it mysssself one day," the attacked answered.

Two large leathery wings beat rhythmically and kept Amica's assailant afloat. The strangely attractive feminine beast had reddish skin, fiery blue eyes, and thin arms with long blade like talons on her digits. The digits of her right hand tightened around Amica's throat.

The tree sprite managed to squeak, "Why should you need my name? Why do you accost me? I'm but a friend of the forest!"

"You are a menace, an aggravation, and a nuisssssance. I'll take your name, becaussssse I like it. Right now I'm deciding whether to end your missssserable life! But you *are* of the foresssst. That'ssss where I need your sssssscrawny *ssssssss," the winged creature declared.

"You are powerful. I am weak. As you just ssssaid, I've a scrawny ***," the dryad said.

Amica stopped struggling against her controlling adversary. The she-beast held the dryad tightly with her left hand's talons, extended the first talon of her right hand, and opened a shallow wound on the tree sprite's left butt cheek. The she-beast allowed a drop of the little dryad's deep blue blood to collect on the end of her talon. She then muttered a few phrases, which were foreign to the tree sprite. Amica's blood droplet burst into a spray of colors. Shimmering lights of all colors extended from the droplet and surrounded the dryad. The larger winged creature then took a small fragment of gray rock, inserted it into the wound on the sprite's backside, and then held the edges of the wound together. The she-beast then muttered another spell and healed the wound over the little stone. At the same time other scratches over Amica's body healed.

"Ow! Why? Why have you wounded, and then healed me? Why do you hurt me?" Amica cried.

"It'ssss what I do, you little blighter. Now lisssssten! I have casssst a Bane Sssspell upon you. You musssst do what I tell you. If you remove the pebble I placed under your sssskin, you will die. You'll ssssuffer a horribly painful death. If you dissssobey my orders, you will die. Do you undersssstand?" the Deceiver asked.

95

"Yessss," Amica answered.

"You can't ressssissssst being a ssssmart *ssssssss, can you? Let me squeeze you a little tighter. It'll help ussss get to know each other better. Maybe it'll get your attention, Amica Carmisssssino," the she-beast muttered as she tightened her talons around the dryad's neck.

"OK! OK! OK! I'm listening. What would you have me do?" Amica shouted painfully.

"You know the foressssstssss of the Drelvissssh people, don't you? You know the Green Vale. Magick deniessss me accessss. The curssssed treessss thwart my every move. I have tried… never mind. That'ssss where you come in. I am going to give you a tasssssk. It will require only the usssse of your talentsss and what I am to give you. Watch," the she-beast ordered.

The she-demon moved her right hand and slowly opened and extended her palm. A cylindrical tube appeared. Many runes covered the scroll tube. Amica understood none of them.

The dryad or tree sprite matron asked, "What is this?"

"A gift. A Rune Sssscroll. It contains the power of a Temporal Stassssisss Spell. Uh, Temporal Stasis Spell…Ninth level Magick. But it workssss only once," the she-beast answered.

Hiding her deception was easy. The Deceiver discerned the dryad knew little of potent Magick. One Ninth Level Spell was the same to her captive as another.

"Ninth level Magick. I am not a sorcerer, great one. Though you squeeze the life from me, I cannot understand and cast such a spell. The term level has no meaning to me. Magick…I have no idea how I am able to do the things that I do. I just do them. I'm not as beautiful or beguiling as you, great one," Amica answered submissively.

"You don't have to undersssstand. The pebble beneath your grimy sssskin will give you the power you need. It does that and nothing more. Anssssswer my questions?" the Deceiver demanded.

"Yes, I know the ways of the Drelves. I enjoy shadowing them, but they guard closely their treasures and the sanctity of the Green Vale. It's only one of two places in the World of the Three Suns where plants are green. I do well with trees. I can move about and through the woods. I have to avoid the tree herders. They don't cotton to mischief. I've been to the Green Vale. They have allowed me to sample the enhancing root. It really doesn't do much for me. But I can't effect any change. The Teachers watch over the Drelvlings too well. I…I don't know how to address you, great one," Amica, answered truthfully.

"*Great one* workssss fine. Or you can call me Alice if you want. While we speak, the Teacher leadsss a group of Drelvessss and Sssspellweaver to Green Vale. You sssshould go and addressss the Sssspellweaver," Alice said.

"Spellweaver. You didn't say there was a Spellweaver. There hasn't been one in many seasons of the enhancing root. Spellweavers are privy to powerful Magick, great Alice. Maybe even you should fear them," Amica warned.

"The Sssspellweaver issss the reasssson I want you to go to Green Vale. You musssst do exactly as I ssssay, or you will die, mosssst horribly. Do you undersssstand?" Alice answered.

"Yes. I understand," Amica Carmisino, the dryad replied.

The Deceiver released her grip on the terrified tree sprite matron, gave her the Rune Scroll, and unveiled the details of her plan.

Amica sighed with relief. She listened intently. When the she-beast finished her dissertation, the tree sprite matron sped away toward Green Vale.

The Deceiver descended to the ground, applied a sticky unguent to her right foot, placed a blue flattened tile on the ground, muttered a few phrases, and disappeared in a flash of blue light.

Clarke continued his vigil in the everred tree. He squinted, peered through his fluted looking glass, and looked for the Drolls. Initially he heard nothing. Then in their distance, he heard screams.

First of anger, vulgarities, and frustration…

Then, horror…

Then, silence…

Overwhelming silence…

Calls of birds, beasts, and insects ended,

The voices of the Drolls and Kiennite fell silent.

The old Drelve watched the forest closely. The enemies faded from sight and sound.

CHAPTER 16
Tomayo's Dream

The Drelvish Ranger Tomayo slept fitfully. Dreams filled his mind. His mind's eye saw the Green Vale and recalled his first trip and harvest when he was thirteen years old. The greenness of the enhancing plant's vale faded to red.

Wisps…

Threads…

Threads of Magick…

Threads of fate…

Threads of time…

Threads connecting worlds …

Dreams connecting worlds …

Dreams of Magick…

The Magick of Dreams…

Magick connecting dreams…

Magick connecting worlds…

Dream raiders…

Elf pressure…

Albtraum…

Albträume, elf dreams, nightmares…

Dreams…

Brilliant red light flashed and then a face entered his dream. Horrific and vaguely female, the creature had fiery red eyes, unsightly wings, and long gnarly arms ending in long curved talons. Dark ichors covered the talons. Still the creature was strangely attractive. She pursed her lips, blew the sleeping Drelve a kiss, and simply hissed, "Hello, sleeping beauty!"

Alarmed, Tomayo leapt up, ran through the tree's bark, scurried up the tree, and went to Clarke.

"Report!" Tomayo ordered.

"I saw five of the enemy. Something befell them. I…don't know…" the old Drelve's voice faded.

He scanned the field through a small flute looking glass.

Clarke regained his composure and reported what he had seen. Tomayo led three scouts to the spot the old Drelve had seen the enemies. A Droll lay on he ground, pierced by a small arrow.

"Is he dead?" young Loganne asked.

"No. He sleeps. That is a tree sprite's arrow. He is afflicted by sleep poison," the experienced Tomayo replied to the young scout.

Loganne, the youngest daughter of Moblee one of the most respected elders of Alms Glen, had earned her spot in the scouts through skills of archery and tracking. The young Drelvish female touched the sleeping Droll with her finely leathered boot. The big beast stirred but did not awaken.

"What do we do with him?" she asked.

Tomayo paused briefly, scanned the area, and then said, "We have no quarrel with this Droll. I detect no predators in the area. In fact I sense little of anything. The remarkable silence continues. Leave him. The poison will wear off soon. He will arouse and return to his ilk. We…we should return to the safety of the forest across the way," Tomayo urged.

"What about the others?" Loganne asked.

"I don't think there are others, at least not alive. The stench of death is nearby. I don't know what befell them, but we shouldn't tarry here to find out. Run. Now!" Tomayo commanded.

The four Drelves hurriedly moved along the circumference of the meadow until they reached the familiar forest. They scurried up friendly red oaks and watched the fallen Droll. After a time, the big wolf-faced beast stood, looked around bewilderedly, and then walked on unsteady legs northward toward the Peaks of Division.

Slowly the sounds of the forest and the meadow returned. Tomayo dispatched Loganne to Alm's Glen to report the events to the elders. When she arrived, Loganne learned the Teacher and his eight companions had departed to Meadowsweet.

The elders doubled the guard at the Lone Oak.

The veteran Tomayo's nightmare continued to unnerve him a bit.

The Deceiver arrived in the familiar barren rocky cavern in a flash of red light. Its lone inhabitant Arachnis raised his head and stared at her with his eight eyes.

"You've been gone long enough! I hope this escapade is worth the cost of an Alter Reality Rune Scroll. The artifact was likely unique. Did you succeed?" the demon asked.

"He ressssisssstssss," she hissed defiantly.

"Probably for the better. We spread ourselves thin. The Master has tasks for you. Work on the lisp!" the eight-eyed beast muttered.

"Kisssssss my *sssssssss, Arachnisssssss," the she-demon hissed.

Arachnis smirked and asked, "Did you accomplish your task?"

"Sssshe will do fine. Sssshe thinkssss sssshe issss under a Bane Sssspell," the Deceiver chuckled.

"She what?"

"It wassss only a Dancing Lightssss Sssspell, but sssshe thinkssss it carriessss the threat of death. Sssshe will do well," the Deceiver answered confidently.

The demons burst into laughter.

CHAPTER 17
Meadowsweet

The preceding amber period, Edkim had stood at the edge of the forest and stared dejectedly toward the woods across the way. Using an odd cylindrical fluted looking glass, the Teacher scanned the woods for signs of the lost young Spellweaver, but Yannuvia had not returned to Alms Glen. The great Lone Oak stood in the center of the large meadow separating the forests. Its red leaves fluttered in the gentle breeze. Disappointed, the Teacher had returned to Alms Glen. He gathered the Chosen to make final preparations.

"Now it is time for you to learn of the greatest treasure of our people, the enhancing root. It is time for the harvest. The dark period is nigh and this is the best time to gather the matured tubers," the Teacher said.

"How do you know the roots have matured?" Gaelyss asked.

"It is my place to know. You and your friends will accompany me to the ground where the plants thrive. Our brethren tend the forest at Green Vale. It is a journey of note. Make ready," Edkim announced.

Gaelyss and four other Drelvlings named Bryce, Debery, Zack, and Meryt went to their homes and gathered provisions for what would be a journey of several thousand paces. Bryce, Meryt, Zack, and Debery were born during the same Approximation as Gaelyss and his twin brother Yannuvia, but Gaelyss's four friends were not Spellweavers. They were very promising students and worked very hard. Harvesting the enhancing Root was an honor among the Drelves and only the best students were rewarded with trips with the Teacher to Meadowsweet. Three adult Drelves armed with long bows and swords stood with Edkim. Gaelyss recognized his father Glinne's friend Rumsie. Sergeant Major Rumsie had earned the reputation as an excellent tracker and had ascended to a position of leadership among the defenders of the realm of Alms Glen.

"The armed escort seems a bit unnecessary," Gaelyss remarked to his companion Bryce.

"The enhancing root grows only in areas near the fringes of our secure neighborhoods. Our hardiest people live there at some peril. We risk capture or worse. My mother insists that the sentries go along," Bryce replied.

"If we live in fear and cannot feel safe in gathering that which we need, then our society flounders," Gaelyss scoffed.

"My mother also says that running is always a perfectly good option when one is faced with conflict," the Drelvling named Debery added.

"But what if your enemy runs faster?" Gaelyss asked.

The Teacher Edkim interrupted the youths.

"We must be underway. Rumsie will lead us trough the forest. He, Beaux, and Klunkus have earned a trip to Meadowsweet through their service. The root must be harvested while the light is dim," the Teacher said. Edkim added, "We have a long walk. When we arrive at Meadowsweet we will take nourishment and a brief rest."

"Meadowsweet?" Gaelyss queried.

"Our ancestral home. The Drelves have long lived at Meadowsweet. Our forebears expanded into the forests. It is every Drelve's heritage. The plants flourish under the great red elms and in the soil of the meadows. The waters of the brooks in the meadows are sweet. Thus, the name," Edkim said.

"What is the origin of the enhancing root, Teacher?" Meryt asked.

Meryt was not the sharpest Drelve in the forest, but he at times asked intriguing questions.

"That's like asking where the Drelves came from, little one," the Teacher answered kindly.

"That means he doesn't know," the mischievous Zack whispered to Gaelyss.

"It doesn't mean my hearing is impaired, Zack," Edkim scolded. "You may clean everyone's moccasins when we reach Meadowsweet."

Cleaning the footwear was important. The finely made shoes aided quiet travel and limited the damage the Drelves did to the grasses and underbrush as they walked. Every Drelve meticulously cleaned his moccasins at the end of the day to protect the fabric of the shoes as well. Cleaning nine pairs would be no fun!

"I'll help you Zack," Gaelyss said and laughed slightly.

"I won't," Debery declared.

At the first radiance of the new light period, Edkim, Gaelyss, Rumsie, Debery, Meryt, Bryce, and Zack, and two veteran Drelves named Beaux and Klunkus began the journey to Meadowsweet. The elders and most of the community assembled to wish the party well.

The group left the confines of Alms Glen and headed into the forest. The Drelves moved through the underbrush with great respect, scurried across the reddish meadow, splashed through a shallow stream, and quickly went back into the cover of the forest. Leaving the chore of observing the rear to Klunkus, Sergeant Major Rumsie led the youths and the Teacher rapidly along a threadlike pathway deeper into the beautiful extraterrestrial forest. Beaux kept a wary eye skyward. The dense foliage and unfamiliar plants astonished Gaelyss. Though he had read extensively of the floras around Alms Glen, Gaelyss had not explored the fringes of the community to the extent his brother Yannuvia. The nine Drelves moved quietly and walked for... Gaelyss realized that he really had no concept of direction or time.

Loganne reached Alms Glen and learned the Teacher had departed. She dutifully reported to the elders and returned to Lone Oak.

Not as adventuresome as his brother Yannuvia, the young Spellweaver Gaelyss only knew the vicinity of Alms Glen. Going between his home tree and the homes of his friends at Alms Glen never posed a threat. Choosing well-defined destinations, his little excursions into the woods were always along well-traveled paths. Gaelyss marveled at the skill of the veteran Drelve Rumsie exhibited in leading them through the dense woods. Looking ahead of them, it seemed that there was no path to follow, but the skilled guide negotiated each cluster of plants. The underbrush gave the impression of opening its red and orange leaf-covered branches and pulling back its thorns as the leader moved along the pathway. Paths in the forest didn't appear to open before them; paths in the forest *did* open before them.

Once a large red elm tree "stepped" aside and allowed them to pass. Rumsie acknowledged the tree herder's politeness. At times tree herders mimicked red elms.

When Gaelyss turned to look in the direction from whence they had come, the neophyte saw no path. Occasionally, they crossed paths with an exotic bird or a small animal. Respecting his fellow creatures, Rumsie paused and allowed them the right of way. Once a rotund furry creature asked Rumsie for directions. Blending into the forest completely, the Drelves respected every blade of the reddish grass, and their gentle steps reflected their love for the land. In areas where the paths were more visible, Gaelyss saw more of the Drelvish people peeking from behind or perhaps from within some of the larger trees. The red, yellow, and orange foliage even yielded to allow a rare bit of green.

Fatigue gripped his muscles. The youngsters had difficulty measuring distance, direction, or time. Soft yellow light bathed the group in cleared areas, but the thick canopy of the forest obscured the amber sky most of the time during their journey.

The party paused at the edge of a clearing and took nourishment of the trail mix they carried. Above, the beautiful amber sky darkened slightly as they walked along the pathway. The light of the three suns merged to create the amber color. The huge black sun Orpheus remained unmoving high in the sky. As always, the small yellow sun Meries danced in the sky and produced the greatest light. As the small sun drew larger in the sky, the light brightened and the air warmed. Although the temperature increased a bit, the forest was never uncomfortable. The appearance of the third sun, Andreas the Wanderer intrigued Gaelyss most. The gray sun had not drawn near in one of its ultra rare Approximations in the thirteen years since his birth. When he saw Andreas in the sky and stared at its faint outline, the Spellweaver sensed familiarity and felt strength enter his body. When Gaelyss stared at Andreas, the gray wanderer seemed to stare back. He longed, as did all Drelves, for an Approximation. During an Approximation, lights came on deep within a Spellweaver's mind, reawakened the knowledge of spells long absent, increased the Spellweaver's repertoire of Magick, and strengthened from the repertoire of the Drelve's defenses.

The nine Drelves moved silently along the cushioned ground. Plush, dense moss covered the ground. The moss was a myriad of colors but mostly deep orange intertwined with bright red and blue hues. Stepping on the moss gave the sensation of walking on air. Breathtakingly beautiful great red oak trees towered above the surrounding forest. Except for their coloration, the red oaks were similar to the great green oaks located in the forests of the Emerald Isle. The Teacher described the green trees in his lessons.

Occasionally a face peered out from the bark. Not all Drelves lived in communities. Occasionally a lone Drelve or a small family inhabited a large tree in an isolated area of the forest.

Abruptly Sergeant Major Rumsie held up his hand, motioned for the party to stop, paused on the pathway, and gave a pleasant whistle that mimicked the purring of a meow-meow skat. New mothers treasured the meow-meow skat's company. The rare feline's gentle purring sounds soothed a restless babe and helped bring sleep, the forest's gentle nurse.

After a few moments Rumsie motioned for them to continue. The small group came to a clearing. An edifice crudely constructed with large rocks filled the center of the area. The rocky building blended into the natural landscape and minimally disturbed the environment. The ever-present multihued moss covered the building. When the Teacher Edkim led the group into the clearing, a hundred Drelves came out of the forest and surrounded him. Some older, some smaller, some fetching females, the Drelves were an extension of the forest.

An older Drelve emerged from the largest tree in the central area. Carrying an oaken cudgel and wearing a crown of woven vines, the elder

Ulysses said, "Welcome to Meadowsweet. The time of the harvest is nigh. We need your skills Teacher."

Addressing the older member of the community, the Teacher Edkim said, "Elder, we have neophytes. They come to gather the enhancing root. We have a Spellweaver of great ability."

The older Drelve nodded and added, "Though we thought two Spellweavers would accompany you, the presence of one blesses us. We have been without Spellweavers for a long time. Our beloved forests ever face jeopardy from the Drolls and Kiennites. Sojourners tell us other peoples stir in the distance near the fringes of the great Plain of Ooranth. If an Approximation approaches, even the most mundane of the world's creatures may develop skills of Magick. I hope the gray sun will draw near and strengthen our young Spellweaver. Harvesting the precious enhancing root involves all Drelves, including Spellweavers and Teachers."

A group of Meadowsweet residents led Edkim to a small chair, ceremoniously asked the Teacher to sit upon it, and brought nourishment to him. Others wrapped beautiful garlands of blue and violet flowers around the Drelve. A particularly lovely young female named Morganne carried a mug of beverage to Edkim and cast a glance toward Gaelyss.

Did Gaelyss detect a smile?

Suddenly he felt hot and befuddled. When their eyes briefly met, both young Drelves blushed. Morganne left the mug in the hands of the thirsty teacher and took a seat on the plush moss by Gaelyss. She delicately placed a small finger against his hand and hooked it around his fifth finger. Gaelyss enjoyed the warm innocent touch of her hand.

The Teacher sipped for a while and then sat the tankard on a nearby stump and spoke. "As the spiritual leader of the Drelve people, my role is the education of our community. Gather all around and I will give a brief discourse while we wait the darkening of the sky. The dark period approaches. Then we will enter the forest and harvest the root. I have great knowledge of the World of the Three Suns, but I've never taught a Spellweaver. Young Gaelyss and his brother Yannuvia have great potential. I hope the fortunes of our people are to change.

"Ours is a beautiful world, bathed by the light of three suns. The gray Wanderer Andreas variably bathes the land with its gray light. Andreas holds to no schedule but its own. On rare occasions, the unpredictable Gray Wanderer comes very near the land. We call this time of great Magick the Approximation of Andreas. Darkness as total as that of the subterranean caves never covers the surface of our world, because the greatest sun, the dark Giant Orpheus, never changes its position in the sky. We do experience dark periods. Our dark periods occur at regular intervals. We experience the beginning of one now. The brief repetitive light and amber periods relate to the position of the small yellow sun Meries in the sky. Most refer to amber periods as rest periods. Some call the cycle of Meries, one light period and one amber period, a *day*. Cycles are broken into the time period we, again arbitrarily, call hours. Hours are broken into minutes, and minutes into seconds. A second is about the length of a heartbeat, but more precisely the heartbeat of a nightwing. The heartbeat of the rare nightwing never varies. Because it doesn't have wings, the nightwing cannot fly. In some places the small beasts are called minutemen. Their hearts consistently beat 60 times in a minute. Since they are small, they are called *minute* minutemen."

"Excuse me Teacher, but how do you know of such creatures?" the inquisitive Morganne asked.

"Time and its measurement have always been an interest of mine. A Mender, a rare creature of our world, gave me information. But that's not important for you to remember. Measurements of Nature's phenomena are always given arbitrary names. Creatures who don't value the enhancing root would never measure their lives in seasons of its harvest, would they, little one?" the Teacher kindly answered.

"Please continue, Teacher," the Meadowsweet elder Ulysses implored.

"Every day, every cycle of Meries includes light and amber periods of equal time-spans of eight hours. The times of greatest light are called light periods, the lesser light are amber periods, and the cyclic extended periods of grayness are called dark periods. The dark period is important to all of the peoples of the World of the Three Suns, including Drelves. We must harvest enhancing root during the dark period. Though the dark sun Orpheus gives little light, the unmoving spiraling darkness controls the movement of Meries. Andreas, the Gray Wanderer, appears in the sky at irregular intervals, usually as a gray speck on the horizon but now and then the gray sun wobbles a bit closer. The gray light of Andreas is more in force during the dark periods, though the intensity of the grayness depends on the nearness of the Wanderer. A season of the harvest encompasses eight dark periods, 480 cycles of light and amber periods, and the equivalent of 120 days of dark periods. Should the Gray Wanderer draw near, light, amber, and dark periods give way to the grayness of Andreas.

"Drelves usually mature in fifteen to thirty seasons, mate when they find love, and live several hundred seasons if blessed by good health. Teachers often live longer, and Spellweavers have uncommonly long lives. A Droll's axe or Kiennite's bow can change that very quickly.

"The enhancing root is so important to our rituals and health. The tubers must mature for eight dark periods before they are harvested. This insures the potency of the root and preserves the wellness, safety, and importantly the survival of the plant. Harvesting the enhancing root properly is the primary mission of the Teacher and his charges, the keepers of Green Vale. Young Morganne has performed well in her function as keeper's apprentice of Meadowsweet. I'm told the plants thrive. I, we, the Drelvish people, thank you, people of Meadowsweet. Your deeds are so valuable to Drelvedom," the Teacher recited.

Edkim paused for a moment and drank from his mug.

Recognizing the Teacher's compliment, Morganne blushed and coyly squeezed Gaelyss's hand.

The Teacher Edkim continued, "Other peoples of our world also value the dark period. This is particularly true of our greatest adversaries. By the way we measure direction, giants inhabit the lands to the center of our world. Lore holds other hardened peoples desire total dominance of these lands. The Drolls and Kiennites have little respect for the forest and the natural world. Their wars have cost our world dearly in the past. The Drolls meander somewhat, but consider the lands near the Mountains of the Great Sea their domain. The terribly powerful Drolls are tribal, but unite to strike against other foes.

"The Kiennites number sorcerers among their populations. They are less powerful than Drolls physically and similar to our size, but their features are hardened. Kiennites have strong hatred in their hearts for all other races, including the Drolls. But they usually will unite with them against common enemies. The Kiennites have a hierarchy, organize in societies called warrens, and congregate at a place called Aulgmoor, where they have a center of leadership.

"Being a peaceful people, Drelves rarely become involved in the great struggles among the other peoples of the World of the Three Suns. Unfortunately we are frequently innocent victims. Conflicts and battles purge our lovely forests. Historically, only the skills of our Spellweavers and our allegiance with the forest keep evils at bay. We must defend our lands where they border the red meadow of the Lone Oak. In other directions the depth of our forest serves us well. The woodland defends itself. Beyond the lands around Alms Glen to an area toward the Great Sea and away from the Peaks of Division, the diverse flora provides a barrier even the greatest beasts can't breach. Swamps, flesh-eating plants, unfriendly walkabouts, exploding peashooters, grab grass, and many other inhospitable vegetations bar the way. Our enemies fear the Magick of Spellweavers. We have been without Spellweavers for generations, but the enemies don't know this. Their fears have kept them at bay," the Teacher concluded.

Adjusting to the light in the intriguing woods was second nature to Drelves. Because Alms Glen was deep in the woods and there were no large clearings near their homes, observing the sky's beautiful brilliant amber color was a new experience for the five Drelvlings. When they studied the skies from the clearing of the Drelvish village of Meadowsweet, the neophytes saw not only the small yellow star Meries reaching its nadir to signal the dark period but also something wondrous.

The gray sun was drawing nearer!

An elder of Meadowsweet named Morin spoke to Gaelyss, "You are welcome in Meadowsweet, Spellweaver Gaelyss. Please rest and regain your strength."

The elder's acceptance of Gaelyss pleased Edkim.

The Teacher said, "Young Gaelyss accompanies me on my quest for the enhancing root. With the approach of the gray sun Andreas, all things Magick will flourish. The tubers will never be more potent. I've only read of harvests during an Approximation. If a harvest has coincided with both an Approximation of the Gray Sun and the thirteenth season of a Spellweaver, it's neither recorded in the annals nor sung about by the campfires."

The community leader Morin handed an oaken cudgel to young Gaelyss. It felt good in his hand.

Feeling strong Gaelyss enthusiastically said, "I look forward to helping harvest the enhancing root. I hope to ever serve Drelvedom."

The elders Ulysses and Morin gave Morganne the task of orienting the youths to the area. After getting Zack, Debery, Meryt, and Bryce situated in guest saplings, Morganne led Gaelyss to lodging within one of the largest red oaks. After exchanging another brief glance, making eye-to-eye contact with Morganne, and sharing another blush with the she-Drelve, Gaelyss walked to the deep red tree. The great red oak beckoned to and welcomed him. The young Spellweaver stepped forward and literally through the burgundy bark of the red oak. Within the great tree, Gaelyss found simple and comfortable accommodations. He felt oddly safe and strong. The air energized him. He sank into a thick growth of reddish moss on the *floor.*

Was the floor merely part of the tree? The floor shifted with his steps. Sleep came easily, and Gaelyss welcomed Nature's gentle nurse. The great red oak tree was more a *host* than a dwelling. The gentle great tree's respirations synchronized with his breathing. The spirit of the great tree had been a part of the forest for a long time.

The young Spellweaver dreamt of warm light periods as a nymph with his mother Carinne. Then his mind's eye saw the excitement of the feasts celebrating the harvests of the enhancing root. Gaelyss genially recalled time spent both in lessons and play with Meryt, Zack, Debery, and Bryce. The great tree nurtured him. The images faded to redness.

Wisps…

Threads…
Threads of Magick…
Threads of fate…
Threads of time…
Threads connecting worlds …
Dreams connecting worlds …
Dreams of Magick…
The Magick of Dreams…
Magick connecting dreams…
Magick connecting worlds…
Dream raiders…
Elf pressure…
Albtraum…
Albträume, elf dreams, nightmares…

The Spellweaver sensed a warm red light, and a lovely feminine face appeared. The youthful face was not Drelvish. Nor did it match the descriptions the Teacher had given of dryads and tree sprites. Dryads appeared as incredibly lovely extensions of the great oaks to which they were bound. Tree Sprites were a bit smaller and less migratory. Some held dryads were merely tree sprite matrons; others held dryads were merely large migratory tree sprites. The womanly person in Gaelyss's dreams was different. Her arms bristled with well-defined musculature. Greener than any other color, her smooth skin changed in the dancing sunlight and produced chameleon-like changes in her color. Her eyes were deep hazel and piercing. Though her voice was something between a minstrel's lyrics and a soft breeze, the young Spellweaver detected firmness in her words as she spoke.

"Young Spellweaver, you sit on the verge of the greatest moment in your young life. At the end of the rest period in this nightless land, you will go with your Teacher to harvest the precious tubers. You will see wondrous things in the Green Vale. Pay heed to the area of the Thirttene Friends. Listen carefully and remember everything you hear. Sleep well," she said softly, faded from his dreams in gentle blue light, and left him.

Gaelyss continued to sleep comfortably. Sounds of activity awakened the young Spellweaver. Sweet aromas filled the air. The Drelves were preparing the first meal of work period.

Feeling remarkably refreshed, the young Spellweaver stood, stretched his frame, extended his arms, and touched the mossy ceiling of the *room* with his fingertips. At thirteen years of age Gaelyss had already attained his adult height. Towering five feet tall, Gaelyss and his brother were taller than their friends and rivaled the stature of a young Droll. Although the chamber within the red oak lacked an obvious egress, Gaelyss intuitively knew where to exit. He *walked* through the wall of the great tree just as he had entered. He never tired of entering and exiting the red trees. The large red oaks enjoyed Drelves passing through them. Experienced Drelves gently and carefully sculpted the rooms from the interiors of the great trees and avoided the veins and neural structures of the living tree. Knowing the *feelings* of the flora of the forest was an innate ability of the Drelves. *Nature* termed the relationship symbiotic.

Gaelyss sensed the spirit and the feelings of the great tree more at Meadowsweet than he did at his home.

He pondered, why?

Was it the proximity of the growing fields of the enhancing plant?

The maturing of the tubers of the plant...

The dark period...

The approach of Andreas...

Magick?

Meadowsweet bustled with activity. A glance toward the skies revealed the position of the suns. Meries reached its nadir. The great dark spiraling celestial body Orpheus lingered at its fixed position. Andreas grew larger by the moment.

Morganne led the visitors to a nearby rivulet where they refreshed. Afterward the Meadowsweet hosts treated the group to a fine meal of the fruits of the forest. Though meat was conspicuously absent, the wealth of the forest provided quite a nutritious repast for the travelers.

The Teacher Edkim approached the center of activity and said, "Gather to me."

The Meadowsweet Drelves, Gaelyss, Meryt, Debery, Zack, and Bryce approached Edkim. Gaelyss again caught the gaze of Morganne's bright eyes. The young she-Drelve crossed the clearing to the mossy knoll where Edkim stood.

"How far must we walk to reach the place where the enhancing plants grow, Teacher?" the inquisitive Meryt asked.

"We have a journey of a two thousand paces to reach the Green Vale, young Meryt. I thank you for the care of my boots. They feel good against my skin and almost purred as I put them on my feet this morning. In all of the World of Three Suns, there are but two known green places, the Green Vale and the Emerald Isle. The Emerald Isle is in the great sea to the west, the left as we face the Peaks of Division. It is there that the Blackthorn grows. We know of the Emerald Isle by legend and stories of seafarers, not by witness. Now we go to the Green Vale," the Teacher responded.

CHAPTER 18
Green Vale

Rumsie and Morganne took the lead. The large group followed the path that exited Meadowsweet to a dead end. A massive cluster of red oaks blocked the way, towered over the path, and blocked out the receding rays of the suns. Edkim moved to the front and spoke ancient phrases in a whispered voice. The great trees responded to the ancient message, moved apart, and revealed the Green Vale.

Green!

The red and orange foliage changed to deep green. Taller trees and bushes rimmed the entire roughly circular area, but a valley filled with short shrubby plants made up the greatest part of Green Vale. A hill in the center of the valley obscured the far side of the circular vale. Bright green plush grass covered a rim that extended several paces. At the edge of the green moss, the terrain inclined gently at about fifteen degrees for thirty paces and reached the floor. The floor of Green Vale extended several hundred paces, rose gently in several areas, and circled the central knoll. A grassy upslope began where the floor ended and extended fifty or so paces to the top of the central hill. Many small rivulets coursed through the landscape. A gentle breeze crisscrossed the warm valley. The odd sky overhead had some blueness intermingled with the ever-present amber light, but now the gray light emanating from the advancing Andreas dominated the sky and merged with grayness of clouds.

Shrubby enhancing plants filled the hillsides and the floor of the Vale. The enhancing plants did not grow in rows. Instead the plants were arbitrarily set in the gently rolling terrain. None grew on the central hill. Very few other plants intermingled with the enhancing plants. Instead of enhancing plants, a myriad of bizarre plants covered the top of the central knoll. Gaelyss and his companions could not determine the dimensions of the hillock from the vantage point the group had taken.

The Drelvlings had never witnessed such greenness!

Enhancing plants were about waist high to the average Drelve. The bushes bore bristles of green leaves and bright red flowers.

Edkim led the party of Drelves into the Vale. Once they entered, the great red trees closed the opening behind them. Sergeant Major Rumsie remained at the now hidden entryway. The young Drelves found the greenness quite strange and alien. Gaelyss and his young friends had heard older Drelves speak of harvesting the enhancing root. Actually being in the green region...

The inquisitive Meryt approached one of the nearest bushes, reached out, and touched the bright red flower.

"Ouch!" Meryt shouted. "It bit me!"

"Plants do not have teeth!" Zack muttered.

Chastising young Meryt, Edkim said, "Well, some do. However, these do not. But they have feelings and deserve our respect. You must approach the plant in such a way that it knows you appreciate its meaning and value."

"Teacher, what are the plants on the hill in the center? They are so strange? Many bear fruits," Zack asked.

"They are the *Thirttene Friends*," the Teacher answered.

"Aren't all plants our friends?" Meryt asked.

"Yes. But like the enhancing plant, these are special. The Thirttene are unique. They *are* Magick. Even when we are without a Spellweaver, we are not without the Thirttene. Their gifts have saved us many times. But we must reserve their fruits for times of need. We are now given Spellweavers," the Teacher answered. Edkim continued, "Now the time has come to harvest the root. Gather around the shrubs. I'll show you the proper way to approach the plants. We always harvest the tubers in the dark period while the light is dim. That's when they have greatest potency. Now the Approximation makes the dark time even grayer. Our ancestors' experience proved the Approximation grants even greater potency to the tubers."

The Teacher went to the first plant on the downward sloping terrain. The older Drelve sang in a low soothing voice. The plant curled its leaves and retracted its barely visible needle-like thorns. The Drelve then tenderly touched the spine of the upper leaves of the plant. The enhancing plant pulled its limbs upward and inward. This in effect changed the plant from a full bush to a thin narrow plant. Edkim then removed a small spade from his pack and knelt at the base of the plant. The Teacher delicately inserted the spade into the ground, moved the digging instrument around the base of the plant, gently pulled the entire plant from the soil, held it aloft, and exposed the roots to the graying light. The gray light from Andreas concentrated on the roots. The entire plant emitted a gray aura. Edkim expertly exposed several thumbnail sized tubers dangling from the uncovered roots. He gently pulled the tubers from the roots, but very carefully left one of the tubers undisturbed. He then gently stroked the roots of the plant and carefully placed the plant back on the soft dark ground. The enhancing plant's roots plunged back into the soil. The Teacher Edkim sang again, and the little bush expanded its branches and reopened its red flowers.

"That's how it's done," the Teacher said matter-of-factly. "Disturb only the plants with flowers. That's the sign that their roots bear mature tubers. Once we have harvested, I'll tell you more of the Thirttene."

The Drelves went about the task laboriously. Meryt and Zack had difficulty in getting past the thorns. As a vocalist, Meryt left much to be desired, and Zack was a bit clumsy in stroking the spines of the leaves. Edkim applied unguent to the wounds left by the thorns. The older Drelves quite capably harvested the tubers, and Gaelyss learned the process quickly. The central hillock and its circle of green trees kept the young Spellweaver's attention.

Wait...

While gazing at the Thirttene friends on the hillock, Gaelyss detected a subtle movement amongst the trees. *Was someone standing on the grassy knoll?* He stared at the area in question. Nothing...

The Teacher Edkim called the five youths together and directed them to follow him to the hilltop. Warm sweet air, a fair breeze, and pleasant light greeted them and created the overall sensation of a warm eve either just before or after a cooling rain. Covering the graying amber sky, blue-gray clouds gathered above them and yielded grudgingly to the ever approaching gray sun. A few raindrops drizzled downward from the low-lying clouds. Thunder rumbled faintly in the distance. When they approached the central hillock, the group defined the dimensions of the mossy grassy knoll. The radius of the perfectly circular knoll was one hundred and sixty-nine feet. A circle of thirteen exceptional trees of various shapes and sizes occupied the top of the knoll. Many of the trees bore fruits. Like the enhancing plants, the trees at the top of the hill were mostly green.

The same plush green moss covered the ground of the hillock. Gaelyss and his comrades shook off the trepidation of walking on the strange green colored moss and enjoyed the feel of the mossy floor. Drelves were wary of unusual grass. Most stories they'd heard of odd grasses warned of danger. The young Drelves remembered shocking grass shocked, grab grass held on tightly and wouldn't let go of one's shoe, and centipede grass uprooted in sprigs of one hundred and walked around. The green grass was *odd*. To the young Drelves' surprise, the mossy ground of Green Vale was plush and comfortable.

Thunder rumbled.

As the youths watched closely, a geyser erupted from the very center of the knoll ahead of them and bathed the trees on the hilltop with waters of many hues. The geyser erupted for thirty-nine heartbeats.

Then the thunder ceased and the area remained quiet.

"I'm wary of the rain from the geyser," Meryt said. "It only extended to the area just beyond the trees. I...I wouldn't allow it to fall on me."

"I agree. I am concerned about the cloudy sky as well. Meryt, let's wait near the trees and watch the skies. This fertile ground is very moist, but it didn't get water from the geyser's eruption! It must rain often. The rain may also fall in many colors! I don't want to get wet!" Zack rambled.

Meryt and Zack gazed upward and watched the sky.

Gaelyss laughed, "Do you feel safe, Zack? Are you worried about those evil raindrops?"

Zack answered, "Very funny, Gaelyss! I don't fear clear waters that fall upon our forests from friendly clouds! Rain replenishes the forest. I don't want green and purple rain falling on me!"

The Teacher Edkim interrupted the neophytes and said, "The same rain falls upon us from the skies in Green Vale and Alms Glen. As young Zack has said, the rain is our friend. What spews from the geyser is not rain. The Thirttene Friends and the geyser that gives them life predate our spoken and recorded histories. Legend holds the Thirttene are older than the Lone Oak. The geyser is old, but not faithful. An entire dark period may pass without an eruption. Sometimes the geyser erupts thrice in succession. It always erupts for thirty-nine heartbeats. I don't think you have to fear the waters of the geyser. They are Magick. You should respect, but not fear Magick."

"Teacher, is it not prudent to fear stuff we don't understand? I talk to plants and animals every day. Animals and plants talk to me. I understand plants and animals. I don't understand this greenness!" Zack answered.

Edkim pensively looked at Debery, Meryt, Zack, Bryce, and then Gaelyss.

"The enhancing plant is green. It's among the most glorious things I've seen. When I came to Green Vale a long time ago as a neophyte, I must confess I felt much like the five of you. But now *I've* been here with a Spellweaver. I understand more of the mystery of Green Vale. I am learning as we speak. We have done well. The tubers we have harvested will strengthen our poultices and give our people the energies they need. Please follow me to the center of the circle of Thirttene at the summit of the green knoll. I'll tell you what I know of them. Perhaps we'll see the Lady of the Trees," Edkim answered.

Rumsie and the older Drelves collected the harvested tubers. The Teacher led the five Drelvlings to the hillside where the strange trees stood. The six crossed several rivulets and streams and passed many enhancing plants. Soon they stood upon the hill. Gaelyss reported that the trees, the unique fruits they bore, the waters, and the entire Vale had auras of Magick. The Spellweaver felt a light touch on his shoulder, turned quickly, but saw no one. Meryt's quiver dropped from his back and spilled his arrows on the ground. At the top of the hillock, thick grass cushioned their steps. The youths adjusted to the pretty green colors. The geyser pool in the center of the flattened top of the hillock had a diameter of thirteen paces. Iridescent lights flickered in the clear sparkling waters of the geyser pool. The overall diameter of the top of the hillock was about thirteen times the diameter of the geyser. Noting the gentle effervescence of the liquid in the basin, Zack and Meryt braced, but the geyser did not erupt.

Separated by equal distances and differing dramatically the *Thirttene Friends* circled the geyser.

Meryt counted the trees, confirmed that thirteen exceptional trees stood on the hillock, called the closest to the Drelves' left number one, and numbered the others leftward two to thirteen.

About the height of three Drelves or thirteen feet, the first tree bore red luscious unfamiliar fruits. Varying in size and shape, one hundred and sixty-nine fruits grew on the tree. Typical for plants in the Green Vale, the tree had green leaves. The tree's light pink blooms brought to mind the common bluerose plants.

Also thirteen feet high, the second tree bore only thirteen fruits, which were rounded at their end and smaller toward the stem. The tree had blooms similar to the first tree. In some distant past, both must have been related to the bluerose and other rose plants.

One hundred and sixty-nine white berries covered the third tree, which was more like a bush.

The fourth tree had thirteen elongated purple fruits that were about six inchworms lengths long. Several intricate webs intertwined in its branches.

The fifth tree was a large oak forty feet tall. But its leaves were green, not red! Its bark was brown, not burgundy. Faint auras of Magick surrounded the tree. The large green oak tree bore no fruit.

Small cherry sized fruits covered the sixth tree, which was thirteen feet tall. The little fruits were red, green, blue, black, white, and chromatic (multiple colors). The little green tree bore thirteen fruits of each variety.

Fourteen feet tall, the seventh tree had a thick truck and bore no fruit.

One hundred and sixty-nine speckled berries covered the eighth tree, which was more like a bush.

Gems of thirteen colors covered the ninth tree.

The tenth tree was a silver maple, thought to be extinct. Most of its prized leaves were made of silver! The old tomes spoke of this legendary tree. The silver maple had thirteen green leaves. Since the extinction of silver maple trees, silver was found only in rare underground veins and mined from the ground.

The very large eleventh tree bore huge orange fruits. Thirty-nine feet tall, the l'orange tree bore thirteen large fruits. Its leaves were deep blue green. Even though the temperature of the Green Vale was comfortable, thin slivers of ice covered the leaves of the l'orange tree. At least the orange color of the fruits was more familiar.

The twelfth tree was a Sick Amore. It bore heart-shaped fruits. According to legend, ingestion of its fruit was the equivalent of imbibing a love potion. Some thought the bittersweet fruit was poisoned. One who consumed the fruit might become intoxicated, lose reason, and long for more. Not surprisingly, the Sick Amore tree bore thirteen fruits.

Also thirteen feet tall, the thirteenth tree had thirteen branches, a trunk with a diameter of thirteen inches, leaves divided by thirteen veins, and thirteen fruits. The fruits were shaped like small silver scroll tubes.

Were the odd thirteen-inch long fruits actually Magick scrolls?

Were they simply flutes?

Gaelyss reported only faint auras of Magick.

Close inspection revealed that the little scrolls had clear lenses at either end and other holes spaced along the slender tube. If one peered through the end of the flute-like structures, the lenses magnified objects viewed in the distance.

The fluted tube was a looking glass!

If one flipped the lenses to the side, blew air through the end of the device, and covered the other holes along the length of the devices, he played different notes. The neophytes now recognized the legendary "toot and see scroll" tree, the source of the rare and sought after looking glasses the Drelvish veterans used to survey the red meadow.

The young Drelves studied the Thirttene Friends and their fruits.

Bryce asked, "What do we do? How do we investigate the fruits? In what order should we proceed? Are we to sample the fruits?"

Gaelyss went to the seventh tree.

After studying the thick bark, the young Spellweaver spoke in the direction of the thick tree, "What is the riddle of this hill?"

Meryt, Bryce, Zack, Debery, and Edkim looked quizzically at the Spellweaver.

Speaking rapidly in a dialect that the Drelves understood, the great tree answered, "I'm surprised to find a Spellweaver among the gatherers of the tubers. I'm a tree shepherd and the voice of the Thirttene Friends. Allow this respite of Nature and Magick to refresh you. Magick and the Gray Wanderer Andreas replenish the fruits and sustain the Green Vale."

Bewildered, the Teacher Edkim stood back with Meryt, Bryce, Zack, and Debery. As Teacher, Edkim had participated in thirty-nine harvests of the enhancing root and walked among the Thirttene Friends over a hundred times. The waters of the geyser had bathed him. For the first time, the Teacher heard the great tree speak. Edkim searched his memories and recalled his readings in the annals.

Had Spellweavers communicated with the Thirttene Friends?

Had a Spellweaver assisted in the harvest during an Approximation of the Gray Sun?

Gaelyss was in Green Vale at the time of the harvest during an Approximation of the Gray Sun.

Had this ever happened?

A long time had passed since there had been a Spellweaver.

By the moment, the wandering sun Andreas drew nearer, evermore filled the sky, and intensified the gray light.

Edkim allowed, "I planned to tell you more of the Thirttene. Now the tree shepherd speaks. Who better than one of *them* to tell you of the Thirttene Friends? Continue, Spellweaver."

Gaelyss asked, "How do you come to be on this hillock?"

"I've always tended trees. These trees needed tending, so I made them my flock. There are always waves in the sea of Magick. I suppose a great wave of Magick swept me to this place. I've only been here a little while, not more than eighty thousand harvesting seasons or so. It's hard to tell. Without the influence of the sun and moon, my circadian rhythm suffers. My internal clock is off a bit," the tree shepherd replied.

"Moon? You also said sun, not suns," Gaelyss queried.

"One sun gave warmth and light to the world I came from. The moon…I do miss the moon. But this is a very pleasant place and I'm doing what I love most, attending gentle trees. I would never have such diversity of dependents in my old wood. Are you going to stay?" the tree shepherd replied.

"What is your name?" Gaelyss asked.

"Only a jackleg tree herder would tell you his name, my young friend. What is your name?" the tree shepherd returned.

"I'm Gaelyss, Spellweaver of the Drelves," Gaelyss replied.

"How refreshing! I've seen Spellweavers among the harvesters, but not in a long time. You are a rarity, young one. I could use companionship. The trees don't say much. Rustling of leaves is beautiful to my senses, but I enjoy conversation and other things of beauty," the forest guardian evasively answered.

Spirits of the forest safeguarded their personal identities tenaciously to resist losing control of their fate. Greedy woodcutters, insalubrious lumberjacks, Drolls, Kiennites, and giants had cut down many trees, killed tree shepherds, and notoriously and wantonly destroyed forestland.

"We must proceed. Tell us of the riddle of the trees," Gaelyss requested.

Edkim remained silent. The Teacher was now a student.

The great tree herder began a dissertation.

"Explaining our presence equates to explaining Magick. I can't you *why* are in Green Vale, but I'll tell you *who* we are. The first tree is an apple tree. We don't have apple trees in Donothor, where I sprouted. But for this friendly tree, I don't think apple trees exist in *this* world. Where apple trees are native, an adage says 'an apple a day keeps the doctor away.' Those folk call healers *doctors*. Doctors are very poor sorcerers. Menders are much more capable than doctors. This tree comes from a stand of trees called an orchard in a place called Virginia. A good chap named Garnet planted it. The apples are delicious. You'll notice different varieties. Some are winesaps, red delicious, golden delicious, mutsus, staymans, galas, pink ladies, and Brittany.

"The second tree is a pear tree. It also bears delicious fruit. The third tree with the white berries is a snowberry bush. If one places the little berries in liquid, the snowberries chill the liquid and create a pleasant beverage for a hot afternoon. That's all they do. The fourth tree is a purplanana bush. The fruit is very good. The tree has passengers, the purplanana spiders. I'm afraid the spiders are very poisonous. You must be wary when picking the purple fruits.

"The fifth tree is a great oak. A tree sprite lives within it. The nymph is away from the tree. When she is away, the great oak feels great sorrow. I don't know where the tree sprite goes on these forays.

"The sixth tree is a rainbow bush. The differently colored fruits have different properties. Each person can only try one. If you eat one of the red berries, you will feel hot; the white you will feel cold; the green you will taste mint; the black you will feel a slight burn to you skin; the blue you will feel a little shock; the chromatic you will have brilliant hues to your skin. The sensations won't last long. Once eaten, the berries grant lingering resistance to the breath attack of dragons and other fanciful beasts of the same color. One other thing... if you throw them, the red ones explode. Some call them cherry bombs."

"The seventh of the trees…hmm…wait, that's me! Let's see…what was I doing? Yes…

"The eighth tree with the speckled berries is a Jellybean bush. Even though the Jellybeans look the same, they taste differently. I'm told you'll never have two of the same flavor. The ninth tree is a gem bush. It bears gems, including extremely rare red diamonds. The tenth tree is a silver maple. Its leaves are priceless. The eleventh tree bears delicious l'oranges. The twelfth tree is the Sick Amore. I would avoid its bittersweet fruit. The thirteenth tree is a 'toot and see scroll' tree. The 'toot and see scrolls' are very popular toys with children," the tree shepherd concluded.

Using her illusory talent, the tree sprite Amica mimicked the appearance of the young Drelve Kirrie from Alms Glen. Amica thought she only read the dweomer Temporal Stasis from the ultra rare rune scroll. Actually the transformed tree spirit perfectly uttered the incantation of the more powerful Alter Reality Spell. Anyone who touched the shores of the great sea of Magick sensed the wave created by the potent spell. The spell stopped time, but the enchantment specifically spared its caster and the young Spellweaver Gaelyss. The vellum crumbled as the dryad Amica uttered the final phrase of the incantation. The *other* effects of the Alter Reality Spell took effect immediately.

Suddenly stillness surrounded the Spellweaver.

Gaelyss pulled his short sword from his scabbard, touched the tip to the bark of the great tree, and shouted with alarm, "Something is amiss!"

From out of nowhere, *Kirrie* stood by him. Gaelyss became aware of the young Drelve female who was so fond of his brother Yannuvia. Turning quickly, the Spellweaver saw his friends and the Teacher standing like unmoving statues. In fact, nothing moved. A raindrop stopped in mid air about two feet from his face.

"Spellweaver! You must learn to detect invisible beings! You must learn to detect Magick! Have you not sensed my presence?" the young female Drelve scolded.

Gaelyss shouted to Meryt and the others, "Make ready to defend yourselves!"

Hearing no response, Gaelyss stammered, "It was you! I saw you on the hill! My brother and I are the only Spellweavers! Unless Yannuvia plays a spiteful gag upon us and now pretends to be you, my brother did not accompany us to Green Vale. Who are you? You are no Drelvling. How can you do such Magick? Nobody has the power to suspend life."

The ersatz Kirrie waved her right hand, removed the Illusory Magick, and no longer appeared a young she-Drelve. Instead the Spellweaver saw the womanly person who had visited his dreams. Her arms bristled with well-defined musculature. Greener than any other color, her smooth skin changed in the dancing sunlight and produced chameleon-like changes in her color. Her eyes were deep hazel and piercing.

"Are you a dryad?" Gaelyss asked.

The female raised both hands defensively and said, "Relax! Your friends are fine. It's only a simple Temporal Stasis Spell. They are merely caught between heartbeats. I bear no animosity toward Drelves. *I wish every Drelve touched by the waters of the Geyser of the Thirttene Friends this day also be touched by Magick and given the power of casting a spell!* I'm not an enemy. I'm simply a messenger sent to give you a warning. You were spared the effect of the Temporal Stasis. I must warn you of your brother Yannuvia. It is you, Gaelyss, who should lead the Drelves. Your brother treks down a dangerous path. He'll return one day and profess loyalty to your people. You shouldn't believe him. He'll stress striking against your enemies and use Magick to bring them down with spells of fire. He will have *changed.* At this moment, only you and the tree shepherd can see and hear me! Please trust me."

"I'm not sure. I'm just beginning to learn Magick, but I know the Temporal Stasis Spell is high-level Magick. I've read of the spell in my texts. It's unclear whether *any* Spellweaver ever mastered the spell. Who…what are you? How do you know my brother's plans? Do you have an idea of his whereabouts?" Gaelyss wondered.

"I'm only a simple tree sprite, a forest nymph. Call me a dryad if you want. Some do. Don't miss this opportunity. Heed my warning. I speak the truth. Guard your people. You swear no fealty. Don't misuse what you have learned today," the nymph warned.

"The Teacher tells us of tree sprites and forest nymphs. You're more than that! You foment mischief. You are a sorceress of sorts. But I don't fear you!" Gaelyss declared defiantly. His stern resolution belied his thirteen seasons.

The beautiful female turned, leaped into the great oak, and vanished. The suspended raindrop fell upon Gaelyss's face. Then the Spellweaver heard the shouts of the Teacher and his friends. Gaelyss ran, followed the ersatz Kirrie to the large oak, and rubbed his hands across the bark.

"What are you doing, Gaelyss?" Meryt asked.

"How did you get to the tree and draw your sword so quickly? I didn't see you move," Bryce added.

"Yeah! Are you fighting the tree?" Debery chortled.

"I hope you can prevail against the big vicious oak tree," Zack joked.

The four Drelves burst into laughter, but the Teacher asked, "What has *happened* Gaelyss? How *did* you move to the tree without our noticing?"

Gaelyss realized he faced the great oak with sword drawn. Clearly none of the others had knowledge of the events that had transpired. How did he begin to tell them? *Had time stopped for them?*

The Spellweaver returned his attention to the tree shepherd. He whispered, "What did you see?"

"I've seen eighty thousand seasons. I see you, young Spellweaver, with a blade pointed toward me. Why do you threaten me?" the tree shepherd answered quizzically.

"You didn't see her?" Gaelyss queried.

"Do you speak of the tree sprite who lives in the fifth tree? I told you she is away," the tree shepherd replied.

"I'm..." Gaelyss stammered.

"Gaelyss, why re you whispering?" Edkim asked.

"I'm sorry, Teacher. I'll continue. Please tell us of the geyser, tree shepherd," Gaelyss requested.

The tree shepherd replied, "Sheath your blade. The tip makes me nervous. The Geyser of the Thirttene Friends erupts and brings rain whenever it chooses. Oh...I see the geyser is erupting now. You are going to love the rain's effect. If it hits you during *this* time of Approximation of the Gray Sun Andreas, it will endow you with Magick. But Spellweaver... you will find the rain more than cleansing. You will grow stronger with each drop that strikes you. Can you feel the effects of the waters?" the tree shepherd asked.

Just then the shadow of Andreas completely filled the sky and bathed the entire area with deeper gray light. The geyser's shower continued. When the drops splashed to the ground, each spattered with the iridescence of an elf's tear.

Meryt ran.

The old tree implored, "You need not flee, young one. Only one who disdains Magick need fear and flee the rain. The raindrops will impart Magick to you, but won't make you a Spellweaver."

Meryt stopped. He remained nearest to the geyser pool. The thirty-nine heartbeat long shower sprayed, refreshed, and soaked the six Drelves on the hillock.

"Gracious host, the geyser's showers have soaked Drelves many times. The waters only refresh us," Edkim said cautiously.

"Not this time, wise Teacher," the tree shepherd countered.

Wet and despondent, Meryt looked at Edkim, sighed, and said, "He's... he's right! I'm endowed with Magick! I'm given the power of a continuous Shield Spell. I'll not have to carry a shield again. I no longer fear the Magick Missiles thrown by the Kiennish shamans."

Andreas complemented the cloudy gray skies.

Zack added, "I have been given the spell Haste."

Debery said, "I can become Invisible."

Bryce informed them, "I can form Mirror Images."

The Teacher Edkim sighed, "The Tree Shepherd speaks the truth. I can now cast a Magick Missile against an enemy. This puzzles me. I have stood in the rain of Green Vale many times. The geyser has sprayed me scores of times. Teachers have harvested the enhancing root in the gray light of the Approximation of Andreas. The geyser's waters have fallen on Teachers in the gray light and never empowered them with Magick. Now I am so empowered, and I don't know whether I can manage the skill. I have never taken a life, even the life of an enemy. Now I am given a destructive spell. I've seen but never touched the shores of the sea of Magick. The great sea... of Magick...why? I..."

The tree shepherd interrupted the befuddled Teacher, "Why, you ask? Magick chooses you, wise one. You do not choose Magick. I have seen you in the Vale many times. You are a loyal servant to your people. But you have never been in the Vale *with* a Spellweaver *during* the Approximation of the Gray Sun. The geyser sprays you during *this* Approximation. I have sensed powerful Magick this day. This is a day like no other. The geyser's rain didn't touch your comrades who did not stand on the hillock. Why? The rain, the presence of the Spellweaver, the benevolence of the Gray Wanderer, but in the end...Magick."

Meryt said excitedly, "If we stand in the rain again, will we learn more Magick?"

"No," the tree shepherd said without hesitation.

Gaelyss left the great tree and walked to the geyser pool. The water gently effervesced. After briefly standing by the geyser pool, the Spellweaver sheathed his sword and returned to the great oak.

The tree shepherd sent a *silent* message to Gaelyss, "What say you, Spellweaver? What have *you* learned?"

The young Spellweaver *silently* replied, "I've learned to beware of gifts. You *did* see and hear her. *Where is she? What did she do?*"

The tree shepherd laughed *aloud*, "Ha! I echo those sentiments. Suspicion can be strength. Trust can be weakness. What can one trust other than Magick? Yes, I've heard ancient phrases this day."

Gaelyss went back to the fifth of the Thirttene Friends, the great green oak. The Spellweaver rubbed the great oak tentatively but jumped back when a small blue-haired nymph walked quickly through the bark.

After sleepily rubbing her dark purple eyes, the diminutive forest creature gently stroked Gaelyss's long silver hair, winked at him, and asked, "Why are you rubbing my tree? Who are you, pretty thing?"

Indignantly Gaelyss challenged the cute little feminine being, "You look *different*. Tell them what you did! Tell them about the spell you cast. Tell *them* what you told me, dryad!"

"Of what do you speak? I'm not a matron! Dryads are huge, nigh as big as Drelvlings, four feet tall! I'm a simple sprite! I've been sleeping in my tree having the best dream. I was drinking the juice of byneberries. I've never seen you, young...ooh! Spellweaver! You are a Spellweaver! You are posing a riddle! Is it a game? I'll play. I've not seen a Spellweaver since...I don't remember. Oh, hello, Teacher. I see you've brought neophytes. I suppose they'll want to sample *my* fruits. Don't you have any pretty ones? These guys are rather homely. Well, all except this one," the sprite warbled chaotically.

Gaelyss protested, "You...you *were* here! You stopped time! You told me...you said..."

Edkim interrupted, "Sometimes the wonders of Green Vale overwhelm us, young Gaelyss. You mind is sensitive to Magick. The events of this gray day have forever changed *me*. I've been here many times and brought many neophytes, but before this day none have ever learned Magick. Now that has changed. I know your experience differs from ours. This has been an exceptional day. We perhaps tarry too long in the Green Vale."

The tree sprite coyly said to Gaelyss, "You are a bit confused, Spellweaver. Maybe *you* had a draught of the byneberries before you came to the Green Vale."

"You've changed your appearance! Why do you torment me, little vixen? What have I done to you? Why do you dislike me?" Gaelyss pleaded.

"To the contrary, Spellweaver. You are cute. I've never told anyone my name, but I'm tempted to tell you. Would you like to come into my tree and share a few moments? I have some passion fruit," the svelte little tree sprite replied seductively.

"He'd best stay with us, Lady of the Trees," Edkim kindly interjected.

"I won't keep him long, Teacher," the tree sprite answered coyly.

"Oh, I suspect your beauty would forever detain him, my Lady," Edkim said complimentarily.

The tree sprite blushed, but her bright green skin turned purple instead of red. Gaelyss studied the cute little creature. The tree sprite's blue hair and purple eyes contrasted with her bright green skin. The greenness returned after her blushing ended. Though totally out of place in most of the World of the Three Suns, the little creature appeared perfectly at home in the Green Vale. As tall as thirty-six inchworms stacked end-to-end, the three foot tall sprite was about two-thirds the height of Meryt, who was an average sized Drelve.

Knowing the sprite's vanity might be used to their advantage and hoping to spare Gaelyss more indignation, the Teacher Edkim said politely and redundantly, "Thank you for allowing our eyes to behold your beauty, Lady of the Trees. It's been too long. We can't all be as beautiful as you. Please bear with us, and we thank you for allowing our glances."

The tree sprite accepted the compliments and offered, "You may try some of *my* wondrous fruits."

Edkim interjected, "Ahem. We'll accept the fruits of the trees, Lady of the Trees."

"But they are so few," Gaelyss objected.

"*The Lady* has given us permission, Gaelyss. Remember the tree shepherd's words. Magick and the Gray Wanderer Andreas replenish the fruits and sustain the Green Vale. The Magick that sustains the Thirttene will replace a fruit as you take it. You must never take the entire crop. And show respect as you take the fruit."

The young Drelves took a fruit from the Apple and Pear Tree. The tree sprite walked over to the tree shepherd, whispered something, returned to the fifth of the Thirttene Friends, and passed through the odd dark brown bark. Gaelyss asked the tree shepherd several questions, both verbally and silently, but after the tree sprite departed, the tree shepherd said nothing.

Taking advantage of the Approximation of the Gray Sun Andreas, the Teacher Edkim harvested one of the thirteen fruits from the 13th tree in the circle of Thirttene Friends. Immediately the nubbin of a new fruit appeared in its place. The new fruit would mature in time. The fruits of the "toot and see scroll" tree could only be harvested one at a time during the times of the Approximation of the Gray Sun. Should the enhancing plant tubers be immature and an Approximation occur, the plant tenders of Meadowsweet entered the Green Vale and took one of the *toot and see scrolls*. The last had been taken thirteen years ago.

Rumsie shouted from across the way, "If you have finished your exploration, we'd best be getting back to Meadowsweet."

Edkim gathered his charges, gave the "toot and see scroll" to Rumsie, and led the group from the Green Vale.

CHAPTER 19
Amica's Reward

The dryad Amica scurried through the treetops and occasionally into willing red oaks. The tree sprite matron had followed the she-beast's instructions to the tee. Overcoming the bungling inhabitant of the fifth of the Thirttene Friends in the Green Vale had been her easiest task. One sip of the byneberry juice, and the sloe-eyed occupant of the great oak fell fast asleep. The fifth Friend's inhabitant was the sort that gave tree sprites and dryads a bad name. Amica didn't kill the Green Vale tree sprite as the she-beast commanded. Though mischievous, Amica was reluctant to harm one of her own.

Wanting to preserve the precious the rare shiny silver, Amica opened the Rune Scroll carefully. The dryad unrolled the scroll and noted the intricate runes etched on the ancient vellum. Reading the verses of the spell ingrained the incantation in her mind. After she read the spell, the vellum disintegrated. Undaunted the dryad hid the silver scroll tube. Amica suffered a mild burning pain in her gluteal area, where the she-beast *Alice* had placed the little gray pebble.

Amica did *so* want the pebble removed. It was literally a pain in the butt.

Doing as she had been told, initially the tree sprite matron mimicked the Drelve Kirrie. Then Amica waited in the tree until she saw the Drelves enter the Vale. She exited the tree and carefully moved among the Thirttene Friends and green underbrush. When she saw young Gaelyss looking toward the hillock, the ersatz Kirrie pulled up the short walking skirt she wore and tantalizingly exposed and extended her upper thigh. She then blended invisibly into the greenery and waited. When the young Delves appeared on the hillock, she gingerly applied a droplet of thick amber to the shoulder of the one called Gaelyss, and stole several arrows from the quiver of one they called Meryt. Amica recited and pronounced the incantation of the spell perfectly. Unbeknownst to the caster, she actually pronounced a Limited Wish, or Alter Reality Spell, the full extent of which the dryad would never know.

After addressing the Spellweaver as *Kirrie*, she meticulously altered her appearance and presented the image the taloned beast had described and demanded. Then Amica spoke to the young handsome Spellweaver and recited *everything* precisely as she was told.

I wish every Drelve touched by the waters of the Geyser of the Thirttene Friends this day also be touched by Magick and given the power of casting a spell!

Having done everything (except killing the Green Vale tree sprite) the she-beast demanded, Amica Carmisino hoped to receive a great reward and get the pebble removed from her buttock.

Amica reached the tree where she first met the she-beast and waited. From the lofty perch she saw the great Lone Oak towering over other trees in the distance. Though she found the Lone Oak beautiful, Amica avoided the great tree. Her forebears told stories of bad experiences in the branches of the great tree. Personally, she had never met anyone who had frolicked in the Lone Oak.

As she waited the tree sprite matron noted one grisly detail. The bodies of the Drolls and Kiennite remained on the forest floor. Inexplicably, the denizens of the forest had ignored the carrion. A flash of red light bathed the area.

She arrived.

The she-beast grumbled, "I hate this gray light!"

Amica smiled and reported, "It's done. The young Drelves are gullible. I took some of their arrows as you asked."

The tree sprite passed several finely made Drelvish arrows to the she-beast.

The Deceiver answered, "Yes, *they* are gullible."

"Am I going to get what's coming to me?" Amica eagerly asked.

"Yes, *you are going to get what's coming to you,*" the Deceiver answered flatly.

"OK. Let me have my earnings," the tree sprite added.

"First, I'll be taking your name," the she-demon said wryly.

"Why?" the little sprite queried.

"You won't be needing it," the she-demon answered icily.

The tree sprite matron died quickly.

The she-demon assumed Amica's svelte form but added macabre mauve wings and a scorpion's tail. The ersatz Amica scattered Drelvish arrows among the corpses of the fallen Drolls and Kiennish shaman. She then flew to the edge of the forest. She smiled wryly. The Droll named Gruth had awakened. Only incapacitated by the doomed tree sprite's arrow, he had survived. The pseudo-Amica continued her plan and flew to the gap in the great Peaks of Division in the center of the World of the Three Suns. Changing to the form of an injured Kiennite, she approached the guard at the gate of the old keep maintained by the Kiennish warlords. She told the guard she'd witnessed an attack on a Kiennish noble and group of Drelves and had barely escaped with her life. Noting her wounds, the guard did not question her, called for a Mender, and went to his superiors. The commanders of the keep dispatched a group of fleet Drolls to the meadow of the Lone Oak. Visiting the Keep, the Mender Fisher answered the guard's summons but found no trace of an injured Kiennite.

Commanded by the very able Moochie, thirteen Drolls ran quickly toward the meadow of the Lone Oak. Ahead they saw one of their own stumbling through the underbrush.

"That's Gruth! He accompanied Lord Melphat," the Drolls' leader exclaimed.

The Drolls ran to Gruth, who babbled incessantly, saying, "Charms! Arrows from above! Beware! Gone! All gone! The stench of death! Woe! Woe!"

The big Drollen lieutenant named Moochie noted, "You smell of Drelve! Who attacked you?"

"I did not see! I did not see! Woe!" Gruth rambled.

Moochie not so gently slapped Gruth and said, "Pull yourself together. Where are Lord Melphat, my brother Phastin, Tenate, and Addipex? Tell me!"

Fearing another slap, Gruth came to his senses and said, "By the red meadow, in the shadow of the cursed great tree! I don't know what happened. We were assailed from above, by slings and arrows of misfortune!"

"Shut up! You sound like a poet! Stay here. Barefoot, wait with him. You others, come with me. Make haste!" Moochie commanded.

The Drollen commander led his party quickly through the woods along familiar paths. Soon the Lone Oak loomed in the distance. Moochie commanded his twelve charges to remain near the forest line of the wild woods.

In the trees across the way, the Drelvish ranger Tomayo looked through a "toot and see scroll" looking glass and saw thirteen Drolls run to the site where the sleeping Droll had been.

Tomayo used the fruit of the thirteenth tree in the circle of Thirttene Friends at the knoll in the Green Vale as a looking glass. During times of relaxation, the device doubled as a musical instrument. Oft times beautiful flute Musick wafted among the trees as the Drelve sentries played. Children used the rare devices as toys, but the monoculars were invaluable in scanning the distal reaches of the red meadow. Though flat, the expanse of the Lone Oak meadow challenged even the keen vision of the Drelves.

Unfortunately the fluted looking glasses were a bit fragile and wore out with use. Ironically, without the touch of a hand or being played, the devices crumbled even more quickly.

"Odd little devices," thought Tomayo.

Use them and lose them.

Don't use them and lose them.

Peering through the looking glass, Tomayo saw the group of Drolls enter the woods and disappear.

The Drelves stood at ready.

In a little while Moochie's party came upon the corpses of their dismembered comrades. The grisly findings confirmed his worst fears. His brother Phastin, Addipex, and Tenate were dead. The Droll's commander noted several arrows with uniquely Drelvish fletchings among the bodies.

"The vile Drelves caused this carnage. The fallen Kiennite among our dead brothers carries the Scepter of Aulgmoor. It is Lord Melphat. We must report back to the forests beyond the Ornash and gather our strength. Lord Saligia must learn his brother's fate. Carry the scepter to the Keep at the gap in the Peaks of Division. We'll make the Drelves and their allies pay for this wrongdoing," the Droll's leader Moochie growled.

Peering through the "toot and see scroll" looking glass, the Drelve Tomayo saw the Droll's leader step to the edge of the red meadow and utter expletives. Then the thirteen Drolls left the meadow. Tomayo noted smoke from the wild wood.

"What does this mean, Sergeant Tomayo?" Loganne asked.

"Undoubtedly, the heavy dark telltale smoke comes from a death pyre. I suppose the Drolls have found their comrades, whom we saw enter but not exit the woods. From this distance I cannot hear his words. I don't understand his outburst. Grief does strange things to people," the older Drelve wisely answered.

"What do we do?" Loganne asked.

"We watch," Tomayo answered.

The Droll scout reached the ancient Gap Keep, reported to its Kiennish commander, presented the Scepter of Aulgmoor, and gave the account of Melphat's demise. Sentries could not find the wounded Kiennite who had brought the original word of an attack on a Kiennish noble. The commander of the Gap Keep dispatched a courier to the stronghold of Aulgmoor.

The courier wore wyvern hides and carried the Scepter of Aulgmoor.

CHAPTER 20
Ill Tidings

Droll scouts brought word of the fall of Lord Melphat and had taken the fabled Scepter of Aulgmoor from the central forests past Mirror Lake and Mirror Mountain to the ancient Gap Keep in the gap in the Peaks of Division, the central mountain range which divided the large land area of the World of the Three Suns. The Keep commander charged the courier with delivering the news of his brother's demise to General Saligia at Aulgmoor. The wyvern-hide courier's forte was speed and stamina. Rather than crossing the mountains and passing through unfriendly territories, the runner left the keep, crossed the gap, and reached the River Ornash where he crossed by ferry. When the ferryman saw the wyvern hide and the ornate scepter, he dared not ask for payment.

The courier trekked across the plain to the Doombringer Mountains, which surrounded the homeland of the Kiennish noble. Accessing a narrow heavily guarded passage, which led to the environs of Aulgmoor, the runner hurried to the largest community in the Kiennish realm.

The ragged messenger finally saw Aulgmoor in the distance. There was no great edifice at Aulgmoor, but the homes of the gnarly ilk's leaders were far more opulent than the simple thatched cottages of the smaller groups and the animal hide tents, pergolas, and stick lean-tos that most Drolls called home.

The messenger rushed to the leader's quarters.

"Halt!" the heavily armored much taller guard commanded.

Breathless, the runner answered, "I bear tidings for General Saligia."

"The General is not to be disturbed. He is...busy," the guard answered evasively.

"I must be heard!" the messenger replied, and bent down and grasped his tattered leggings for support.

"You can tell me," the guard haughtily answered.

"You don't want to be the bearer of these tidings," the messenger sighed.

"Why not?" the guard queried.

"I'd best tell only the general," the runner insisted.

"Then you can wait here until he wakes up. Lord Saligia was involved in negotiations of the highest order with the Drollen chiefs. Something's afoot. I don't want to wake him. He awaits the return of the High Shaman Melphat. I think the brothers plan something major, messenger. I really don't want to awaken the General," the guard insisted.

"My friend, the general must hear my communication. I'm not going away," the tired sprinter continued.

"It's your funeral! Go on in, but I warn you, the General had a lot of the Drolls' mead. I suspect he is quite hung over. Come with me," the guard answered.

The guard led the messenger down a dimly lit corridor to a heavy wooden door. Tentatively the guard raised his hand and pecked on the door.

"He'll never hear that," the envoy fumed.

"OK! OK! I fear for my hide! You are getting us both tarred and feathered!" the guard argued. He hammered on the door.

A disgruntled voice answered from within, "This had better be good."

"I'm sorry, my lord. There is a courier from the Gap Keep. He insists on hailing you," the guard submissively replied.

"Enter," the gruff voice commanded.

The messenger sighed and stepped forward as the guard opened the door to the General's chamber.

"My lord, may I speak?" the exhausted courier asked.

"I certainly hope you have something to say. I was dreaming of the Belles of Thabell, the most beautiful ladies of our ilk. Say your peace and let me return to my rest. In fact, I want you to sing your message," the hulking Kiennite demanded.

"It's difficult, Lord Saligia…" the courier stammered.

"Get on with it!" Saligia demanded.

"I can't sing, Lord Saligia. And the matter…" the envoy pleaded.

"Sing! **** you! Sing!" the commanded demanded.

"I…I should like…" the beleaguered messenger pleaded.

"I'm not going to say it again! Sing!" Saligia commanded.

"Yes, Lord Saligia. Please remember you insisted," the cowering courier added.

Saligia clenched his fist and muttered, "Sing!"

"La, la, la, la, la, la, your brother's dead!" the messenger crooned.

"What? What the…" Saligia gawked.

"La, la, la, la, la, la, he fell in the woods near Alm's Glen," the messenger continued, plaintively trying to carry a tune.

"Shut up!" the guard demanded.

"Do you speak the truth?" Saligia asked.

"Unfortunately, Lord Melphat was found dead near the Lone Oak. He and four Drollen companions were slaughtered. Lieutenant Moochie of the Drolls found only the veteran Gruth alive. Moochie's brother Phastin was among the dead. The Drolls found Drelvish arrows among the carcasses. Here is the scepter Lord Melphat carried. I was dispatched to inform you," the courier added.

He extended the scepter of Aulgmoor and gave the old ornamental device to Lord Saligia.

"The Scepter of Aulgmoor. My brother would never part from this in life," Saligia muttered.

"I'm sorry, Lord Saligia," the wyvern hide clad courier muttered.

The guard looked to the courier and said, "You should be sorry. You are the worst vocalist I've ever heard."

"Idiots! Leave me!" the general demanded.

The Kiennite leader wailed long into the amber period.

CHAPTER 21
Return to Meadowsweet

Laden with their precious enhancing root, Edkim, Gaelyss, and the group of Drelves followed Rumsie back to Meadowsweet. Rumsie paused intermittently and used the small fluted looking glass Edkim had given him to scan the path ahead.

Gaelyss thought mostly of the bizarre interlude with the ersatz Kirrie who became the ersatz tree sprite. Perhaps the tree sprite was a genuine sorceress. He spoke no more to the others about the encounter. His thoughts wandered to his brother Yannuvia, who had missed the marvel of Green Vale and the harvest.

Where was Yannuvia?

What was his brother fomenting?

Had the temptress spoken the truth?

Why was the experience so surreal?

Several brief rain showers freshened them on the walk. Above, the Gray Wanderer Andreas remained near, filled the sky, and bathed the land with its gray light. The effects of the uncommon and unpredictable Approximation were evident all around the travelers.

A red bird changed to blue.

Brown eyes turned blue.

Water flowed upward.

Yellow geese got down and danced.

Snakes flew.

Flying snakes always flew, but the airborne reptiles lived only in the deep forests.

Knowing the Drelves of Meadowsweet joyously prepared for celebrations honoring the Approximation, Rumsie quickened the pace and soon the group arrived at Meadowsweet. Edkim, Gaelyss, Meryt, Zack, Debery, Bryce, Rumsie, Beaux, and Klunkus would share this Approximation of Andreas with their brethren at Meadowsweet. The elders Ulysses and Morin met the reapers and sent the tired harvesters to their guest trees. Everyone anticipated a wondrous feast after the rest period and distribution of the precious tubers.

Too excited to sleep, Gaelyss slipped from the great red oak tree, walked into the dark gray light, and ambled to the periphery of the quiet village.

His keen senses detected the fragrant aroma of the Teacher's pipeweed. He found Edkim leaning against a red oak. Sergeant Major Rumsie stood by the older Drelve.

Edkim acknowledged the young Spellweaver's approach and bade Gaelyss sit beside him. Rumsie nodded respectfully and walked away into the forest. As the youth sat on the thick moss, Gaelyss saw the Teacher held a small leather bag in his left hand. Edkim pulled his briar pipe to his lips, took a long slow drag, exhaled, and filled the air with aromatic smoke. Edkim didn't waste his energy blowing smoke rings. The enjoyment of the pipeweed was sufficient for the oldster.

Gaelyss stared curiously at the rucksack.

The Teacher took another draw on his pipe and then said, "Are you not tired? The day was long."

"I could not sleep," Gaelyss confided.

"Green Vale overwhelms all of us. Even now, the greenness of the enhancing plant's Vale astonishes me," Edkim confessed and drew again on his pipe.

Gaelyss continued, "I have many questions, Teacher."

"I may not have answers to all your questions. To be honest I have a few unanswered questions," Edkim honestly answered.

Gaelyss sighed and admitted, "I don't understand what happened to me on the hillock by the geyser pool. Otherwise I found Green Vale exhilarating. I've been told many stories of gathering enhancing root but none do the beauty of Green Vale justice. Just knowing such wonders exist is reassuring. I don't think I'll find sleep this rest period."

"I fear some of this day's events are my fault. I've delayed telling you many things. I'd hoped to talk with you and your brother together. It's time I told you more. The nearness of the Gray Wanderer gives me strength. I've helped many of our people face the questions and trials of maturing. Walking in Green Vale, gathering the enhancing root, and standing within the circle of Thirttene Friends intimidates the most experienced Drelves. I've watched your eyes and noted your silence. More is at play and something troubles you, young Gaelyss. You were very pensive on the walk back to Meadowsweet. I see concern in your eyes. If something troubles you, it troubles me. Ask your questions, Spellweaver. I'll answer as best I can," Edkim poignantly answered.

"Thank you, Teacher. First, has the tree shepherd spoken to other Spellweavers?" Gaelyss asked.

"A question I cannot answer, young one. Before you and Yannuvia, I'd never taught a Spellweaver. Before this day, I had not heard him speak," Edkim replied and took another long draw of his pipe.

"Some of his words appeared in my mind. I didn't hear them," Gaelyss remarked.

"I only know the words he spoke aloud. Did he communicate disturbing thoughts to you?" Edkim asked.

"No. He was only gracious and informative. Regarding the Lady of the Trees, must one have her permission to partake of the fruits of the Thirttene Friends?" Gaelyss asked tentatively.

"The Lady of the Trees is very pretentious and vain. I don't think she has the power to deny access to the fruits of the circle of Thirttene, but the compliments we give her cost nothing. It takes no longer to say something nice than to say something vindictive. So I, like my predecessors, the Teachers who came before me, humor her. Haven't you encountered other forest sprites?" Edkim asked.

"No, Teacher. Is the Lady of the Trees to be regarded with suspicion? She appeared to me while we were harvesting. She appeared taller," Gaelyss answered.

"I know she disturbed you. I sensed you were troubled when you rushed to her tree. Let's talk more of her. Tree sprites and dryads are capable of Illusory Spells and mischievously changing their appearance. In the World of the Three Suns, Dryads are simply mature tree sprites. Dryads are taller and less migratory. Other than the fact she's greener, the Lady of the Trees is not that different from other tree sprites. Tree sprites can be quite seductive. It's best you didn't enter her tree. I've heard lore of them having the ability to charm, and the gray sun Andreas enhances all Magick. You stood in the place of greatest Magick in the entire world, so far as I know. You are young. She is mischievous. We've never documented any harm she's done. I suspect she *charmed* you. I'd not tarry in thoughts of her. Are you still fearful of the Lady of the Trees?" the Teacher asked sincerely.

"I don't fear the tree sprite, dryad, or whatever she is called," Gaelyss declared.

"Good," Edkim surmised and took another long draw on the old pipe.

Summoning courage, Gaelyss continued, "Teacher, what do you know of dreams? My uncle Sigmund says they have great significance."

"Your Uncle Sigmund was thrown off a horse when he was young. Dreams…some say dreams are the mind's attempt to sort out our feelings? Others say bad dreams are caused by mythical beings called elves sitting on the dreamer's chest. Elfdreams…elf pressure. Dreams are just dreams, Gaelyss. But I'm neither a Spellweaver nor an interpreter of dreams. But you may tell me of yours," Edkim answered.

"I've dreamt of females, or more specifically, a female. I think it was the Lady of the Trees. Or another tree sprite," Gaelyss answered.

"Tis not an unpleasant thing, Gaelyss, to dream of females. Our Drelvish ladies are amongst the most beautiful of the forest. I find the feminine Drolls strangely attractive. Can't say much for Kiennish females, though I've heard their Belles of Thabell are quite attractive," the Teacher answered.

"I did not dream of Drelves. My schoolbooks portray Drolls and Kiennites. My father Glinne described sprites he had seen in the wood. Though uncommonly pretty and intriguing, the tree sprite we saw at Green Vale had blue hair, purple eyes, and bright green skin and stood about two-thirds the height of an average sized Drelve. The very different womanly image from my dream is taller than a Drelve. Though of slight physique, she appears powerful in other ways. Her arms bristle with well-defined musculature. Her smooth skin is greener than any other color, but like *us* the changing suns' light changes her color. Her piercing eyes are deep hazel. Her voice is something between lyrical and a soft breeze, but I detect firmness in her words. Teacher, I saw her *on the hillock at Green Vale,*" Gaelyss confessed.

"Young Gaelyss, I never left your side in Green Vale. I saw only the tree sprite. Perhaps you experienced a daydream," Edkim suggested.

"It wasn't a dream. Twas Magick, Teacher. She stopped time. She… offered…offers me things," Gaelyss answered.

Noting the youth's consternation and without reason to doubt Gaelyss's word, Edkim replied, "Gaelyss, the Magick you describe is legend. I can't explain how you moved on the knoll. Look. I presented a Spell Book of the Drelves to both you and your brother. Yannuvia remains away. Though I retain a copy, the spell book of the Drelves is beyond me. Now that I feebly touch the sea of Magick, I realize how little I know. Knowing one paltry spell doesn't make one a Spellweaver. As I said, neither your Uncle Sigmund nor I can deduce the meaning of your dream. Unequalled as a storyteller, Sigmund just thought he could.

"But you…are a Spellweaver. You'll read of spells that freeze time. Not even the greatest Spellweavers of old cast such a dweomer. We're taught and in turn teach that only Andreas chooses Spellweavers and only Spellweavers receive the gift of Magick. Though not a Spellweaver, I have a spell at my beckoning. To the best of my knowledge, this hasn't ever happened, Gaelyss. None of the journals of our people speak of such an occurrence. Before this day I'd never been at Green Vale with a Spellweaver, but other teachers had many times. Many times our people have harvested the enhancing root during the Approximation of the Gray Sun. Some force gave Magick to Meryt, Zack, Bryce, Debery, and me. Was it our standing in the rain from the Geyser of the Thirttene during the Approximation while in your presence? I'm not sure. I can't explain the gifts the four neophytes and I received. Usually verbal, somatic, and material movements are required to make spells work. The spells we learned have simple verbal commands, a single somatic movement, and no material component. It's not *natural* Magick," Edkim rambled.

"*Natural* Magick? Isn't that a contradiction of terms?" Gaelyss asked.

"Well, it's not the *usual* Magick. During Approximations, Magick flourishes. Many folk detect and employ things Magick, but only Spellweavers utter spells. Kiennish shamans have powers of Illusory Magick. Magick is innate to some creatures, such as dryads and tree sprites. Because you're a Spellweaver and study Magick, your understanding is beyond mine. Meryt, Zack. Debery, Bryce, and I should *not* know Magick. I don't understand," Edkim rambled.

"Nor do I understand, Teacher. Perhaps my command of Magick is insufficient. Have other Spellweavers mastered the book when they had seen thirteen harvesting seasons?" Gaelyss asked.

"Thirteen. It seems you were just born. Where does the time go? I don't know, Gaelyss. Some Spellweavers study the book throughout their lives and never comprehend the more powerful spells. The night of your birth, elders noted unparalleled nearness of Andreas. Maybe you are *different*," Edkim said.

"I can't imagine the sun nearer than it is at this moment," Gaelyss replied as he glanced at the dark skies.

Edkim glanced upward and acknowledged, "True. I don't fully recall the Approximation thirteen tears ago. I was caught up in the excitement of your birth. Twin Spellweavers! Now your brother is away. We must guard you. Your safety is a priority for all our people. You must study incessantly and become stronger," Edkim said determinedly.

"Teacher, I want no special treatment," Gaelyss insisted.

"I'd hoped you'd share this day with your brother Yannuvia. His absence worries me," Edkim sighed.

"His absence worries me as well," Gaelyss answered.

The Drelve remembered the words of the *transformed* tree sprite during the time stoppage at Green Vale.

Did he really see her?

Was he simply charmed?

How did Edkim, Bryce, Zack, Debery, and Meryt attain Magick?

Edkim remained silent.

Gaelyss chagrinned, "I've lots of studying to do."

"In good time. First, we'll enjoy the celebration of the Approximation of Andreas with our brethren. Next season you will be more experienced and better prepared. This day Magick has entered my consciousness. In this regard, you are the veteran," Edkim clamored.

"Only by thirteen harvesting seasons," Gaelyss reminded the Teacher.

"Perhaps you should rest a bit," Edkim gently suggested.

"Thank you, Teacher. I appreciate everything you do," the young Spellweaver answered.

Gaelyss stood, excused himself, and returned to his guest tree. Too excited to sleep, he flipped through the pages of his spell book. Eventually fatigue overcame him, and the young Spellweaver dozed for a while. When he awakened, Gaelyss found the knowledge of three new spells within his acumen. He heard singing outside his red oak, placed *The Gifts of Andreas to the People of the Forest* inside his pack, and exited.

Drelves of all ages danced and sang in the cleared area in the center of Meadowsweet. Gaelyss recognized Morganne, the elder Ulysses, the elder Morin, and the members of his party from Alms Glen. Meryt, Bryce, Zack, Debery, Beaux, Rumsie, and Klunkus sang and danced with their hosts. For the ceremony the Drelves changed from their usual garb to brightly colored tunics and cloaks.

Deep gray light replaced the usual amber light. Above the bizarre gray star filled the entire sky and imparted Magick to the realm. Some effects were whimsical. Stones spoke, trees walked, elephants flew, and slow birds caught worms. The effects from the Approximation of the dark sun always varied, but the Gray Wanderer always endowed Magick to mundane creatures and things. The celebration lasted two days. Slowly Andreas drifted away from the world and reclaimed its temporary gifts. However, Edkim, Debery, Bryce, Zack, and Meryt retained their newfound powers of Magick. The Teacher prepared his charges for the return to Alms Glen.

The Meadowsweet Drelves escorted their guests to the fringes of their lands. Rumsie took the point, Klunkus watched the rear, and the group returned uneventfully to Alms Glen. When they returned, the group learned there was no word of Yannuvia. The elders informed the Teacher of Loganne's message about the Drolls. Rather than going to his tree to rest, Sergeant Major Rumsie departed immediately for the perimeter at the Lone Oak meadow. Gaelyss went to his tree home to study *The Gifts of Andreas to the People of the Forest.*

CHAPTER 22
The First War Machine

Tomayo had taken few respites since the thirteen Drolls had searched the area of the wild woods where the Kiennite and three Drolls had earlier disappeared. Old Clarke had served well. Rumsie returned from Meadowsweet and relieved his stalwart comrades.

The Drelvish sentries alternated scanning the far woods with *the toot and see scroll* looking glass. As Rumsie watched the woods to the north nervously, he heard shouts in the distance. The Sergeant Major alerted his fellows and sent Loganne to Alms Glen to find the Teacher Edkim.

In a few moments, several heavily armored Drolls appeared in the northernmost area of the red meadow. The Drolls entered the meadow and stood in the ankle high red grass. Extending their spears into the air, the large hominids shouted in unison. Though fluent in the Drollen tongue, Rumsie didn't translate the phrases to his younger comrades.

Old Clarke shrugged and said, "Rather innovative grouping of expletives. I'm not sure I've ever heard that combination of insults. Why are they angry at us?"

"Drolls don't require a reason to be angry with Drelves. We'd best prepare," Rumsie answered succinctly.

Already archers climbed into the trees and Drelves lined the areas between the heavy shrubs among the trees and also armed themselves with bow and arrow. The Drolls remained beyond bowshot, about a thousand Yardley paces, or yards away. The number of Drolls increased as Rumsie watched. Abruptly twenty Drolls broke into a run and headed for the forest edge where the Drelves waited. After the first group advanced fifty yards, a second group of Drolls charged forward. Another twenty followed the second group at about the same interval. The long legs of the heavily armed Drolls covered a hundred yards quickly. Soon five groups charged toward the tree line, and the first group was 600 yards away.

"The wave. It's the way they always attack. I've witnessed this many times. They have little regard for individual lives. Their leaders use this tactic at times to count the number of archers opposing them," Clarke suggested.

"Make ready. At three hundred yards, fire!" Rumsey commanded.

The first group of Drolls shouted loudly and reached a pitch that old Clarke found uncomfortable. When they were 300 yards away, the bowstrings of the Drelves twanged loudly and a shower of arrows filled the air. Each Droll in the front rank was struck with at least two arrows as most of the long-range bows found their marks. Twelve Drolls fell; the others ran forward another few yards. Then another volley of arrows brought them down.

The second tier of attackers reached about 250 yards when the third volley of arrows rained upon them. Most fell, but a few charged forward. The third tier ran past their fallen comrades and reached two hundred yards. By now they were in range of the shorter-range bows of the Drelves on the ground. Arrows rained from above and directly into the attackers. The fourth tier of attackers was struck down by 150 yards and the fifth and final group fell a hundred yards from the trees. Only seven volleys of Drelvish arrows struck down a hundred of the wolf-faced enemies. The Drolls never came near the tree line.

Rumsie's people heard a roar beyond the trees across the meadow and several hundred Drolls erupted from the trees and charged toward the Drelves' positions. The mass attack focused on the two areas from which most of the Drelvish arrows came. Rumsie anticipated this tactic and had his people shift their positions as the Drolls charged. Once again the archers fired accurately into the Drolls. The Drolls' commanders had their warriors run in a serpentine manner. Still the Drelves' short-range bows fired into the attackers. Only a few Drolls actually reached the forest edge, and even then the thick underbrush impeded them and made them easy targets for the short-range bows. The enemies fell without any hand-to-hand combat and the Drelves suffered no losses. With only sixty archers and thirty ground fighters, Rumsie repelled the attackers. The red grass of the Lone Oak meadow was covered with the carcasses and thick blood of the Drolls.

"What a foolish attack. No tactics of note! Were Kiennites among them?" Tomayo asked.

"I saw none. Lust and anger fueled their attack. I think...it can't possibly be over," Rumsie said.

The others noted uncharacteristic uncertainty in the veteran Drelve commander's voice. Scouts in the upper section of the forest edge reported seeing movement among the trees on the opposite side of the forest.

"Refurbish your supply of arrows. Stay at ready!" Rumsie ordered.

Loganne returned with Edkim, Meryt, Debery, Zack, and Bryce.

The Drelves weathered three other Droll attacks during the next three cycles of Meries. Every time the enemy numbered only a few hundred.

Rumsie and Edkim chose to avoid bringing young Gaelyss to the front and using Magick.

On the fourth day, the Drolls actually inflicted casualties. Several Drolls assembled a large ballista about four hundred yards from the tree line. Drelve archers fired long-range shots into the Drolls to create a nuisance and delay the assembly. Eventually the Drolls managed to load a large bolt and fired into the trees. The crude attack was effective. The quick Drelves easily avoided the large missile, but the ballista bolt crashed into the trees forcefully and knocked several Drelves from the trees. The falls killed two Drelves and injured others. The fatally wounded Drelves were named Lynne and Russell.

Archers fired gallantly toward the ballista but the device was beyond range of accuracy. The Drolls reloaded the device.

"They are beyond range," Rumsie chagrinned.

"I can't believe they have constructed a war machine. I haven't known them to do such things," Clarke added.

"Get our people out of the trees. Here comes another missile!" Rumsie warned.

A second bolt fired from the weapon crashed a few yards in front of the tree line and uprooted a clump of red grass. The red meadow immediately healed its wound.

"Were we only able to do what the grass does," Edkim moaned.

"You'd best get ready to do what healing you can. They are massing at the edge of the wild woods, and they are firing the ballista," Tomayo shouted. "Furthermore we have lost the vantage point of the trees. We will have to attack them from ground level."

"Then it will be hand to hand and branch to branch. Even with the forest as our ally, I don't think we can keep them at bay. They will be too many!" Loganne added.

Rumsie sighed and said, "Then we'll have to take out the ballista by hand. We should reach it before they can arrive in force. Prepare a party at once."

"I'll go!" Loganne shouted.

"Wait!" Edkim interrupted. "We'll lose too many lives!"

"I see no alternative!" Rumsie shouted as another large bolt crashed into the trees and severely wounded a tree herder. Violet sap flowed from the Drelves' friend's horrific wound.

Edkim stepped past Rumsie, walked to the edge of the forest, directed his left hand in the direction of the Drolls manning the war machine, and fired a mauve bolt of energy toward the Drolls. The Magick Missile unerringly traveled to the ballista and struck the nearest Droll. The large beast fell to the ground and dropped the bolt he carried toward the device. A second Droll reached for the bolt, but Edkim sent a second spell toward the enemies and dropped him.

Sweating profusely, the Teacher slumped to the ground and panted, "I'm sorry. I can do no more this day."

"The device remains intact," Rumsie noted.

Several Drolls ran from the far side of the meadow to reinforce their comrades at the ballista. Rumsie sent a number of Drelves to gather torches and oil to burn the war machine.

"Wait. I can help! Give me the torch and oil," Debery said hurriedly.

The young Drelve took the implements, uttered a phrase in Old Drelvish, and vanished. In a little while the wooden ballista broke into flames.

The remaining Drolls shouted, broke away from the burning ballista, and ran toward the trees. The activity in the trees across the meadow ceased.

In a short while a Drelve scout ran to Rumsie and said, "They are withdrawing. I heard them shout 'Spellweaver' as they retreated."

Debery reappeared by Sergeant Rumsie.

Meryt asked the Teacher, "Why did you and Debery use Magick? We were ordered not to attack."

"You did as you were told. We can't let the enemy know all our resources. The fire appeared, much like a fire spell. The Drolls assumed Magick Missiles and Fire Magick attacked them. We have fought only Drolls, but I surmise a Kiennite fashioned the war machine for them. Stay at ready," the Teacher answered.

"Should I summon the Spellweaver? Should I summon Gaelyss?" Loganne asked.

"He knows only defensive spells. I don't think he can help us at the moment. I want him to study *The Gifts of Andreas to the People of the Forest*. Given some time, he'll master more spells. For now we must defend the forest against our enemies," Edkim answered.

"Mind you, we have only seen skirmishes. The Drolls have sent only probing attacks. If they attack in force, we'll be stretched to the limit. Also, the only evidence we have seen of the Kiennites is the machine. They can bring Magick to the fray," Clarke said.

"The departure of the Gray Sun has leveled the playing field. It would have been a great ally," Tomayo added.

"You forget Kiennish shamans are born during the Approximations. Though five of our number received the power of spells during the Approximation when we were at Green Vale, we gained no Spellweavers as we did thirteen seasons ago, and Yannuvia remains missing. We must prepare for more attacks," Edkim sagely advised.

Ten cycles of Meries passed and the Drolls did not attack, but Tomayo noted Drolls sneaking around the northern end of the Lone Oak meadow on several occasions. Rumsie gave Meryt, Zack, Debery, and Bryce supervised shifts among the trees at the edge of the red meadow to allow them to gain experience. The Sergeant Major, elders, and Teacher worried regarding their inexperience but nonetheless pressed the youths into service. On three occasions Drolls charged onto the meadow and feigned attacks. Oft times the enemy attempted to bait the Drelves into coming onto the meadow where the larger Drolls had an advantage over them in hand-to-hand combat. Rumsie and Tomayo gave strict orders forbidding this action.

The erstwhile neophytes Gaelyss, Meryt, Debery, Zack, and Bryce learned on the job.

CHAPTER 23
Saligia's Assault Begins

Far to the north in the Doombringer Mountains, the Lord of Aulgmoor, the leader of the Kiennites, surveyed his gathering forces.

"Lord Saligia, we have word of a battle on the meadow of the Lone Oak. Droll legions have attacked the Drelves," the courier panted.

"I assume the Drolls were defeated," Saligia answered flatly.

"Uh...yes. A Spellweaver repelled them. I'm sorry to report, Lord Saligia, but your war machine was destroyed," the courier reported.

The wyvern hide clad courier remembered Saligia's reputation of blaming the messenger for bad news and cringed.

"Fools! They reacted with a knee jerk! The Drelves simply slay them at will. They should have waited for my orders. What word is there from the other Drolls and the Kiennish warrens to the north?" Saligia replied.

Relieved the General did not berate him, the courier added, "They mass at the River Ornash as you commanded. Only Moochie's warriors attacked. The loss of his brother Phastin overwhelmed him."

"I also lost a brother. It's a reason to plan, not act rashly. We'll attack the Drelves in force when the time is right. For now, allow the Drolls their impulsive attacks. Tell Moochie to continue to send probing attacks into the red meadow. This will make him feel important. Send word to my cavalry to make ready. Make sure my armored divisions are set in motion. The Drelves will rue the day they crossed my family," Saligia icily said.

Back at Alms Glen, the young Spellweaver Gaelyss read incessantly for fourteen days, stopping only to catch naps and respond to his mother's demands that he take nourishment. His mind blossomed after the trip to Green Vale and the Approximation. He easily translated the incantations in *The Gifts of Andreas to the People of the Forest*. Understanding the spells included the realization that many required rare ingredients, or material components. Gaelyss had never heard of some of the items to which the spell book referred.

Gaelyss spent little time with Meryt, Zack, Debery, and Bryce and missed their persistent efforts to entice him to play. The newfound strengths of the young Drelves enabled them to assume greater roles in the defenses of the forests of Alms Glen. Traveling to Meadowsweet and the Green Vale to harvest the enhancing root was a rite of passage from Drelvling to adult Drelve. Usually neophytes had time to transition into roles in the community. Gaelyss, Meryt, Bryce, Zack, and Debery enjoyed no such luxury. Necessity forced the five young Drelves into positions of responsibility.

At mealtime and his infrequent rest periods, Gaelyss found solace in the company of Kirrie. Kirrie was just entering her thirteenth season as Gaelyss began his fourteenth. They talked of his missing brother Yannuvia. Gaelyss knew that Yannuvia had been her favorite. Kirrie's exceptional skills and knowledge assured she would be one of those chosen to accompany the Teacher during the next harvest. Happenstance determined that all five neophytes of Gaelyss's group were male Drelvlings. Moblee's daughter Loganne had been the best student of her year. After her trip to Green Vale, Loganne trained four years. At the edge of seventeen the elder's daughter assumed her role defending the perimeter.

At the Lone Oak meadow, the Drolls infrequent attacks occasionally wounded and rarely killed Drelves. Sergeant Major Rumsie organized the Drelvish rangers in strong defensive positions. The dense forest protected the Drelves and kept the defenders' casualties down. Tension mounted with each passing cycle of Meries. Parties of Drolls ambled onto the field and fomented just enough mischief to prevent Rumsie from standing down from high alert. Dark period after dark period passed, and the Drolls did not attack in force and mount a major offensive. The enemies' patience was unusual. Reinforcements rotated from Meadowsweet and other communities. Young Morganne served one dark period's time at the perimeter and briefly visited Gaelyss. Thereafter, she returned to Green Vale to tend the enhancing plants.

Gaelyss was a more committed student than his missing brother Yannuvia. The Teacher and the elders feared Yannuvia had likely fallen to a marauding enemy patrol or a wandering monster. Remembering the warning the mysterious female gave him at Green Vale, Gaelyss feared Yannuvia's return.

CHAPTER 24
Another Harvest

Eight dark periods passed and Yannuvia remained away.

The time came to harvest the enhancing root tubers. Edkim and Rumsie discussed the upcoming harvest.

"Teacher, I am concerned for your safety. I agree that a small contingent draws less attention. Having accompanied me many times, Klunkus can capably lead your party to Green Vale. Should the Spellweaver Gaelyss accompany you? He might fall into the enemies' hands," Rumsie cautioned.

"Last season's harvest the presence of the Spellweaver may have aided my and the four neophytes' enhancements. Meryt, Zack, Debery, and Bryce have been invaluable in the defense of the perimeter. Keep the four caballeros, as they call themselves, at Alms Glen. Gaelyss can defend us on the journey. Perhaps Yannuvia will return. The power we gain from the enhancing root warrants our risk. Young Kirrie shows great promise. It would be wrong to deny her the rite of passage. We'll leave on the morrow," Edkim asserted.

Rumsie respectfully accepted the Teacher's decisions.

Meryt, Zack, Debery, and Bryce remained at Alms Glen and assisted Rumsie with the defenses of the area. Gaelyss accompanied the Teacher Edkim. Klunkus served as guide for the group. Three neophytes, including Kirrie, accompanied the Teacher. Edkim hoped until the last moment that Yannuvia might return.

Edkim, Gaelyss, Klunkus, the experienced archer Balewyn, crusty old Clarke, Kirrie, and two other neophytes named Zachary and Taylor set out for Meadowsweet. Along the way denizens of the forest made the long trip easier. Rambling ramble bushes uprooted and moved along both sides of the party. The rambling ramble's brambles made snapping sounds and covered any slight noise made by the stealthy Drelves' footsteps. Water lilies sprayed fresh sweet water from their roots and refreshed the group. Gaelyss's thoughts returned to the previous season. He had enjoyed the trip with his four lighthearted friends. Now he thought of them guarding their homes and preparing for an all out assault by the Drolls, which could occur at anytime.

As they crossed clearings in the forest, each peered upward to the sky. Only Meries and the ever-present Orpheus gave light to the world. The Gray Sun remained but a dot in the horizon. The amber skies darkened as the dark period approached. As always the harvest would occur during the time Meries was at its nadir. Gaelyss recognized some of the unique massive trees. Occasionally a Drelve waved to them from one of the smaller trees. Sometimes the young Spellweaver pondered whether the solitary Drelves were at greater peace. Of course there was strength in numbers if enemies appeared. But he envied the amount of time the dwellers of the deep forest had to themselves, time which could be used for study. He had so much to learn.

Soon a familiar voice beckoned to them.

"Welcome. We have prepared a banquet for you. The elders Ulysses and Morin await your arrival. We have learned of your tribulations against the Drolls. Please follow me," Morganne requested.

Gaelyss marveled at how a year had changed her. Being from Meadowsweet, the eighteen-year-old Morganne helped tend the plants at Green Vale and expertly harvested the tubers. Morganne carried a long bow across her well-defined shoulders and wore a short sword on her belt. Her garment enabled the she-Drelve to blend into the forest.

Drelves lovingly harvested the thick fuzzy bark from fur fir trees. The bark yielded durable lightweight material. If it was carefully harvested, the fur fir tree's fuzzy bark grew back rapidly. But for being orange, the needles of the fur fir tree were similar to fir trees of other lands.

Morganne moved effortlessly and fluently through the underbrush and gently pushed aside branches to avoid injuring the plants. Knowing they had nothing to fear from the Drelves, small animals stayed their ground and birds remained on their nests.

Soon the group reached the hidden village of Meadowsweet.

The elders Ulysses and Morin greeted them and invited the group to partake of the wealth of the forest. After the meal, the hosts led their guests to comfortable trees. Morganne eagerly volunteered to show Gaelyss the way to his tree.

"I hope you are well, Spellweaver. How are your studies progressing?" Morganne asked politely.

"I…I am well. The spell book challenges me. I work no harder than any of my people. My task is just different," Gaelyss answered.

"You are modest. I'm sure you are a great Spellweaver. Here is your tree. I hope you are comfortable. There is a nice stream nearby, where warblers always entertain. It's my favorite place. It's so restful. Let me know if I can do anything to make you more comfortable," the she-Drelve sincerely offered.

"Thank you," Gaelyss replied and entered the tree.

The Spellweaver sat on the soft bedding and placed his pack on the floor. The tree separated part of its bark and allowed him a view of the darkening amber sky. Meries had faded to a dot on the horizon. Gaelyss was briefly disappointed that Andreas had not wandered into the sky as the gray sun did the season before. However the beauty of the dark period removed his regret. The wonderful repast settled well, but the young Drelve still found sleep difficult. He walked through the tree into the common area. Morganne was leaning against a lamppost tree in the center of the clearing. The lamppost tree produced faint light, which was prized more if one lived in a world where total darkness followed daylight. In the dark period, the tree accentuated the faint light. Reflecting the glow of the plant, Morganne appeared quite lovely.

"Can't sleep?" she asked.

"I've tried. Could we visit your favorite place?" Gaelyss answered.

"Follow me, please," the she-Drelve replied happily.

Morganne led Gaelyss along a narrow path through the thick varied flora that surrounded the common area of Meadowsweet. Soon the Spellweaver and his hostess reached a little meadow. A babbling brook coursed through the small field. Collectively, the plants produced an extremely pleasing aroma. The sweet fragrances gave the Drelvish community its name Meadowsweet. Rainbow fish playfully leapt from beneath the shallow waters. Many birds nested in the low-lying branches of the trees above the brook. Even in the reduced light of the dark period, Gaelyss appreciated breathtaking beauty of the meadow. The two Drelves sat by the side of the stream, slipped off their finely made boots, stuck their feet in the rippling waters, and wiggled their toes.

"It's lovely," Gaelyss sighed.

"I'm glad you enjoy it. I come here to clear my mind and do nothing," Morganne admitted.

"I can see why you do," Gaelyss agreed.

The Spellweaver shyly avoided looking directly at the young she-Drelve.

"Are you lonely, Spellweaver? You have so much responsibility," Morganne asked genuinely.

"I have lots of friends. It's just...we all have so much responsibility now. And please, call me Gaelyss. Everyone's important. For instance, look at all you do, Morganne. You tend the irreplaceable enhancing plants. In addition, you don a bow and warrior's garb and meet us in the forest, and only at eighteen seasons," he replied.

"I do my tasks happily. It's a joy to care for the plants. They purr when they are happy. Did you know?" Morganne answered.

"Uh, no. I have seen many wondrous plants. The tree herders, the orange triffids, and the Tree Shepherd I met last season are among them. I can't say I've ever heard them purr," Gaelyss conceded.

"Plants share their essences with us. Giving them kindness in return only makes sense. Have you prepared the roots?" Morganne asked.

"No. I've missed the lessons. The Teacher said I should study the spell books. So you see, you and others who prepare the enhancing root serve important roles. Just as important as mine," Gaelyss apologetically answered.

"Preparing the roots is simple. One must show them some love. Watch, Spellweaver, I...I mean Gaelyss," Morganne said.

She reached into a pocket on her outfit and removed a slightly oblong thumbnail sized tuber. Gaelyss recognized the enhancing root tuber. Fully developed tubers were rather uniform in size.

Morganne spoke softly, "If I attempted to cut the surface of the tuber with my edge, and it's finely honed, I could not cut through the skin. But a gentle touch..."

The she-Drelve gently rubbed the rough surface of the small tuber, brought the bulb to her lips, and gently bussed the surface. The shell of the tuber opened and revealed a buttery violet pulp.

"This root was harvested last season. We carry one with us when we are on patrol. The pulp can sustain us for seven cycles of Meries. I don't want to waste this, will you share it with me?" Morganne asked.

"I'm not hungry, but I cannot refuse the offer of such a treat. I've had the root prepared in many ways, but never like this. Thank you," he answered.

Morganne dipped her long fingers into the pulp and gently removed some of the nourishing fleshy tissue of the tuber. She slowly and gently extended her fingers to Gaelyss's lips and allowed him to take the rich nutrient into his mouth. She then removed the remainder of the luscious tuber and placed it into her mouth.

"It's pleasing," Gaelyss said.

"The taste is unique. We derive exceptional energies from the plant. The tubers sustain us," Morganne replied.

"I see why you are fond of this place," Gaelyss reiterated.

"The stream, the plants, and the birds expect nothing from me. I suppose we should get back. The morrow will be long," Morganne said reluctantly.

Morganne led Gaelyss back down the path to the common area and his guest tree.

When they reached the red oak, she said excitedly, "Good night, Spellweaver. I am glad that you have returned to Meadowsweet. I had feared responsibilities would keep you away. I will go with you to the Green Vale on the morrow. We will have the best harvest ever!"

"Good night, Morganne, and please…again, please call me Gaelyss," the Spellweaver answered.

CHAPTER 25
Morganne's Dream

Exhilarated as she had never been in her eighteen seasons, Morganne literally skipped back to her humble red oak sapling. The austere little tree welcomed her as always, and she fell onto her bed.

"I think I'm too excited to sleep," the she-Drelve allowed, but fatigue from the long wait for the visitors in the forest took hold and she slept.

Soon, dreams came.

Beautiful fields, a kiss from Gaelyss by the babbling brook, a floral leaf in her long silver hair at a ceremony of life-long commitment...

Then a flash of red light filled her mind.

Wisps...

Threads...

Threads of Magick...

Threads of fate...

Threads of time...

Threads connecting worlds ...

Dreams connecting worlds ...

Dreams of Magick...

The Magick of Dreams...

Magick connecting dreams...

Magick connecting worlds...

Dream raiders...

Elf pressure...

Albtraum...

Albträume, elf dreams, nightmares...

Dreams...

Then, a face...

Morganne's mind's eye stared into the fiery eyes of a winsome female. The young she-Drelve had seen few females of other ilk. The foreigner's face was powerful and strangely attractive, much like the wolf-faced Drolls. Old Ulysses had seen a Giantess a long time ago. When he talked to the youths by the firesides, the elder described the large person as looking like an outsized Kiennite.

Did she dream of a giantess?

Could a giantess be this enthralling?

Intimidated by the vision, the young she-Drelve perspired profusely as she slept. The very tall alluring female in her dream had smooth reddened skin, fiery red eyes, and wore a blazing red dress. Long green hair fell provocatively across her back and chest and produced a disheveled look. The female walked proudly back and forth across a field of green grab grass. Purplish flowers dotted the field. Morganne knew grab grass grew in the woods east of the Drelves' central forest.

But grab grass was red!

The blades of the red grass tenaciously held fast any poor creature that stumbled upon it. The grab grass's victim usually starved or fell to a predator. This green grab grass tantalizingly grasped and released the female's powerful lower legs. Even dreaming, Morganne shuddered when she noted the female's strong hands with their long sharp talons. Tiny sparks of flame burst from the talons as she rubbed them together. The vision perplexed and terrified the sleeping Drelve. Black and red flower petals showered around the striking feminine being. The female pursed her lips, emitted small bursts of hot breath, and burned the vibrantly colored petals as they neared her. Morganne felt the warmth of the she-creature's breath. The Amazon rolled the digits of her left hand, created a small ball of deep green flame, and playfully tossed the little flaming orb up and down. She gently inhaled and then slowly exhaled gray smoke. The smoke enveloped the little ball of flame. Smiling wryly, the female allowed the smoke enshrouded green fireball to rest in her palm. The smoke condensed and cleared. The green ball transformed to a smooth round gray stone.

"Let's have some girl talk. He's very handsome, isn't he, my pretty?" the matron said glibly in Drelvish tongue.

"Who...is who handsome? Who...who...what manner of ilk are you? Why do you disturb my sleep?" Morganne said, her lips trembling.

"Don't be coy. You know what I'm talking about. I see how your mind's eye beholds the young Spellweaver. Why not reveal your torrid feelings for him, sweets?" the deep voice asked the sleeping she-Drelve.

"I'm...I don't understand such words. I respect the Spellweaver. He is... my leader," Morganne protested.

"Nonsense! You melt when you see him. Admit it! I know what thoughts lurk in your conniving little head. I know why you took him to the creek. What manner of treats will you give him next time?" the uninvited visitor to Morganne's dream demanded.

Morganne sniffled as she replied, "Why do you say such hurtful things? Who...who are you?"

"I'm the one who's telling you what you really feel, right? You're going to have to fight to win him. Watch the filly that accompanies him. Your

Spellweaver is young, and weak. He lacks the intensity of his brother. He is a pseudo-leader. False!" the woman said.

Deep maroon and red auras surrounded her features.

"Gaelyss is a great Spellweaver. He loves us! He loves his people! I adore him!" Morganne protested.

"A-ha! You admit it, you little vixen. You just as much a deceiver as I am. ****! ****! ****! You're better than I am. Gaelyss loves himself! Otherwise, he'd be in the trees that border the red meadow. He's weak," the she-creature answered.

"Well, I never…such language. I didn't know the Drelvish tongue could be bent into such words. Had I said such, my mother would have washed my mouth with creeping Clorox flox. There's no more nasty plant in all the wood, but it'd be appropriate to treat your filthy mouth. You should get on your knees and beg forgiveness! You do have knees, don't you? Morganne retorted defiantly.

Anger replaced fear.

"You little urchin! *If I had permission*, I'd rip off your ssssorry…do *I* have kneessss! Look upon thessse!" the she-creature countered.

She raised the clinging red dress and exposed long curvaceous legs. Her hair changed from the playful green to the darkest black. Blue fire sparked from her eyes.

Morganne again shuddered in her sleep.

The she-beast regained her composure and hissed, "All thingssss being equal, your lover boy issss weak. You can help him. I'm loath to do it, but I'm told to bequeath you a pressssent. Remember, you'll have to fight to win a Spellweaver. Sleep well, little tart."

Following a flash of blue light, the vision faded from her mind's eye. Morganne entered deep sleep and dreamed no more this rest period. She awakened with an enormous headache and sat up on the edge of her cozy bed. The she-Drelve reached beneath the bed and retrieved an enhancing root tuber. She stroked the tuber gently and brought it to her trembling lips. An iridescent tear fell from her cheek and struck the enhancing root. The plant opened immediately when the tear fell upon it. Morganne removed the pulp, munched on it, and briefly closed her eyes. The nourishing herb immediately eased Morganne's headache. The she-Drelve stood and took a deep breath.

Something moved within her sanctuary!

A small gray stone hovered near the foot of her bed. Gray light emanated from the stone and slowly filled the inner tree with grayness. Reflexively Morganne reached out and grabbed the stone. Initially cold, it warmed in her hand. Originally a perfect sphere, the rock molded to fit her grip.

Fearful, she placed the little rock within her walking cloak. The stone bonded to her.

How?

Did she still dream?

She noted the scents and sounds of Meadowsweet and knew she was awake.

Morganne closed her eyes and remembered the face from the dream.

What powers did the gray stone possess?

Was the device beneficial?

Could it harm Gaelyss?

How did the vile visitor know she thought of Gaelyss with every breath?

And had since she met the young Spellweaver during the last harvest...

The highlight of her seventeenth year had been the trip to Alms Glen. Fraught with emotion, Morganne removed the gray stone from her cloak and stored the strange little rock in a chest beneath her bed. She covered the chest with a small piece of invisimoss, which hid the container from both normal and Magick vision.

Still trembling, but resolved to do her job, the young she-Drelve exited her abode and joined the enlarging group of Drelves in the common area of Meadowsweet.

CHAPTER 26
Kirrie's Dream

Morganne and Klunkus led Edkim, Gaelyss, Kirrie, and a large contingent of neophytes to the Green Vale. The weather remained lovely. The dark period gave the land an eerie but familiar deep golden hue. Andreas remained only a distant speck in the sky, itself no larger than the retreating Meries. Edkim, Gaelyss, Klunkus, Balewyn, Clarke, Kirrie, Zachary, and Taylor represented Alms Glen, the largest community of Drelvedom.

Once they entered the luscious green valley and approached the enhancing plants, Edkim painstakingly instructed the neophytes in the proper technique to harvest the root tubers of the delicate sensitive plants. Morganne tirelessly harvested the tubers. When she was not directly working with a plant, the young she-Drelve assisted any neophyte having problems. Assisted by tree herders, orange triffids, and wandering red oaks, Klunkus, old Clarke, and Balewyn the archer stood guard. The massive red oaks concealed the entrance to the vale after the Drelves entered.

Young Kirrie learned quickly. Her small hands speedily and carefully removed the tubers from the roots. The Teacher Edkim praised her work. In her thirteen seasons Kirrie had seen the effects of war. Family members and friends had been maimed and killed in the conflict with the Drolls. She had watched and waited hopefully for Yannuvia's return, but there had been no word from the missing Spellweaver. Kirrie had attended every assigned class, performed all tasks assigned her, and studied all her lessons. In Yannuvia's absence, seventeen year-old Loganne had been Kirrie's role model. Deeply within her heart, Kirrie constantly feared for Loganne's safety and spent many sleepless rest periods pondering Yannuvia's fate.

Kirrie had always respected Gaelyss. Drelvish tradition mandated such respect. All Drelvedom realized the rarity of Spellweavers. Gaelyss seemed more aloof than his missing twin brother. While Yannuvia explored the forest, Gaelyss studied books. Kirrie appreciated the rarity of participating in a harvest with a Spellweaver.

Kirrie occasionally felt watched. On one occasion, she caught the stare of the tall Meadowsweet she-Drelve Morganne. At eighteen, Morganne was five years older.

Kirrie pondered why she suffered Morganne's derision or disapproval.

Kirrie had seen the Meadowsweet Drelve once when Morganne visited Alms Glen. During her visit, Morganne wedged between Kirrie and Gaelyss and sat by the Spellweaver's side while the Teacher Edkim talked of camouflage and the chameleon effect. Intent on absorbing the content of the Teacher's lesson, Kirrie made little note of Morganne's actions.

The chameleon effect was the ability of Drelves to blend into their forest environment. The forest ilk adeptly blended into the orange and red forests of the World of the Three Suns. The Teacher proposed Drelves would be blue in a blue forest. Kirrie realized now the Teacher's supposition was true. Looking around she noted she and her comrades blended into the greenness of Green Vale. Her skin wasn't permanently green. It absorbed, reflected, or copied the greenness of the enhancing plants. The green color suited Morganne. Kirrie managed a chuckle. A harrumph from the Teacher returned her to her tasks.

Gaelyss spent most of his time on the hillock in the center of the Green Vale among the Thirttene Friends. Rarely and briefly the geyser in the spring in the center of the hillock erupted and sprayed the trees and the surrounding area with rainbow colored water droplets. Whenever the geyser erupted, Edkim remembered the marvelous events of the previous season and ushered the neophytes up the hill to stand in the falling droplets. Gaelyss stood in the shower each time. The interval of the geyser's eruptions varied, but the geyser always spewed for thirty-nine heartbeats. The Teacher described the geyser as old but not faithful. Unfortunately for the Drelves, anyone who stood in the rain only became wet. The rainbow waters did not impart powers of Magick as they did the season before to Meryt, Zack, Debery, Bryce, and the Teacher Edkim.

Gaelyss inspected the Thirttene Friends. The Tree Shepherd remained silent. Twice the playful blue-haired tree sprite came out of her tree, ran over to Gaelyss, kissed the Spellweaver, and left a shiny blue imprint of her lips on his cheek. The young neophytes laughed at the tree sprite's antics. If anything, Morganne turned a deeper green. The tree sprite giggled as she returned to her tree. Trying to concentrate on his work, Gaelyss found the tree sprite's mischief perturbing and removed the blue imprint with a simple Dispel Magick Spell. Though the dark period always lasted exactly fifteen days, measuring time *during* the dark period was difficult. Light and amber periods were equal. One day described one light and one amber period of Meries. The term *tomorrow* described the next light period. *Tonight* described the present amber period. The dark period was simply called the *dark period*, though again it was never as dark as the underground caves. An hour was one-eighth the length of a light or amber period. If Andreas drew near the world, its gray light influenced all periods.

During the dark period, somnolence and tired muscles, not the three suns, told the Drelves the lateness of the hour.

It was *time* to rest and take nourishment. Though the Drelves received no fortuitous gifts of Magick, they gathered a bountiful harvest. The Teacher Edkim allowed each neophyte to pick a single piece of fruit from the apple tree and pear tree. Each warrior took a cherry bomb. After carefully replanting the last enhancing plant, Edkim gathered the erstwhile neophytes around him.

"You are no longer neophytes. You have passed your challenge. Every one of you has performed well and will now join their communities as adults. Drelvedom welcomes you. We must gather our wares and return to Meadowsweet. Normally we tarry and enjoy the beauty of the Green Vale. Circumstances, specifically the threats to all our homes and our beloved forests, necessitate our departure. Klunkus and Morganne, will you please lead us? Clarke, your wise eyes should watch our flanks. Balewyn, keep your bow at ready. I sense…never mind. Make ready," the Teacher said.

Gaelyss reluctantly left the hill.

Seeing the gleam in young Morganne's eyes when she looked upon the Spellweaver, the veteran Klunkus smiled and suggested, "Morganne, I'll take the point. Will you grant me the favor of walking beside our Spellweaver and assuring his safety?"

Morganne blushed and answered, "It will be my pleasure."

Kirrie sighed derisively. *Morganne understood why she suffered Kirrie's derision and disapproval.*

Klunkus expertly led them out of the Green Vale and along the trail back to Meadowsweet. Back in the village, the elders Ulysses and Morin greeted them. After brief refreshment, villagers led the tired harvesters to their trees. Morganne again walked Gaelyss to his guest tree.

"Thank you for your help, Spellweaver," she said respectfully.

"I did little. Your efforts exceeded mine. I should thank you, and your community for the assist you've given the Teacher and our people. I personally thank you for sharing the peaceful interlude by the brook. I'll think of that solitude in difficult times. Have a well deserved and good rest, Morganne of Meadowsweet," Gaelyss said respectfully.

"Good night, Spellweaver Gaelyss," the she-Drelve replied.

Kirrie watched the Spellweaver and the older girl saying their good rests. Fatigue overwhelmed her and she slipped through the bark of the small everred guest tree. The comfortable little bed beckoned to her and the little Drelve slept in no time. Her sleeping mind returned to the marvelous experience of tending the enhancing plants and the beauty of the Green

Vale. Then Yannuvia's face appeared as it often did. Kirrie had admired him so much.

Why had he left?

Where was he?

She languished as much in her dreams as she did while awake.

Then calmness took over. Kirrie saw slowly moving beautiful white clouds in an alien blue sky. She sensed a soothing breeze and her tired hands felt warm. She never felt so comfortable, so relaxed. Redness gently filled her vision.

Wisps...

Threads...

Threads of Magick...

Threads of fate...

Threads of time...

Threads connecting worlds ...

Dreams connecting worlds ...

Dreams of Magick...

The Magick of Dreams...

Magick connecting dreams...

Magick connecting worlds...

Dream raiders...

Elf pressure...

Albtraum...

Albträume, elf dreams, nightmares...

Dreams...

Then a face appeared.

Kindly and beautiful, the matronly female had smooth, lovely white skin and deep blue eyes. Soft blonde hair fell gently down the length of her back. She was as tall as a Droll, which made her twice Kirrie's height. She wore a long flowing robe made of cottony fabric that exposed smooth hands with well-groomed nails.

She spoke barely above a whisper, saying, "You have labored long, my little one. I won't long disturb your needed rest. You are no longer a child. You have great skills."

"Who are you? You are not of the Drelvish ilk. You are so beautiful. Your voice...it soothes my aching bones. Why do you compliment me? I only did my job," Kirrie asked.

"*Who I am* is not important. Think of me as a Good Witch. It is you that matters. Your Spellweaver needs you. He must get stronger. Your people's survival depends on him," the kindly matron reported.

"But what of Yannuvia? I await his return. All my people do," Kirrie queried.

"He is away. I don't know his fate. But you have one Spellweaver among you who wants to do well. You can help him, Kirrie. Support Gaelyss. Make his burden lighter. As you grow older, be by his side. He needs a shoulder. He needs a companion," the matron implored.

"Gaelyss has his studies. It seems he wants little else. To Gaelyss, the forest is an after thought. But all my people support him," Kirrie answered.

"Beneath the surface, beyond the Spellweaver, beyond the seeker of Magick, there is a feeling, needing person. He needs love. You can help him now," the matron said sincerely.

"I'm only thirteen seasons of age. He's fourteen. We've only begun life. I don't know how to love him," Kirrie mumbled.

"That will happen in time. For now, just be there for him. Certainly evil will befall your Spellweaver if affairs proceed as they are. I can assist," the lovely visitor insisted.

The Good Witch rolled the digits of her left hand and created a small ball of deep green flame, which she gently tossed up and down. She softly inhaled and then unhurriedly exhaled gray smoke, which enveloped the little ball of flame. Smiling kindly, the female allowed the smoke enshrouded green fireball to rest in her palm. The smoke condensed and cleared. The green ball transformed to a smooth round gray stone.

"You must tell no one of our get-together. I can't help you if you do. Think of your people. Think of your Spellweaver Gaelyss. He is *your* destiny. Don't dwell of those who have departed. If you can't be with the one you want, love the one you're with. You have rivals for his attention. Don't yield to them," the kind voice added.

"What is the import of the little gray stone?" Kirrie asked.

"The stone in my hand? Seek it. *Should* you find it, you, and only you, can use it to greatly assist your Spellweaver. Now you must rest, Kirrie of Alms Glen. Kirrie, of the Drelves. Kirrie, friend of the forest. Rest well," the Good Witch said.

Subtle blue light surrounded the Good Witch, and the image faded from Kirrie's mind. The little she-Drelve awakened, sat up, and suffered a terrible headache. Remembering what she had learned, Kirrie took one of the enhancing tubers she had harvested, gently rubbed its rough surface, and softly kissed the shell. The shell opened. Kirrie ingested the delicious purplish fruit and soon her headache abated. Still tired, the young Drelve fell backward onto the bed, sighed deeply, and fell asleep.

Soon a gentle peck on her tree told her it was time to awaken and begin the return to Alms Glen. Kirrie awakened and rubbed her still sleepy eyes. The dream festered in her mind. Trying to brush the images aside, she stood, stretched, and began to gather her belongings.

Wait!

Grayness bathed her room.

The flickering gray light mimicked the previous season's Approximation of the Gray Wanderer Andreas. Kirrie peered quickly through the tree's bark, noted the dark period continued, and did not see the wandering sun Andreas. The she-Drelve heard a faint humming sound and saw something spinning in the *grayness* of the little tree's interior. The gray light emanated from a small spherical stone hovering in the corner of the little room.

Was the deep gray rock ...the stone she had seen in her dream?

Kirrie reached out and quickly took the stone from the air. When the she-Drelve touched the floating stone, the artifact warmed, altered its shape, and conformed to the size and shape of the little she-Drelve's hand. Kirrie placed the gray stone in the pocket of her walking cloak. The stone pressed against her orange-yellow skin and meld with the she-Drelve. Inexplicably, Kirrie felt comforted.

In a few moments another knock on the tree reminded her of the time. The little Drelve finished gathering her few items, cleaned the interior of the guest room, passed effortlessly through the red oak's thick bark, and exited the tree.

Uncharacteristically, the Teacher Edkim slept poorly. A master at self-discipline, the Teacher usually slept efficiently. He kept sensing indistinct images akin to someone attempting to pry his or her way into his subconscious. Finally his mind found the rolling grasses of the great plain of the Ornash River with its peaceful breezes and gentle bird songs.

The Teacher rested.

In the morning Edkim awakened with a headache. The Teacher placed his thumbs on either side of his neck and vigorously massaged the tense muscles. After several attempts, he managed to ease the spasms and the headache abated.

Time was wasting.

Edkim gathered his artifacts and made ready for travel. His great responsibilities precluded the interference of a headache. Exiting the tree, Edkim went to pay his respects to the elders Morin and Ulysses, his Meadowsweet hosts.

The veteran Klunkus stood impatiently as the Teacher bade good byes.

"We must return to Alms Glen," Klunkus insisted.

"I agree," Edkim replied.

Clarke took the Teacher aside and asked, "Teacher, are you well?"

"I'm well enough. Why do you ask?" Edkim answered matter-of-factly.

"No disrespect intended, Teacher, but you have the look I have after an evening of too much mead. I'll be on my way," Clarke allowed.

Morganne attempted to stand by Gaelyss, but Kirrie stepped between the Meadowsweet maiden and the Spellweaver and said, "You should scout ahead and help assure safe passage for the Spellweaver."

"I will assure he has safe passage from Meadowsweet. Can you assure me that he will be safe in Alms Glen?" Morganne icily answered.

"I'll see he's well *attended*," Kirrie answered smugly.

This day Drelvish scouts did not carry the sharpest daggers in their finely made sheaths. The sharpest daggers came from the eyes of Kirrie and Morganne as they parted ways.

CHAPTER 27
Kirrie's Decision

The small party of Edkim, Gaelyss, Klunkus, the archer Balewyn, crusty old Clarke, Kirrie, Zachary, and Taylor returned from Meadowsweet. Refusing to take a rest period, Klunkus left for the Lone Oak meadow. Immediately after leading the group back to Alms Glen, Edkim allocated the fruits of the harvest to the various families. The Drelves stored most of the enhancing root. Older Drelves prepared some of the tubers for use in potions and unguents. Others made jellies and jams, mixing the vitamin enriched enhancing root tubers with fruits, berries, and ever-popular blue bee honey.

Kirrie had tenaciously shadowed Gaelyss throughout the trip back from Meadowsweet. The young she-Drelve had paid him little mind before the journey to Meadowsweet and the Green Vale, but now she seemed quite interested in the Spellweaver's every move. Gaelyss politely thanked her for her efforts and retired to his tree. Without stopping to turn down the enticing bed's covers, the Spellweaver relieved the burden of his weathered pack and dropped onto the soft mossy coverlet. Soon he slept.

Kirrie's mind swirled. She had learned so much in the past few days. As she had walked back beside Gaelyss, her thoughts had returned often to the kindly face in her dream.

Why had the benefactor insisted on silence?

What was the purpose of the little gray stone she carried in her pocket? Intermittently the outsized pebble had emitted low-pitched droning sounds and pulses of gray light. At times she felt warmth from the stone. Was the rock alive?

Should she tell the Spellweaver?

Should she tell the Teacher?

The burden was more than her thirteen-season-old mind could bear. Kirrie stood up, exited her tree, went to the Teacher's abode, and knocked politely on the bark of the Old Orange Spruce.

Teachers had lived in the ancient tree as long as anyone remembered. As far as the Drelves knew the Old Orange Spruce was as old as the Lone Oak. Both trees were older than Dirt, the first Teacher to write about them in the annals.

Kirrie started to turn away when the Teacher sleepily answered, "Who calls at this hour? Are we attacked?"

"No, Teacher, it is Kirrie. I had a …question," Kirrie asked.

The Teacher's kind but firm hand reached through the bark and helped the little she-Drelve through the wall of the Old Orange Spruce. The aroma of blood oranges filled the air.

"Please enter, Kirrie. What is your question?" Edkim asked.

"Can you tell me about dreams?" Kirrie asked tentatively.

The Teacher sat by his desk and replied, "Recently a young Drelve asked me about dreams. He then slipped away into the forest and has not returned. I speak of Yannuvia. The last young Drelve…just say it's becoming a common question for me. Tell me what troubles you, my lady."

Kirrie blushed at being called lady instead of child or neophyte.

She answered, "I'm not going anywhere Teacher, unless you direct me to do so. I wonder…what do the annals say of dreams?"

"The annals are the record of Drelvedom, the story of our people, as recorded by the Teachers of each generation. Dirt was the first writer's name. That's the reason *'your name is Dirt'* is such a great compliment. The records belong to all Drelves. Dreams belong to the dreamer. We all have dreams. The annals speak of deeds and actions, not dreams, Kirrie. What troubles you?" Edkim asked.

"Oh, I am not troubled, Teacher," Kirrie lied, "At least, no more than any of our people. It's just, I…don't understand…I've…"

"Perhaps you should tell me about your dream?" Edkim judged.

"She told me not to…but you are the Teacher. You are wise. I am not," Kirrie stammered.

"*She?* Of whom do you speak?" Edkim queried.

"She told me not to tell anyone about the encounter, but I fear for our people, Teacher. What is a *Good Witch*?" Kirrie asked sincerely.

"Good witch? I don't know such an ilk, Kirrie. Where have you heard the name?" the Teacher asked.

"I…I saw her in a dream, Teacher," Kirrie confessed.

"Well, describe her," Edkim suggested.

"The Good Witch was kindly and beautiful. The matronly female had smooth, lovely white skin and deep blue eyes. Soft blonde hair fell gently down the length of her back. She was as tall as a Droll, which made her twice as tall as I am. She wore a long flowing robe made of cottony fabric and exposed smooth hands with well-groomed nails. She spoke with a soothing voice. She was very convincing that she had my interest in mind," Kirrie honestly related.

"I suppose the name *Witch* implies Magick, but the word *good* confuses me. Magick is neither good nor bad, it's just...Magick. You describe someone who seems sincere, but things aren't always, as they seem. I'd say, it was just a dream, Kirrie. I've seen Drolls, Kiennites, Giants, Ogres, Dryads, Sprites, Huldra, Centaurs, and I've read of hundreds of different folk in the annals. I've neither seen nor heard of one such as you describe, though I hope I dream of her," Edkim said, ending with a chuckle.

"Teacher, I...excuse me," Kirrie yawned.

"You should find sleep now, Kirrie. We'll talk more on the morrow. I hope Rumsie is well. I asked Klunkus to request the Sergeant Major come to Alms Glen and give me a status report from the front. Let's rest," Edkim suggested.

"As always, your advice is sagacious, Teacher. I'll say good night," Kirrie sleepily responded.

Kirrie exited the Old Orange Spruce, crossed the quiet common area of Alms Glen, and reentered her tree. Though she feared retribution from the Good Witch, the she-Drelve could not fight sleep. Kirrie's mind returned to a warm light period when she walked with Yannuvia at the fringe of the forest. As Drelvlings, both knew trekking so far from the security of Alms Glen was forbidden and they risked punishment from the elders and their parents.

Yannuvia used a patch of rare invisimoss to hide them and rancid gray berries to cover their scent. The Drelvlings avoided detection by the keen noses and eyes of the guards and saw the Lone Oak. Like a sentry, the great tree watched over the wide field of red grass. Excited, Kirrie saw the wild wood in the far distance.

Young Yannuvia serenaded his companion.

The little Spellweaver sang, "Oh, Kirrie, Kirrie, it's a wild wood. It's hard to get by with just a smile, Kirrie. Oh, Kirrie, Kirrie, it's a wild wood. Stay close by my side, Kirrie; it's a wild wood."

Yannuvia sang quite poorly. His singing had been a bad move in more ways than one. Gray berries hid one's scent; invisimoss made one invisible, but not inaudible. The sentries caught the young Drelves. Getting caught meant cleaning lots of Rangers' boots and several light periods of reading and writing. But they spent time together. Kirrie supposed it wasn't such a bad punishment and cherished the memory of Yannuvia. The young Spellweaver had disappeared just before he was to go to Meadowsweet and Green Vale for the harvesting of the enhancing root. A year had passed since she had looked upon his face.

Kirrie dreamt of Yannuvia. In her dreams she was in Yannuvia's arms, where she wanted to be.

CHAPTER 28
The Teacher's Dream

Older than his years, the Teacher Edkim had seen more of his people fall in his tenure than the previous five Teachers combined. He had just returned from Meadowsweet and accomplished a great harvest. Edkim pondered Kirrie's questions, which he'd been unable to answer. The Teacher watched Kirrie return to her home tree. Edkim slipped through the thick bark of the Old Orange Spruce. His tomes said nothing of Good Witches or the interpretation of dreams. For that matter, the annals said nothing of witches at all. Campfire songs told of mythical beings called elves. The same songs asserted nightmares were the results of elf pressure. The malevolent beings created the disturbed sleep by sitting on the dreamer's chest. Some superstitious Drelves carved figures on their trees to guard against the mythical elves. The Alfkors guarded against malevolent elves and resembled a five-pointed star. Edkim saw such a figure craved into the bark of the tree he occupied in Meadowsweet.

For the entire duration of the trip from Meadowsweet, Edkim had battled headache. Finally, he gave in and used one of the precious tubers he carried in his pack. The enhancing tuber remedied his headache, healed the bruise he had suffered at the Green Vale, sealed a cavity in a molar, and repaired a small cut on his finger. With his pain eased, the Teacher went to his bed and soon slept.

Images flowed past his sleeping eyes. Deeper into the stages of sleep…a flash of red…

Wisps…

Threads…

Threads of Magick…

Threads of fate…

Threads of time…

Threads connecting worlds …

Dreams connecting worlds …

Dreams of Magick…

The Magick of Dreams…

Magick connecting dreams…

Magick connecting worlds…

Dream raiders…

Elf pressure…

Albtraum…

Albträume, elf dreams, nightmares…

Dreams…

The Teacher stood at the edge of a small clearing in the outskirts of Alms Glen. Staring across the meadow, his mind's eye saw a matron walking toward him. Clearly Drelvish, she wore a simple dark orange dress and cork wood sandals. Her long brown hair gave away her age. Drelves' hair changed from silver to brown as seasons passed. As she approached, he saw clarity in her sparkling eyes and gentleness in her smile. Her right forearm bore a distinctive purplish birthmark. She bore a linear scar on her chin and favored her left leg. Edkim's senses detected the floral fragrances of her hair and essence. She smiled.

"Mother?" the Teacher queried.

"You labor long and hard for *your* people. What do you do for yourself? Do you ever smell the roses that you so carefully tend? You suffer pain for an entire cycle of the sun before you utilize an enhancing root tuber to gain relief. For what reason?" she asked gently.

"I am the Teacher," Edkim answered matter-of-factly.

"You are also a person," the matron answered.

"Who are you? Why and how do you invade my sleep?" he asked.

"Does the image not please you?" the figure replied.

"My mother Estelle left us twenty seasons past. She would never question my dedication to the role my people give me. Again, I ask, who are you?" Edkim asked.

"Just consider me a Good Samaritan. You handle yourself well. You couldn't answer the young one's questions. Made you uncomfortable, didn't it?" the ersatz Estelle observed.

"What is a Samaritan? What makes a Samaritan *good*? You haven't answered my question," Edkim persisted.

"A Samaritan is…a helper…one give gives of himself, smart ***," She answered.

Her tone changed.

Edkim detected a bit of anger.

"Ok, you're a helper. Why do you care about Drelves? We are but a simple people. We don't seek power or wealth. We only want to live our lives at peace with the forest and its denizens. How does invading my dreams and disturbing my sleep help me?" Edkim asked.

"I care about the forest, the world, and Magick. I care about what is right. As I said, I am a Samaritan. I'll help you answer the urchin's questions. I chose an image I thought you'd find pleasing. I am a Good Witch," she answered.

"The term *witch* means nothing to me. If you are *good*, then stop perverting the memory of my mother and reveal yourself. Then we can converse, though I don't understand how we are talking in my dreams," Edkim persevered.

"I am a Dreamweaver of sorts. It's easier to communicate this way. *Must* you define how we understand one another? Do you try to define Magick? I'll show you my true colors," the ersatz Estelle replied.

The image before Edkim's mind's eyes changed from his mother to another beautiful matronly female. The female had smooth, lovely white skin, deep blue eyes, and soft blonde hair that fell gently down the length of her back. She was as tall as a Droll, which made her time and a half the Teacher's height. She wore a long flowing robe made of cottony fabric and exposed smooth hands with well-groomed nails.

She spoke with a compassionate, soothing voice, "Is this better?"

"I'm not sure it's *truthful*, but you now appear as Kirrie described. State your business, or else allow me to sleep," Edkim insisted.

"You are difficult. I *knew* she'd come to you. I *intended* she do so," the Good Witch answered.

"It's hardly what I'd call *good* to invade the mind and sleep of a child, Good Witch. I concede that one cannot define Magick. You are saying that you are a witch, and witches are Magick. I accept that as axiomatic. Are you a Spellweaver? If so, have you *charmed* Kirrie? Do you intend to *charm* me?" Edkim asked incredulously.

"Gaelyss is the only Spellweaver in *these* woods, Teacher Edkim. Young Kirrie can support and be an important asset to him. The fate of your people, all Drelvedom, parallels his success. Gaelyss *needs* Kirrie. That's the reason I contacted her," the Good Witch answered.

"Gaelyss *has* the support of all Drelvedom. Kirrie is talented, dedicated, and strong-willed, but a single harvest separates her from being a neophyte. Kirrie can only make a small contribution to Gaelyss's course. Though he is our *only* Spellweaver, he grows stronger and will carry his burden well," Edkim said deceptively.

"You don't have to conceal Yannuvia's absence. Yes, I know of Gaelyss's missing brother. Kirrie dreams only of Yannuvia. But what you say is true, Teacher. Gaelyss *is* your only Spellweaver. Kirrie, you, and all Drelvedom should abandon the foolish hope that the other will return. Could anyone survive a full year in the wild woods?" she argued.

"You don't know Yannuvia. He is one with the woods. I don't know how, but I think I'd know if he were dead. Kirrie is fond of him. I don't know how you gain your information, but I doubt you are all-knowing," Edkim countered.

"Don't underestimate me. Edkim, I know Magick touches you, but a simple Magick Missile does not give you the power to know Yannuvia's fate. The Drolls and Kiennites amass near Aulgmoor. Your defenders have only skirmished with probing parties. Yet they have suffered losses. The forests cannot help you much longer. The tree herder wounded by the ballista died while you were at Meadowsweet. Morale falls among the defenders at Lone Oak. When Rumsie reports on the morrow, he will confirm all these things. Trust me when I say you have only one Spellweaver, and he is your people's chance for survival. Neither he nor you can be tentative. Your salvation lies in Magick. You know I speak the truth," she said succinctly.

"If you are correct about the Drolls and Kiennites, how can Kirrie and I change the course of such a tide? We are but two," Edkim countered.

"The answer lays with the girl, Teacher. Your role is the instruction of the Spellweaver and guiding Kirrie to his side. This must be your course. I can help, but only indirectly. I am, after all, a dream," she chided.

The Good Witch rolled the digits of her left hand and created a small ball of deep blue flame, which she gently tossed up and down. She softly inhaled and then unhurriedly exhaled gray smoke, which enveloped the little ball of flame. Smiling kindly, the female allowed the smoke enshrouded blue fireball to rest in her palm. The smoke condensed and cleared. The blue ball transformed to a smooth round gray stone.

Edkim stared at the beautiful image. Such a lovely creature could not be deceitful! She wouldn't betray him.

He winced and shouted aloud, "Am I charmed?"

If someone had stood within ten paces of the Old Orange Spruce, he would have clearly heard Edkim's outburst. Yet the Teacher remained asleep.

"Do you *want* to be charmed?" the Good Witch answered coyly.

The matronly Dreamraider caressed the little stone.

"What trickery do you hold in your hand? Traveling minstrels transform flame to stone. It's not even Magick. It's illusory," Edkim argued.

"I'm no minstrel. I hold power in my hand. You might call the stones, destiny changers. Seek them, Teacher of Drelvedom. Mind you, do not opine for your missing Spellweaver. Go with the bird in your hand rather than the one on the wind. Heed my advice. The morrow approaches. You should, in point of fact, sleep. Do you want to see your mother again?" the Good Witch offered.

"My mother is dead! Your name! What is your name, Good Witch?" Edkim demanded.

"My name is Amica. Amica Carmisino. Does that help you, Teacher?" she answered.

Blueness surrounded the matron. The Dreamraider changed briefly to the dreamy image of Estelle, mother of the Teacher Edkim. She smiled, blew a kiss toward the Teacher, and faded from his dreams.

Edkim slept.

CHAPTER 29
Sergeant Major Rumsie's Concerns

All too soon Edkim heard the knock upon the Old Orange Spruce.

Rumsie's voice asked, "Teacher, are you home?"

"Yes, my friend, enter," Edkim, replied.

The veteran Drelve entered the foyer of the Teacher's home. Several small rooms divided the inner sanctum of the great orange spruce where the Teachers had lived for generations. The outermost, or foyer, served as a place of consultation. A small spiral staircase meandered upward and downward from the foyer. The Teacher slept in the uppermost part of the great tree. The lower chamber housed the artifacts under the Teacher's care, including the annals, the history of the Drelvish people. The inner portion of the great tree had a pleasant orange aroma, thus, the name. As far as the Teacher knew, the Old Orange Spruce was unique in the woods around Alms Glen.

"How was the harvest?" Rumsie asked.

"Bountiful! Klunkus, Clarke, and Balewyn protected us. Young Kirrie bested the efforts of Zachary and Taylor, the other neophytes, but all performed well. We have three more members of our community to share our burdens. The Spellweaver Gaelyss has served well again. Morin and Ulysses, the elders of Meadowsweet, were gracious hosts, as always. One of the Meadowsweet group, a young girl named Morganne shows great promise. She has tended the plants for five seasons and now serves as sentry on the route to the Green Vale. But more importantly, how are affairs at the red meadow?" Edkim asked.

"I would like to give you a better report, Teacher. The situation could have been worse. Since your party left for Meadowsweet and the Green Vale, we have seen no major attacks. Drolls meander through the trees on the far side of the red meadow. Occasionally they run onto the meadow, taunt us, and then fall back into the woods. A griffon rider named Lapaglia reported large numbers of Drolls massing in the Doombringer Mountains near the Kiennite stronghold Aulgmoor. We still don't know Yannuvia's fate. There's still no word of him. We'd hope he'd return for the harvest season. Our rangers have seen only skirmishes and probing parties. Yet we have suffered losses. The forests cannot help us much longer. The tree herder wounded by the ballista died while you were at Meadowsweet. Rangers searched unsuccessfully for a Mender. Our best efforts could not stop the loss of the tree herder's life's sap. I never learned the tree herder's name. His speech mimicked a whispering wind on a mountaintop. He talked of an ideal place with endless meadows, fresh breezes, warm sunshine, and refreshing waters. He called it Elysium. I hope our ally has found the Fields of Elysium. The rangers grow tired. We've been wary an entire year, eight dark periods. Your return from the Green Vale with a fresh supply of enhancing root tubers will boost falling morale. Had only Yannuvia returned! He had such passion. I still remember his song to little Kirrie. He was ever getting her in trouble," Rumsie said, managing a half smile.

His loyal ranger and friend's words confirmed the statements made by his ersatz mother the Good Witch. Taken back, Edkim remained silent for a moment.

Then the Teacher said, "The tree herder was a good friend. He did not have to stand by us, yet he did. The Drolls have never used war machines. Unpredictable tactics! Kiennites must have fomented the deed! Immediately upon my return and before I retired, I instructed the matrons and cooks to prepare enhancing root stews for the front line rangers. Hopefully this will revitalize their strengths and spirits. I also had hoped for young Yannuvia's return. I am encouraged by Gaelyss's progress. I'll double my efforts to teach him. Unfortunately we received no additional boons from the Green Vale. Are the four young spell casters well?"

"Meryt, Zack, Debery, and Bryce have been valuable in the defenses. Debery's Invisibility Spell has enabled him to spy on the Drolls' activities. We used gray berries to hide his scent. Still the Drolls almost caught him. He gains experience. The defenders will appreciate the enhancing root stews. Klunkus reached us last evening, told us of your and Gaelyss's return, and lifted our spirits. Klunkus went to the upper boughs to take his watch, and I came here to speak with you. The griffon rider Lapaglia had to depart for the coast. We saw wyverns in the sky toward the great sea," Rumsie replied.

"Griffon riders risk all every time they ascend on their steeds. Wyverns and griffons are natural enemies. I'm glad we received Lapaglia's intelligence. Otherwise we would not have learned of the enemies' strength. Finding Menders is difficult. I'm sorry your efforts did not save the tree herder. Have someone relieve Klunkus. He must rest. I am calling a meeting of the council. I want you to stay in Alms Glen for a time," the Teacher requested.

"I'm needed at the Lone Oak, Teacher," Rumsie protested.

"I want you to instruct Gaelyss, Kirrie, Zachary, and Taylor in hand to hand combat. Balewyn will help them with archery. We must hone their skills," Edkim insisted.

Rumsie clearly disliked the idea of being away from his charges at the red meadow, but acquiesced to the Teacher's request. The Drelves' leaders exited the Old Orange Spruce and went to the common area of Alms Glen, which bustled with activity. Matrons, older males, and young neophytes fed roaring fires beneath large iron pots. Other Drelves brought fruits of the forest and placed them in the pots. Kirrie, Zack, and Taylor busily utilized their new knowledge of opening the enhancing root tubers, tenderly shelled the tubers, and then placed the precious pulp into the large pots. Wonderful aromas filled the air. Drelvish rangers arrived from the front with crystal gourds to carry the stew to the defenders at the Lone Oak meadow. Older more experienced Drelves opened the tubers and carefully placed them in small odd cooking vessels over small fires. These Drelvish alchemists made concentrated potables from the enhancing root and rare medicinal herbs gathered from the forest. Rumsie and Edkim smelled rosemary, basil, ginger, onyums, garlic, thyme, blue cohosh, canterberry, gooseberry, and even rare booderries, harvested at great peril from the depths of the subterranean caves. Only the most experienced alchemists utilized the noxious byneberry. The collages of fragrances invigorated the Teacher and the Sergeant Major. They saw no sign of young Gaelyss.

Seeing Kirrie, the Sergeant of the Guard Rumsie approached her and queried, "Have you seen Gaelyss?"

Noting the concern in his face, Kirrie answered, "Sergeant Major Rumsie, I knew the Spellweaver would be tired from the trip. I carried him some of the first batch of enhancing stew and encouraged Gaelyss to rest. He must maintain his energies to help his studies of Magick. Gaelyss's success is paramount."

Edkim nodded appreciatively to the young she-Drelve, winked, and said, "Very good, Kirrie. I *dreamed* you'd care well for the Spellweaver. You are a *Good Witch*."

"I understand, Teacher. I *dream* of helping Gaelyss," Kirrie answered, smiled, and remained at her tasks.

Rumsie looked briefly with puzzlement at the Teacher and his young comrade. Then the Sergeant Major acquiesced to his hunger and dove into a bowl of enhancing stew.

CHAPTER 30
War Council of Aulgmoor

Far to the north in the Doombringer range, envoys from the Kiennish warrens and Drollen clans reached the inner ward of the Kiennish stronghold Aulgmoor. Traditionally the most powerful Kiennish warren leader resided at Aulgmoor, but the individual warrens maintained some autonomy. As the commandant of Aulgmoor, Saligia exercised authority over several spell casters and lieutenants, who in turn recruited roving bands of Drolls to foment trouble. Easily defended and centrally located, Aulgmoor served as a rallying point for the Kiennites in times of duress. The Kiennites' traditional adversaries, including Drelves, Giants, Ogres, Hobgoblins, and Flugzeugs, had never mounted a successful offensive against Aulgmoor.

General Saligia paced impatiently in his war room and heard a knock at the heavy copperwood door. Copperwood hardened over time.

"Enter," Saligia commanded.

"Lord Saligia, they have arrived. The Drollen chieftains grow more impatient by the moment. Shall I bring them?" the viceroy asked.

"Yes, yes, yes, you wimp! Don't cower before them! Send them to me," Saligia growled.

In a while, several ornately clad Kiennites and battle-seasoned Drolls entered the war room. A central table made of polished rare red cedar dominated the chamber. Braziers lined the walls and produced a light similar to the highest illumination of the light period. Chemical fires produced the light from the braziers, and the compounds gave off a slight sulfurous odor that gave pleased and enticed the Drolls and Kiennites. Chairs made of hard yellow wood were placed around the table, and the tanned hides of Baxcats, Leicats, meow-meow skats, noir skats, and wailers lined the walls. The felines had fallen victim to many generations of Kiennish Generals' hunting forays. The current General and commandant of Aulgmoor Saligia cared little for hunting, but he humored his followers and kept the hides on the walls. As far as Saligia knew, many of the animals were now extinct. At least he'd never seen them in the wild.

Various and sundry representatives of the Kiennish warrens entered and took seats at the table. Dressed in full battle regalia, Saligia stood at the head of the table and carried the staff his fallen brother Melphat had borne in life. The General recognized Woodrow, Wilson, Calvin, Coolidge, Theodore, Delano, and Roosevelt, leaders of the Seven Warrens of Kiennites. The Drolls sent envoys, but Saligia did not know their names. As per tradition, only the Kiennites remained the war room. Saligia greeted the Drolls and thanked them for coming, and then the General's subordinates led the Drolls' clan leaders to a large assembly room where the wolf-faced allies feasted on mead and meats from the Kiennish kitchens. Saligia's actions didn't offend the Drolls. Drolls preferred eating, drinking, and fighting to planning and negotiating. After scanning the group of Kiennish warren masters gathered in the war room, the General began to speak.

"Where is Pierce? Where is Piercie? Where is the commander of my Firehorse brigade?" he asked.

An older Kiennish warren lord named Delano stood nervously and looked about the table at his cohorts. Obviously he had drawn the unenviable task of addressing the powerful Kiennish General.

Delano began, "Piercie has changed his name to Tumuch. He always hated the name his mother gave him. He waits at the Gap Keep with a hundred cavalry mounted on flame horses. Bluthgar and Dolenz ride as his second and third in command. Pierce's, I mean, Tumuch's brigade is finely tuned and itching to fight. On your order, he will attack the vile red meadow defenders in force. Drollen infantry waits at the gap to the plain above the Ornash with our Kiennish regiments. The Drolls have answered your call. Moochie Korcran remains at the Lone Oak with his advance units. By your command, they have only made harassing maneuvers. We... uh, they don't understand the tactic, Lord Saligia. Nine dark periods have passed since Melphat fell. This enabled the Drelves to see another season of their harvest. Their Spellweavers have had another nine dark periods to further their foul Magick. Fortunately for us, the gray sun has not drawn near in this time frame. Why do you tarry?"

"A tired enemy is a vulnerable enemy. Have not our numbers increased? Have we not constructed the war wagons? Have you suffered losses? Moochie's legion suffered during their rash attacks! Have you no faith in me?" Saligia growled menacingly.

"Now, now, now, I have *ever* served you, Lord Saligia. I...we have followed your instructions, though we don't understand them. We are warriors. Our warrens seek blood for blood. We just want to fight the Drelves. We want to avenge Lord Melphat," Delano replied submissively.

"As do I. The time is nigh. Send a spider rider to Moochie. Tell him to attack the ****** tree," Saligia said bluntly.

"I'm sorry, Lord Saligia, did you say, 'Attack the tree'?" Delano queried.

"Can you not hear? I said 'Tell the Droll Moochie to attack the ******* tree.' The Lone Oak bears great significance to the Drelves. It means nothing to us. It fills a great area of the field of battle. Destroying the Lone Oak will demoralize the Drelves and clear the way for our all out assault," Saligia clarified.

"Lord Saligia, the Lone Oak has great Magick. If we attack this symbol of the forest, all sorts of Magick will deluge our forces. Should we take such a rash step?" Delano asked fearfully.

"Simpleton! Have you ever seen the tree cast a spell? Does any among you know of the tree casting a spell? If we destroy this symbol, the Drelves will cower before us. We can rout them, destroy the central forests where they make their homes, and rid the world of their pestilence," Saligia said powerfully.

"If you are wrong, Lord Saligia, Moochie's troops will be fodder," Coolidge bravely suggested.

"Look about! Do you see Drolls seated among you? Will any Kiennites fall if the tree mystically destroys the Droll's infantry? Would you rather have *our* people attack the tree?" Saligia countered.

"I'd rather not attack the tree at all, Lord Saligia," Calvin declared.

"We will find out what happens when the tree is attacked, Calvin. I say we have Moochie attack the tree. This will force the Drelves to show their hand. We don't know how many Spellweavers live among our enemies. Now, take some red ale with me. I've had a griffon rider carry it from the Emerald Isle. Drink to our victory," Saligia stated authoritatively.

The viceroy Chamberlain carried a tray bearing eight large mugs. He dutifully sat a mug before Saligia, Woodrow, Wilson, Calvin, Coolidge, Theodore, Delano, and Roosevelt.

"We'll drink for Piercie. I want his firehorse cavalry in close reserve to the Drolls. Seeing them will enhance the morale of Moochie's brigade. Tell Piercie to go to Moochie and tell the Droll that he may plunder the Drelves' homes. He gets dibs on the…just tell him he can do whatever he wants," Saligia muttered evilly as he tipped his mug and drank deeply of the fine rare red ale.

"You are the commander. We'll follow your orders. But Lord Saligia, do you trust the Griffon riders?" Delano asked.

"No," Saligia answered succinctly.

"Then, why…?" Delano asked.

Saligia stopped him amid his question and said, "I tire of your questions, Delano. Do you want to challenge me? I can arrange it! No one can bring the red ale from the Emerald Isle as quickly as the griffon riders. Besides, they are loyal to no one. They don't have much of a chance at long life.

Sooner or later, they encounter the griffon's traditional enemy, the wyvern, and become wyvern bait."

"No, my Lord Saligia. I don't want to fight you. I'll shut up and drink my ale, and be grateful for it. I'll send my personal courier to the Gap Keep to give the orders to Pierce, I mean, Piercie. Do you mind too much if I call our comrade Tumuch? He prefers it," Delano asked submissively.

"It's not too much to call him Tumuch. Tell him he's always Piercie to me, unless of course, he is victorious. Now, be off with you. We will mobilize the main force from Aulgmoor to follow the Drolls from the Ornash plain. The Drelves have seen their last harvest," Saligia growled.

With the conclusion of the meeting, Woodrow, Wilson, Calvin, Coolidge, Theodore, Delano, and Roosevelt left the room. Saligia breathed deeply, clutched the hilt of his broadsword, and hoped his blade would find the neck of the scoundrel that killed his brother.

A gentle knock disturbed his vengeful thoughts.

"What now?" Saligia grumbled.

A calm voice asked, "General, do you require my assistance?"

"Actually, Fisher, some of your sleep poultice would be nice. I understand you've been rather busy since the Drolls arrived. Enter and report to me," Saligia commanded.

The Mender Fisher opened the door, and entered the chamber, approached the General, and answered, "Yes, Lord Saligia. I treated many walk-ins, crawl-ins, and split ends. Once your visitors partake of the mead and vintage, they squabble among themselves. I patched up quite a few. I'd hate to see the damage they'd do to an enemy. I'll prepare a sleep poultice."

Fisher was typical of the ultra rare Menders. In the World of the Three Suns, the snow-white skinned, pigment less Menders possessed unique healing ability. Kiennish shamans, Drelvish elders, and ultra rare Drelvish Spellweavers did not understand the nature of the Menders' talent. Camps of the various combatants sought Menders during many conflicts in the troubled land. Given their choice, the reclusive healers preferred to live alone in the great highlands. Pacifistic and never offering resistance to capture, Menders shared their talents indiscriminately. Given the opportunity, a Mender would first heal a warrior, any warrior, and then his enemy. Mender's nature precluded haughty eyes, a lying tongue, hands that shed innocent blood, feet swift to run into mischief, deceitful witness that uttered lies, and sowing discord among brethren. Menders were neither loyal nor disloyal. Menders did not display lust, gluttony, greed, sloth, wrath, envy, and pride. Likewise Menders did not show signs of chastity, temperance, charity, diligence, patience, kindness, and humility. Menders did not seek adultery, fornication, uncleanness, lasciviousness, idolatry, witchcraft, hatred, variance, emulations, wrath, strife, seditions, heresies, envying, murders, drunkenness, revelings, "and such things."

Menders understood mending.

For many generations the ancient Menders had lived among the other peoples and exchanged their talents for sustenance. Although the Kiennish General considered them spineless creatures, Saligia appreciated the value of the Menders. Had anyone seen a female Mender? Or a little one? Come to think of it, he'd only seen Fisher. Fisher had served Saligia's father Dydracks. The pale healer never aged, never changed. Lore held all Menders looked and acted the same. The healers were totally neutral…what an odd alignment!

The Mender had treated Saligia for many infirmities.

Menders didn't cast spells. The pale healers commanded great knowledge of natural and herbal remedies. Fisher's sleep poultice contained thirteen herbs and spices. Specifically, valerian root, dream fruit, passionless fruit, booderries, byneberries, melon toning, butter fly, slumber berry, nodding ham, kava kava, lavender, rose petals, and a live cricket. The identity of the ingredients was commonplace knowledge. Only Menders knew the secret of mixing the ingredients and creating the cataplasm.

Ingredients…

13 herbs and spices…

Fisher approached the General and said, "The poultice works quickly. Are you ready to retire?"

"I've a big day on the morrow. My mind races. Work your Magick, Mender," Saligia ordered.

"I'll apply the poultice to your brow when you are ready. It's not Magick, Lord Saligia. It's skill," Fisher platonically replied.

Fisher took a soft fabric from his old mooler hide bag and produced a rare pewter container. Delicately the Mender reached his long thin white fingers into the unguent, removed some of the thick aromatic dark green substance, and applied the goop to the fabric. Fisher then placed the saturated fabric onto Saligia's broad forehead.

The Kiennite took a deep breath and said, "Well done. Your services are well worth what you are paid. Do you want for anything?"

"General, you should recline. Soon the poultice will induce sleep. Rest well," the Mender answered.

Saligia nodded and turned toward his large bed.

Fisher cleaned the green poultice from his fingers, gathered his implements, and left the General alone. The healer walked passed the guards outside Saligia's quarters and followed the familiar corridors to his lodgings. Fisher entered his quarters and sat on the firm bed in his austere room. Aulgmoor had been his home for... a long time. The Kiennites provided what the Mender needed. He did not know hunger. He was warm and comfortable. He wanted nothing more. He practiced his trade. The Drolls and Kiennites gave him plenty of work.

His treatments did not require prior approval.

Drolls paid co-payments of ale, mead, and blue bee honey.

Saligia demanded no formulary restrictions.

His services did not require a referral.

Menders needed no insurance.

Menders followed no treatment guidelines.

Menders had no peer review; they seldom saw another of their ilk.

Menders had no certification exams.

The healers did not undergo Recertification.

Being a Mender didn't require licensure.

Once a Mender, always a Mender...

There was no Mender Board.

Menders didn't belong to the Mender Association of Parallan.

Menders were just Menders.

CHAPTER 31
A Gift for the Teacher

The dark period ended.

The Drelves busily prepared stews, poultices, potions, and unguents from the bountiful harvest of the enhancing root. Rumsie had worked with Gaelyss, Kirrie, Zachary, and Taylor. Edkim used the time to talk with the elders about the trek to Meadowsweet. Clarke and Klunkus returned from the red meadow and joined Edkim and Rumsie for a repast in the bright light of the light period. Little Meries shared its rays of its warm reassuring light with the world. Gaelyss excused himself to study the spell book. Balewyn took Kirrie, Zachary, and Taylor aside and worked with their archery skills. As the light period gave way to the amber light of the so-named period, fatigue overcame the industrious Drelves.

The Drelve leaders sat by a small fire and enjoyed a few moments to rest and recollect. Edkim, Rumsie, Klunkus, Clarke, and Balewyn knew the defenses were in the good hands of Beaux, Loganne, Meryt, Bryce, Zack, and Debery.

Kirrie walked from the common area of Alms Glen into the forest. She stretched her weary arms and yawned. A bluebird rested briefly on her shoulder as she stood quietly. She heard a rustle in the hedgerow.

"Sleep, child," a matronly voice murmured soothingly.

Kirrie dropped to her knees, leaned onto a plush bed of orange moss, and fell asleep.

By the fire, Edkim said, "Klunkus you have worked beyond expectations. I want you to spend this amber period sleeping. Go to your tree. Take a bit of time to be with your family."

"I work hard to make life safer for them. My mind wanders to them often. Does this weaken me as a ranger?" the veteran Klunkus asked.

"It goes both ways, my friend," Rumsie answered. "Thinking of my life-mate Poohbie energizes me. My daughter Sara Jane attains her twelfth season. If all goes well, she'll go to Green Vale for the next harvest. My son Landon is seven. I find solace in my time with them, and thinking of them warms the long periods on the perimeter. My family makes me a better Drelvish ranger, I think," Rumsie said.

"Clarke and I have never taken a life mate, so we can't give a perspective on this issue," the Teacher Edkim added.

"Clarke is too ornery, too crusty. No self respecting she-Drelve could put up with him," Klunkus chided.

Clarke drew on his briar pipe, exhaled sweet smelling smoke, and replied, "Very funny, Klunkus. You must have found some charming weed and used it on my brother's daughter Diana Maceda. Your beautiful life mate Diana never saw it coming!"

"Charming weed! I wooed Diana with *my* charm. Where could you find something as rare as charming weed? You old blighter!" Klunkus parried.

"Now, now. Old friends shouldn't barb one another. Enjoy your pipeweed, Clarke. Klunkus, I think you'd have calmer time with your family," Edkim said, but couldn't hold back a chuckle.

"No offense, my good friend," old Clarke said, as he smiled and extended his wrinkled hand to Klunkus.

"Certainly none taken, you old buzzard," Klunkus answered.

He patted his oldest friend Clarke on the shoulder, stood, bowed to the Teacher, saluted Rumsie, and went off toward the yellow poplar tree he and his family called home.

Clarke blew a few smoke rings. The smoke changed to red, blue, then violet color as it left his old pipe, a Maceda family heirloom. Klunkus's life-mate Diana Maceda was Clarke Maceda's niece. Clarke was Diana's godfather.

"Klunkus is a valuable talent. I'd like him to be more careful," Rumsie added.

Clarke asked, "Teacher, why are you not espoused? Is it a tradition for Teachers to be bachelors?"

"No, not necessarily. It's an individual matter," the Teacher answered. His long time friends noted discomfort in his tone.

"I realize, we've never talked about this. Clarke, why are you a bachelor? Is Klunkus correct?" Rumsie asked his friend.

"There're reasons we haven't had this discussion, fellows. Let's change the subject. Wait! Someone approaches," Clarke answered.

Clarke wasn't worried about an enemy. He didn't want other Drelves to hear their personal bantering. Young *Kirrie* approached the three patriarchs of Alms Glen.

"Kirrie, you should be resting. How may we help you?" the Teacher Edkim asked.

"I sorry to interrupt your quiet time, Teacher. I cannot sleep. I hope to spend time with the Spellweaver on the morrow. I was wondering if I might consult the tomes in your library for a time. But if you are going to be away from your tree, I don't want to inconvenience you," Kirrie asked apologetically.

"Rumsie, Clarke, and I have much to discuss, so I plan to be up a while. You won't disturb me. As you know the Old Orange Spruce always permits your entry with me, but I need not be with you. You can enter by whispering my daily pass code to the old tree. Just say 'Yannuvia's return' and the bark will permit you to enter. As you know the library is in the lower chamber. I just returned the last volume of the annals before I came to the common area," Edkim answered.

Kirrie answered, "Thank you, Teacher. Excuse my interruption, rangers. I'll leave you to your discussions. By the way, Clarke, *I* find you very handsome."

Edkim and Rumsie laughed.

Clarke harrumphed and said, "Now there's a she-Drelve with good taste."

Kirrie left the threesome and they resumed their reminiscences. They discussed plans for the next few periods' defensive rotations. Rumsie hoped to get the veterans a bit more rest. Edkim reiterated his goal to advance the Spellweaver and young community members' training. Clarke planned recruiting trips to settlements deeper in the Central Forest. Individual Drelves showed up daily. The Drelves' numbers at the Lone Oak meadow had never been greater.

Still the Teacher worried.

Why had the Drolls and Kiennites not attacked?

Why did the sentries note the absence of the gnarly Kiennites?

Was the griffon rider accurate in his estimation of the numbers of Drolls near the Ornash?

Was it worth the risk to send a scouting party to the fringes of the realms of the Kiennite in the Doombringer Mountains?

Questions...

Edkim pondered these and many other questions as he made his way back to the Old Orange Spruce. He glanced at the sky. Orpheus sat dark and unchanging high in the sky. Meries sat at midpoint, typical for its location in the amber period. He realized half a period, about four hours, had passed since he had sent Klunkus off to bed. His aching bones yearned for the softness of his bed.

The Teacher reached the old familiar tree and effortlessly passed through the outer bark. Quickly Edkim realized he was not alone. The Good Witch sat comfortably on the settee in his foyer. The beautiful, mature female had smooth, lovely white skin and deep blue eyes. Soft blonde hair fell gently down the length of her back. She was as tall as a Droll, which made her time and a half as tall as the Teacher. Now she wore a short white dress made of cottony fabric, which stopped alluringly several inches above her knees and exposed her smooth long legs. Her silky hands ended in long fingers with well-groomed nails.

She spoke with a sultry voice, "How do you like this, Teacher? Is this better?"

"How'd you get in here?" Edkim exclaimed.

"Are you sure you aren't *dreaming*?" she asked coyly.

"That's the one thing I am sure of at this moment. You didn't answer my question," Edkim demanded.

For once, he wanted for a weapon. He readied the Magick Missile command in his mind.

"You invited me. 'Yannuvia's return', indeed. You obviously cling to the hope your lost Spellweaver will walk through the wall of your tree at any time. You didn't listen to me, you bad boy! Should I punish you?" the Good Witch asked as she seductively crossed her legs.

"Kirrie! What…what have you done to Kirrie?" Edkim stammered.

"The little fairy is having a nap. She's fine. She needed rest. I wouldn't hurt her. Her tortured mind would not allow her to sleep. You know I am right. She must, like you, stop yearning for something that won't happen. Yannuvia is gone. Gaelyss is here. My Sleep Spell helped accomplish two ends. Kirrie needed sleep, and I needed to talk to you. Are you interested?" she asked seductively.

"I am interested in the welfare of my people, Good Witch, or whatever your name is! How can you know so much about our lost Spellweaver and us? I should be rid of you," Edkim declared.

The Teacher extended his left hand and prepared to use the spell he had learned at Green Vale.

"Don't you remember from your dream? Amica. Amica Carmisino. My name is Amica Carmisino. Please don't hurt me, Mister Magick Edkim. I only want to help. Check the plush moss by her tree. You'll see Kirrie is fine. I'll wait for you. But time wastes. Thundering hooves head your way. Have you considered the damage a hundred firehorses would do to a forest?" the Good Witch answered.

"I might just go to Kirrie's tree. But…for some reason I believe you about Kirrie. Rumsie confirmed everything you relayed to me while I slept. It's odd to say such a thing! For some reason I believe…blast you, are you *charming* me?" Edkim stammered.

"You are tired, Teacher. I mean you no harm," she replied calmly. "If you want to attack me with a Magick Missile, I won't resist. Should I open my raiment so you can more clearly see the path to my heart?" she replied.

The Good Witch stood, walked across the small foyer, and placed one hand on each of the Teacher's shoulders.

Edkim noted the sweetness of her breath. She dropped her left hand, took his left hand, and slowly led him to the settee.

"Sit. Rest. Know that your charges are safe this evening. I don't know what the morrow holds. The future of *this* world is complex. The future of Magick rests in your hands…and the hands of your Spellweaver. I'll help you however I can. Close your eyes. Put your feet upon my lap. Relax," she caringly whispered.

Edkim sighed. Had she wanted to attack him, she certainly could have done it by now.

He relaxed.

"Be my burden," she whispered.

Edkim leaned back of the soft settee and closed his eyes. Soft light enveloped him and he felt comfortable. The Good Witch extended her left arm and gently rubbed his long browning hair. Vestiges of youthfulness remained in his locks. Her touch rejuvenated his spirit. He opened his eyes and stared into her ashen face. A flicker of red penetrated the deep blueness in her eyes. Still she was beyond beautiful.

"What do you want?" the Teacher asked.

"Only the continuation of what is good is this world. Only the betterment of the World of the Three Suns. Only the success of your Spellweaver. Edkim, let me help you," the Good Witch asked.

"You say you want those things most important to me. Is that what you say to all whose dreams you violate, Dreamraider?" he asked.

"That was not nice. You are tired. Like Kirrie, you need sleep. Nature's gentle nurse will restore your reasoning. First I must give you a gift," *Amica* said alluringly.

"I do not seek pleasures of flesh, Good Witch," Edkim insisted.

"I haven't offered them! *Yet!*" Amica answered indignantly.

She removed her arm from his shoulder, pushed his legs from her lap, and stood.

Smiling caringly, the Good Witch rolled the digits of her left hand and created a small ball of deep blue flame. The blue flame emitted no heat, but instead chilled the entire foyer. She softly inhaled and then unhurriedly exhaled gray smoke, which enveloped the little ball of flame. Amica Carmisino then allowed the smoke enshrouded blue fireball to rest in her palm. The smoke condensed and cleared. The *icy* blue fireball transformed to a smooth round gray stone.

Slowly the temperature in the great tree returned to normal. Edkim sat up and stared at his visitor and the little stone.

"Cold Stone. I offer you this gift. Use it wisely, Teacher. In the hands of a Light Sorcerer, Dark Sorcerer, Witch, or Spellweaver, its use is limitless. In your hands, it may only be used once. When you are facing fire, Teacher, only then should you play this ace. The power of the Cold Stone is beyond young Gaelyss. Given time, that may change. For now, the Cold Stone is your charge. Of the stone, tell only those you feel you must," the Good Witch stated convincingly and extended her hand to offer the gray stone.

Edkim reflexively jerked his left hand backward, then quickly extended it forward and accepted the stone. The rock was initially cold and firm, much like a stone plucked from the bottom of a cool stream. Then the stone felt warm and soft like willing flesh. The softened stone conformed to the shape of the Teacher's left hand.

"It's alive!" he stammered.

"Oh, not like you and I. It's Magick. It's from the *source* of Magick, Teacher. Just for fun, use it to chill your beverage on a hot day. Remember my words," the Good Witch explained.

"You are beautiful. I don't understand. I can't control my mind when I am around you, whether dreaming or awake as I am now. My world is usually so ordered. I have thoughts I'd normally not have. I have urges...I..." Edkim said, his voice fading.

The womanly figure smiled again and gently touched his cheek with her left index finger.

She cooed, "Maybe you should you give in to your feelings. I'm here. You're here. Now, *I'm offering...*"

Edkim shook his head negatively. "I am the Teacher. I will accept the gift of your Cold Stone, though I understand neither how you invade and speak to us in our dreams nor why you offer the stone to me."

She smiled and said demurely, "Mysterious. That's the idea."

For a moment they stood together, and she held his hand softly. Then she bent forward, gently bussed his lips, released his hand, turned, and walked through the door. Edkim stood alone in the foyer of the Old Orange Spruce. The stone in his hand was again cold. The Good Witch's delightful scent lingered in the room. The Teacher did not tarry in the foyer. He rushed through the tree. A brief flash of blue light interrupted the amber light. Hurriedly, the Teacher ran to Kirrie's modest home tree.

He tapped on the bark and said, "Kirrie, are you within your tree?"

"Teacher?" a sleepy voice within the tree replied.

"Yes, may I enter?" Edkim asked.

"Certainly," she answered back.

"Are you well?" he asked frantically.

"Yes, is it time to begin the day's work? I fell asleep on the trail and lost track of time. I notice, though, the amber period continues," Kirrie asked sleepily.

"Is it really *you*?" he queried oddly and touched her forearm slightly.

"Teacher, are *you* well? Do you have fever? Did you sample the mead?" Kirrie asked.

"I'm…I'm OK. I just had a dream. If you know what I mean," the Teacher answered ashamedly.

"I know *exactly* what you mean, Teacher," Kirrie responded. "Do you want me to walk you to your tree? Would you like to stay here? I'll sleep on the floor," Kirrie offered.

"I…no, I'll return to my home. The amber period is only half over. Give no one your pass code, Kirrie. Meet me by the Spellweaver's tree at the beginning of the next amber period," Edkim requested.

"Teacher, that's a period and a half from now. Shouldn't we be working?" the young she-Drelve queried.

"I think we both need rest, and I have some serious reading to do," Edkim replied.

"I could help," she offered.

A flash of red light heralded her arrival in the barren rocky cavern. Its lone familiar inhabitant raised its massive head and turned its eight eyes toward her.

"You've been gone long enough! Did you succeed?" the demon asked.

"Yessss. I did what I wassss told to do, you big horse's ********," She hissed defiantly.

"We spread ourselves thin. The Master has tasks for you. Work on the lisp!" the eight-eyed beast muttered.

"Kissssssss my ********, Arachnissss," the she-demon hissed.

She turned defiantly, stepped on the blue stone, and disappeared in a flash of blue light.

Arachnis smirked.

CHAPTER 32
Mobilization

To the north, Saligia made ready. Already the seven warren lords of the Kiennites, Woodrow, Wilson, Calvin, Coolidge, Theodore, Delano, and Roosevelt had departed.

General Saligia dispatched couriers to the Gap Keep to give word to Tumuch, the erstwhile Piercie, to move forward with the firehorse cavalry, one of the most fearsome of the Kiennites' armaments.

Most Kiennites couldn't control the large firehorses. The Kiennish noble Tumuch shared the Korcrans' exceptional farrier skills and approximated Drollen stature. The Korcran clan chose Drollen firehorse riders from the multitude of Drollen warriors of the northern clans. Fire riders were highly trained and indoctrinated in the care of the rare temperamental animals. The Kiennish warren lord Tumuch commanded a force of a hundred such firehorses and riders. The Korcran clan had always managed to capture the volatile steeds. Now the clan's leaders muttered about a "lost treasure." The Kiennites Saligia and Tumuch weren't privy to all Korcran dealings.

Saligia also sent envoys to the Drolls' leader Moochie who maintained the force harassing the Drelves at the red meadow, the realm of the Lone Oak. Frustrated by nine dark periods of waiting, the big Droll was unhappy with the envoy's instructions to delay any attack against the Drelves. To this point, only small numbers of warriors from the many Drollen clans arrived each period. His orders had been clear.

Language was finicky.

To some, a thousand of his folk were a thousand Drolls; to others, a thousand Droll; a village might be called Drollen, simply Droll, but not *Drollish*. *Kiennish* described something related to Moochie's gnarly allies, the Kiennites. But *Drollish described* nothing. *Drollish* was thought superfluous. The big warrior thought all this foolish, but some of his ilk would fight over the pronunciation of their names. However, none of Drollen ilk was as bad as the Kiennites. He thought of the Kiennish warren lord Pierce, who changed his name to Tumuch, because others teased him "too much." Moochie chuckled. One named Moochie couldn't belittle another's name *too much*. The name had served the big Droll well, and Moochie had smacked many who belittled his moniker. He enjoyed smacking people around. Their teasing him about his name just gave him another reason.

Moochie laughed aloud and startled the subordinates who stood around him at the fringes of the western border of the red meadow.

"Keep the Drelves on edge but don't fully engage them," the communiqué had clearly stated.

But with the orders the courier had brought kegs of the best mead and bundles of the best smoking weed. After nine dark periods of inaction, Moochie just wanted to fight. Otherwise the Drollen clan leader was happy with his relationship with the Kiennites. Though disgruntled, Moochie followed his orders.

Clattering hooves and neighing beasts of burden lifted the Drollen commander's spirits, until Moochie realized horse and mooler-drawn wagons, and not cavalry, approached. The wagons carried large axes. Field laborers followed them.

The wyvern hide clad courier ordered, "Note well these orders. 'Equip your warriors with axes. Send them into the wild wood. Harvest the trees. Bring the timbers to the edge of the wood. Construct battlements by these drawings and instructions.' The orders bear the signature of Lord Saligia of Aulgmoor."

"Bah! My warriors want to draw blood, not sap! Why do we delay? My horses are champing at the bit, and my warriors are gnawing the rawhide that binds the pack animals," Moochie chagrinned.

"Why don't you tell Lord Saligia you disagree with his orders?" the envoy Neville smirked.

"Don't get smart with me! I'll whip you just for the fun of it!" the Droll growled.

The much smaller gnarly Kiennite drew back and stuttered, "You…you best not lay a hand on me! I wear the garb of the wyvern! I am the emissary of the Lord of Aulgmoor."

"I know! I know! If I were going to maim you, you'd already be maimed! Tell your boss we are following orders and being good boys," Moochie conceded.

"I'll tell *our* boss you have a bad attitude but carry out his orders," Neville responded.

"All Drolls have a bad attitude. It's what makes us Drolls! Now get out of here!" Moochie growled.

Neville departed.

Moochie gathered his subordinates and growled, "OK, you blokes, grab an axe and hit the woods. I mean literally hit the woods. The boss in Aulgmoor wants us to fell some trees. Maybe it'll make the Drelves mad and they'll come out of their trees, run over here, and pick a fight. Looks like that is the only way we're getting to fight. I want to hear some timber falling. And try not to land any trees on another Droll or Kiennite! If a tree falls on one of your hard heads, it'd damage the wood!" Moochie shouted.

The grumbling Droll warriors reluctantly dropped their broadswords and bows, took axes from the wagons, dispersed into the trees, and began to chop away.

Across the way the Drelvish archer Balewyn sat upon the tallest red oak and used his "toot and see scroll" looking glass to look toward the north. His keen eyes picked up the arrival of the Kiennish emissary and several heavy horse drawn wagons. Somewhat relieved that the hooves he had heard approach were not cavalry, the veteran archer had nonetheless alerted his fellows to the increased activity in the wild woods on the far side of the red meadow. In a few moments, Rumsie was by his side.

"What have you seen, Balewyn?" the Drelve's Sergeant Major asked.

"The Drolls have descended into the woods with axes. They are chopping down large numbers of trees. I hear the timbers falling. My spirit feels the pain of the trees," Balewyn sighed.

"As do I. Why are the Drolls cutting down the forest? Drelves don't live in the wild woods. Drolls are not woodsmen. They are jackleg lumberjacks. I'm sending for the Teacher and the Spellweaver," Rumsie answered.

Balewyn continued to watch the bustling activity.

Edkim arrived with Gaelyss. Gaelyss cast a Detect Magick Spell and shook his head negatively. The young Spellweaver then cast Speak with Animals and communed with a small furry beast that had fled from the wild woods.

"The Drolls are wantonly chopping down trees. They carry the felled trees to a central area where they are assembling...rafts, or picket fences, or a stockade, or a fort. They are grumbling constantly and their morale is low, according to my friend the woodchuck. I detect no Magick among their work, but from this distance, assessment is difficult," Gaelyss reported.

"Should I go investigate under the cover of invisibility," Debery asked.

"No. It's too risky. They'd smell you and hear you. If the Drolls want to build a fort, they can rot inside it. We shan't attack them, for I have no desire to occupy the wild woods. We'll hold our ground. Spellweaver, can you assist us with Entangle and Plant Growth Spells. There are a lot of Drolls in the area. They could attack at any time. Do you have any suggestions, Teacher?" Rumsie asked.

"I don't know why the Drolls would build a fortress. Kiennites build edifices, but Drolls are largely nomadic. Blanchard has told us he saw a large fortress near Aulgmoor. The griffon rider Lapaglia told us he saw many Drolls and Kiennites in the area, but I don't know how much I trust him. I've pondered whether we should risk a recon into the area around Aulgmoor," Edkim answered.

"A recon to Aulgmoor! Teacher, the way is too hazardous!" Balewyn said dumbfounded.

"True. But the Drolls disdain the underground caves. Our archives tell of pathways through the caverns. The entryway is somewhere near the Alluring Falls," the Teacher answered.

"Getting to the underground caverns would be nigh impossible. There's no way to avoid open ground near Mirror Mountain. The Alluring Falls are cursed! If you make the caverns, beasts of untold vileness roam in the darkness. The darkness…how you'd propose we'd see in the darkness?" old Blanchard asked.

The elder had arrived from Alms Glen to join the discussion.

"I suppose you're right. It would be hazardous. I would like to know what's going through the Kiennish leaders' minds. Drolls follow brute force. In a hand-to-hand fight, the wily wolf-faced beasts are second to none, save maybe an ogre or giant. But the Kiennites are cunning and intelligent. We have felt the power of their spells. I lost the neophyte Bystar to a Magick Missile cast by a Kiennish shaman. Time isn't on our side. When they unite against a common enemy, in this case us, the Drolls don't battle among themselves and their numbers increase. They hate us. The Kiennites always bear us ill will, but usually don't attack us without reason. They are envious, conniving, ill tempered, and unpredictable. They ally with the Drolls. I certainly would like to know what has riled them up against us," the Teacher pondered.

The veteran Tomayo had been listening to the discussion and interjected, "Remember the wounded Droll we found nine dark periods ago. We surmised a tree sprite or a Dryad attacked him. His comrades were likely lost in the wild woods."

Loganne, the seventeen year-old daughter of the elder Moblee, said, "The arrow was clearly not Drelvish. How could they blame us for whatever befell their comrades?"

"Tree sprites are mischievous and aggravating, but I don't see how a thousand of them could take out a group of Drolls and Kiennites. Kiennites and Drolls don't need a reason to attack us. They are malicious," Clarke added.

As time passed prominent Drelves continued to arrive. Now the elder Blanchard, old Clarke, Tomayo, young Loganne, Rumsie, Meryt, Bryce, Debery, Zack, the Teacher Edkim, the Spellweaver Gaelyss, the archer Balewyn, Klunkus, Beaux, and young Kirrie gathered by the tree herder they called Old Yellow. Tree herders had names but they were unlikely to give them up. Old Yellow had been around a long time and had a preponderance of yellow leaves. He was old, yellow, and liked the name Old Yellow. The Drelves used the shade of the aged golden tree for strategy meetings. Of course the location changed because the tree herder uprooted and meandered along the fringe of the forest to groom his flock of everreds and red oaks. The younger Drelves separated from the main group and sat beneath a Rose Maple to take nourishment before resuming their watches.

"I would like to see Yannuvia return," Kirrie whispered to Loganne.

"Don't waste your breath, young one. He's gone," Loganne answered.

"Who's watching Alms Glen, if we are all here?" Kirrie asked.

"Every Drelve is a fighter in these times, Kirrie. The common area is in the good hands of Glinne, Carinne, and my father Moblee. Zachary and Taylor are becoming more proficient by the cycle of Meries. So are you, Kirrie," Loganne responded.

"I hear more Drelves are coming to the area. Perhaps a contingent from Meadowsweet will arrive soon. The Teacher feels we should reinforce the defenses of the Lone Oak meadow," Meryt said.

"Meadowsweet? Would not reducing our strength at Meadowsweet jeopardize the safety of the enhancing plants and the Green Vale? I thought their roles indispensable," Kirrie asked.

"Old Morin and Ulysses are pretty tough. The trees surrounding the Green Vale heartily protect the area. Magick guards its own," Loganne answered.

"And no Droll could find the path to the Green Vale. Giant fly traps and the wayward triffids would feed on trespassing Kiennites," Bryce guffawed.

"Wayward triffids? What are wayward triffids?" Kirrie asked.

"The orange triffids you see about you are our friends. Wayward triffids have a yen for flesh, and they don't mind if it comes from a Drelve," Debery added.

"Why does the Teacher not tell us of these beasts?" Kirrie queried with concern.

"Because they don't live in these woods," Edkim's voice sternly answered. "Flesh eating triffids live far from Alms Glen. It's more important you learn things of greater immediacy."

"Yes, Teacher. We'll be getting back to our watch," Debery quickly responded.

Two dark periods passed.

The Drolls busily worked in the wild wood forests across the way. During that time many Drelves arrived and reinforced their brethren.

CHAPTER 33
The Battle of Lone Oak Meadow Begins

Moochie awakened in a particularly bad mood. His warriors had become wood workers. Finally the courier Neville returned from Aulgmoor.

"I have orders. You are to attack the great tree on the morrow. Lord Saligia will arrive soon. Tumuch rides from the Gap Keep with a hundred firehorses. Your attack will precede the arrival of the cavalry," the Kiennite said and handed a letter to the big Droll.

"Why attack the tree? I've never seen it do anything more than give shade. There are legends, but that's all they are. A hundred firehorses! They won't leave anything for us! My boys have labored in these woods for 150 cycles of Meries, including the dark periods. Now you tell me the fun of ravaging the Drelves falls to a bunch of horsemen. After we've done all the work here! Balderdash! ****!" Moochie complained.

"Just stop complaining. Lord Saligia has sent barrels of mead! You should shut up and drink your mead!" Neville smirked.

"Some day!" the big Droll countered. "I tolerate you because you bring such grand brew."

"You tolerate me because you are ordered to do so," the Kiennite smugly answered.

Moochie fumed, but even orders to attack the great tree meant at least something was happening.

Tomayo sent word to Rumsie of the arrival of a Kiennish contingent.

On the morrow, at the beginning of the light period, Moochie stepped to the edge of the expansive red meadow.

"Archers! Move onto the field. Advance to a hundred paces of the great tree. Wait for my command!" Moochie bellowed.

The yellow, orange, red, and violet leaves of the great masterful Lone Oak fluttered in the morning breeze.

On duty at the tallest red oak, old Clarke jumped with alarm. Hearing an ominous sound in the distance, he motioned to the chattering Drelves around him and asked them to remain as quiet as possible. In the distance he heard the low rumble of thunder but the amber skies were clear. Across the way many Drolls' harsh voices shattered the quietness of the morning. Shortly thereafter a large number of Drolls moved onto the red meadow at a rapid pace. Armed with long bows, the Drolls stopped a hundred paces from the Lone Oak.

"Make ready! They come!" Clarke bellowed.

The trees on the Alms Glen side of the red meadow burst into activity. (This would be the eastern side of the red meadow if one held a compass.) Drelves scurried up the larger trees and runners left for the common area to summon reinforcements. Rumsie kept half the adult Drelves at the front at all times. Many Drelves of Alms Glen referred to Meryt, Zack, Bryce, and Debery as Receivers of the Gift of Magick. The four young Drelves preferred the four caballeros. Two of the four caballeros always stood at ready. The foursome managed some fellowship at the change of duty but otherwise duties kept them apart. The Teacher usually remained at the common area to instruct the young, and Gaelyss spent most of his time studying *the Gifts of Andreas to the People of the Forest*. Per chance both the Teacher and Spellweaver were at the front line when the Drolls ran onto the meadow. They joined Rumsie and Clarke in the high branches of the great red oak. Rumsie and Clarke stared thorough looking glasses on the field.

"Don't waste arrows. Every shot must count. They outnumber us. Wait until they come into range before you fire!" Rumsie commanded.

A hundred longbows trained on the advancing Drolls. The Drolls ran to within a hundred paces of the Lone Oak, halfway encircled the great tree on the western side, and faced the Drelves in the Forest of Alms Glen. The big warriors halted their charge and began to shout taunts toward the Drelves.

"I estimate they number five hundred. Why have they stopped? Watch the trees behind them. All the clearing they've done exposes their positions. Fools!" Clarke reported.

"I see Kiennites and more Drolls in the trees. They are bringing something forward. It looks like...it can't be...they've constructed a giant moving wooden fortress... a log wall. It rolls on hewn logs. Slowly...the walls are made of whole trees bound together by pitch and adherer hides. There're other bizarre constructions! The Drolls have stopped the machines at the wood's edge. The Drolls near the great tree carry bows. They are insulting our mothers and fathers," Tomayo reported.

"Words will not hurt us. Nor will their bows from this distance. Hold your fire," Rumsie ordered.

"Adherer hides? What are adherers?" Kirrie asked Loganne.

"Beasts covered by sticky goop. Weapons stick to them. You'll stick to them if you strike or touch them. Evidently lots of the slimy bear like beasts roam the high forests of the Doombringers near Aulgmoor. You wouldn't want to meet one. I'm told adherers are fond of Drelve. But now's not the time for a bestiary lesson," Loganne replied. "Listen!"

Again the Drelves heard a distant roll of thunder to the north. The sound was barely audible over the shouts of the Drolls on the meadow. The large wolf-faced warriors worked themselves into frenzy. Typically Drolls carried long broad swords or two-handed axes, disdained shields, and carried longbows strapped across their broad backs. One of the larger Drolls moved nearer the Lone Oak, spat on the great tree, and made an obscene gesture toward the Drelves.

"What's the point of that behavior? The spittle will nourish the tree. He expends energies needlessly. What are they doing?" Rumsie pondered as he looked through the glass.

Across the field, Moochie the Droll clan leader moaned, "What are we doing? I've seen adolescent boondoggles, moon doggies, and baby boomers accomplish more. When may I attack?"

Neville replied, "What are boondoggles, moon doggies, and baby boomers?"

"Nothing is as slow and inefficient as a boondoggle, but if they are properly prepared, the giant slugs make a tasty stew. Moon doggies just lie around all day and soak up the suns' light. Unfortunately their apathy is contagious. Boomers are ground nesting birds, which get their name from their loud calls. Bust your eardrums if you aren't careful. Dangerous beaks. Baby boomers are little boomers. They're easy to find because they make lots of noise and easy to catch because they are slow. You Kiennites don't get out in the world much, do you?" Moochie sardonically answered.

"We do what we must. We have others, my comical friend, do the more mundane tasks like catching fowl for the table. The rolling fortresses are almost in position and I see the smoke from the approaching firehorses. You may attack the tree soon."

"Thank you for small favors. I've sent my warriors to beat up on a piece of wood. But the Lone Oak is an important landmark to the foolish Drelves. Our actions might draw them out of their hiding places, cowards that they are," Moochie surmised.

"Very insightful, comrade. You may show promise yet," the Kiennish wyvern clad courier Neville replied.

A rider approached.

"A rider approaches the far wood!" the sentry Clarke shouted.

Sergeant Major Rumsie and the Drelvish leaders peered through "toot and see scroll" looking glasses and monitored the situation across the way.

The Kiennite Neville and the Droll's clan leader Moochie walked to meet the messenger, a wiry Kiennite who rode in on a large wolf spider. Smaller Kiennites oft times used the big furry spiders as steeds. Eight legs were better than two, four, or six. Drolls preferred the arachnids in stews or roasted over the fire.

The rider panted, "A message from Lord Saligia. He will arrive on the morrow. He wants the attack on the tree to begin. Observe the Drelves' response."

"I am Neville. I call the shots here! Show me your authentication," Neville demanded.

"I have ridden this cursed spider for a period and a half. I'm hungry, thirsty, and tired. I'm the personal envoy of the warren masters. My name's Chamberlain, Neville! The warren lords Woodrow, Wilson, Calvin, Coolidge, Theodore, Delano, and Roosevelt have concluded meetings with Lord Saligia at Aulgmoor. If you don't follow this order, Lord Saligia'll feed you to this spider. He's as hungry as I am and a lot more ornery. Blighter tried to bite my legs several times. I thought he was spider-broken. Where are you from, Neville?" the spider rider quipped.

Noting the big arachnid's drooling, Neville replied timidly. "I serve, as did my father, at the Gap Keep. But I've been to Aulgmoor many times! Lord Saligia favors me!"

"Lord Saligia favors me! I ride his spider!" Chamberlain countered.

"I wear the wyvern hide!" Neville argued.

"So do I!" Chamberlain quarreled.

The Kiennites traded barbs a few times. Then Chamberlain showed Neville an amulet bearing the seal of Aulgmoor, which validated the spider rider's message.

Moochie grinned and enjoyed the Kiennites' bickering.

"What are you waiting for, Commander Moochie? Attack the ****** tree!" Neville barked.

"As you wish, *my little masters*," the big Droll replied and bowed facetiously.

The immense Droll walked onto the red meadow and raised his war lance.

Across the way, Clarke relayed, "The Kiennish rider sat upon a great black spider. After some discussion, they've sent a Droll onto the field. He's signaling the warriors in the field. The warriors are arming their bows."

"This doesn't make sense. We can't reach them with our bows. They certainly can't reach us. The Long Oak stands in the center of the circular shaped red meadow. The meadow has a periphery of 6765 Yardley paces, or yards. The Lone Oak stands roughly a thousand paces from our perches. The Drolls stand another hundred paces beyond the tree and carry crude bows. The bowyer BJ has armed us with the finest bows and arrows. Most longbows have a range of about 200 yards. Our best modern bows may have a range of 360 yards. Silk gathered during an Approximation and used as bowstring doubles the range. The bowyer BJ's unique techniques produce the finest arrows. His arrows give another 100 yards of accuracy and distance. But 800 yards still won't reach the great tree. The enemies and the tree are too far away," Rumsie observed.

The Teacher Edkim agreed.

"The Drolls are stabbing their arrows into the ground before them. Teacher, what does this mean," Clarke reported.

"It reduces the time it takes to notch. They can fire more often. Also, the point of the arrow is more likely to cause an infection. I'm told Drolls use adherer glue to attach their arrowheads to the shaft. Removing an imbedded Drollen arrow is difficult, if not impossible," Edkim answered.

"How *does* one remove an arrow, Teacher?" Loganne asked.

"Dowels of wood soaked in blue bee honey will reduce the risk of infection. Increasing the size of the dowels widens the entry point and enables extraction of the arrow. I'd imagine it's quite painful. Enhancing root balms will help ease the pain. Let's hope you evade the Drolls' and Kiennites' slings and arrows," the Teacher answered.

"You may as well give us another lesson, Teacher. The Drolls continue to file around the Lone Oak. None have advanced toward our positions. Wait…they have fired a volley of arrows into the branches of the great tree! They are assailing the Lone Oak!" Clarke reported.

Five hundred or so crudely made arrows ripped through the branches of the Lone Oak. Many tore through the large yellow and red leaves. Some penetrated the thinner bark of the Lone Oak's limbs. Others reached the massive tree's truck, and either bounced off or barely pushed into the bark. Dark maroon sap flowed from the wounds created by the Drolls' arrows.

Every Drelve who had access to a "toot and see scroll" monocular peered through the looking glass. Many legends told of consequences of striking the tree or removing a leaf from the Lone Oak. Horrified, the Drelves watched as the Drolls' arrows ripped seven great leaves from the tree. The large leaves fluttered downward and came to rest on the ground.

The Drolls reloaded their longbows.

"I feel his pain," the tree herder Old Yellow communicated to the Drelves.

Occasionally tree herders spoke aloud. For the most part, the forest wonders communicated their thoughts telepathically.

"I do as well, old friend," the Teacher mumbled compassionately.

The Droll archers fired another volley. Hundreds of arrows cleaved more leaves from the Lone Oak's branches. Observers on both sides watched tensely and awaited the great tree's response. Numerous leaves fell upon the red meadow's grass. More dark sap flowed from the tree's wounds.

Mimicking the anguished screech of a dying night bird, Old Yellow wailed, "I can't endure this carnage!"

The tree herder pulled his massive roots from the ground and moved forward a few yards.

"No, my friend. The Drolls are taunting us! Please hold your ground," Rumsie pleaded.

The tree herder paused. Deep audible sobs emanated from the massive plant. On the field, the Drolls launched a third volley into the Lone Oak. Sap rolled like tears down Old Yellow's trunk.

"Sergeant Major Rumsie! Teacher! How can we watch this slaughter?" Loganne shouted.

Dragging his great roots behind him, the tree herder Old Yellow inched forward and now stood at the very edge of the red meadow.

"Great Tree Herder, you compromise our defensive line. You must hold your position! We depend on you! The Lone Oak seems little phased by the arrows. Please stay where you are, lest you break our line," Rumsie pleaded.

"How can I stand and do nothing?" Old Yellow sobbed.

"You must. For all our good," Edkim advised.

At the western edge of the red meadow Neville, Chamberlain, and Moochie watched the first three volleys. The Kiennites felt angst as the leaves fell from the Lone Oak.

Smirking, the Droll Moochie asked, "You High And Mighty Kiennites expected something mystical to happen, don't you? It's just a big, old tree. Its leaves fall to the ground and the enemy still hides in the far side of the wood. How long do we continue this charade?"

"Our orders, your orders are to attack the Lone Oak," Chamberlain and Neville chimed together.

"Their arrows aren't piercing the central trunk. Volley fire! Watch your aim, you idiots!" Moochie screamed.

The Droll archers fired one, two, three more volleys. By now leaves steadily fell from the Lone Oak's branches to the ground.

"Watch the field! Watch the tree line to our right! Stay at ready! Beaux, shore up the line behind Old Yellow. Where his movement has disrupted the underbrush, a direct assault will easily break through. Gaelyss, can you help?" Rumsie shouted, giving orders continually as he peered through the looking glass.

"Many Drolls lurk in the far wood. I can't discern their armament. The Droll commander shouts orders behind the archers. He stands with Kiennites. Here comes another volley!" Clarke shouted.

The Drelves watched three volleys of arrows deluge the Lone Oak and cause many wounds. Rivulets of maroon sap trickled down the trunk and limbs of the tree. The many arrows rapidly separated leaves and denuded the Lone Oak's branches.

"We are not really inflicting much damage on the tree. Leaves will grow back. Do you *mind* if I engage the tree with fire?" Moochie asked the Kiennites facetiously.

"Go ahead and fire the tree," Neville replied just as scathingly.

"Bring oil!" Moochie commanded.

Several Drolls carried large vessels from the trees to the proximity of the archers. A number of archers dipped arrows in the thick gooey tar. Other Drolls used a flint stone, created sparks, and ignited their arrows. The next volley included fifty or so flaming arrows. When the flaming arrows struck the Lone Oak, some created small fires, but the Lone Oak's dense wood and flowing sap prevented any major fires. Leaves now littered the ground and covered the red grass.

"Now the Lone Oak must endure fire! Tis more than I can bear!" Old Yellow the Tree Herder wailed.

The forest leviathan moved forward.

A wide gap appeared in the tree line where the tree herder had stood. Drelves quickly moved old brush into the area and the Spellweaver Gaelyss cast an Entangle Spell, which intertwined the existing vines. He followed with a Plant Growth dweomer. The spells partially filled the area vacated by the large tree herder. Though the tree herder's speed would win few races, Old Yellow's still pace surprised both Drelves and Drolls.

"I see movement across the way. Someone...something moves out from the tree line of the Drelves' forests. Have the Drelves constructed a war machine?" the Kiennite Chamberlain shouted with alarm.

"Well. It seems we've flushed out an opponent. We have another tree to fight," Moochie stated mockingly.

"Fool, that's not a tree! That's a tree herder, a shepherd of the woods. Your warriors are going to be in for a tussle with him," Neville chimed.

"Anybody he can catch deserves to die," the big Droll said wryly. He then added confidently, "The monstrosity moves toward the Lone Oak. He'll just be another target. This becomes target practice. My archers will mow them both down!"

"So far all they've only knocked off a lot of leaves. The wood of the great tree does not burn. The oil and flaming arrows have done little. Your attack is ineffective, Droll!" Chamberlain the envoy from Aulgmoor judged.

"You may address me as Lord Moochie, or Commander Moochie, or Boss, but you will show me respect, Kiennite! I've been sweating it out down here on this cursed meadow for over nine dark periods. My warriors have performed every menial task your liege of Aulgmoor has demanded. Now we have to fight the way you want. I say, let's go over to the trees and thrash the Drelves! Every passing period their Spellweaver casts more protective spells. We don't know how much Magick is at the bidding of the scum of Alms Glen. What say you?" Moochie angrily responded.

"I'd ask if you have a plan to attack the walking tree, *Commander* Moochie," Chamberlain sarcastically.

"I say you are insubordinate! If the Lone Oak still stands on the morrow when Lord Saligia arrives, the General will not be happy. We'll allow you to explain it to him, *Lord* Moochie," Neville answered contemptuously.

"With friends like you guys, who needs enemies," Moochie grumbled. Then the Droll commanded the archers on the field, "Fire, you dummies, fire at will!"

Hearing the command, five hundred Drolls repeatedly fired arrows into the Lone Oak.

CHAPTER 34
Old Yellow's Stand

Old Yellow dragged his roots along behind him and moved toward the great tree in the center of the red meadow. The tree herder's roots generated loud rumbling sounds akin to a landslide, but his tremendously heavy roots left the red grass undamaged. Old Yellow disdained hurting plants of any sort, even those as small as a blade of grass.

Gaelyss hurriedly cast spells. Beads of iridescent perspiration dripped from the young Spellweaver, fell to the ground, and burst into an array of colors. Refusing to stay in the rear, Kirrie wiped the Spellweaver's brow, gathered vines for him, and followed him along the edge of the forest as he worked. Beaux and his life-mate Maggie followed the Spellweaver and Kirrie closely with bows ready. For the moment Gaelyss concentrated on casting Snare Spells. The Snare Spell created a circular trap that blended into the red grass. Only Magick detected the snare. The spell entrapped any unfortunate creature that stepped into the circle of Magick. The Magick snare then dragged the victim upside down and suspended him from everred trees at the edge of the forest. The Spellweaver used small pieces of vine, snakeskin, and strong sinew as the spell's material components. Kirrie carried snakeskin and sinew for the Spellweaver. The Drelves had a very limited supply of such materials, and Gaelyss soon used up his stores. However, he had cast several snares, each of which could incapacitate one opponent. The Spellweaver informed the Drelvish sentries of the snares' locations. Gaelyss cast a Wall of Thorns Spell to fill the space vacated by Old Yellow. The spell created a barrier of very strong pliable red bushes bearing needle sharp thorns as long as a Droll's finger. Passing through the barrier caused serious injury. The Wall of Thorns covered an area about thirty paces by ten paces and plugged most of the gap created when Old Yellow uprooted.

The distraught tree herder now reached a point halfway to the Lone Oak.

"Nice work, Gaelyss," Rumsie commented. The Drelve's Sergeant Major continued, "I note the Drollen archers are slowing their fire."

Moochie the Drolls' tribal leader dryly commented, "We have a limited supply of arrows. I can't allow my archers to empty their quivers. My warriors' arrows have knocked thousands of supposedly enchanted leaves to the ground and effectively denuded the big tree, but the Lone Oak still stands. The cowardly Drelves remain hidden in their trees. My warriors have tested and shown to be false the foolish folklore surrounding the tree. Where is the Magick, my Kiennish friends?"

"Don't be a smart ***! I'd suggest you change tactics, *Boss*," Neville chided.

"We have two trees to fight. We'll attack hand to hand, or hand to limb! It's time to chop some wood. My troops have certainly *logged* enough experience lumberjacking. Five hundred warriors attack two trees, and only one is mobile. What a lark of a battle! What a waste of time! To axes!" Moochie commanded.

"Should we also attack, Commander?" a burly Droll asked from the woods behind the leaders.

"No. A hundred or so will surround the Lone Oak," Moochie moaned.

The veteran Drelve Clarke shouted from the highest tree, "The archers have dropped their bows and taken axes. They advance toward the Lone Oak."

"Sergeant Major Rumsey, Old Yellow is only halfway to the Lone Oak. Five hundred Drolls bearing axes charge the great tree. What should we do?" Tomayo asked.

"We lack the numbers to face them hand to hand. The attack on the Lone Oak is a ploy to draw us into the open. Clearly some force other than the brutish Drolls masterminds this battle plan. In my years I've never seen the great tree leafless. Yet the Lone Oak doesn't respond. Legends…are just legends, I suppose," Rumsie sighed.

"Teacher, what say you?" Tomayo continued.

"Probably our enemies the Kiennites foment this travesty. I see things I hoped I'd never see. Alas! Old Yellow should have remained at his post! Now he is in jeopardy. As soon as the Drolls destroy the Lone Oak, they will attack Old Yellow. He stands alone in the center of the field of red grass. We can only watch! All Drelvedom is in jeopardy. Be ready to defend these woods and our homes. Spellweaver, how can we help you?" Edkim meekly answered.

"I have cast what protective spells I can. Why doesn't the Lone Oak retaliate against the Drolls?" Gaelyss responded.

The Drolls on the red meadow gave a chorus of blood curdling shouts, raised their axes, and charged toward the Lone Oak. Out of the blue, Old Yellow moved 600 yards in less than a heartbeat. The sudden movement placed the tree herder in a position between the charging Drolls and the iconic tree.

Astonished, Moochie asked, "How'd he do that?"

"How'd he uproot and move around, Commander?" the Kiennite Neville countered.

"How did Old Yellow move so quickly, Teacher?" Rumsie asked.

Edkim replied. "Tree herders manage limited teleportation. It's an innate ability, not a spell. Can you enlighten us, Gaelyss?"

Still breathless and exhausted from repeatedly casting spells, the young Spellweaver replied, "No, Teacher. What I know of tree herders, I've learned from you. My brother, not I, spent lots of time with Old Yellow."

Kirrie said, "Teacher, may I speak?"

"Yes, Kirrie," Edkim answered.

"I spent time with Yannuvia and Old Yellow. Once Yannuvia and I saw an eight-legged horse descend from the upper limbs and talk to Old Yellow. The tree herder is Magick. Though he's not a Spellweaver, Old Yellow does many things to help care for the forests. Old Yellow attends the Lone Oak. He removes fallen leaves from the red meadow and grooms the great tree's bark. Old Yellow swore he'd always protect the great tree of the meadow. That's what he's doing now. Old Yellow loves us. I don't think he'd want us to run after him," young Kirrie answered.

"He could use some eight-legged horses now! The Drolls are attacking," Rumsie shouted as he peered through the looking glass.

Positioned between the charging Drolls and the Lone Oak, the tree herder extended his largest bough, brought it back to his thick truck, ripped out a piece of his heartwood, and hurled it into the charging Drolls. The large spear impaled four Drolls. By now large numbers of Drolls bearing axes reached the tree herder. Old Yellow began to twist violently at the base of his trunk. In so doing, he thrashed his lower limbs about and sent many Drollen warriors flying unceremoniously through the air. Several Drolls dodged the big tree herder's limbs, managed to get near his trunk, swung their large axes, and landed a few blows. Old Yellow ripped his roots through the air and knocked them away. The tree herder ejected another large piece of heartwood, clutched it with a flexible middle bough, and stabbed the attacking Drolls. The wolf-faced attackers' casualties mounted.

"Cursed tree! Bewitched *wood*! My warriors fall like splinters before him! You Kiennites do nothing!" Moochie growled angrily.

"It's no fault of ours that your soldiers are inept," Neville smirked.

On the field, many Drolls skirted the tree herder's position, encircled the Lone Oak, and attacked the great tree from the eastern side toward the Drelves.

"Old Yellow fights with great tenacity. Many Drolls fall. I'd say a hundred or so already, but the enemies are too many. Drolls circle the Lone Oak and attack from this side. Oh, my! Their axes are cutting through the bark and digging into the flesh of the Lone Oak. Maroon sap pours from the great tree's wounds," Rumsie reported.

Continuing to thrash his boughs about, Old Yellow knocked many Drolls off their feet and numerous others into oblivion. More astute warriors stood back and hurled spears toward the angry behemoth. The spears broke off a few of the tree herder's smaller limbs. Additional Drolls saw the futility of rushing the tree herder and fell back. Eventually fifty or so Drolls circled the big yellow tree. All the while their comrades took advantage of the 89 pace circumference of the Lone Oak and continued to attack the great tree's bark in force.

Old Yellow sensed the outcries of the injured Lone Oak and moved laterally and around the tree. Drolls fired more spears toward the tree herder but caused little injury. Old Yellow actually pulled three Drolls' spears from his trunk and returned them lethally to their senders. Shuffling through the fallen leaves of the Lone Oak, Old Yellow removed a seven Yardley paces long section of his heartwood from his center and moved against the Drolls attacking the eastern side of the Lone Oak that faced the Drelves. Urgency spurred the big uprooted tree's movement. He remained strong, repeatedly used the great section of his heartwood, and sent Droll after Droll to the netherworld. Ripping out the heartwood created a deep wound in Old Yellow's trunk. To this point, the Drolls' spears and axes had inflicted less damage. Soon the tree harder had smote or chased away the Drolls attacking the eastern side of the Lone Oak. Unfortunately the enemies' numbers enabled them to close on the western side of the great tree and hammer the Lone Oak with their axes. The upper limbs of the Lone Oak trembled from the repeated blows.

"Old Yellow has slain over two hundred Drolls, but the enemy still confounds him. They are too many, and now attack the western side of the Lone Oak. The great tree shivers from the blows. Scarcely a leaf remains on the stately boughs. My heart breaks," Clarke reported.

The 1106 year-old Drelve wailed as he peered through the looking glass.

"My legions begin to turn the tide. The cursed tree herder cannot defend both sides of the Lone Oak. Send reinforcements with bows and spears to the near side of the tree," Moochie the Droll shouted proudly.

CHAPTER 35
Zack's Sacrifice

On the red meadow, the Drolls encircled Old Yellow. Moochie's warriors carefully remained a safe distance away and avoided the tree herder's heartwood spear and violently thrashing limbs. Moving slowly, the tree herder Old Yellow trudged back around the great tree and chased away the Drolls attacking on the western side. As soon as Old Yellow vacated the area, Drolls charged and attacked the eastern side of the vulnerable Lone Oak.

Zack watched intently from his perch on a low-lying limb of an everred tree. Only a season away from his first trip to the Green Vale, the young Drelve surveyed the events on the red meadow.

Zack went to his cohorts Debery, Bryce, and Meryt and said resolutely, "It's more than I can bear to watch, my friends. The tree herder fights like a yeoman but he is outmaneuvered. It's time the Drolls faced speed. Will you give me the red fruits that we took from the Thirttene Friends at the hillock in the Green Vale? There's something I must do," Zack said resolutely.

"You can't go onto the field. First, Edkim and Rumsie ordered us not to enter the fray, and secondly, it'd be suicide!" Meryt objected.

"It's not a matter of debate. Will you give me what I ask?" Zack continued.

Meryt reached into his raiment and gave Zack three round red objects. Zack dropped from the tree to the ground and approached the edge of the red meadow. Observing the action intently on the field, Rumsie and Edkim failed to see the young Drelve approach the red meadow's edge. Zack crawled under the underbrush, carefully avoiding the Wall of Thorns. The Magick needles injured anyone attempting to cross them, including a careless Drelve. Suddenly Zack emerged from the underbrush, stood on the fringe of the red meadow, and enjoyed the touch of the ankle high red grass to his lower calves. The young Drelve uttered several phrases of the Old Drelvish tongue and started toward the carnage that enveloped the Lone Oak. Initially Zack moved at normal speed, but soon ran across the red meadow with the speed of a Cheethra. The speedy Cheethras had the body of a woman, the head of a predatory cat, flowing manes, long tails, sharp fangs, and deadly venom. Ancestral enemies of the Drolls, the rare she-cats inhabited the plains east of the Ornash River and beyond the central forests of the Drelves. No land creature moved faster than Cheethras. Now empowered with the Haste Spell bequeathed by the Green Vale's Magick rain, the Drelve Zack equaled the speed of the legendary Cheethra.

"Zack! Stop!" Kirrie shouted.

Rumsie and the Teacher echoed her warning, but now the young Drelve raced pell-mell toward the battle in the center of the red meadow. Zack covered the thousand Yardley pace distance quickly.

On the far side of the meadow, Moochie stood impatiently with the two Kiennites, Neville and Chamberlain.

Staring across the field through a primitive scope, a Droll lookout placed in one of the taller wild wood oaks shouted, "Commander Moochie, there's activity from the far woods. Coming out of the trees…it's…"

"What are you saying, Brutus? Is our ploy working? How many?" Moochie shouted back.

"One… it's a Drelve. A single Drelve…just one…He's attacking. He moves with the speed of the wind," the lookout Brutus reported.

"With that swiftness, it's got to be a Spellweaver! Fetch my horse, bow, and quiver!" Moochie shouted.

Old Yellow reached the side of the Lone Oak facing the wild woods and scattered the attacking Drolls. The wolf-faced warriors drew back, avoided Old Yellow's powerful attacks, and outflanked the slower moving tree herder. In frustration the tree herder hurled his heartwood pole and killed six taunting Drolls. Unfortunately Old Yellow effectively kept the Drolls away from only one side of the Lone Oak.

"A Drelve attacks with great speed! Close and engage him before he has time to place spells upon us. Destroy him! Charge!" Beefcake, the ranking Droll on the field shouted.

The Drolls left the Lone Oak and rushed toward the rapidly approaching Zack.

"Zack's maneuver has drawn them away from the Lone Oak for the moment. I don't know what else he can accomplish," the Teacher Edkim observed.

Zack ran rapidly to the left of the Lone Oak and stopped. Quickly the Drolls ran toward him.

"Encircle him!" Beefcake screamed and ran toward the Drelve.

Zack waited until the first group of Drolls were fifty paces away from his position and then hurled a round red object into the charging Drolls.

The device landed at the feet of the nearest Droll and exploded with great force. Red grass, mounds of dirt, and twenty Drolls flew into the air. The explosion left a defect fifteen paces wide in the red meadow. Zack turned and ran with *Haste* directly south, away from the Lone Oak. Bewildered, many Drolls turned and ran northward.

Beefcake growled, "Don't you dare turn away from him! Close before he throws more spells upon us! Now!"

"Woe! It *is* a Spellweaver," Neville moaned.

"What are we to do?" groaned Chamberlain.

"I suppose it's up to me," Moochie growled.

A farrier arrived with Moochie's armored warhorse and the Commander's war lance, bow, and quiver of arrows. Moochie's longbow was Drelvish. If truth were known, Moochie's great grandfather Walt took the Drollen commander's longbow from a dead Drelvish Sergeant Major in a bygone battle. Moochie slung an ornamental quiver across his broad shoulders with the longbow and mounted the steed.

"Take us to war, Velvet," the Droll commanded his steed, and the warhorse broke into a gallop toward the Lone Oak.

"Cherry bomb! Zack used a cherry bomb. The Drolls pursue him. Old Yellow makes headway against those away from us. He's hurling pieces of himself into them. He sacrifices himself!" Rumsie shouted.

Every Drelve's eyes remained fixed on the battlefield. Everyone who had access to a looking glass employed the device.

The Drolls chased Zack, but fell behind the fleet runner.

A much larger party of Drolls moved around Old Yellow like a swarm of bees. Occasionally one of the enemies delivered a stinging blow, but more often the forest guardian squashed the attackers with his powerful branches or impaled them with missiles ripped selflessly from his heartwood. Copious streams of deep yellow sap flowed from Old Yellow as he chased his tormentors.

Clarke shouted from his position high in the tallest red oak, "A rider! A rider moves across the meadow on a steed black as the darkest cave. He moves from the wild woods toward Zack."

Zack ran a hundred paces, turned, and faced the charging Drolls. The Drelve waited until his enemies were thirty paces away, and then hurled another cherry bomb into them. Another deafening explosion rocked the battlefield, shook the ground, wounded the Drolls' field commander Beefcake, and sent forty Drolls to their nevermores. The force of the explosion created another great hole in the red meadow and sent tremors felt by both the Kiennites that stood and impotently watched the battle and the Drelves that stood in awe of the destruction. Ever thinking ahead, Zack ran to the southwest away from the Alms Glen forest and the Lone Oak. Fearing the wrath of the now wounded Beefcake, befuddled Drolls followed Zack. Old Yellow again ripped a piece of heartwood from his trunk, staggered as he ripped the vital support from his being, swung the heartwood through the Drolls, and bashed many of them.

The rider avoided the tree herder. Old Yellow could not attack him.

Zack turned and faced his dwindling number of enemies. Between the efforts of the Drelve and tree herder, over four hundred Drolls lay dead on the field. Two hundred Drolls now chased Zack. Another hundred harassed the tree herder and fired spears into Old Yellow's wounds. The tree herder groaned loudly when spears drove deeply into his already deep wounds. The tree herder bent his trunk, shortened his height, inserted his trailing roots into the red grassy meadow, and stabilized his position. However, this sacrificed his mobility, and Drolls surrounded him.

Zack had stopped running near the southern end of the red meadow.

The injured and quite angry field commander Beefcake ordered the Drolls approaching Zack, "Surround him. Stay at a distance. He's mine!"

Growling and snarling, the Drolls surrounded young Zack. The Drelve stood quietly as 200 Drolls surrounded him.

"Zack has stopped running. Why is he standing still? Many Drolls surround him. He could have easily outrun them and got back to our tree line!" Clarke shouted.

"Old Yellow stands unmoving as well. Drolls also surround him. The dark rider has moved past the Lone Oak and tarries about three hundred paces from Zack. I don't see how we can help," Rumsie reported.

Edkim added, "Unfortunately I agree. Watch the woods."

Beefcake limped up, and joined his circle of his friends who surrounded Zack, and drew his great axe. The little Drelve stood alone defiantly.

"You can't take us all Spellweaver! Prepare to meet your doom!" Beefcake growled angrily.

The massive Drollen field commander limped toward Zack. When Beefcake was forty paces from him, Zack hurled a red fruit toward the hulking Droll, rapidly turned ninety degrees, hurled a second cherry bomb toward the advancing Drolls, turned another ninety degrees, hurled a third bomb, turned another ninety degrees, and then hurled a fourth little red fruit. Enabled by the Haste Spell, Zack threw the four cherry bombs to their destinations in resounding and deadly chorus.

Boom!
Boom!
Boom!
Boom!

The four explosions rocked the red meadow. The first bomb exploded at the big brute Beefcake's feet, obliterated him, threw thirty Drolls advancing with the field commander into the air, and opened a thirty pace wide crater. The second bomb exploded, killed fifty Drolls, and opened a crater twenty paces deep. The third bomb hit a Droll directly, fell to the ground, exploded a split second after the others, created a shallower crater, and slew ten Drolls. The fourth cherry bomb devastatingly fell among the largest group of Drolls, opened a crater forty feet wide, and smote nigh a hundred wolf-faced warriors. After the fourth explosion Zack faced only ten disoriented and deafened Drolls.

Moochie struggled to maintain Velvet's reins. The very ground rumbled beneath him, six explosions hurt his keen ears, and smoke and the heavy stench of death permeated the air. The cherry bombs created six massive craters and littered the ground with the dead. Gaining control of his steed and filled with hatred, Moochie angrily glowered at the Drelve. Surrounded by four large craters, Zack stood about two hundred paces away.

"Zack still stands. The rider yet sits upon his black horse. The action around Old Yellow has waned. The shock and awe created by young Zack has at least temporarily slowed the attack against the Lone Oak and the tree herder. I've never seen so many dead on a field of battle. Nigh eight hundred Drolls have fallen. Zack's bombs disrupt the red grass and create deep craters. The red grass has always replenished its losses. How can Nature and Magick heal such wounds?" Clarke reported.

"Perhaps the enemies will turn and run. At least Zack has given Old Yellow and the Lone Oak a chance," Rumsie added.

"Woe! The power of a Spellweaver! Should we retreat?" Neville screamed.

"We already stand in the rear more than a thousand paces away. The spells haven't touched *us*. The Drolls bear the brunt of the Spellweaver's assault. The tree herder and great tree are damaged, perhaps mortally. The fool Moochie has softened the enemy for Lord Saligia's attack. The Drelves have revealed their hand and played their highest card," Chamberlain argued.

"Who's to say the Spellweaver won't turn his attention to us. Lord Saligia has yet to arrive," Neville countered.

"The *fool,* as you called our commander, still stands on the field. If my eyes tell me the truth, he trains his bow on the Drelve," Chamberlain reported as he stared through his looking glass.

"He is then a fool! The commander sits astride a horse and aims a bow at a target two hundred paces away. It'd be an impossible shot for the best Kiennish archer. Drolls are hack and slay fighters, not bowman. Their inept assault on the big tree proves it," Neville answered.

The lone horseman held his ground about two hundred paces away. The few surviving Drolls near him didn't mount a threat. Zack felt fatigue in his muscles for the first time. Haste enabled one to move twice as fast but also sapped one's energies twice as quickly. Still the Drelve felt he had the strength to make it back to the woods. He had given the tree herder a chance. From his position, Zack could not see Old Yellow. Mounds of dirt, smoke, and the Lone Oak obscured his view. Though the distance was great, the Drelve felt the rider's gaze, and a cold chill coursed down his spine. Keeping an eye toward the rider, Zack began to weave his way eastward through the craters made by the cherry bombs.

Moochie sat high on Velvet. The Droll brought his bow about and pulled a long deep red arrow as long as his longbow from his quiver. The arrow glinted in the amber light. As the Droll notched the arrow in the Drelvish longbow, the red color of the shaft darkened. Unlike most arrows, the shaft, fletching, and arrowhead blended to a single unit. Zack saw the rider draw his bow, but the retreating Drelve felt the great distance gave him chance to evade the projectile. The tired Drelve *hastily* negotiated his path past the greatest crater and moved wearily toward the safety promised by the forest of Alms Glen.

Haste and fatigue…

Nature and Magick…

Moochie pulled the bowstring taut. Zack ran more quickly. Taking a deep breath, the Droll unleashed the arrow. The projectile flew high into the smoky skies. Higher and higher…

Zack felt a sense of panic. Even arrows fired from the finest made bows never reached such a height. He *was* in range.

Not to fear…

The Drelve moved quickly to the right. High in its course the arrow changed direction, followed the Drelve's movement, and began to descend.

Bewildered, Zack ran left, right, left, and right again.

The descending arrow mimicked his movements.

Zack turned and ran straight toward the horseman at breakneck speed.

The arrow fell further and turned backward.

Zack screamed, turned, and ran as fast as Haste took him toward the sanctuary of the Alms Glen forest.

Two hundred paces from the forest's edge…

One hundred and fifty paces…

Zack heard the encouraging shouts of his fellows.

One hundred paces…

Zack heard an ominous humming sound.

Then a sickening thud…

Horrified, the young Drelve saw the angry barbed tip of the projectile protruding through his chest.

Brief excruciating pain…

Zack fell fifty paces from the forest's edge.

Beaux, Klunkus, and Loganne broke from the woods, ran to their fallen comrade, picked up Zack, and carried his body to the forest edge.

The lone horseman watched from the desecrated red meadow.

CHAPTER 36
The Felling of the Great Tree

Gaelyss, the Teacher Edkim, Rumsie, and Kirrie ran to the fallen Zack. Edkim touched his lifeless body.

"I cannot remove the arrow," the Teacher said.

Rumsie shouted upward to Clarke, "Watch the horseman! Watch the field! What do you see?"

"He has not moved...wait, his steed trots toward the Lone Oak. Many Drolls emerge from the far trees. They run to the rider, not to further the attack on Old Yellow. The tree herder has not moved. He stands or slumps near the Lone Oak. Smoke fills the air. It's hard to see, even with the looking glass, Sergeant Major Rumsie," Clarke answered.

Across the way the Kiennite Neville said with amazement, "The Droll has felled the Spellweaver. Some force of Magick guided his arrow along an extended and sinuous course. The Droll is a spell caster."

"And we have insulted him. We'd best clean up our acts. He's sure to gain favor in the eyes of Lord Saligia," Chamberlain agreed.

"Aye, but the great tree still stands, and the tree herder, though weakened, remains on the field, and the walking tree beast has killed more Drolls than the Spellweaver," Neville observed.

On the field several hundred Drolls ran to Moochie and his steed Velvet. Cheering raucously they praised their commander and his victory over the *Spellweaver*. Moochie basked in the moment briefly, then turned his head toward the mangled Lone Oak. Drolls' axes had cleaved through a third of the tree's diameter, and a torrent of thick maroon sap flowed from the wounded tree. The yellow tree herder darkened the red grass with its deep yellow ichors. Several broken branches dangled from the injured tree herder, and the tree herder had opened great gashes in his wide trunk from which sap flowed freely.

Moochie said, "Thank you, my warriors, but it is you who have fought long and hard on this field. We still have work to do. The tree still stands."

The Drolls shouted and started toward their fifty or so comrades who still stood near the tree herder.

"Wait! Enough of you have died fighting this abomination. Stand clear!" Moochie ordered.

The Droll urged his steed Velvet forward and closed to within a hundred paces of the tree herder. The Droll's commander pulled another red arrow from his quiver and notched it to his bowstring. Moochie pulled the bowstring taut, aimed the bow toward the tree herder, and released the arrow. Unlike the missile launched at Zack, this arrow followed a straight course into the deep wound in Old Yellow's trunk and disappeared into the wound. Old Yellow moaned loudly and crashed lifelessly to the ground.

Seeing the tree herder fall, the Drolls went into frenzy and descended on the Lone Oak. As many as possible crowded against the trunk and pummeled the great tree with their axes. Moochie triumphantly rode over to the Kiennites and dismounted.

"Woe! Old Yellow has fallen to another of the vile arrows unleashed from the horseman's bow. The Drolls attack the Lone Oak with full force," Clarke reported.

Moochie gloated, "Neville. Chamberlain. When your Lord Saligia arrives, you may tell him that *I* have slain the Spellweaver and the tree herder. My warriors finish the cursed tree, the icon of Drelvedom, and crush the enemies morale."

"Yes, Lord Moochie! We will relay your message. Scouts convey Lord Saligia will arrive on the morrow. I...we must say this has been a glorious day for our alliance. The arrows...how do you come by the arrows, Lord Moochie?" Neville asked submissively.

"We have only killed two trees and one Drelve, and at the cost of almost a thousand alliance warriors. Many were your blood kin, Commander Moochie. We have not fired the first shot or taken the first blow against the Drelves in their forest. The cursed forest is their strongest ally. I doubt you have enough of those fancy arrows to eliminate all their allies," the viceroy of Aulgmoor Chamberlain observed.

"It's obvious Drolls' blood means little to you, viceroy. The thousand warriors had names, families, and plans. If you continue to belittle the efforts of my warriors and fail to show me respect, I may have an arrow for you, Chamberlain. Worse yet for you, I might tell Lord Saligia you have stood tentatively by the sidelines whilst lowly Drolls destroyed a Drelvish Spellweaver and an evil tree herder. What say you?" Moochie growled.

"I say Lord Saligia, not you, commands this campaign. I am impressed with your victories on the field this cycle of Meries. I will relay your bravery and tenacity to Lord Saligia when he arrives," Chamberlain grudgingly acknowledged.

A tremendous crash reverberated across the red meadow as the Drolls' axes brought down the mighty Lone Oak. The tree fell toward the wild wood. At the moment the tree fell, every blade of red grass on the field wilted and turned brown.

"The red grass wilts, Chamberlain," Neville reported.

CHAPTER 37
Moochie's Triumph

Rumsie, Edkim, Gaelyss, Clarke, Beaux, Klunkus, the elder Blanchard, Ulysses the elder from Meadowsweet, and Loganne gathered at the base of the tallest tree to discuss the tragedies of the day. Kirrie sat with Meryt, Bryce, and Debery, young Zachary, and Taylor. The younger Drelves served mostly as messengers.

Every Drelve mourned the loss of Zack and Old Yellow and feared the consequences of the felling of the Lone Oak. Coincidentally Morganne arrived from Meadowsweet and volunteered to assume the duty of studying the field. As she ascended the tree, the she-Drelve cast a glance toward Gaelyss and received a subtle frown from Kirrie.

Morganne surveyed the field through her looking glass.

Exuberant Drolls gathered at the fringe of the wild woods and raised their voices in song. Crude growls characterized the wolf-faced warriors' usual speech and Drolls emitted mournful howls when they were lonely or hunting. When raised in unison Drolls' voices were oddly lyrical. The warrior in Morganne appreciated the enemies' songs of victory.

Morganne had met Zack briefly when the fallen Drelve came to Meadowsweet and helped the young neophyte learn to properly harvest the enhancing plant root tubers at Green Vale. The tree herder Old Yellow had visited the folk of Meadowsweet many times to help attend the great red oaks that surrounded and defended Green Vale. Like all Drelves, Morganne of Meadowsweet mourned the loss of the Lone Oak.

The great tree lay on its side in the center of the meadow. Drolls hewed boughs from the tree to fuel their victory fires. Standing on the eastern side of the fallen tree with bows drawn and arrows notched, another hundred Drolls faced the Drelves' forests.

Having heard the old veteran Clarke's warnings about the rider of the black horse and his lethal arrows, Morganne kept a keen eye through her "toot and see scroll" looking glass and scanned the field. She saw no riders.

At the forest's edge, Edkim the Teacher said, "There's no time for mourning. A great party of Drolls remains just across the dying meadow."

"Why don't they attack?" Beaux asked.

"They relish the malice they've fomented!" Klunkus added bitterly.

Ulysses remarked, "Drolls showing such discipline is unusual!"

"Teacher, why did the great tree do nothing to defend itself? It fell like any other tree. Why do we see no effects, no consequences of the Lone Oak's demise?" Loganne asked plaintively.

"The red grass dies. Our hearts break. The world lost a thing of beauty. I'd say there are grand consequences to the fall of the great tree, young Loganne," Edkim responded quietly.

"Yet it simply lays on the field, felled by crude axes. Why has Magick abandoned the old tree?" the she-Drelve persisted.

"Evidently the Lone Oak was more of Nature than Magick, Loganne. We are bereft of Old Yellow, the Lone Oak, and brave young Zack. We cannot dwell on our losses, my friends. We must prepare to battle whatever the Drolls throw at us. This rider concerns me greatly. The projectiles fired from the dark rider's bow traveled unerringly to Zack's heart and drew the life from the tree herder. The rider appeared Droll. How did the Droll obtain Arrows of Slaying? Woe to us, if the Gray Wanderer granted them a Spellweaver," Edkim sighed.

"Doesn't Magick always touch Kiennites born under the gray sun, Teacher?" Loganne asked.

"You remember your lessons well, Loganne. Kiennish shamans have some powers of Magick. These powers are purportedly illusory Magick," Edkim answered.

"It wasn't an illusion that pursued the *hasted* Zack across the red meadow and smote him, Teacher," Clarke added.

"I don't have answers. Rarely the enemies fire Magick Missiles and fire spells. Remember we lost the neophyte Bystar to such a shaman seven years ago. We must do what we can, old friend. Take rations and try to rest. The Drolls must also attend a great pyre this amber period. I look to the skies for Andreas, but the gray wanderer remains away," Edkim replied.

"The gray sun doesn't cotton to the whims or needs of simple folk," Rumsie added simplistically.

The Drelves ate trail mix and sipped teas made with forest herbs and enhancing root extract. Though the victuals couldn't uplift their spirits, the nutritious foods certainly refreshed their bodies.

Morganne peered at the Drolls on the far side of the meadow, which was riddled with bomb craters and the fallen trees. Until this moment, the red grass grew back. Now the field withered.

Drolls chopped timber from the Lone Oak, built a great fire, and piled their dead on the burning wood. Dark smoke filled the sky.

The Kiennite Neville sipped mead from the crude vessel the Drollen quartermaster had given him. The dour expression on the Kiennite's face reflected his dislike for the brew. Kiennites preferred red ale and distilled beverages from the Emerald Isle and wines from the vintners of the highlands near the Doombringer Mountains. Now Neville had to show some solidarity with the Drolls whose yeoman's work had at least won this day's battle.

Day…

Neville thought of time.

Kiennites disdained the term *day,* which many peoples of the World of the Three Suns used to describe a cycle of a light and amber period. Others gave each light and amber period an arbitrary length of eight *hours,* so a *day* was 16 *hours.* Every sixty days the dark period arrived, and it lasted 15 days. The Kiennites preferred the term cycles of Meries, and counted longevity by dark periods. The Drelves placed great significance to the maturation of the tubers of the enhancing plant, which occurred after eight dark periods. Eight cycles of dark periods made what the forest people called one season. A season encompassed 600 *days.* All folk divided time into *minutes.* "Just a minute" meant the same to everyone. "Hold on a second" had a consistent meaning. Sixty minutes made an hour. Sixty *seconds* made a minute. A *second* was the precise time between the heartbeats of a peculiar person called the *minute* minuteman. If one had precise means to measure time, a season of the harvest on the World of the Three Suns was 611 cycles of Meries. A dark period lasted 832,040 minuteman heartbeats or seconds. The interval between dark periods was 3,524,528 seconds. A full season was 39,088,169 seconds.

Interesting numbers…

Might numbers be Magick?

Did Time belong to Nature, Magick, or both?

Did science belong to Nature, Magick, or neither?

Bottom line…

Neville the Kiennite certainly thought little of the Drolls' mead. Moochie enjoyed a respite and the brew.

"Your master will find the field to his liking," the Droll said smugly.

"He will. Lord Moochie, you are such an important liege of your people. Why do you not ride a firehorse?" Neville queried.

"It is a great honor for a Droll to be a fire rider. Piercie the Kiennite warren leader strives to maintain the standard of excellence of the honored fire riders. I'm sorry; I forget he now prefers the name Tumuch. Having Velvet as my steed is a greater honor for me. Her mother Lizzie bore my father into battle. Her ancestor Pennie carried my grandfather over the

Doombringer passes many times. Firehorses are undisciplined. They run away if given the chance. Velvet and I are a team," Moochie proudly answered.

Wearing also the same look of disdain on his Kiennish brow after tasting the mead, the spider-riding envoy from Aulgmoor Chamberlain asked, "Are your warriors resting?"

"Drolls at war do not rest, Kiennite. My forces keep vigil on the field and attend the pyres of my fallen. Your master Lord Saligia has requested that we not attack. For that reason, and only that reason, the cowering Drelves find rest this amber period. Cowards they are, the forest scum sat hidden behind their trees and thorns while their Spellweaver, the tree herder, and the Lone Oak died. Their time of reckoning is nigh. We'll wait for your master," Moochie answered and drank deeply from his tankard.

"Your refreshment is well earned, Commander Moochie. I don't suppose you'd share with us the secret of your quiver," Neville persisted.

"A Droll must have some secrets," Moochie responded mockingly.

In reality, the big Droll had no idea how the arrows derived their power. Moochie had never heard of a Tuscon, the bird whose feathers gave the lethality to the arrows.

Moochie walked away from the Kiennites to the simple pergola his quartermaster had set up for him. The tent had served him well. The massive Droll had spent many rest periods within the canvass waiting for a day like the one just past. His forces suffered extensive losses. For that the Droll privately mourned.

The Drelves lost three stalwarts.

CHAPTER 38
Firehorses

High in the red oak, 800 paces away, and beyond the range of the wolf-faced warriors' bows, Morganne spent an entire cycle of Meries watching the activities on the dying meadow. The flames of the massive pyre for the many Drollen warriors and the tiny pyre for little Zack waned. Ultimately the celebratory chants of the Drolls diminished and silence covered the field. The Drolls standing at ready in the middle of the field moved only when relieved. The horseman who fired the lethal arrows against Zack and Old Yellow had not reappeared.

Morganne's arrival allowed Clarke, Beaux, Klunkus, and Rumsie some much needed rest. Little Meries moved nearer, brightened the sky, and ended the amber period. The she-Drelve watched another changing of the Drollen archers. Nothing warranted disturbing the leaders' hard earned sleep. Her keen ears detected the slow roll of thunder in the distance. Thinking the thunder heralded a nice gentle rain to benefit the distraught Drelves, Morganne sighed deeply, looked to the north, but saw no clouds in the skies. From the low foothills just beyond the horizon to the north a dusty smoky cloud rose from the ground. The thunderous sound persisted and grew louder.

Morganne sent the young Drelve Forbin to alert the leaders of the unusual sounds and sights. Though he had seen sixteen seasons of the harvest, Forbin had not been to Meadowsweet. The young Drelve had been born in a year with several exceptional neophytes. What Forbin lacked in ability, he made up for in enthusiasm. He scurried down the tree to inform the Teacher and Rumsie.

Soon the Alms Glen leaders joined Morganne in the high perch and also heard the cumulative sounds of many footsteps. Morganne, Rumsie, and Edkim looked through "toot and see scrolls."

Riders on exceptional mounts appeared at northern end of the meadow. A contingent of Kiennites followed the riders. The hoof beats of the steeds drowned out the cheering of Drollen warriors in the meadow and the woods beyond. Two huge Kiennites as big as Drolls rode at the head of the bizarre column. Riding a large stone pony, the Kiennite on the left wore lavish robes and around his neck an amulet with a rose colored stone in its center. The massive Kiennite on the right carried a war hammer and wore rare wyvern hide, which was usually reserved for the Kiennish couriers. Possession of such armament indicated an individual of great import. His firehorse trotted methodically and effortlessly down the path and onto the meadow. The gleaming red animal emitted little sprays of flame from its three nostrils as it galloped along the trail. Without an armed rider, the horse would still be a deadly opponent.

Snorting red sparks and hot steam and effortlessly carrying heavy burdens, ninety-nine additional massive firehorses bore huge Drolls who wore plate mail armor. Knowing one horseman on an unexceptional mount smote Zack and Old Yellow, the Drelves gasped at the sight. A hundred firehorses and their riders fit more suitably in one's worst nightmare. The firehorses appeared to glide along the road. Several hundred Kiennites and a huge force of Drolls followed the firehorses. Marching thirty across and over a hundred orderly rows deep, the impressive force jeopardized the future of all Drelvedom.

The Teacher and Rumsie summoned Gaelyss. An all out alert brought every available Drelvish defenders to the fringe of the Lone Oak to battle for their lives, forest, and existence as a people.

General Saligia, the Lord of the Kiennites and liege of Aulgmoor rode on the left and Lord Tumuch, Kiennish firehorse master, rode on the right at the heads of the column. Neville and Chamberlain ran to the Kiennites' leaders and bowed down before them.

"Lord General Saligia, long have we awaited your arrival. We have a great victory! As you see, the Lone Oak is destroyed. Also, the Drolls felled a Drelvish Spellweaver and a walking tree. Over a thousand Drolls fell, but no Kiennites have died," Chamberlain eagerly reported.

"So you consider the loss of a thousand of my loyal warriors a victory, Chamberlain?" the Kiennish General muttered.

Saligia was not overly fond of Drolls, but the Kiennites' leader disdained his subordinate's attitude toward his allies.

"Oh, I only meant, a strategic victory. A Spellweaver, Lord Saligia, has fallen! What are the odds the Drelves could have more than a single Spellweaver?" Chamberlain continued.

The Droll Moochie approached the General and said respectfully, "Lord Saligia, your arrival is opportune. We have had all we can handle. Your force will crush the enemies."

"Thank you, Commander, I mean, *Colonel Moochie*! I name you ranking officer of the Drollen clans. You have followed your orders well. I thank you," Saligia commented.

Moochie looked toward Tumuch who sat arrogantly upon his snorting firehorse. Neither Droll nor Kiennite spoke, but each nodded respectfully to the other. Moochie recognize the efforts Tumuch made to secure and train the horses and their Drollen riders. Moochie disdained his given name Kevin; Tumuch disdained his given name Piercie. Though necessity frequently allied Droll and Kiennite, Moochie the Droll and Tumuch the Kiennite were true friends.

Both Neville and Chamberlain held back telling the General of the Droll's impatience.

"Their leaders gather. I fear an all out attack comes soon," Rumsie warned. "Everyone should take his or her position and prepare for the worst."

Gaelyss responded, "Sergeant Major Rumsie, I have cast Wall of Thorns Spells along much of the frontline. The Magick thorns resist normal fires, but the firehorses' breath may be another matter. Also, if the Kiennites number spell casters, they may be able to dispel the Magick."

"None of us can resist the power of the lone horseman's bowshots. If he appears, we must swarm upon him like Drolls. His bow fires only one arrow at a time," the veteran Clarke strongly suggested.

"This is enough talk. Make ready. I imagine they will attack while the light is high and Andreas the Gray Wanderer is gone from the sky," Edkim said.

Across the way, Saligia ordered sharply, "The Drelves are demoralized. The purveyor of Magick, the gray sun, is away. Let's begin our attack. Colonel Moochie, send archers. Intersperse Kiennites with Drolls. Don't risk lives unnecessarily. Attack with flaming arrows. We'll see how the Drelves respond."

Rumsie shouted, "Drolls and Kiennites approach. I'd say three or four hundred Drolls and a hundred Kiennites. Bowmen. Archers. Some carry torches. Make ready our longbows. In each volley, I want every other archer to fire. I want them to neither know our strength nor pinpoint our positions. Please allow our plant allies and Gaelyss's spells to protect us while they will. Good luck to all. May Andreas arrive soon?"

Shouts erupted in the woods to the west, and Drolls and Kiennites filed onto the field in three ranks, walked toward the center of the browning meadow, and joined the group of Drollen archers who stood just beyond the destroyed Lone Oak. Following Saligia's direction, Kiennites alternated with Drolls, and the bowmen stood a body length apart. Every fourth warrior carried a lighted torch. The hundred firehorses and their riders stood at ready by the Kiennites' General. Moochie mounted his steed and galloped behind his archers as they marched toward the center of the meadow. Four Kiennites wearing ornate robes rode on stone ponies behind the rows of archers. Steadily the force approached the waiting Drelves.

"The horseman!" Clarke warned.

"He's but one of over a hundred now. His bow threatens us one at a time. I worry about the four riders behind the advancing archers. Needless to say, the horsemen in reserve are ominous indeed. Gaelyss, can you determine anything from this distance?" Edkim asked.

"The closest archers are 500 Yardley paces away. That's twice our bow range. I don't know if a Magick Missile will do much damage from this range. I can try," Gaelyss volunteered.

"No! It'll alert them to your presence and provide the dark horse's rider with an idea of your location. He more than likely carries more Arrows of Slaying! Can you check for Magick among them?" Rumsie asked.

Gaelyss conjured briefly, studied the advancing formation of Drolls and Kiennites, and concentrated on the rider of the black warhorse who had smote Zack.

"It's too far to be specific. Faint auras surround the four Kiennites on horseback. The fire carried within the ranks is *normal* fire. I find no aura of Magick about the torches. The archers are 500 paces away, and the dark horse and its rider are a hundred behind them. The rider of the beautiful black horse carries something of import. Even from this great distance...its aura of Magick is...intimidating and beyond anything I've sensed, Teacher. If Magick touches someone, it gives him a unique aura. Others touched by Magick recognize these auras. Yannuvia had strong auras about him. Since the rain fell upon them during the trip to Green Vale, Zack, Meryt, Bryce, and Debery have auras. You, Teacher, have an aura. The tree sprite has an aura. The big Droll has no aura. It's what he carries that worries me," Gaelyss reported.

"Must be the arrows. Let's hope he has nothing else of such power. How *does* a Droll come to possess Arrows of Slaying?" Rumsie pondered.

"Suffice it to say that he does!" Edkim warned.

Colonel Moochie watched his warriors advance to within 300 yards of the cursed enchanted forest and enter the range of the Drelves' longbows. The Droll urged Velvet and rode to the rear guard of the advancing troops. The four Kiennite horsemen struggled to maintain control of their steeds, but the dark horse Velvet obeyed her rider.

"Steady. Move forward another hundred paces," Moochie commanded.

"The dark rider charges! No, he stops," Clarke, shouted.
Two young Drelves fired arrows sent toward the Drolls, Kiennites, and riders. One arrow found a mark in the thigh of a Droll in the first rank. The other thudded into the ground harmlessly among the enemies. The wounded Droll wailed inconsolably.

"Hold your fire!" Sergeant Major Rumsie shouted.

"At the quick step, advance!" Moochie commanded. Remaining in formation, four ranks of bowmen charged forward a hundred paces and reached points 200 paces from the Drelve lines.

"Halt! Light your arrows!" Colonel Moochie ordered.

"Notch your arrows!" Rumsie ordered.
Drelvish archers up and down the tree line notched arrows into their bows and pulled their bowstrings taut.

The flame bearers moved among the ranks of Droll and Kiennish archers and applied fire to the peat soaked arrows, which broke into flame.

"Fire!" Moochie ordered the Drolls and Kiennites.

"Fire!" Rumsie commanded the Drelvish defenders.

Flaming arrows flew from the longbows of the alliance of Aulgmoor. Bowstrings hummed from all areas of the trees and underbrush at the edge of the forest. The arrows rose high into the air and crossed paths at their courses' pinnacles. Opposing arrows defied probability and actually struck one another in mid flight. The Drelvish archers fired from finely made longbows and rained death upon the Drolls and Kiennites who stood in the open field. The volley fired by Moochie's warriors rained into the trees and underbrush. If the flaming arrows struck the area where Gaelyss had cast Wall of Thorns and Entangle Spells, the flames simply died. However, any flaming arrows that struck Nature's flora ignited fires. Smoke and heat rose from the resulting fires. A blind squirrel sometimes finds a nut. Three of the enemies' four hundred arrows struck Drelves, and caused mortal wounds. On the field over a hundred Drolls and Kiennites fell.

"Reload and fire!" Moochie shouted.

Several Drelvish arrows came within ten paces of the Colonel's position behind the ranks. The flame bearers scurried to light as many arrows as they could.

"Bring down the flame carriers, then fire at will!" Rumsie commanded.

"It's like shooting fish in a barrel," Clarke commented.

The Drolls and Kiennites managed another fiery volley. None of the arrows found a Drelve, but fueled the fires in the underbrush. Drelves scurried to extinguish the fires, but the burning oil created a good bit of heat. A second volley rained from Drelvish bows in all areas of the woods and felled most of the flame bearers. Little fires erupted in the browning grass.

General Saligia hired a mercenary named Locum Tenets. Half Drelve and half something else, Locum appeared Kiennish and swore fealty only to material goods. Calling himself wyvern master and rat master, the half-Drelve bravely and skillfully entered the vigilant winged serpent's nests and took the young soon after the eggs hatched. Only a wyvern could viably hatch a wyvern egg. Stealing an egg accomplished very little. For a price, Locum had agreed to assist in the assault against the Drelves at Lone Oak.

Now Saligia summoned the mercenary and muttered, "Are you prepared to attack?"

Locum answered, "Yes, Lord Saligia. The wyvern will perform well. I can't say much for the fellow you chose to ride the hippogriff. I've trained him as best I can."

The General growled, "I've paid you a small fortune. You'd best do a yeoman's job, Tenets! Get to it!"

Locum scurried away. In a little while two specks appeared in the sky

Moochie shouted, "Fall back!"

The Drolls and Kiennites rapidly moved out of the Drelves' longbow range, but a few well-placed shots found their mark. Moochie cursed loudly and urged Velvet backward. The masterful black horse walked backward and avoided one of the craters created by Zack's cherry bombs.

The two flying shapes rapidly approached the Drelves.

"What trickery is this?" Clarke asked.

CHAPTER 39
Many *Bryces*

"A wyvern! It bears a rider! And a hippogriff also bears a rider. They carry large vessels. Woe! They approach rapidly!" Edkim screamed.

"Concentrate all fire on the flying enemies! Can you do anything, Gaelyss?" Rumsie implored.

"No! Don't use a spell. The dark rider may pinpoint your location," Edkim shouted.

Arrows zipped toward the approaching wyvern but the gnarly rider expertly guided the great beast higher into the sky. The wyvern moved with tremendous speed and swooped downward. The wyvern rider guided a payload of oil onto the biggest fire. The oil splashed and a great flame gushed from the burning brush. The flames consumed two Drelves who tried to extinguish the blaze. Moving evasively, the wyvern escaped the buzzing arrows, but the beast's rider lost his grip and fell to his death. Now free of its yoke, the wyvern flew southward toward the distant mountains and disappeared.

"That's one less enemy," Rumsie surmised.

The hippogriff and its rider drew near.

With the body of a horse and the head, wings, and claws of a griffin, hippogriffs flew slowly, but they did fly. Horses and griffins were traditional enemies. The bulky cross should have never been possible, since lore held griffins were fond of horsemeat. An old adage, "I'll do it when horses and griffins mate" came to mean *"sometime never."* Most considered Hippogriffs uncontrollable mounts, and the Kiennite aboard this one quickly learned that painful lesson. Carrying a huge vessel and scrawny Kiennite, the massive hippogriff made an easy target for the Drelves' archers. As soon as the beast came into range, several archers fired arrows into its wide chest. The hippogriff screeched, flew wildly, threw the Kiennite from his saddle, and streaked angrily toward the area from which the arrows flew. After its rider fell to his death, sheer anger drove the monster. Time and time again the Drelves' arrows hit the great beast and finally robbed it of its life. Unfortunately for the Drelves, the erratically flying hippogriff fell amidst three archers who battled a fire near the forest's edge. The oil carried by the beast fell into the flames, created a fireball, and immolated the three Drelves. The beast's massive body fell into the flames and burned.

Now two great fires and many small ones burned at the edge of the Drelves' forest.

Colonel Moochie sat on his black steed, watched the fires burn, and smiled wryly. Several ambitious bowshots fell near the Droll, and Moochie raised his dragon scale shield and stopped an arrow. Moochie glowered at the Drelve forest, pulled his longbow from his shoulder, notched a deep red arrow, and fired it blindly toward the woods. The arrow flew over 250 paces, evaded the trunks of several large everreds, rose sharply at a sixty degree angle, and struck a she-Drelve archer named Nicole Petraliddes squarely in the chest. Nicole fell limply from the red oak perch and died before she hit the ground.

"Cursed Death Magick! Who can stand against it?" Bryce screamed.

The young Drelve raised his bow, broke through the smoke of the burning underbrush, and ran to the edge of the dying red meadow.

"Bryce, stop," Loganne shouted futilely.

"Bryce, the odds are impossible! Stop!" Rumsie added.

Little Bryce bravely shouted and charged onto the field. The four mounted Kiennites galloped to the side of the dark rider. The four shamans Paddywhack, Knickknack, Clyburn, and Rucker had remained tentatively in the rear.

Bryce charged toward the five riders.

Several retreating archers turned but Moochie said, "You have done your duty. You leave 300 of your fellows dead on the field. Retreat to the woods."

"Are you scared, Lord Moochie?" the wiry bloke Paddywhack asked facetiously.

"Are you kidding? Anger or grief spurs a single Drelve. He'll be good sport," Knickknack held.

Still holding his longbow and ancient dragon shield, Moochie growled, "I am not scared."

A Drelve's arrow remained lodged in the scales of the glistening shield.

Bryce ran rapidly. When the lone Drelve was about a hundred paces from the five riders, the four Kiennites moved in front of the massive Droll. Bryce then uttered a few phrases of old Drelvish tongue. Thirty-four shimmering images of the little Drelve formed on the field. Performing indistinguishably, every image drew its longbow, notched an arrow, and made ready to fire.

The Kiennish shaman Knickknack growled, extended his gnarly left hand, and muttered, "Be gone!"

223

A violent violet ray of Magick streaked toward the images of Bryce. The Magick Missile sailed though the thirteenth image from the horse riders' left, or west. The image vanished. In its place, additional images formed. Now 55 images of the Drelve appeared.

"I'm scared now," Paddywhack admitted.

"We face a Spellweaver," a third Kiennite Clyburn chagrinned.

Moochie readied his longbow.

Because the four Kiennites had positioned themselves between the Drelve and the Droll, Bryce had no shot at the ominous rider on the dark warhorse. From a hundred paces, the Drelve aimed carefully and fired his arrow. The projectile drove deeply into Knickknack's chest, and the Kiennite fell dead from his horse. The horse galloped away, tripped, and fell whinnying into a nearby crater.

When the Kiennites' shaman fell, Drelves' cheers erupted from the Alms Glen woods.

"The Mirror Images give the young fool a chance!" Clarke shouted.

"Magick poisons his mind," the Teacher Edkim somberly added.

The fourth Kiennite Rucker uttered, "May death take you!"

Rucker extended his hands and sent a Flaming Hands spell in the direction of the rightmost 13 images of Bryce. The Magick of the spell obliterated those thirteen images, but in their place, others formed. A total of 89 images of the little Drelve now shimmered a hundred paces from the three remaining Kiennites and the huge Droll.

Though unnerved Bryce aimed his bow, fired a second arrow, squarely struck Rucker, and the Kiennite shaman fell dead from his horse. The steed bolted and ran directly toward the Drelves' forest.

"Scum bags! Idiots! Hold your spells! They only strengthen him!" Moochie chided.

The Droll Colonel's warning came too late. Both Clyburn and Paddywhack sent Flaming Hands Spells toward the many images of Bryce. Clyburn's spell obliterated the eight central images, but immediately enough images formed to create a total of 144 shimmering Bryces. Moments later Paddywhack's spell crashed into the 21 images on the extreme right. Those images faded, but instantly more formed. Now 233 *Bryces* appeared on the field. Bryce calmly fired first at Clyburn and then Paddywhack. Both Kiennites fell from their horses, slain by the Drelve's accurate shots.

233 shimmering images of young Bryce now lined up against the big Droll. Bryce reached for an arrow, as did Colonel Moochie. At the same time, Rucker's steed reached the edge of the wood. The she-Drelve

Morganne took the horse's rein and leapt upon the scared animal. Saying a few calming phrases the she-Drelve started toward the many images of Bryce and Colonel Moochie. As she expertly rode the animal, Morganne drew her longsword.

The retreating Drolls stopped and looked back at the bizarre scene. Colonel Moochie gave no orders. The firehorses remained sequestered at the edge of the wild woods. The Kiennish General Saligia and his commanders in the wild woods looked upon the developing battle through ornate looking glasses.

233 Bryces aimed carefully at the big Droll.

Moochie notched a deep red arrow into his bow and nonchalantly fired the arrow toward the many Bryces. The deep red arrow covered the hundred paces quickly, buzzed around several images, and moved left and right. Appearing mesmerized by the red arrow's movements, the 233 identical images of Bryce stopped attacking and followed the arrow. The red arrow paused abruptly in mid flight, coursed to the 89th image of Bryce from Moochie's left, struck the image, and fatally wounded young Bryce. For a moment 377 images of Bryce flickered on the field and then all the images instantly disappeared. Cheers erupted from the Drolls and Kiennites that stood about two hundred yards away, in the center of the brown meadow, and the edge of the wild woods.

At the moment Bryce fell, Morganne reached Colonel Moochie. Mounted on Rucker's horse, the she-Drelve shouted, thrust her vorpal blade into the Droll's left side to its hilt, and penetrated his heart. Cut down by Morganne's blade, the big Droll fell from his beloved Velvet. Colonel Moochie had little time to relish his victory over the second *Spellweaver* and never used two red arrows remaining in his quiver. Unlike the wyvern and the steeds ridden by Knickknack, Paddywhack, Rucker, and Clyburn, the dark horse Velvet remained by the fallen Droll's side. Comforted by his loyal steed Velvet, Moochie drew his last breath thinking of the face of his beloved Hannah Dakota and believing he had brought down two Spellweavers in a single cycle of Meries.

Morganne expertly halted Rucker's steed, turned, and rode back to the fallen Droll, dismounted, and grabbed the dragon shield, longbow, and quiver carried by the dark horse's rider. Just as several arrows landed near her, Morganne leapt back onto Rucker's horse and rode quickly to where Bryce fell. With great effort the she-Drelve lifted Bryce and took the little Drelve's broken body back to the forest of Alms Glen.

CHAPTER 40
Pyres

General Saligia screamed, "He has taken down another Spellweaver, but Moochie Korcran has fallen! Send riders to retrieve his body. Cursed luck! ****** Drelves! Two Spellweavers in a single generation! They will all pay! Recall the warriors from the field. Colonel Moochie will have his pyre! If I get my chance, I'll make steak out of that ****** wyvern!"

"I won't allow the Drelves to defile my friend's body. I'll retrieve Commander Moochie," Tumuch growled.

The Kiennish horse master kicked his fiery steed's sides, and the firehorse snorted, broke into a gallop, and headed toward the fallen Drollen commander.

"Lord Saligia, it's a great victory. To this point, two Spellweavers have fallen. The Drelve forests are ablaze. The wyvern rider and hippogriff rider's attacks looked awkward but proved very effective. The Drelves have likely suffered greater casualties than we know. We should press our advantage," Neville urged.

"If the wyvern master weren't dead, I'd *knight* him. Let the fires burn awhile. Let the Drelves stew in the bitter knowledge they've lost two Spellweavers," Lord Saligia stated authoritatively.

Morganne rushed through the burning underbrush with Bryce's body and the goods she'd taken from the fallen Droll. Rumsie, Edkim, Gaelyss, Beaux, Klunkus, Clarke, Kirrie, and the elder Ulysses from Meadowsweet quickly gathered around her.

An expert in using innovative combinations of the enhancing root, the elder Ulysses enjoyed an unparalleled reputation in the healing arts. Drelves lacked facial hair, but old Ulysses' wrinkled face gave the appearance of a short beard. Typical of an aged Drelve, his hair was now completely dark brown. The aged Drelve checked Bryce's body and shook his head negatively. Before he returned his pouch to his raiment, Ulysses gave Kirrie a supply of medicinal herbs.

"Alas! A fire rider rides toward us! Make ready!" the sentry Coweta shouted.

The Drelves' leaders turned and faced the field.

The sentry yelled again, "The firehorse reached the fallen Droll. The rider dismounted, took the fallen leader's body, and threw it upon the dark horse. They now ride back toward the far woods. The fallen commander's noble steed follows close behind the firehorse."

"The enemies regroup. More than a thousand have fallen and Bryce eliminated four shamans. Morganne has rid us of the Drollen commander, the bane of Bryce, Zack, Nicole Petraliddes, and Old Yellow. The fires have damaged our perimeter. We lost 10 comrades this period. All had names, families, dreams, and loved ones. I'm broken. But we have no time to mourn. Zack, Bryce, Old Yellow, and Nicole Petraliddes fell to the arrows fired by the Droll chieftain. Juliebee of Meadowsweet, Annaleigh of Alms Glen, and Gretchen of the Vale Road were killed when the hippogriff fell upon the forest fires and augmented the flames. The first volley of the Drolls arrows killed Fennick, Tanyalee, and Heyerdal, three of our veteran archers. The names of those who fell in battle will be etched in the annals, the history of our folk, and remembered in our songs," Edkim relayed.

"Our comrades dig shallow trenches, remove brush, and struggle to extinguish the fires. Throwing water on the burning oil does no good. When the fire runs out of fuel, Nature will extinguish it. Morganne of Meadowsweet risked her life to slay the Drolls' commander. But importantly she also retrieved his shield, longbow, and cursed quiver. We thank you Morganne, but I urge everyone to await orders before you act. We can ill afford more losses," Rumsie counseled.

Morganne placed the longbow, quiver, and dragon shield at the feet of the leaders.

"Sergeant Major Rumsie, Teacher Edkim, elder Ulysses of Meadowsweet, I didn't intend to be insubordinate. I thought the Droll endangered Gaelyss the Spellweaver. The big Droll slew Nicole Petraliddes with a blind shot. It's only by the grace of the forest he didn't hit the Spellweaver. He still carried two red arrows in his quiver. My life meant...means nothing compared to the life of the Spellweaver. If I fall, others can ably assume my role," Morganne declared and bowed deeply and submissively.

"Stand, warrior. You need not bow. Your efforts saved many lives, at least for the moment. Morganne of Meadowsweet, you shall henceforth be called Droll's bane! Our progeny will sing of your bravery by their campfires." Edkim said.

Morganne stood, nodded to the Teacher, and addressed Rumsey, "Bryce mesmerized the Droll. His spell enabled me. Bryce deserves the credit for bringing down the commander. What will you have me do?"

"Stand by us. You've earned the right to do so," Rumsie answered.

"I agree. We must study these items. Gaelyss, what can you tell us?" Edkim continued.

Kirrie and Morganne glanced at Gaelyss and then exchanged glowers. Gaelyss noted the she-Drelves' glances. Though the heat caused by the fires waned, his face burned briefly.

The young Spellweaver sighed, raised his right hand, uttered an old Drelvish phrase, and then said, "The two red arrows in the quiver radiate Magick of the highest order. The other arrows ... nine, rival those carried by our Drelvish archers. The finely made bow bears markings. The letters are Drelvish! B...G...BG. This is a Drelvish self-bow! The bow and nine arrows are products of Nature, not Magick. The shield is made of overlapping scales from numerous species of dragon. I see red, black, yellow, and, oddly, green scales. One peculiar little gray scale with very strong auras sits in the handhold of the shield. I've never read of green and gray dragons in our texts, Teacher. Perceiving the protective power of this shield doesn't require Detection of Magick," Gaelyss reported.

Klunkus reached for the quiver with the red arrows.

"Don't touch the vile things!" his close friend Beaux warned.

Klunkus jumped back. Beaux placed a concerned hand on his shoulder.

"Probably good advice for the moment," the Teacher Edkim agreed. "We must learn more of the arrows. What else can you tell us, Gaelyss?"

The young Spellweaver concentrated and considered his limited alternatives. Unbeknownst to the focused Gaelyss, both Kirrie and Morganne edged nearer him.

"Um, I need a piece of dung," the Spellweaver said.

"Excrement?" Beaux queried.

"For a spell. I'll try to define the arrows with the spell Detection of Evil," Gaelyss answered.

Kirrie, Morganne, Beaux, and Klunkus rushed into the nearby woods. Gaelyss stared at the red arrows.

"Please continue, Gaelyss," Edkim urged.

"Does anyone carry incense?" Gaelyss asked.

Loganne stepped forward and volunteered a long piece of thin bark. "It's from the red basil bush. I soaked it in pyroprika crystals. It smells nice when it burns."

Rumsie accepted the incense and handed it to Gaelyss.

The Sergeant Major shouted, "Sentries, what's happening on the field?"

The veteran Glinne shouted, "The smoke clears slowly. The enemies gather their dead. The large cavalry force has not moved from the forest's edge across the way."

"We shouldn't tarry. Gaelyss," Rumsie said with concern.

The Spellweaver looked anxiously toward the forest. Klunkus came from the woods sporting the dropping of a small creature. Kirrie, Morganne, and Beaux followed soon. All managed to find some excrement.

"Use mine, Spellweaver. It's dried firfer dung," Klunkus implored.

Beaux countered, "Firfer dung? How do you know it's firfer dung? What makes you a dung inspector, Klunkus? Why must the stuff be dried?"

"So it'll burn, silly," Klunkus answered.

Gaelyss extended his right hand, took the material from the veteran Drelve, uttered a simple phrase, snapped his left thumb and third finger, and produced a small flickering flame at the tip of his index finger. The flame emitted no heat. The Spellweaver ignited the small piece of firfer dung Klunkus had given him, slowly walked around the red arrows in the Droll's quiver, and muttered arcane phrases as he walked.

Firfers were furry little beasts, which gathered roots and berries. When war did not grip the forest, firfers filled the air with pleasant cooing sounds.

Gaelyss took the red basil and pyroprika incense from Rumsie, lit the incense, and finished the incantation. Fine plumes of sweet smelling smoke filled the air and covered the stench of death and dung. Many Drelves gathered around.

Gaelyss finished the spell.

"The red arrows pose no threat as they lie. The Detection of Evil dweomer defines items or foes that…it's hard to explain. Evil is relative. When the meow-meow skat purrs a sweet song and calms a fussy child, the feline is a true friend to the child's fatigued mother; however, the same beast is evil to the mouse that becomes the feline's meal. That's over simplified, my friends, but suffice it to say, I don't feel the red arrows threaten us," Gaelyss struggled.

Edkim said, "Just the same, I want everyone to stand back while I examine them."

The Teacher picked up the longbow and studied its markings and workmanship. Edkim then gingerly reached into the quiver and removed one of the red arrows.

Edkim stated, "Gaelyss is correct. The bow is Drelvish. The Drolls took this from one of our forebears. The bowyer's insignia is engraved on the back of the bow. BG. I wonder, did Byrum Goodale create this device? BG was his logo. He labored five hundred seasons ago. We must learn more of these implements. Summon the bowyer BJ Aires."

The archer Tomayo ran into the forest, found BJ laboring in his workroom, and soon returned with the bowyer, a Drelve of average height and size but exceptional dexterity and keen vision. Since hostilities began, BJ had not left his workplace and incessantly created arrows for the Drelvish archers.

"You summoned me, Teacher," BJ said respectfully.

Edkim extended the fine longbow and pair of odd red arrows to the tired bowyer.

The Teacher said to BJ, "Morganne retrieved these weapons from the Droll's fallen commander. The bow appears Drelvish. The initials BG are engraved in its wood. I'd say it's the work of the great Byrum Goodale. What can you tell us about the bow and arrows, BJ?"

BJ inspected the bow and red arrows. The arrows had smooth scratch-free surfaces. The arrow's shaft, arrowhead, and plume formed a single unit. Gaelyss, Edkim, Rumsie, and Clarke watched intently.

BJ Aires began, "This is a self-bow. Its inner heartwood resists compression and the outer sapwood performs better in tension. This makes a natural laminate effect in a single piece of wood. A concoction of wax, resin, and fine tallow makes the wood water resistant. I quickly recognized the fine workmanship. You are correct, Teacher. This bow bears the mark BG. My instructors talked of the abilities of Byrum Goodale. It would be hard to duplicate this self-bow. It's remarkably well preserved. The Drolls cared for the artifact well. Most bowstrings are made of hemp, flax, or silk. BG harvested and made bowstrings from the silk of purple glowworms. We harvest this silk in the dark period. However, harvesting such silk when the gray sun is near amplifies the silk's power. Most longbows have a range of about 200 yards. Our best bows have a range of 360 yards. Silk gathered during an Approximation doubles the range. I'm told the Droll fired this exceptionally well made self-bow from a distance of 200 to 250 paces. The bow has a far greater range. My guess is the Droll didn't know its significance.

"I can't define the Nature of the red arrows. As I hold this one, I see it's a single piece of material. There's no fletching...well, the end of the arrow does form the shape of a plume. Darned if I know what the material is, Teacher. It's light. I've never seen this red wood. For the most part I work with materials of Nature, the wonders of the forest. Only during the Approximations of Andreas am I able to create exceptional weaponry. Based on what you've told me and not knowing their origin, I'd not trust these arrows," the bowyer reported.

Rumsie quickly agreed, "I totally agree."

"Have you tried notching one of the red arrows?" BJ asked.

"No. To this point, every time one of the red arrows has been fired from the longbow, one of our most stalwart friends has died. The Droll thrice struck down our people with red arrows fired from this bow. A fourth shot dropped our great ally the tree herder," Rumsie quickly remarked.

"Then the Droll must have been a Spellweaver! The evidence tells me this is nothing more than an exceptional longbow. Its maker used the same silk from purple glowworms that I use. One *must* harvest the silk during the dark period. This is very good string! I don't know when it was harvested. I know naught of auras and the like. Firing at a target tells me more about a weapon. May I fire one of *my* arrows from the bow?" BJ asked.

"You are too valuable to us, BJ. I don't want to risk you," Rumsie replied.

"Zack, Bryce, Nicole Petraliddes, Old Yellow, Juliebee of Meadowsweet, Annaleigh of Alms Glen, Gretchen of the Vale Road, Fennick, Tanyalee, and Heyerdal made the ultimate sacrifice. I must contribute whenever, wherever, and however I can. I can't imagine a Drelvish bow harming me. Has the Spellweaver detected any malice from the longbow?" BJ asked.

Gaelyss commented, "Intense auras of Magick surround the arrows. The bow has no aura. I'm a Spellweaver and know little of armaments, but I recognize the bow's workmanship."

"Then it's time to test the weapon. All my life I've wanted to fire a bow created by Byrum Goodale. Do Drolls yet stand on the field?" BJ asked.

"Describe the field, Coweta," Rumsie shouted.

"The smoke has cleared. Drolls stand about midfield. The leaders tarry at the forest's edge. Those in the field are about a thousand paces away, near the middle of the meadow. They are armed with bows. Under the cover of the smoke, Drolls may have occupied the deep craters made by Zack's bombs. If so, the nearest would be within 400 paces. The horsemen remain at the right end of the meadow, from my perspective," Coweta dutifully reported.

"Teacher, what say you?" Rumsie asked.

"Bowyer Aires, if you have no misgivings about this bow, I feel comfortable with the weapon in your hands. Please proceed," The Teacher Edkim answered.

"Let's see what this can do," BJ the bowyer said.

Taking the old bow Morganne had taken from the Droll, BJ stepped to the edge of the wood. The bowyer looked through an unusual looking glass and said, "987."

"What?" Rumsie asked quizzically.

"Your observer is incorrect. The Drolls are not a thousand Yardley paces away. They are 987 paces away," BJ muttered.

BJ pointed the longbow toward the Drolls.

From above Coweta yelled, "The Drolls stare through glasses as we do. If my eyes don't deceive me, they are laughing at you, Master BJ."

BJ removed the quiver from his back and revealed four exceptional arrows. The arrows had dark blue shafts, fletchings of many colored feathers, and deep gray arrowheads. The arrowheads glinted in the amber light, and the fletchings reflected lights of many colors.

"Are those fletchings made of…phoenix feathers?" Gaelyss asked.

"I don't know. I've never seen a phoenix. I've only read of them. I doubted their existence. Now that I've seen these feathers, I'm not so sure," Edkim replied.

Sergeant Major Rumsie walked to the edge of the wood among the burned out brushes, stood by BJ, and remarked, "How exceptional! The blue arrows are beautiful. May I study your wares, fletcher?"

BJ offered the Sergeant Major the first arrow from the sturdy wyvern hide quiver. Rumsey stroked the deep blue shaft of the arrow, marveled at the beauty of the ever-changing fletching, and pondered the lethality of the deep gray broad head. The experienced archer looked for bodkin points along the shaft but the shaft seemed a single piece of wood. As Rumsie manipulated the arrow, those around him saw all the colors of the spectrum in the darkening light.

The light period gave way to the amber time.

Rumsie commented, "It has so little weight and I see no bodkin points. I'd say it feels strong. The blue wood of the shaft, the fine fletching, and the metal creating dangerous point are foreign to me. How did you come by such materials?"

"The materials are not of *this wood and time.* Just call them a trade secret. A bowyer and fletcher must have some secrets. I will say I constructed these arrows during the last Approximation. When the Spellweaver stood in the Green Vale, the Gray Wanderer drew near, and the geyser's rain fell on the neophytes and the Teacher, wonderful things happened. During this time I labored in my workroom in the Shad Cove. Gray light fell upon me while I assembled the four projectiles. I have saved them for a time of need. It appears now is such a time," BJ Aires answered.

Rumsey stared quizzically at BJ.

Then the Sergeant Major said, "Coweta has said the enemies stay in the field. Some may be nearer than we know, lurking in the craters. The grass is burned. Drolls and Kiennites prefer scorched earth. They run faster on bare ground. The distance is too far to allow you a shot. Drolls on horseback could easily overtake you before you made your way back after taking a shot. I cannot allow you to sacrifice yourself."

"I'll worry about that," BJ answered.

The bowyer and fetcher walked onto the edge of the charred tormented erstwhile red meadow. BJ rubbed his forefinger deftly against the nock on the bluewood arrow, placed the arrow against the bowstring, and pulled it taut. When he released the arrow, sweet string Musick filled the area around them. The blue arrow streaked from the bow and flew higher and higher into the air. Stationed in the center of the field 987 paces away from BJ and Rumsie, Drolls saw the rapidly moving arrow flying high over their wolf-like heads. The warriors stopped laughing, turned, and began to wave frantically at their commanders gathered at the edge of the wild woods.

Perched high in the red oak tree at the edge of the Drelve woods, Coweta and Tomayo stared across the red meadow.

Tumuch the Horsemaster sat proudly upon his firehorse. The large Kiennite had worked many seasons to fine-tune his force. Now the chance to crush his ancestral enemies had finally arrived. His firehorse brigade would demolish the Drelves' defenses and save many Drolls' and Kiennites' lives. Though Kiennish by birth, Tumuch loathed sharing the glory of victory with the gnarly warren leaders of the Doombringers and the leaders of Aulgmoor. The Horsemaster endured the obligatory pleasantries with Neville and Chamberlain. Moochie's death genuinely affected Tumuch.

Suddenly the Kiennite Neville blurted, "Why do the Drolls in the field turn and wave to us?"

"What do you see?" Chamberlain shouted to the lookout on the war machine's tower.

The lookout answered, "Nothing. No Drelves occupy the field. Wait… wait… incoming! Be on guard!"

Tumuch had no time to react. The broad head tip of the blue arrow fired from over 2000 paces away ripped through his powerful chest. The oversized Kiennite moaned meekly and fell to the ground by the side of his firehorse with a resounding thud.

General Saligia reflexively raised his shield. After Tumuch fell from its back, his great firehorse turned, and bolted, and ran northward away from the meadow.

Coweta turned to Tomayo and said, "Unbelievable. The fletcher's arrow has evidently slain the enemies' Horsemaster."

BJ turned, gave the bow and quiver with its three blue arrows to Rumsie, and said, "Now we only have 99 firehorses to fight. Use these well."

"How?" the Teacher Edkim muttered with amazement.

"The Droll evidently didn't realize what he had. This is a Bow of Striking. Byrum Goodale harvested its bowstring during the Approximation of the Gray Sun. He must have also assembled the bow when the gray sun was near. I created the arrow in the gray light. Alone, as fine as it was, I don't think the arrow would have traveled more than half the meadow's breadth if fired from my best self-bow. I'd say this bow likely has a range three or four times that of our best longbows. I'd estimate, about 987 paces, with one of my usual arrows" BJ suggested.

"Let me test your theory," Rumsie added.

The Sergeant Major took a finely made arrow from his quiver. A red falcon had donated the fletching. Rumsey placed the arrow's nock against the drawstring of the longbow, pulled the string taut, and fired. The arrow sailed through the air.

The Drolls in the middle of the field still stood in awe at the sight of the fallen body of Lord Tumuch. Most had turned their backs to the Drelves' wood. For one Droll, this was a fatal mistake. After flying 987 yards Rumsie's arrow drove deeply into the unfortunate Droll's back and felled the inattentive warrior. The fallen Drolls' fellows shouted and broke for the woods on the far side of the field.

General Saligia saw Tumuch fall from his steed and howled inconsolably. Seeing fear in the eyes of his colleagues and hearing the screams of the Drolls' scouts running from the field angered the Kiennish General further.

Neville squeamishly wailed, "Woe! Woe! Woe! This attack must be the work of a Spellweaver. Who else can deliver a death stroke from 2000 paces?"

"Could the Drelves have had three Spellweavers?" Chamberlain asked as he cowered behind a nearby firehorse.

"Enough!" Saligia bellowed.

The General's shout immediately quieted Neville, Chamberlain, and the others. The Kiennites' commander drew his iniquitous curved blade and snarled, "I'll slay the next coward who runs from the field myself! We have a mighty force. The Drelves cower behind their trees. This is some trickery on their part to demoralize us, and by **** it's almost working! Who stands second in command to Piercie?"

"Who's Piercie, Lord Saligia?" Neville queried timidly.

"Piercie was Tumuch's given name, you idiot! Piercie! You've got to be the worst **** viceroy any commander's ever had! I will suffer you to prevail against the Drelves. Who's second in command of the firehorse brigade?" Saligia shouted.

A massive Droll bellowed, "That'd be me, General Saligia."

"And you are?" Saligia asked impatiently.

The older Droll answered, "I'm Bluthgar, of the Korcran clan. Twas I who trained young Piercie, uh...Tumuch. I also trained many of our fire riders. Moochie was my nephew. He was my brother Mickey Korcran's son.

"Well, Bluthgar of the Korcrans, we've ****** around too long. It's time to end this thing. I hope you're a bit more wary than your nephew. Fire the field! Burn the grass," Saligia ordered.

Neville motioned to the woods, and several torchbearers started toward the field.

"Not torches, you idiot! Torches are simply natural fire. Use the firehorses! The firehorses will quickly immolate their beloved field and wither the Drelves' spirits."

Tomayo stared through the looking glass and said, "The great horses and riders move forward."

CHAPTER 41
Bluthgar

Bluthgar of the Korcran clan of Drolls beseeched his commander for one favor before proceeding to the field.

"With your permission, Lord Saligia, I'd like to give Tumuch the fallen Horsemaster and Moochie my nephew and your loyal soldier, the honor of the pyres they should be afforded."

"You may proceed," Saligia muttered.

The General feared a mutiny amongst the Drolls if he refused. The powerful wolf-faced allies had lost both Moochie and Tumuch on the field of battle. Though Tumuch was Kiennish, he was beloved by the Drolls.

Bluthgar directed three other fire riders to help him surround the fallen horsemaster's body. According to Droll tradition, Bluthgar removed none of Moochie's gear. He left the fallen commander's war lance, and replaced his bow, quiver, and shield. On Bluthgar's signal, three Drolls, all members of the Korcran clan, nudged their steeds. The four firehorses reared on their hindquarters, gave heinous blood curdling neighs, and then inhaled. The great beasts brought their forelegs downward, crashed their hooves to the ground, shook the earth, and then snorted blazing flames from their mouths and nostrils. The four columns of flame met at the seven and a half foot (two and a half Yardley paces) frame of the fallen Droll. In a short while the flames emitted by the four firehorses consumed the Droll's body. After Bluthgar's charges afforded their fallen leader his pyre, Saligia's minions prepared Tumuch. The fire riders and horses afforded the Horsemaster the same honor.

Clarke and Rumsie joined Tomayo and Coweta in the observation area of the tallest red oak. Peering through the looking glasses, they saw activities across the way.

Coweta reported, "Four firehorses immolated the body of the fallen Drollen commander and the Horsemaster. I don't suppose you have a hundred of those fancy arrows."

Rumsie replied, "I... we have only three. I lack BJ's skills as bowyer and fletcher. He says the bow will work in the hands of any Drelve, or any one with training. Byrum's longbow will be kind to its wielder. I suppose BJ and I have only stirred up the enemies. It was our hope that the attacks might demoralize them and send them packing. We also have the two red arrows Morganne took from the dead Droll. We've chosen not to use those."

"I...I see movement. The great horses are taking the field. Twenty, thirty, forty, fifty, eighty, ninety-nine... Our estimate was correct. I see the war machines the Drolls constructed at the forest's edge. One is a great log house, or...log wall. It rolls on logs. Oh, my, the others are catapults," Coweta answered.

"No, those are trebuchets. The Drolls maneuver a rolling wall, behind which they'll advance their trebuchets, their siege engines," Clarke said.

"What's the difference between a catapult and a trebuchet?" young Morganne asked.

Morganne had rejoined the group in the lookout and prepared to relieve her friend Coweta. The Teacher Edkim climbed with the she-Drelve and joined the Drelves' leadership high in the upper branches of the great red oak.

Tomayo added, "I've never seen such devices. In the last battle the Drolls manned a ballista that cost us dearly. Now they have construed these war machines. I wouldn't have dreamed of them creating such machines."

"Perhaps *they dreamed* of the devices..." the Teacher Edkim pondered.

Rumsie, Clarke, Coweta, and Klunkus looked quizzically at the Teacher. Morganne, Kirrie, Tomayo, and Gaelyss identified with the comment.

"Trebuchets have greater range and heavier payload and smash castle walls," Edkim threw in.

"We don't have a castle," Morganne argued.

"We have these trees which defend us. Kiennites must be behind this planning," Rumsie entered.

"The enemies have bantered in the wild woods for many dark periods. We've seen the smoke of their many fires," Clarke said.

Coweta sighed as she continued to survey the field, "The war machines still sit at the forest's edge. Only the great horses and their riders enter the field. They'd be just a speck without the looking glass, but through the magnifying lens they are horrifying!"

"Yes, they are indeed," Clarke, commented.

Now under the command of Bluthgar, the ninety-nine fire riders brought their steeds onto the field. The horses fanned out at about two degrees of separation to maintain an equal distance between them. Six craters pockmarked the landscape and in some areas fires had denuded the formerly red and now brown grass. The Lone Oak lay prostate in the center of the field and the shattered remains of the tree herder lay nearby. For the first time on record, the damaged red grass failed to repair its injuries.

Abruptly the ninety-nine fire horses broke into a gallop. Sparks and flecks of fire erupted where their hooves hit the ground. Smoke rolled from their nostrils. 99 clouds of dust followed the devilish steeds. The Drelves rushed to their defensive positions. Gaelyss stood by Edkim and awaited instruction.

At 1500…

1300…

1100…paces the enemies were too far away.

900…700…500…300 paces…

They stopped.

Gaelyss felt chilled.

Kirrie stood behind Gaelyss and placed a hand on his shoulder. Morganne moved down from the high watch, ran to Gaelyss side, and drew her short sword. Kirrie's eyes met Morganne's for a brief moment. Even the threat of immediate battle failed to ease the tension between the she-Drelves.

The firehorses remained about three hundred paces from the Drelves. At Bluthgar's command, the fire riders spurred their mounts, and the massive animals reared on their hindquarters. Smoke rolled from their ears and nostrils. The animals belched out flame from their mouths. The firehorses' breath spewed forward in an arc that reached a hundred paces and created fires in the withering red grass. Each fire rider then walked his steed backward fifty paces and repeated the maneuver. The horses returned to all fours and puffed smoke, then again reared on their hindquarters, kicked their forelegs violently, and again spewed forth flames. The fire riders repeated the tactic. Gradually the entire meadow erupted in flames behind the retreating firehorses. Some riders altered their courses to avoid the craters left by the earlier bombs. When they reached the fallen Lone Oak and tree herder, Bluthgar directed his charges to surround the great trees. At the surrogate commander's signal, the riders spurred the horses. All 99 steeds reared, kicked, and spewed fire. The cumulative effect of the fire breaths ignited the fallen structures of the great trees. The remnants of the trees burned brightly. Smoke of many colors wafted into the sky. Soon the white-hot fires totally consumed both the iconic Lone Oak and the remains of the steadfast ally of the Drelves.

The Drelves could only watch the spectacle. Gaelyss and Morganne rejoined Edkim, Tomayo, and Rumsie in the high watch.

"Why do the enemies raze the ground and wantonly destroy living plants?" Morganne asked.

"The grass slows the progress of their attacks," Tomayo guessed.

"It's more likely they just hate the grass, like they hate us," the older Clarke said cynically.

"Listen! That sound!" Morganne shouted.

"Is it thunder?" young Gaelyss asked.

"No! It's war machines!" Clarke answered as he stared across the smoldering, charred field through the looking glass.

Great contraptions moved toward the Drelves. Great red oaks felled and stacked upon one another created the facade of the first device. The stacked trees created a wooden wall forty feet high and four hundred feet wide. The apparatus rolled on huge wooden wheels. Droll and Kiennite *power* moved the apparatus. Aided by yoked moolers and red mastodons, many Drolls and Kiennites pulled and pushed the great device. Behind the wooden apparatus, in essence a moving wall, the Drolls moved four enormous trebuchets. The Drolls had also yoked moolers to the trebuchets and assisted the great bovines in advancing the enhanced catapults. The huge wooden wheels produced the sound of rolling thunder. The entourage of destruction inched forward slowly across the scorched grass.

"Why don't they use the firehorses?" Morganne asked.

"I suppose the equines don't cotton to menial tasks," Clarke surmised.

"The tactic advances their machines such that our archers won't be able to directly assault the drudgers while they advance the machine. Close combat favors the Drolls because they are so powerful individually. Are our preparations completed?" Rumsie asked.

Klunkus said, "Beaux and I have done as you suggested. We widened the path toward Alms Glen. Now ten Drolls can walk abreast down the path. We've added brush and recruited walkabout bushes to fill in breaks along the path. The Spellweaver Gaelyss added some Plant Growth and Entangle Spells."

Morganne asked, "How does one *recruit* a thorny walkabout bush? Just catching one is nigh impossible."

"Having the Spellweaver charm the blighter helps?" Beaux answered.

Looking awestruck, Morganne said, "Spellweaver, you are so talented!"

Blushing, Gaelyss said, "I simply used Commune with Plants and *charmed* a few of them. Walkabouts are not bad fellows, if you get to know them."

Clarke harrumphed and said, "You ask a lot of questions, Morganne."

"I hope you fight as well as you talk, old fellow," Morganne quipped and smiled.

"Old! I'm only 1106! I'm in my prime!" Clarke returned also with a smile.

"I'd say both of you have proven your worth," Gaelyss answered.

"War is upon us, my friends. Let's put all our efforts into defending the forests," Rumsie ordered.

The Drelves assumed their assigned defensive positions. On the field the Drolls steadily moved the large fortress on wheels and four huge trebuchets across the ravaged meadow. The Drelves nervously watched the fire riders on their frightening mounts.

CHAPTER 42
War Wolves

General Saligia and the seven warren lords of the Kiennites, Woodrow, Wilson, Calvin, Coolidge, Theodore, Delano, and Roosevelt sat upon warhorses. The warren lords made up the Council of Aulgmoor, which is where the lot would have preferred to remain, but General Saligia insisted they follow the war legions into battle. Now the warren lords marveled at the spectacle of Saligia's forces moving onto the field. Many had thought the General's ideas folly, but now they saw the massive war machines and thought better. Saligia called the trebuchets his *war wolves*.

The Drelve leaders met just behind the dense tree line at the fringe of the forest, their first line of defense. Most of Gaelyss's spells remained intact, and the Drelves had hurriedly reinforced areas damaged by the wyvern rider and the ill-fated hippogriff. Though awkward, the airborne attacks had been remarkably successful and wreaked havoc.

"I feel we're watching molasses flow," Clarke grumbled.

"It's more like watching hot lava flow from a volcano and not being able to run away," Tomayo chimed.

"They would like nothing more than to draw us into the open field, my friend. We must wait and make our shots count when they are in range," Rumsie answered.

"Yes, but they will have the cover of the siege machines. The great catapults have greater range than our longbows. Behind the cover of the siege machine, the enemy will be able to duck and cover," Clarke added.

Saligia studied the field and looked toward the amber skies. The time reached about mid light period. Farriers tended the thick hooves of the firehorses and quartermasters brought a steady supply of fresh mooler meat to feed the great beasts. Legions of Drolls and Kiennites labored to move the siege machines into their planned positions. Saligia ordered the field commanders to place the rolling log-walled fortress about three hundred paces from the fringe of the Drelves' forest and the trebuchets another hundred paces behind the wooden wall. By the beginning of the amber period, the fortress was near that point. The Drolls had difficulty moving around the craters in the meadow. In fact, the southernmost war machine almost fell into the largest crater. Many Drolls scurried with tools to fill in some of the crater. Swords and axes were poor substitutes for shovels.

Saligia's minions positioned the four trebuchets about two hundred paces apart. More Drolls led mooler drawn wagons carrying large boulders into position behind the machines. The delay frustrated the Kiennish General, but he waited for the machines to near his planned positions. The delays gave the Drelves time to shore up the weakened areas of the forest edge. The little Drelve Zack's efforts still benefited his people.

Saligia sent a fire rider across the scorched meadow to give directions to the field commanders. Meanwhile very youthful appearing Kiennish shamans went from fire rider to fire rider and muttered incantations. Faint purplish lights appeared about a half pace in front of the riders. The odd purplish lights formed the shape of a warrior's shield and remained in front of the fire riders when the firehorses moved.

Drolls pushed the log-walled fortification forward and their fellows began to move the four trebuchets from behind the fortress into positions equidistant from the Drelves' forest and one another. Saligia insisted the devices be placed 233 paces apart and their arms the equivalent of 21 paces in length.

As the Drolls advanced the central rolling log barricade, Rumsie shouted to his archers to make ready. The Sergeant Major took the longbow he had gotten from BJ, notched an arrow, pulled and extended the bowstring, and released the arrow. The missile soared over the rolling fortress and struck an unfortunate Droll who pushed the trebuchet nearest the rolling log wall. The warrior yowled in pain and fell. The dead Droll's name was Shaggy Korcran.

The Drolls hesitated briefly, snarled, cursed the Drelves, and then returned to their tasks.

The inexperienced Kiennish shamans laboriously cast their 99th spell. Now all fire riders now had a purplish glow before them. Saligia motioned to Bluthgar. The Horsemaster nodded his understanding.

Bluthgar made a sweeping forward motion with the war lance in his left hand and shouted, "For Lord Moochie!"

The 99 fire riders in unison shouted the same and charged forward. In only a few heartbeats the riders reached the midpoint of the meadow where the great tree had stood. Cheers erupted from the Drolls on the field as the riders passed.

"What are the purple lights?" Chamberlain asked.

"Simple Shield spells. They'll stop normal arrows and some Magick. Although the shamans were all born during the last Approximation of the

Gray Sun, these blokes aren't as versed in Magick as my brother Melphat. But the dweomers will protect the riders a bit," Saligia grudgingly answered.

"Too bad old Tumuch didn't have one of them," Neville chimed.

"Wouldn't have helped! The shield's protection is unidirectional and Lord Tumuch was nefariously attacked from the rear," General Saligia murmured. "Now follow me to the center of the field."

Reluctantly the Council of Aulgmoor, Neville, and Chamberlain mounted stone ponies and joined Lord Saligia. The General rode a saber-toothed mare. In comparison to the great firehorses, the Kiennish leaders rode mediocre steeds.

"To the second line," Rumsie shouted.

Drelve defenders vacated the trees at the edge of the field and moved to a row of trees immediately behind the front line. Archers remained at the edge of the forest, interspersed among the shrubs and Wall of Thorns Spells cast by Gaelyss.

"Stay your hand until they are in range. Fire one volley and then fall back. We've seen the range of the firehorses' breath. Someone must stand by the Spellweaver. My friends… please shoot well!" Rumsie ordered.

"I'll stand by Gaelyss," Morganne quickly offered.

The she-Drelve ran to the Spellweaver, who stood behind a Wall of Thorns a hundred paces behind the edge of the wood.

"Thank you for defending me," Gaelyss said appreciatively.

"It's my pleasure, Spellweaver. They will be here soon. May I offer you my lips for luck?" the she-Drelve asked.

Gaelyss shrugged and said, "I suppose I should not refuse the offer of luck at such a time."

Morganne kissed Gaelyss gently.

From her position in reserve, Kirrie enviously watched Gaelyss and Morganne's brief kiss. Unable to contain her zeal, the she-Drelve ran to Gaelyss, gave the Spellweaver a passionate kiss, and said, "You can't have too much luck!"

Suddenly the fire riders stopped a few paces to the rear of the Drolls pushing the war machines. Thick sulfurous smoke spewed from the ears and nostrils of the great steeds.

The Drolls shouted and pushed the war machines forward with renewed intensity. Expecting an all out attack by the fire horses, Rumsie had pulled his personnel back to safer ground, leaving only a few designated archers to try to pick the riders off the horses. The Sergeant Major watched the odd tactics on the field.

Clarke shouted, "Orders, Sergeant Major. They are moving those odd catapults into position."

"Archers in the front line, fire! Fire at will when the catapult drivers come into range. Clarke, Coweta make ready. The fire horses are too near to resume the high watch," Rumsie ordered.

"Why do the fire riders not attack? I've never seen such a formidable force. We have nothing to offset them," the veteran Beaux asked.

Neville surveyed the battlefield through his looking glass and asked, "Lord Saligia, the attack stalls. The fire riders have stopped short of the advancing war machines. Why do you halt the attack?"

"Does your great experience in battle tactics make you an expert, Neville?" Saligia answered facetiously.

"No, Lord Saligia, this is my first battle experience. It's just that the firehorses are so powerful. They should obliterate the Drelve defenses. We could walk into Alms Glen," Neville answered defensively.

"The firehorses are irreplaceable. Boulders are replaceable. As you witnessed, when Tumuch fell, his steed bolted away. As much as I disdain many things about our allies the Drolls, the Korcran clan has mastered the art of capturing and training the fire horses. Horse and rider becomes a unit. At all times, each rider has a second, third, and a fourth in training. The horse must never be without a rider. If the horse becomes separated from its rider, the animal runs away. Should all the riders of a given steed fall, the steed invariably returns to the wild. We have many foot soldiers. We have few fire riders. I suppose, viceroy Neville, you know the exact location of Alms Glen. I didn't think so! We have only begun the battle when we win this field. I plan on raining destruction down upon their beloved trees. Behind the wooden fortress our archers can return fire and keep them occupied. Boulders! Boulders, Neville! We'll pummel them with boulders. We've lots of boulders and foot soldiers," General Saligia discoursed.

"Yes, we can always get more rocks and Drolls," Chamberlain chimed sardonically.

"Why don't you go say such to our friend Bluthgar?" Saligia replied.

"I...I just thought you'd be glad I agreed with you," Chamberlain acquiesced.

"I'm impressed with you, Chamberlain. You're right. We can always get more Drolls," Saligia said quietly. "Now watch the effects of my war wolves, the constructions created from my designs."

Saligia extended his war lance forward and shouted, "Death to the Drelves! Avenge Lord Melphat! Avenge Lord Moochie! Avenge Lord Tumuch! Fire!"

Saligia's voice boomed across the field. Sentries saw his motion and went into action,

Drelves fired arrows toward the four trebuchets. The war machines stopped three hundred paces from the Drelves' forest edge. From the distance the defenders could see the details of the devices well. Much like an active hill of ants, Drolls labored to place a stone which weighed at least 300 pounds into the guide chute at the base of the frame of the war wolf.

The machines...

The trebuchet consisted of five basic parts; the frame, which the Drolls had constructed of hardwood hewn from the unwilling trees of the wild woods; the counterweight, which was a large piece of Elberton granite; the beam which was a fifty foot long section of heartwood; the sling, which was made of tough Nuaga lizard hide, and the guide chute fashioned from hardwood. (Nuaga was a big lizard with stretchy but extremely resilient hide.) The frame supported the other components and provided a raised platform from which to drop the counterweight. The counterweight, pulled by gravity alone, rotated the beam. The guide chute guided the sling through the frame and supported the enclosed projectile until acceleration was sufficient to hold it in the sling. The sling accelerated and held the projectile until it was released. One end of the sling was fixed to the beam, or arm, while the other was tied in a loop and slipped over a release pin extending from the end of the beam. As the beam rotated it pulled the sling, with its enclosed projectile, down the guide chute. As the sling exited the chute, it accelerated in an arc away from the beam, but because the beam was still pulling the sling behind, the loop was held on the pin. The sling continued to accelerate through its arc until it eventually swung ahead of the release pin. At this point known as the release angle, the loop slipped off the pin and the sling opened.

The Drolls released the counterweight and fired the mechanism. A loud swooshing sound followed and the war wolf hurled the 300-pound stone through the air toward the forward line of the Drelves. The huge rock crashed into trees, smashing a large red oak and breaking the tree at its midpoint. The tree fell, narrowly missing several Drelves. The Drelvish archers in the front ranks released a volley of arrows toward the trebuchet, but the war wolf was beyond effective range of their bows, and most arrows fell short of their mark. The other three trebuchets sent massive boulders crashing into the trees and fractured several large limbs. In less than a minute the Drolls loaded and fired a second salvo of stones into the woods, knocking down more trees. One stone squarely hit Gaelyss' Wall of Thorns Spells. In this instance, the thorns broke up the rock and gave Magick a small victory over Nature.

Rumsie surveyed the scene and said, "The boulders are smashing our defenses. We will soon be open to a close quarter assault. We shan't fare well in hand to hand battle with the Drolls."

"The machines are too far away. Our arrows don't reach them," Clarke dejectedly answered.

CHAPTER 43
Klunkus's Maneuver

The veteran Drelve Klunkus rushed to a group of archers who had just avoided the second toss of the rightmost war machine and shouted, "Follow me! I shan't just wait to be squashed like a bug by these rock tossers!"

Twenty or so archers followed Klunkus onto the open area of the meadow at a run. Soon they reached an area a hundred-pace distance from the forest and two hundred from the rightmost trebuchet. The group stopped, directed their bows toward the war machine, and fired accurately and effectively from this range.

Eleven Drolls manning the war wolf fell.

Klunkus ordered the group to reload, but a large group of Drolls bearing longswords and halberds ran from behind the rolling log barricade to their left and charged them.

"To the trees! With haste!" the veteran commanded.

Arrows flew from behind the log wall toward the beleaguered Klunkus and his companions.

"Cover them!" Rumsie ordered.

Drelves rushed to the edge of the wood and fired bowshots over Klunkus's retreating party. The archers felled a dozen Drolls who pursued Klunkus's group, but many others zealously chased the Drelves. Klunkus's group narrowly reached the woods ahead of the Drolls. The Drolls fell into lethal firing range and faced of dozens of arrows. Those who did not fall beat a hasty retreat to the cover of the rolling log wall. Klunkus's group's brave efforts slowed the firing of the rightmost device, but Drolls quickly ran to replace their fallen comrades. The other three devices rained boulders into the woods and battered the trees. A boulder fell upon a Drelve named Douglass Cutter from the Vale Road and ended his life. Huge boulders fired from the trebuchets forced the few remaining defenders to abandon their positions and fall back to the second tree line. Only the Walls of Thorns repelled or broke up the massive boulders.

"They'll run out of those big rocks soon," Clarke allowed.

"Not true! I see more war wagons hauling boulder from yonder woods. They are like grains of sand, these Drolls," Beaux observed.

In frustration Rumsie drew his BG longbow, notched an arrow, fired, and slew a Droll manning the trebuchet second from the north. The unlucky

Droll's name was Nick Henshell. Rumsie climbed onto one of the lower branches of a thick trunked red oak. Steadying himself, the Sergeant Major fired repeatedly and scored hits over and over again against the Drolls manning the trebuchets. Soon he exhausted his arrows and called for more. The Drelves' leader saved the three special arrows given him by the fletcher BJ Aires and disdained using the two red arrows taken from the fallen Drollen commander. Rumsie looked beyond the log fortress and trebuchets and stared at the Kiennites mounted on equines and the many firehorses in the middle of the field. Loganne refurbished the Sergeant Major's supply of standard arrows, and he continued to fire. Purplish smoke wafted from the BG self-bow's elaborate bowstring. Fearing damage to the artifact and seeing his efforts barely slowed the attacks of the war machines, Rumsie took the bow from his aching arms and bleeding fingers, and sighed.

"Someone fires at our machines from the woods. I thought you said the Drelves had no bows that would reach our positions on the field," Chamberlain asked.

"If you recall the Horsemaster Tumuch's fate, I'd say again there remains a Spellweaver among them. The best advice I can give you is to keep shields at ready. The shaman did what they could to protect the fire riders, but I wouldn't trust one of their shield spells to protect from such arrows as slew the Horsemaster. I trust this dragon hide shield more. I'd suggest you employ yours, Chamberlain," Saligia grumbled.

The Kiennite raised his shield and looked intently toward the woods. The firehorse commander Bluthgar rode to the General and his viceroys.

"Well, for now their counterattacks have stalled. The long-range arrows have stopped, and our warriors behind the log hide have chased them back into the woods," Neville reported as he stared through his looking glass.

The massive Droll Bluthgar said icily, "At great cost. I've...we've lost many warriors. When may I attack, General Saligia? My people die and I stand back," Bluthgar complained.

"I note your impatience Commander Bluthgar, but please recall the Horsemaster and your nephew's fates. We still face at least one Spellweaver. An unlikely and cursed affair, that the Drelves would have three! Our attacks weaken them by the moment. You'll have your chance. Stand with your fire riders," Saligia commanded.

Bluthgar growled but moved back to his riders.

The relentless attacks from the trebuchets continued.

"Gaelyss and Rumsie have done what they can. We can't withstand this onslaught," Edkim bemoaned.

Klunkus called together Beaux, Tomayo, and Clarke. The four had a rushed discussion, and then gathered groups of twenty or so Drelves. The four groups went to the fringe of the forest, dodging large boulders that crashed around them. Then the groups repeated the maneuver Klunkus had tried. Each group met with some success, dropping a few Drolls at each trebuchet. The attacks disrupted the Drolls efforts briefly, but sheer numbers enabled the large wolf-faced warriors to replace their losses quickly. Again Drolls armed with hand held weapons charged from behind the rolling wall and pursued the four groups of Drelves. Speed allied with the Drelves and each group hustled back to the forest ahead of the pursuing Drills. Drelvish archers fired into the charging Drolls and caused many casualties. Three groups of Drolls again retreated to behind their mobile bastion. The fourth group chased Tomayo's party. Karyl, a she-Drelve from the small hamlet Grove Town slipped and fell. Karyl stood and tired to run away, but the angry Drolls quickly closed on the young she-Drelve. Seeing her comrade's plight, Morganne left Gaelyss, ran to the edge of the wood, pulled several arrows from her quiver, notched the first, fired, and cut down the Droll nearest Karyl. Rapidly Morganne fired thrice and dropped a Droll each time. All but one of the Drolls that pursued Karyl turned and started to run away. Frustrated by other Drelves' escapes, the lone angry Droll growled and raised his battle-axe above his head. Morganne and Clarke fired arrows toward the big warrior. An instant before the missiles struck with lethal precision, the Droll unleashed his great axe and hurled it toward the fleeing Karyl. The weapon struck and smote the young she-Drelve. Karyl and the Droll fell at the same time. Morganne rushed to the fallen Karyl, picked up the she-Drelve's lifeless body, and ran to the forest's edge.

A Droll named Fred Mutts, commander of the trebuchet nearest Morganne and Karyl, grunted, "At least old Mixter took one out as he fell! This one's for you, Mixter my friend!"

Mutts place a huge boulder in the guide chute and dropped the counterweight. The projectile flew over the fallen Mixter, crashed into the woods, killed a Drelve named Lucie Brown, and avenged the Droll.

CHAPTER 44
Meryt and Debery's Plan

Meryt and Debery stood together beneath a hastily constructed shelter behind the lines.

"Gaelyss does all he can. Sergeant Major Rumsie has fought to his and his weapon's exhaustion. Our archers are beyond range unless they enter harm's way. The war machines batter our defensive positions. Bryce and Zack have died in the fray. What do you have left?" Meryt asked.

Debery replied, "I gave Zack all my cherry bombs, save one. My skills with the bow aren't refined. If we only had more of the special arrows and great bows! Rumsie fired the BG longbow until his fingers bled, but the Drolls are too many. He's felled fifty or more."

Meryt said, "I also have one bomb remaining. Seeing the damage Zack did, I think a bomb will bring down one of the war machines. The massive wooden log bastion they've constructed is too big. I can shield us but the Drolls would fell us with their axes before we accomplish the task."

"I agree. We can't do it together. They would certainly see and slay us before we reach the contraption. I can approach the war contraptions unseen. Will you give me your remaining cherry bomb?" Debery asked.

"I shan't allow you to do it alone. They will *smell* you and sniff you out before you get to the apparatus. Let's create a diversion. Our best archer Rumsie is too tired now, but the brave girl from Meadowsweet showed great proficiency with her bow. Let's go to her," Meryt suggested.

After returning with the fallen Karyl, Morganne returned to Gaelyss's side where she found young Kirrie standing by the Spellweaver with weapon drawn.

"You are supposed to guard the Spellweaver, *Morganne*! If you will not, I shall," the younger she-Drelve said stoutly.

"You should go to the rear and tend the injured, little one," Morganne replied coolly.

Several Drelves carried Karyl's broken body past the three young Drelves and minimized the importance of their squabble. Stretcher-bearers carried two seriously injured archers who had been knocked from their perches in the trees. Meryt and Debery approached the Spellweaver, Morganne, and Kirrie, where they stood about fifty paces beyond the range of the war wolves.

"That was pretty fancy shooting, Morganne. Would you come with me please?" Meryt asked.

"I'm told to guard Gaelyss," the she-Drelve replied.

"You abandoned him to try to help Karyl of Grove Town. Now I ask you to do another noble deed," Meryt asked.

Morganne turned to Gaelyss and asked, "What do you want me to do?"

"Do what you can to defend our people," Gaelyss answered.

Kirrie bravely entered, "I'll stand by him!"

The young Spellweaver slumped down on a fallen log and breathed heavily. Gaelyss had cast spells nigh continuously since the altercation had begun. His Magick consisted largely of defensive spells that augmented the powers of Nature and the forest. Many Wall of Thorns, Entangle, and Plant Growth Spells thickened and repaired damage caused by the Drolls' attacks. Kirrie wiped his brow with a soothing aloe leaf.

"Should I face the enemy, I can, for the moment, only wield my sword," Gaelyss admitted.

Meryt talked quietly with Morganne.

Morganne pulled her long sweat-soaked tresses aside and muttered, "It's a lame plan, but at least it's something to try. They are pummeling us!"

Just then a massive boulder crashed into a large everred about twenty paces in front of them. The everred fell, landed upon a Drelve named Jenna Leigh from Warren Town, and snuffed out her life.

Morganne, Debery, and Meryt walked to the edge of the woods. Standing on fairly open ground, an individual Drelve easily evaded the big boulders. Carefully avoiding the Magick barbs, Debery stepped behind a Wall of Thorns. Once again the young Drelve utilized his gift of Invisibility and disappeared from sight. Meryt then raised his left hand and a faint purplish aura appeared about a step in front of him. Morganne checked her quiver, replenished her supply of arrows, placed her fine short sword in its sheath, and carried her bow.

"Are you ready?" the invisible Debery asked.

"Yes. Let's do this! Here comes another boulder! Stay to our right and behind me! Neither the Drolls nor *I* see you!" Morganne shouted.

Clarke saw *two* young Drelves walking onto the field and screamed, "Meryt! Morganne! Don't throw your lives away! We need your bows! The trickery of the Magick shield will deter neither the Drolls' axes nor their fists!"

His words fell on deaf ears.

"Make haste and good luck, my friend. We can't hold them long!" Meryt said.

He and Morganne then walked forward. A massive boulder sailed over their heads and crashed into the woods behind them. Predictably, a number of Drolls ran from around the log hide and moved toward them.

"Ten, twenty, thirty, forty...they must think we're pretty tough!" Morganne muttered.

She allowed the Drolls to close about fifty paces, and then stepped to the side of Meryt. Her bowstring began to sing.

Whoosh!

Whoosh!

Whoosh!

Whoosh!

Four Drolls fell.

"Wait!" Meryt yelled.

He moved to his left a bit and extended his weightless shield before Morganne. Seven Drolls' arrows bounced harmlessly away. Morganne stepped to the right and fired three times.

Whoosh!

Whoosh!

Whoosh!

Three Drolls fell, but now thirty-three closed to about seventy paces from the pair. Then a whine, rock, and great explosion roared to their left. The ground trembled as the southernmost large war machine broke apart and crashed to the ground. The explosion caught the attention of the Drolls charging toward Morganne and Meryt, and the thirty-three enemies stopped. The enemies' hesitation gave the two Drelves a head start.

"Just give me three steps!" Meryt shouted.

Morganne fired three times in rapid succession.

Whoosh!

Whoosh!

Whoosh!

Morganne felled three more Drolls, and then followed Meryt's suggestion of a hasty retreat.

Total chaos enveloped the area around the destroyed trebuchet. The explosion ripped a great crater in the ground and threw large stones into the air. Timbers fell all about. A flying boulder landed on an approaching war wagon loaded with more ammunition for the trebuchets, broke the wagon apart, and scattered the wagon's payload. The six moolers yoked to the wagon broke free and ran toward the Kiennish leaders in the middle of the field. The large purple beasts rumbled across the scorched field and bore down on Saligia's position. Before the massive bovines reached his commander in chief, Bluthgar ordered six fire riders to intercept the erstwhile beasts of burden. The firehorses moved between the leaders and the stampeding moolers. The equines sent forth bursts of flame similar to dragon fire and roasted the moolers.

"Lots of meat for dinner," Bluthgar surmised.

Morganne and Meryt ran quickly toward the forest. The Drelves' spirits lifted as they neared the forest's edge and realized the pursuing Drolls couldn't catch them. Then Morganne recognized the dreaded sound of many arrows in the air. Sickened she turned. The Drolls had stopped and launched a myriad of arrows toward her and the fleeing Meryt. The young she-Drelve took a deep breath and waited for the end. Just as the arrows neared, Meryt knocked her forward to the ground and sprawled on top of her. Meryt extended his hands over his head and shoulders and covered most of their bodies with the purplish ghostly shield.

Realizing Morganne was taller, Meryt shouted, "Draw in your legs."

Reflexively Morganne pulled her knees under her chest.

Thuds!

Many thuds!

Many arrows struck the ground around her.

"Ouch!" Morganne cried.

A twinge of pain in her left leg and a low moan from Meryt told the she-Drelve something was amiss. Encouragingly she heard the whirring of arrows flying over her head from the woods behind her. The Drelvish archers counterattacked the Drolls. Though grievously wounded Meryt still breathed. The power of his Magick Shield wavered. Morganne struggled to her feet. A crude arrow protruded from her left lower leg and confirmed she had been shot. Unfortunately for young Meryt, his legs had extended beyond the protection of the shield and he suffered several wounds. He was bleeding badly and the little Drelve's consciousness faded. Ignoring her pain, Morganne drug Meryt to his feet and struggled toward the waiting woods, which now seemed so far away. Disdaining shields and within a hundred paces of the woods' edge, the Drolls who had pursued Morganne and Meryt were easy picking for the deadly accurate Drelvish archers. The few Drolls not killed immediately turned and ran back to the cover of the log walled fortification.

Tomayo, Klunkus, and two Drelves from Churchill Downs named Big Boy Brown and Tiny Tim rushed from the edge of the forest to their wounded comrades. Coweta ran beside the others with an arrow's nock pulled against her bowstring. Struggling, Morganne pulled the steadily weakening Meryt.

"Cover them!" Rumsie shouted.

Suddenly another massive explosion rocked the battlefield and destroyed the trebuchet positioned just to the left of the rolling log fortress. The explosion opened another great crater in the ground. Many Drolls lost their lives. The commotion gave Klunkus, Tomayo, Big Boy Brown, and Tiny Tim the time they needed to reach Morganne and Meryt. Coweta stood beyond the wounded Drelves and fired one, two, three, four, five, and six arrows into Drolls as the wolf faced warriors appeared from behind the cover of the rolling log hideaway. The seven Drelves remained fifty paces from the woods.

General Saligia had barely time to assess the destruction from the first explosion when the second hit.

His observers reported, "A Drelve stood before the forest edge protected by Magick. His cohort fired arrows with great lethality. Our warriors bravely stood against them. Now great fireballs have destroyed two war wolves. Our warriors battle Magick."

"Spellweavers! Cursed Spellweavers! How many? ****!" Saligia screamed.

Carrying halberds and ugly battle-axes, a hundred Drolls poured from behind the rolling log fortress and ran with reckless abandon toward the injured Drelves and the quintet working to save them. Other Drolls armed with long bows followed.

"Cover them! Cover them! Fire! Fire! Fire!" Rumsie commanded.

Drelves rushed to the edge of the meadow. Twenty archers knelt with bows drawn and twenty others stood behind them. Klunkus, Tiny Tim, Big Boy Brown, and Tomayo struggled to help Morganne and Meryt. Coweta bravely stood her ground and fired until she emptied her quiver. She then turned and followed fifty paces behind the others. Klunkus, Tomayo, Big Boy Brown, and Tiny Tim reached the woods with Morganne and Meryt. By now, the Drolls were within ten paces of Coweta, who was forty paces away from the woods' edge. Coweta saw her comrades reach the edge of the woods, realized the Drolls were too near, and heard Rumsie's commands. The she-Drelve dropped to the ground and rolled. As soon as Coweta fell to the ground, the first rank of archers fired a volley into the charging Drolls. Immediately the second rank fired, followed by the first rank again. A torrent of arrows rained lethally into the beleaguered Drolls. From the range of forty paces the Drelves' bows were nigh as accurate as a Magick Missile. The Drolls fell in great numbers. While her comrades' arrows sailed over her prone body, Coweta crawled to the relative safety of the edge of the forest.

More Drolls charged from behind the rolling log hideaway. Then from the few still standing trees, Drelves' arrows filled the air and rained down on the charging Drolls. More than thirty fell. Others ran onward, but a second volley felled another twenty. Demoralized, the remainder turned and fled back toward the relative safety of the rolling log. For the moment the two remaining war machines stopped firing.

"Cowards! Fools! Our forces must pursue the Drelves into the woods! Why do they think we pound the barriers?" General Saligia growled as he stared across the field.

"General Saligia, we face *Spellweavers*! Observers described Magick shielding a warrior on the field. At the same time explosions destroyed the war wolves. Two more sources of Magick! How many Spellweavers do we face? Will they attack the rolling fortress next? We now have only two functional war machines. Shouldn't our forces retreat?" Neville suggested.

"You are a simple ****, Neville. The war wolves are ripping down the trees and underbrush. Our forces have killed two Spellweavers already. We'll kill two more! ****** Spellweavers! ****** Magick! My warriors manning the war wolves are dying at the hands of the Drelves who are running onto the field. Neville, make yourself useful! Ride to Commander Bluthgar and ask him to send five fire riders to each remaining trebuchet. This will deter these brazen little attacks," Saligia growled.

Neville shuddered, then said, "Yes, Lord Saligia."

The viceroy urged his stone pony and the little gray equine trotted to the side of the Droll Horsemaster's huge firehorse.

After speaking with Neville, Bluthgar looked toward Saligia, nodded and sent five fire riders to each trebuchet. 89 firehorses remained in the center of the meadow, some five hundred paces from the war machines and two hundred paces from Saligia's entourage. The two remaining war wolves resumed an all out attack and knocked down taller trees. Few arrows now came from the forest. Saligia stared at the disrupted outer section of the Drelve forest a thousand paces away.

The General smirked and said, "89 is a good number. Soon the Drelves will know the meaning of fire and brimstone."

Coweta replenished her quiver and remained at the front line. Klunkus and Tiny Tim helped Morganne to the relative safety of a shelter in the rear. Tomayo and Big Boy Brown carried Meryt. Gaelyss, the Teacher, Kirrie, and the elder Ulysses worked feverishly with Morganne. The Teacher Edkim expertly removed the nasty arrow from the she-Drelve's leg. Assisted by Kirrie, the elder Ulysses applied an ointment made from enhancing root and many forest herbs. Kirrie administered an herbal tea enhanced by the precious tubers. Gaelyss placed his right hand on Morganne's upper thigh above the wound.

Struggling to maintain consciousness, Morganne smiled meekly and said, "Watch your hand, Spellweaver. I usually don't allow such familiarity."

Gaelyss took several small white berries in his left hand, crushed them, touched the juice to Morganne's lips, uttered a few phrases, and completed a Cure Spell.

The spell eased much of Morganne's pain, and she asked, "How is Meryt?"

"We…we have lost him," Edkim sadly reported.

"No! He…saved me," Morganne sobbed.

"Your efforts, though foolhardy, have aided us greatly. How did Meryt hurl the bombs while guarding you with his Shield Spell?" Edkim continued.

"No, it wasn't Meryt! What's become of Debery?" Morganne queried.

"Debery?" Edkim quizzically followed.

"Debery. *He* threw the cherry bombs. Where is Debery?" Morganne asked.

Gaelyss placed his hands on her shoulders, and said, "You should rest."

"We didn't see…oh, no! Debery used his ability again. I'd asked him not to do so. Klunkus! Beaux! Tomayo! Clarke! Look for young Debery," Edkim asked.

After a few moments Clarke reported, "Debery has gone missing."

Gaelyss sighed, stood, and looked toward the field. Morganne rested and breathed comfortably.

The young Spellweaver turned to Edkim and said, "I'll go to the edge of the field and look for him."

"No! It's too dangerous. *I* can't…we can't spare you!" Kirrie protested.

"She's right, Spellweaver. Sentries report several firehorses have moved near the remaining war machines. They could reach us in a flash," Rumsie cautioned.

"I must find my friend," Gaelyss said determinedly.

"Defend him at all cost!" Rumsie ordered.

Accompanied by Klunkus, Clarke, Tomayo, Rumsie, and Beaux, Gaelyss walked to the edge of the woods. Far to his right Drolls placed boulders in the guide chutes of the two remaining trebuchets and then resumed firing the war machines. The Kiennites' leaders and the fire horses remained in the center of the field. Five fire riders waited near both war wolves.

Gaelyss raised his left hand, muttered old Drelvish phrases, and slowly scanned the field. Boulders crashed into the trees about a hundred paces to his right, but the Spellweaver maintained his concentration and unhurriedly moved his extended fingers from left to right.

When he pointed toward and just to the left of the second destroyed trebuchet, Gaelyss stopped and gloomily said, "I detect an aura...an invisible body lies near the ruins of the second war machine."

"Direct me!" Rumsie insisted.

Gaelyss pointed the area where the body was located. Rumsie bolted from the edge of the woods. Clarke, Klunkus, and Beaux followed him. The fire horse riders nearer them noted the four Drelves, but followed orders and held their positions. Drolls behind the rolling fortress poured out onto the field.

Seeing the Drolls moving toward Rumsie, Tomayo shouted, "Charge the war machine! Give the Sergeant Major time!"

A group of fifteen Drelves ran toward the war machine nearer the northern end of the log wall. Seeing the larger group of Drelves running toward the trebuchet, the Drolls changed course, ran away from Rumsie's little group, and rushed toward Tomayo's party.

Tomayo shouted, "Stop! Give them a volley, and then return to the wood. The firehorses are moving!"

When Rumsie reached neared the body on the field, Gaelyss muttered two phrases. The Dispel Magick dweomer removed the invisibility and enabled Rumsie to find the prostrate form. Clarke arrived in short time. The veterans scooped up the small frame and rushed back to the woods. At the same time Tomayo's charges fired a single volley, turned, and ran as fast as they could to the woods. Drelves in the woods fired arrows into the Drolls and slowed them. The fire riders inched forward, but stopped when Tomayo's group retreated. Both Rumsie and Tomayo's groups reached the battered fringes of the woods. Again suffering losses, the Drolls stopped their pursuit and returned to the cover of the log-walled bastion.

Rumsie and Gaelyss ran to the Teacher and Ulysses. The elder still tended Morganne and a wounded Drelve named Kate Hannie from the Vale Road. All the while both war machines pummeled the trees and woods to the north end of the barren meadow and forced the Drelves to retreat further into the woods.

257

A well-made arrow pierced Debery's lifeless body.

"This arrow...is Drelvish. It bears the fletcher BJ's insignia, and the markings say..." Rumsie noted.

"It bears my mark. The missile that killed Debery flew from my bow," a grief stricken Coweta chagrinned.

"You could not see him and didn't know he was there! Your arrows kept them from us. Excepting your efforts, we'd *all* be dead, " Klunkus said sympathetically.

"He took out two war machines and gave us time, though I don't really know why the fire riders tarry," Edkim assessed.

Bearers arrived with two additional casualties. Shelton and Martha hailed from the vintner's community near Mirror Lake. Martha died when a boulder smashed into her hideaway. A Droll's arrow ended Shelton's life.

Gaelyss wept at the loss of his friends.

Edkim gently closed Debery's eyes and solemnly said, "We are bereft of Zack, Bryce, Meryt, and Debery. The four gained the gift of Magick at the Green Vale. Now at the cost of their lives, they have used that gift to aid our cause."

"Perhaps it should be called the curse of Magick," old Clarke chimed.

"Perhaps it should," Gaelyss added cynically.

The Spellweaver's comment startled the Drelves gathered around young Debery's body. The Teacher Edkim, Sergeant Major Rumsie, the old Veteran Clarke, young Kirrie, the wounded Morganne, Klunkus, Beaux, bereaved Coweta, Tomayo, and the elder of Meadowsweet Ulysses stood quietly. A boulder smashed a red oak about fifty paces to the north.

A runner approached General Saligia and knelt to one knee. The General recognized Tessa Long, a Kiennite from Harding's warren. Tessa Long had been stationed in the log-walled bastion.

"Give your report," Saligia commanded.

"Lord Saligia, the Drelves retrieved the body of a frail unarmed Drelve near the ruins of the second war wolf. He had been invisible in life. I also saw a Drelve who protected a she-Drelve archer with a Magick shield fall on the field. It seems the battle has cost them two more *Spellweavers*," Tessa Long reported.

"What has been our cost, Tessa?" Saligia asked.

"Lord Saligia, the invisible Drelve nefariously destroyed two war machines with powerful Magick. I'd number our losses at 800 warriors since the war machines began to fire," Tessa reported.

"Two Spellweavers against only two war machines and a few hundred Drolls! That is a great accomplishment, Lord Saligia! What a strategic victory! When have we seen the deaths of four Drelvish Spellweavers?" Neville chirped.

"You are a fool, Neville. But in this case the sacrifices of our warriors and engineers have not been in vain. The Drelves foolishly expend their greatest assets early in the fray. The war wolves have nigh obliterated the trees to my left. Our greatest force, as *I've* always intended, remains in reserve to immolate the forests and expose Alms Glen. Soon we'll attack in force and rid the World of the Three Suns of the Drelves," Saligia grunted.

CHAPTER 45
Battle Lines

The amber period ended and the skies brightened as the light period began. The Drelves looked to the skies and hoped for a sign of the gray sun. The Kiennites and Drolls scanned the same skies and happily noted the Gray Wanderer Andreas remained but a speck low in the horizon. The Drelves ended an amber period without rest. Many Drolls lay dead on the field. Rumsie could only estimate the enemies' losses. The Sergeant Major knew the name of every Drelve who had fallen. Kirrie sang a dirge for the fallen at daybreak. Clarke, Tomayo, Beaux, and Klunkus accompanied her with mournful Musick played on their *toot and see scrolls*.

Saligia sat upon his saber-toothed mare and surveyed the field. The Drolls manning the trebuchets were about out of boulders, but the machines had demolished the outer curtain of the Drelves' defenses. Outer curtain generally referred to a castle or edifice's outer wall, but the great trees had served that purpose for the Drelves. Following the same analogy, the upper branches of the great trees served as the allure or wall walk for the Drelves. The Kiennite General summoned Bluthgar.

"Let's test the enemies' reserve, Commander. Send the ten fire riders stationed with the war wolves to the wood's edge. Burn the debris. Slay any Drelves who happen along," Saligia commanded.

"Yes, Lord Saligia," the big Droll answered.

Bluthgar started toward the front line.

"Wait! Send thirty-four fire riders to the right and keep fifty-five to the left," Saligia insisted.

"Lord Saligia, those numbers would include my steed and me," Bluthgar insisted.

"Then let Neville deliver the orders," Saligia demanded.

"As you wish," Bluthgar answered snidely.

"Lord Saligia, I'm not a man of war. I'm…I'm just your viceroy. I should stand by and advise you," Neville stammered.

"Take my banner and deliver my orders to the forward fire riders," Saligia growled.

Neville nervously accepted the standard, which bore the insignia of the Aulgmoor warren. Wearing his finely made red tunic across his narrow shoulders made the gnarly Kiennite more imposing. Reluctantly, Neville urged his stone pony and the stalwart equine moved forward.

Coweta stood bravely on the second branch of a mangled red oak some thirty paces beyond what was the edge of the woods. She shouted to Rumsie, "Sergeant Major Rumsie, an elaborately adorned Kiennite bearing the royal insignia of Aulgmoor approaches the forward line. He makes for the fire riders."

Rumsie jumped up and joined Coweta. The Sergeant Major stared at the carnage about him and the scarce cover that remained for his people. The Drelves' commander then looked behind him, scanned the forest, and saw the dead and wounded Drelves. Rumsie remembered the vigor and zest for life shared by Meryt, Zack, Bryce, and Debery. Sadly he recalled the beauty of the Lone Oak. Anger and Dread filled the Drelve's heart as he watched the noble Kiennite approach.

Did this person foment these foul deeds?

Rumsie sneered and drew one of the three exceptional arrows the fletcher and bowyer BJ had given him. The Drelve Sergeant Major placed the nock of the blue arrow against the extraordinary bowstring of BG's self-bow.

Neville reached the sullen fire riders who sat upon the snorting steeds a few paces beyond the war machine. Exhausted Drolls slumped against the support structure of the trebuchet and an empty war wagon. To his right several hundred Drolls gathered behind the rolling log-walled bastion. Many others perched upon the apparatus with bows and scrying devices. Saligia's viceroy tentatively approached the largest Droll who not coincidentally rode the largest firehorse.

Bluthgar's second, a Droll named Dolenz, commanded the fire riders who guarded the trebuchets. Though not Korcran by birth, at an early age Dolenz ran away from his clan in the northernmost regions of the Doombringer Mountains and joined a traveling minstrel show. His travels led the young Droll to the Korcrans. Dolenz had a readily apparent gift for dealing with the temperamental firehorses and remained under the tutelage of Bluthgar and the Kiennish Horsemaster Tumuch.

Neville harrumphed, expanded his chest, and said, "I command you to attack the remnants of the forest. Take no prisoners."

Dolenz answered, "I saw you leave Lord Saligia and Commander Bluthgar's side. You carry the banner of Aulgmoor. For those reasons, and those reasons only, I will carry out these orders. Get back to the rear and *hide,* viceroy!"

261

Dolenz bowed facetiously.

Rumsie muttered to Coweta, "The fire rider bows to elaborately adorned Kiennite! Tis worth this price to be rid of him!"

The Drelve released the arrow, which flew from the self-bow, quickly traversed the distance to the Kiennite, and sank deeply into his chest. Neville meekly groaned, dropped the banner of Aulgmoor, and fell from the stone pony. The little horse galloped toward the Drelves. Quickly a Droll scurried from the trebuchet, retrieved the banner of Aulgmoor, and waved it through the air.

"Good shot, Sergeant Major!" Coweta marveled.

"Neville is slain! Woe!" Chamberlain exclaimed.

"How will we *ever* get by without him?" Saligia said sarcastically. The General hastily added, "Retrieve my banner."

The Droll Dolenz made a forward motion with his war lance, and he and his nine colleagues moved forward. Facing the Drelves' woods, the ten fire riders fanned out and moved past the war machines and the cheering Drolls. With a shout, the ten charged forward. Rumsie fired one of the fletcher BJ's finely made arrows from BG's self-bow. The projectile followed a true course toward Dolenz, but Dolenz turned the purplish ghostly shield into the arrow's path. The arrow stopped instantly when it impacted the Magick Shield and dropped harmlessly to the ground.

The fire horses quickly reached the woods. Rumsie and Coweta barely evaded them. The riders spurred their horrific steeds; the fire horses reared and spewed flames onto the dismantled trees and underbrush. The breath of the horses approximated the breath weapon of small young red dragons. The flames consumed everything except the Wall of Thorns Spells cast by the Spellweaver Gaelyss.

Rumsie gathered his forces and set up a line of defense at a predetermined point some fifty paces back in the woods. Soon thick smoke filled the air, and the fire riders eased into the forest. One rider attempted to spur his horse over the Wall of Thorns. The thorns caught the animal's underside and severely injured the equine. Horse and rider fell to the ground. Drelvish archers slew the Droll. The injured firehorse thrashed about in pain. Clarke hoped to mercifully end the animal's suffering with his blade, but the animal's thick hide turned away the sword. The badly wounded animal attempted to spit flames on the Drelve and prevented further action by the old veteran. Meanwhile the other fire riders steadily broke through the underbrush and penetrated the forests further. Several ranks of Drelve archers peppered the air with bowshots, but the purplish shields deflected the arrows. One Droll moved laterally, exposed his flank, and allowed a well-placed shot from young Zachary's bow to find his left thigh. The rider yelped, corrected his direction, and moved forward.

The Droll field leader Dolenz growled, "Forward you fools! Damage their defenses and take out as many as you can. But stay on course, **** you!"

By design, the Drelves' tactics kept the riders moving in one direction. The firehorses and riders funneled into a narrow pathway the defenders had cut into the woods. At the same time the enemies cut deeply into the defenses.

Morganne donned her buckskin body armor, grabbed her bow and quiver, and shouted, "Follow me! Bows ready!"

The she-Drelve moved to the south, away from the firehorses. Klunkus, Beaux, and four Drelves from Meadowsweet named Hamilton, Joe, Frank, and Reynolds followed Morganne. The seven Drelves looped back toward the scorched meadow, ran onto the edge of the field, ran northward for a few paces, and reentered the Drelves' burning forest. Only small shrubs and stalwart walkabouts, a few Wall of Thorns Spells, and thick smoke separated the seven from the fire riders.

"Are we not committing suicide?" Beaux asked.

"Meryt told me to stay behind him. The protection of a Magick shield is unidirectional. The fire riders concentrate on pushing forward. Our arrows do nothing to the steeds. Zachary has shown us the riders are vulnerable. Firing our arrows from any angle but frontal will injure the Drolls aboard the horses. BJ's arrows will penetrate their armor. Avoid hitting the purplish shields." Morganne said.

Rumsie placed Clarke in charge, broke off from the main group of defenders, and went to Gaelyss. The Teacher Edkim and Kirrie had not left the Spellweaver's side.

Rumsie urgently shouted, "Move to the tree behind us, Spellweaver. Teacher, Kirrie, stand fast! If I fall, he's in your hands. Do whatever you can!"

"The situation looks grim," the Teacher glumly added.

"We must prepare for the worst. Hoping it might disrupt their chain of command, I used one of the three arrows the fletcher BJ Aires entrusted to me and smote a Kiennish noble on the field, but it didn't work," Rumsie quickly added.

Rumsie took a position between the young Spellweaver and the bustle in the hedgerow created by the Drollen fire riders and their ghastly steeds. The Sergeant Major held BG's self-bow and an exceptional blue arrow with its nock against the bowstring and waited. There wasn't much else he could do.

At the point the third war wolf had attacked the woods and caused extensive damage, Morganne, Klunkus, Beaux, Hamilton, Joe, Frank, and Reynolds reentered the woods and moved parallel to the firehorses. Carefully dodging the Magick barbs on a Wall of Thorns, Morganne edged her way along. Wincing to peer through the smoke, the she-Drelve saw the flaming nostrils of the nearest fire horse about fifty paces to the north and hundred or so paces into the woods. Morganne could not see the rider but knew she looked at him from the side. Concentrating, the she-Drelve pulled her bowstring, aimed just above the horse's back near his middle, and released an arrow into the smoke. The seven Drelves heard a loud yelp as the arrow found its mark.

"A piece of luck! A blind squirrel just found a nut," Klunkus commented appreciatively.

Encouraged by Morganne's shot, the others fired into the smoky woods. Thuds and yells followed. Three horses ran rider-less out of the woods and across the field. Shouts of encouragement came from the woods. Arrows flew over Morganne and her group's heads toward the fire riders.

"Those came from our archers! Are they going to shoot us?" young Reynolds asked apprehensively.

"Keep low and hope for the best," the veteran Beaux answered the youth.

The veteran's words did not reassure the youth.

"Keep firing!" Morganne urged.

Their flanking maneuver gave the seven an advantage. The Magick shields stopped frontal attacks against the Drollen fire riders. The lucky seven fired one, two, three volleys into the smoky area and created more chaos. Without riders, two more firehorses ran from the woods.

Dolenz and three other fire riders remained. The big Droll had accomplished his mission. His riders and their steeds had destroyed the rubble created by the war machines, opened a path for the foot soldiers, and killed a few Drelves.

Dolenz wanted more.

The arrows in his left leg were mere nuisances. Cursed Drelves had flanked him and fired around his shield. He'd seen five of his fellows fall, including his cousin Cubby. Once their riders fell, the unruly steeds bolted. Dolenz lacked the skills to capture a fire horse. Few possessed such skills. The Korcran clan had tended equines of all sorts, but the numbers of horses in their possession had diminished in recent time. The Korcrans had not captured a fire horse in several hundred dark periods. Losing the five horses hurt nigh as much as the loss of his brethren.

Dolenz sensed panic in the air. The Drelves retreated in a pattern. They were protecting something, or *someone*! Thanks to his equine's fiery breath, a clear path led into the woods.

Thud!

Thump!

Another Drelve's arrow pierced the neck of the rider to Dolenz's right. The rider gasped, fell from the horse, and the steed predictably ran away.

"Why are we waiting? Let's make a name for ourselves in this battle. The Drelves guard the areas to our left tenaciously. Take that direction! Keep your shield facing forward. It moves with you. Slay all you can!" Dolenz ordered.

The three fire riders urged their steeds forward and charged through the thin remaining underbrush.

Morganne saw another steed run away from the battle. Six firehorses had fled. The death throes of the seventh horse injured by the Wall of Thorns had mercifully ended. Loud shouts, neighs, and screams of horror told her the remaining three fire horses had broken through and charged toward Gaelyss's position. Rumsey had kept the special arrow's nock against his bowstring. Three firehorses charged toward the area where the Spellweaver had worked with the Teacher Edkim and tended the wounded. Kirrie stood strongly by Gaelyss. Morganne's group broke and ran from the field, but they were too far away to help.

Rumsie fired BJ's blue arrow at the nearest stallion. The arrow found its mark in the horse's neck. Though not lethal, the painful injury caused the steed to buck violently. The Droll fire rider struggled to maintain control of the horse and in so doing let down his shield. Three Drelvish arrows pierced his chest, and the Droll fell lifelessly to the ground. The injured firehorse kicked and neighed violently. One of its fore hooves hit a Drelve named Roesgen who hailed from the Vale Road. The firehorse angrily spewed fire, set several trees and shelters ablaze, and then fled from the forest. All the while Dolenz and his remaining comrade headed straight for Gaelyss. Rumsie quickly rolled aside and avoided the charging fire horses. The horses spewed flames toward Gaelyss and Kirrie. Gaelyss threw a drop of shiny silvery liquid into the air, muttered a brief phrase, and cast a spell, which surrounded Kirrie and himself with blue light. Fire bathed them but left the two Drelves uninjured. Taking advantage of his position to the side of Dolenz's subordinate, Edkim sent a flash of blue flame into the rider. The Magick Missile knocked the rider from the horse. Typically the horse fled as the rider fell to the forest's floor.

Now Dolenz and his steed stood alone against the Drelves.

Two additional Spellweavers!

How many walked with the Drelves?

Which should he attack?

Not much time!

Another arrow penetrated his right leg. Dolenz turned toward Gaelyss, drew back his war lance, shouted, and started to hurl the weapon. An instant before the Droll threw the weapon, Rumsie expended his last special arrow. The arrow passed through the Droll's forearm and knocked the war lance from his hand. The lance fell harmlessly to the ground. Disarmed and seeing Gaelyss protected from flames by Magick, Dolenz yelled and directed his horse toward Edkim. The horse exhaled before Rumsie, Clarke, or Gaelyss could react. The flames approached the Teacher, started to engulf him, but then eerily moved around Edkim's frame and singed the grass and trees around him.

Dolenz stared in disbelief.

Then horrific pain…

Several Drelve arrows sank deeply into his wide back. Dolenz thought of the wide meadows of the Nags Head plain high in the Doombringer Mountains where the Droll had spent the finest times of his life. More arrows struck the massive Droll. As Dolenz took his last breath, the Horsemaster reflexively clutched the reins, wrapped them around his left wrist, and nudged the animal. Carrying his dead rider, the firehorse turned and ran from the forest.

Edkim sensed coldness in his raiment.

He shouldn't draw breath!

How did he survive?

Why was he alive?

Had the odd gray stone in his raiment protected him?

Kirrie shuddered, grasped Gaelyss's hand, and sobbed, "You…you saved me…us!"

Gaelyss shrugged and replied, "In so doing, I used my last drop of mercury. I can't produce another Resist Fire Spell."

Rumsie ran to the Spellweaver.

Seeing Gaelyss was unharmed, he then went to the Teacher and marveled, "Mr. Magick Edkim! How many more tricks have you? First the Magick Missile, then the Fire Resistance! Your spell differed from the Spellweaver's? Are you indeed a Spellweaver?"

"Indeed, I am not. I did cast the Magick Missile. The Gray Wanderer bequeathed me the dweomer at the Green Vale. This stone saved me from the fiery death the fire rider intended I endure," Edkim muttered.

The Teacher pulled a simple gray stone from his raiment. The gray rock conformed to Edkim's grasp.

"What is this stone, Teacher?" Rumsie asked.

"An artifact. I…I don't know its origins, but I know its power," Edkim answered.

Gaelyss added, "Teacher, it gives an aura, but it's an aura of mystery. I can't decipher the meaning."

Kirrie eyed the events intently. The little she-Drelve still gripped Gaelyss's hand tenaciously. Morganne, Klunkus, Beaux, and the foursome from Meadowsweet, Hamilton, Joe, Frank, and Reynolds ran to the area.

"Is the Spellweaver unharmed?" Morganne panted.

"For now," Rumsie added.

The firehorse bearing the dead Droll Dolenz neared the center of the field.

General Saligia stared at the woods. He had seen eight unbridled firehorses flee from the field and knew their riders had met their doom. Bearing Dolenz, another horse approached. Observers couldn't account for one fire horse.

Bluthgar sighed and said, "Dolenz serves even in death. Though not Korcran, he was like a brother to me. Thanks to him, we retain at least one of the steeds. Riders I can train. Firehorses are irreplaceable. We lost the Korcran family heirloom that helped us capture the wild horses. Dolenz did what you asked, Lord Saligia, and cleared a path into the depths of the Drelves' defenses. Do you think they could have defeated ten fire riders without the aid of a Spellweaver?"

Chamberlain interrupted, "It's not possible! Lord Saligia has slain four Spellweavers in this conflict. Your riders must have spooked their horses!"

"You scumbag! I ought to skewer you now! Does this warrior look like he spooked his horse? More than twenty arrows impale him, yet he returns with his steed?" Bluthgar angrily responded.

"Chamberlain, do you want to accompany Commander Bluthgar in the attack?" Saligia asked facetiously.

"No…no, General Saligia. I…I must remain near you, so to advise you," Chamberlain stuttered.

"Petty battles have cost us ten riders and nine steeds. May I attack in force and end this thing, Lord Saligia?" Bluthgar asked.

Saligia looked to the east. Thick smoke billowed into the air at the battle site. Large numbers of Drolls gathered behind the rolling log-walled field fort. The war wolves stood quiet. He glanced behind him and saw a legion of Kiennites in reserve. Another legion of Drolls stood at ready. 89 fire riders gathered around the fallen Dolenz.

"It is time. Send forth the ground forces. Prepare for your attack, Commander Bluthgar," Saligia ordered.

CHAPTER 46
Regrouping

Rumsie and the Teacher gathered the Drelves' leaders around, including Glinne the father of Gaelyss, Loganne the daughter of old Moblee the elder of Alms Glen, Debby the Alms Glen elder, and the bowyer BJ Aires. Kirrie and Morganne refused to leave Gaelyss's side. Blanchard and Ulysses the elders of Alms Glen and Meadowsweet respectively gathered the effects of their lost citizens. The veterans Balewyn, Clarke, and Tomayo watched the field. Smoke gradually cleared.

Rumsie said, "They gather a tremendous force, Teacher. Drolls and Kiennites in the thousands! Our arrows can't bring them all down. More importantly eighty-nine fire riders and steeds remain. Defeating ten such enemies extended our resources. Without the uncommon valor of Morganne, Beaux, Klunkus, Hamilton, Joe, Frank, Reynolds, young Zachary, and others, we'd have already lost. Teacher, your unexpected Magick is reassuring. Gaelyss, it's good we have you. What more can you do?"

Edkim answered, "My newly bequeathed power of Magick Missile consumes great mental and physical energies. I feel fatigue I've never felt. I can muster the necessary energy only twice each period, if that! The fire resistance occurred without my knowing and was not of my doing. Our Spellweaver has labored constantly throughout this ordeal and borders on exhaustion. But for his spells, the Drolls would have walked upon us. Gaelyss, have you the energy for a Summoning Spell?"

"For what reason, Teacher? Animals can do little to help us," Rumsie asked.

"I require flight, Sergeant Major. I have an idea of combating the firehorses," the Teacher answered.

"How can we fight such an enemy?" Rumsie challenged.

The Teacher answered, "Obviously, ice opposes fire. Cold opposes hot. Unfortunately our Magick doesn't include spells of destructive cold Magick. Gaelyss?"

Gaelyss sighed, "Teacher, the Fire Resistance Spell sapped me. I can offer no Magick. Give me a bow so I can fight."

"Then all is lost. I'd say we should send the Spellweaver deeply into the forest and make whatever stand we can," Rumsie said dejectedly.

Ǿ ∞ Ǿ

"The Drolls and Kiennites and their firehorses will fire the entire forest. It'd just be a matter of time until he's overtaken. The enemies are too many," Klunkus inserted.

"Perhaps you are right," Edkim conceded

"I can help," Kirrie said softly.

"You have done so much already," Edkim said.

"No. I can help you fly," Kirrie answered.

"My loyal little friend, you are not a Spellweaver," Edkim answered quizzically.

"Yes, how can *you* help?" Morganne added derisively.

"With this," Kirrie answered and produced a spherical gray stone from her raiment.

When she grasped the rock, the stone conformed to the shape of the she-Drelve's small hand. Earlier the Teacher had produced an ostensibly identical gray stone.

"My child, how long have you possessed this?" Edkim asked.

"More importantly, how did you come to posses this?" Rumsie asked.

"Or perhaps more importantly, what does it do?" Morganne queried suspiciously.

"I…I was told not to reveal the stone. But I think the time has come to use this…Summoning Stone," Kirrie answered.

"You didn't answer the question of where the rock's origins," Loganne added.

"Nor will I," Kirrie replied matter of factly.

"Then I shall not," Morganne interjected.

The tall she-Drelve from Meadowsweet produced another similar rock. Edkim produced the Cold Stone. The three stones emitted faint gray light and produced the faintest low-pitched hum.

Edkim said, "Elder Debby, please prepare enhancing root toddies for Gaelyss and the warriors. Rest every moment you can, Spellweaver. Rumsie, you should consider using the red arrows. I must talk with Kirrie and Morganne. Kirrie, Morganne please follow me to Old Orange Spruce."

Kirrie released Gaelyss's hand, turned to Loganne, and said, "Stay by his side!"

Loganne answered, "To my death!"

Gaelyss weakly quipped, "Let's hope it doesn't come to that."

Kirrie, Morganne, and Edkim hastily ran toward Alms Glen.

"Prepare a perimeter. Create ranks of fire. We'll let them know they've been in a fight," Rumsie ordered.

Edkim, Morganne, and Kirrie reached the Old Orange Spruce, entered, and sat in the foyer.

"There's not much time, Kirrie. Tell me everything you can. Like you and Morganne, I never *dreamed* of having such power. Have *you*?" Edkim asked.

"Teacher, actually I *did* dream of the stone. When I told you of my dream in the Old Orange Spruce, I should have told you I had it," Kirrie answered.

"Tell Morganne of your dream," Edkim suggested.

Kirrie relayed to Morganne the details of her dream. "The Good Witch was kindly and beautiful. The matronly female had smooth, lovely white skin and deep blue eyes. Soft blonde hair fell gently down the length of her back. She was as tall as a Droll, which made her twice as tall as I am. She wore a long flowing robe made of cottony fabric and exposed smooth hands with well-groomed nails. She spoke with a soothing voice. She convinced me that she had my interest in mind. The stone appeared after my dream."

"Morganne, what say you?" the Teacher implored.

"I'm not a Spellweaver! Because I was told the device would help the Spellweaver in a time of need, I tried to stay by Gaelyss as much as I could. Duty called me away to help Meryt and attack the fire riders. I did those things to protect *him*!" Morganne said defensively.

"How did you come by the stone?" Edkim gently continued.

"Like you, I *dreamt* of the stone," Morganne reluctantly confided, and then relayed to Kirrie and the Teacher the details of her dream. Morganne said, "My mind's eye stared into the fiery eyes of a winsome female. I've seen few females of other ilk. The foreigner's face was powerful and strangely attractive. Old Ulysses once saw a Giantess and described the large person when he talked to us by the firesides. He said Giants looked like big Kiennites. I thought I dreamt of a giantess. Could a giantess be so enthralling? The vision was certainly intimidating. I perspired profusely in my sleep. The very tall alluring female in my dream had smooth reddened skin, fiery red eyes, and wore a blazing red dress. Long green hair fell provocatively across her back and chest and produced a disheveled look. The female walked proudly back and forth across a field of grab grass. The grab grass was green with purplish flowers. I knew grab grass grew in the woods east of the Drelve forest. But grab grass is red! The blades of grab grass tenaciously hold to any poor creature until it starves or falls victim to a predator. This *green* grab grass tantalizingly grasped and released the female's powerful lower legs. Tiny sparks of flame burst from the long sharp talons of the female's strong hands as she rubbed them together, which perplexed and terrified me as I slept. Vibrantly colored black and red flower petals showered around the striking feminine being. She pursed her lips, emitted small bursts of hot breath, and burned the petals when they neared her. I *felt* her warmth. The Amazon rolled the digits of her left hand and created a small ball of deep green flame, which she playfully tossed up and down. She gently inhaled and then slowly exhaled gray smoke, which enveloped the little ball of flame. Smiling wryly, the female allowed the smoke enshrouded green fireball to rest in her palm. The smoke condensed and cleared. The green ball transformed to a smooth round gray stone. The stone remained after the dream. This is the stone. I have feared it, because of its origins. I…I should have told someone."

Morganne extended her hand with the small gray stone. Eighteen seasons of the harvest had not given her the wisdom to relay the rest of her dream. She *privately* recalled her conversation with the Amazon.

"*Let's have some girl talk. He's very handsome, isn't he, my pretty?*" the matron said glibly.

"*Who…is who handsome? Who…who…what manner of ilk are you? Why do you disturb my sleep?*" Morganne said, her lips trembling.

"*Don't be coy. You know what I'm talking about. I see how your mind's eye beholds the young Spellweaver. Why not reveal your torrid feelings for him, sweets?*" the deep voice asked the sleeping she-Drelve.

"*I'm…I don't understand such words. I respect the Spellweaver. He is… my leader,*" Morganne protested.

"*Nonsense! You melt when you see him. Admit it! I know what thoughts lurk in your conniving little head. I know why you took him to the creek. What manner of treats will you give him next time?*" the uninvited visitor to Morganne's dream demanded.

Morganne sniffled as she replied, "*Why do you say such hurtful things? Who…who are you?*"

"*I'm the one who's telling you what you really feel, right? You're going to have to fight to win him. Watch the filly that accompanies him. Your Spellweaver is young, and weak. He lacks the intensity of his brother. He is a pseudo-leader. False!*" the woman said.

Edkim's voice ended Morganne's private recollection.

The Teacher implored, "Go on, Morganne."

Morganne continued, "Before she left me to my sleep, her features developed a deep maroon hue and deep red auras surrounded her. I have to this point kept the stone a secret. Our situation dictates we utilize anything we have. I know Gaelyss has done all he can. I would like to get back to his side as soon as I can."

"Have you any idea of the stone's power?" Edkim asked.

"No," Morganne answered succinctly.

"And you, Kirrie, what do you know of your stone?" Edkim asked.

"Only that it should be used to help my Spellweaver when the time is dire," the little she-Drelve answered and glowered at Morganne.

"You need not defend yourselves. I have not revealed the presence of my device. Like you, I wasn't sure of its origins. The device unveiled its power when it saved me from the fire horse's breath weapon. Most odd! Magick moves in mysteriously ways. It's only fair that I tell you of my dream," Edkim said.

The Teacher told of his dream. "She appeared compassionate and beautiful. The matronly female had smooth, lovely white skin and deep blue eyes. Soft blonde hair fell gently down the length of her back. She was as tall as a Droll. She wore a long flowing robe made of cottony fabric and exposed smooth hands with well-groomed nails. She spoke with a soothing voice. Morganne, you acted properly. Kirrie, you told me of your dream, but I remained silent, though I experienced a similar dream. The benefactor visited me in this very foyer and called herself a Samaritan, good witch, and friend. She placed this stone in my hand. My stone is a *Cold Stone*."

"Teacher, what have we experienced?" Kirrie asked.

"Albträume," Edkim answered.

"Albträume?" Morganne inquired quizzically.

"Albträume, elf dreams, nightmares… I can't explain how the Dream raiders invade our sleep and cause the dreams," Edkim confessed.

"Why did we leave the field, and the Spellweaver Gaelyss?" Morganne demanded.

"The stones reacted to one another. I worried for the Spellweaver's safety. Thinking it would be the safest place to study them, I brought us to the sanctuary of the Old Orange Spruce. We are removed from the Spellweaver. These stones are, indeed, gifts," Edkim said matter-of-factly.

"I'd like to get back to Gaelyss as quickly as possible," Kirrie quickly said.

"So would I," Morganne also injected.

Edkim noted the quickness of their answers and the glint in their eyes and said, "It's nice to see someone…uh, and so *many* interested in the welfare of our Spellweaver."

The three Drelves placed the gray stones in their left hands and brought them together. Grayness filled the foyer of the Old Orange Spruce. The stones low-pitched hum rose to loud droning. The stones felt warm in their respective hands.

Kirrie said, "It's warm."

Morganne added, "The stone I hold feels warm as well."

Then Edkim remarked, "The stone I hold grows cold."

Bright-eyed, Kirrie asked, "Teacher, what is your plan?"

Edkim answered, "My plan? Our archers and rangers can't stop the fire riders, let alone two legions of Drolls and Kiennites. The enemies' greatest weapons have been the war machines and the fire breathed by the great steeds. Otherwise we simply battle their great numbers. That we can do with tactics and the help of the forest. The Cold Stone provides me an opportunity to stem the tide of the battle. I've just *now* learned its powers. I shan't allow it to leave my hand. We can't cover ground rapidly. The Drolls have positioned themselves throughout the field. I'd need a means to fly over the field. We lack such Magick."

"Perhaps not. My rock is a Summoning Stone. Just this moment, the artifact tells me its history. In the hands of the Korcrans, the gray stone helped gather firehorses. The Drolls' loss is our gain," Kirrie, said.

Excited, Edkim asked, "Can you sway the steeds to our side?"

Kirrie replied, "No. The firehorses serve masters. Evidently the artifact only affects any given beast a single time. Is Magick always this finicky?"

Morganne held the gray stone in her hand and entered, "This stone feels warm. It...*speaks* to the others. But *still* tells me nothing. I...I don't understand."

"Nor I. But I *feel* your stone's interaction with the one I carry," Edkim replied.

"So do I! I sense unspoken words...thoughts...I feel my newfound knowledge of the Summoning Stone comes from Morganne's stone! Her stone awakens mine. Could Morganne hold a Master Stone, Teacher?" Kirrie asked.

"I only know the stone I hold now tells me the powers it possesses. Perhaps I should hold the stone you possess, Morganne," Edkim suggested.

"I...I don't know. I was told it was to benefit the Spellweaver. But it tells me nothing now. Here...take it," Morganne said, and offered the stone to the Teacher.

Edkim still held the Cold Stone in his left hand. He extended his right hand and took Morganne's stone. The second stone meld to the Teacher's grasp. Slowly he brought two stones together until they gently touched. Grayness bathed first the Teacher and then Morganne. The Teacher smiled and returned the stone to Morganne. Morganne took the stone. The gray rock again changed to fit her grasp.

"What did it tell you, Teacher?" Kirrie asked.

"The stone was entrusted to Morganne. She should keep it," Edkim said.

"Would you like to hold my stone, Teacher?" Kirrie asked.

"No. It's unnecessary. Summon a griffin," Edkim replied.

Kirrie smiled and said, "I'll try. But should I do it in the Old Orange Spruce?"

"No, let's do it outside," the Teacher said, managing a smile.

The three exited the tree.

"With your permission, I'll return to the field and Gaelyss," Morganne implored.

"Yes. We'll be along," Edkim answered. Morganne hurried away toward the battle lines.

"How do I do it, Teacher?" Kirrie asked.

"Kirrie, I don't know! I am no Spellweaver. This period and indeed in my last 500 heartbeats, I've learned more about Magick than I knew my entire lifespan. Use your mind, your feelings, your heart," the Teacher answered.

Kirrie held the Summoning Stone in her left hand, closed her eyes, sighed deeply three times, and concentrated. Little beads of iridescent sweat appeared on her brow. The two Drelves heard wings fluttering in the distance, then louder. Screams told them the battle had resumed.

"Woe! A wyvern! Drelvish arrows remain in its hide! It's the very beast that bore oil and carried the Kiennite to his death!" Edkim shouted and dove to the ground.

The wyvern flew overhead.

"Get down, youngster! It's easier for him to pick off a standing target!" the Teacher shouted.

Kirrie stood, remained silent, and kept her eyes closed. The beast circled around the clearing twice and landed about twenty paces from the she-Drelve. The wyvern looked like a dragon with two legs and two wings. The wings bore eagle-like talons at their tips. The beast's long serpentine tail ended with a barbed tip. The wyvern extended its snout with its crane like beak, waddled toward Kirrie, stopped about three paces from her, and sat on its haunches.

Kirrie opened her eyes, turned to the Teacher who lay prone on the ground, and said, "His name is Dallas. He's ready to serve, though he'll only follow my commands. At least that's what he...and I guess the rock says."

Edkim stood.

The Teacher asked, "Isn't Dallas an odd name for a wyvern?"

"He says Edkim is an odd name for a Drelve, Teacher," Kirrie answered.

Glinne, Loganne, Tomayo, and a contingent of warriors arrived to defend Alms Glen from the wyvern.

"Hold your fire!" Edkim shouted. "I'm still sorting things out."

"He won't attack us, Teacher," Kirrie assured Edkim.

The Drelves circled the wyvern, which sat lackadaisically in the cleared area near the Teacher's tree.

"I never thought I'd be glad the battle line had drawn nearer Alms Glen, Teacher, but at least we got to you quickly. We saw the beast appear in the distance. I've never seen a wyvern fly so quickly and purposefully. What are we to do?" the veteran Glinne asked.

Edkim looked into the beast's eyes and said, "Go back to the front lines. At least for the moment, you are not needed. I think Kirrie has everything under control. But send Morganne back to me."

"I doubt she'll willingly leave the Spellweaver's side. Drolls and Kiennites enter the far side of the field. Rumsie thinks an all out assault is imminent. Are you sure we should leave with the beast in the propinquity of the settlement?" Loganne asked.

"Tell Morganne I have directions for her. It'll only take a moment. Tell her to bring two lengths of our finest expandable rope," Edkim said urgently.

Except Loganne, the group reluctantly returned to the battle lines. Loganne insisted on staying by the Teacher's side until Morganne returned. Soon the disgruntled she-Drelve returned with two lengths of Drelvish rope.

"I don't want to be away from Gaelyss. Drolls and Kiennites mass on the field. The Drolls behind the rolling log hideaway make sorties into our positions. Foolhardy sorties, for our bows strike them down. But I'm needed by the Spellweaver's side," Morganne chagrinned.

"Don't concern yourself with Gaelyss! He can take care of himself," Kirrie said viperously.

"What do you care of him? Everything I hear says you paid Gaelyss no mind when his brother Yannuvia was around. You are too young to…" Morganne answered with equal contemptuousness.

"Ladies! We have plenty of enemies. Morganne, thank you for returning with the rope. I *know* your stone's power and the course I must take. Tell Gaelyss to be strong and learn well," Edkim said platonically.

"Teacher, I don't understand," Morganne protested.

"You will," Edkim continued. "Now be gone."

Morganne hustled away.

Following Edkim's detailed directions, Kirrie created reins for the placid wyvern. Once the reins were gently secured, Kirrie and the Teacher mounted the wyvern and flew to the west. Sitting in front, Kirrie guided the fifteen-yard long beast higher into the air. Soon they were over the circular meadow. From the height, the war machines appeared as child's toys and the swarming Drolls and Kiennites looked like small insects crawling on the forest floor. The firehorses were grouped near the center of the field, where the great Lone Oak had stood for so long. Columns of foot soldiers advanced from the wild woods to the east. The extensive damage to the wild woods saddened both Drelves. Drolls and Kiennites had harvested the trees, lived off the land, and damaged the wild woods nigh as much as their war machines had damaged the Drelves' forest. Destruction of the Lone Oak and the loss of life compounded the madness.

Edkim instructed Kirrie, "Take us down to the center of the field, but tell the beast to stay out of bow range."

Kirrie concentrated. Dallas flew in a long sweeping arc toward the field.

Below, a Kiennish lookout shouted, "Beware! A flying beast! Drelves ride the wyvern! Guard the General!"

Drolls and Kiennites scanned upward, and many broke and ran. The wyvern flew quickly, but Kiennish lookouts saw the Drelves. Saligia instinctively raised his dragon scale shield and ducked his head beneath it. Bluthgar circled the fire riders around the General. Chamberlain ran toward the woods.

Edkim gently grasped Kirrie's shoulder and said, "It's time."

Kirrie asked, "What do you want us to do?"

Edkim answered, "You will be at risk. Dallas will have to dive over the leadership in the center of the field. In their zeal to protect their leader, the entire brigade of fire riders have come into the area of effect of my spell. I can only do it once. Are you ready?"

Kirrie replied, "Yes, Teacher. I don't understand your plan, but I will do as you ask."

Kirrie directed the wyvern to fly over the fire riders, and Dallas obliged. Edkim took the Cold Stone from his raiment and held the artifact in front of him.

"Lean forward, Kirrie," the Teacher said emphatically.

The Teacher extended the gray stone and concentrated. As the wyvern neared the Kiennites' leader and his entourage, Drolls fired arrows and hurled spears. The firehorses reared and sewed fire upward, but the arc of flames ended before it reached the speeding wyvern. A great roaring sound emanated from the Cold Stone, followed by a conical flash of white cold. The cone of cold originated at the point of the Cold Stone in Edkim's hand, extended outward in an arc of 120 degrees, and instantly drained all heat over a distance of five hundred paces. Saligia saw the wyvern riders and feared a spell. The General dropped his lance, gripped his dragon scale shield with both hands, held the shield in front of him, and screamed. The cone of cold roared past and froze everything in its path. The Magick purplish shields did not protect the riders and their steeds. In a heartbeat, a massive force of 89 firehorses and riders became frozen dead! The frigid Magick froze Kiennites mounted on stone ponies but spared the little steeds. Cold Magick affected neither stone ponies nor saber-toothed mares. Saligia held his breath but the cold hurt his nostrils. The Magick froze the fleeing Chamberlain and many surrounding foot soldiers in their tracks.

Dallas the wyvern swooped over the field and carried Kirrie and Edkim high into the amber skies. Thousands of Drolls and Kiennites had advanced beyond the area Edkim had attacked and stood confused on the field. Kirrie saw no movement in the area frozen by the cone of cold.

"It seems the leadership has been destroyed. Does this end the war, Teacher?" she asked.

"Perhaps. The defenses to our realm are broken down. Our Spellweaver is exhausted. A great force remains on the field. If they attack, the enemies can walk right into Alms Glen. But this army is a headless snake. Let's make for the lines and consult with Sergeant Major Rumsie," Edkim suggested.

Seeing Kiennish nobles running from the woods to the north and away from the battlefield, Kirrie asked, "Let them have another attack with the Cold Stone!"

"I cannot, young Kirrie. The rock is now…just a rock," Edkim said tiredly.

Agonizing on the ground by his steed, Saligia grasped the horse's reins with numb fingers, struggled to maintain control of the uninjured saber-toothed mare, and remained still. His frostbitten fingers and his numb legs throbbed, but the dragon shield had at least saved his life. The Kiennite risked a glance overhead and saw the wyvern flying away from him.

Cursed Spellweavers!

Cursed wyvern riders!

What treachery!

Dead firehorses and their riders lay frozen about him. Bluthgar's glassy unmoving eyes confirmed the horsemaster's death. Kiennites fled from the woods toward the north. Drolls ran from the front lines. Looking for signs of danger from above, many stumbled and tripped over fallen horses and riders. Grimacing and fighting to maintain consciousness, Saligia stood and supported his damaged body against the saber-toothed mare. The General understood why the huge tusked horses were sometimes called ice mares. Fleeing Drolls saw the General's struggle to stand. His glower stopped them in their tracks.

"Get your ***** back into formation and get ready to fight," Saligia shouted.

Saligia refused help, mustered all his energies, remounted his steed, and rode away from the frozen bodies of the fire horses and their ill-fated riders. Defiantly, the Lord of Aulgmoor raised his war lance and shouted every curse he knew in both Droll and Kiennish. Drolls saw the wounded general riding out from the frozen carnage. The visage spurred their morale, and the warriors shouted, turned about, and charged toward the General. Cheers erupted. The Kiennite council of Aulgmoor halted their retreat and returned. Whether due to loyalty or fear of reprisal, their return spurred the Kiennish warriors to come out from the woods and run toward Saligia.

Kirrie directed Dallas, and the wyvern flew to the cleared area behind the ever-changing frontline. Rumsie moved archers and foot soldiers back further into the woods. Gaelyss managed two Wall of Thorns Spells to reinforce the flimsy line of trees and underbrush.

Dallas landed among the suspicious Drelves. Kirrie and the Teacher released the rope reins and climbed off the wounded wyvern. Dallas gazed into Kirrie's eyes. Kirrie nodded and the immense wyrm began to pluck crude arrows and spears from its wing and underbelly. Dark ichors flowed from its wounds, and the great beast cried like an injured infant.

Kirrie helped Edkim to a large clump of red orange moss in the shade of the Old Orange Spruce. Diaphoretic and ashen, Edkim's chest heaved.

Arriving first, Loganne said, "Teacher, what can I do to help you?"

Edkim weakly shook his head.

"You really came through, Teacher. We have a chance now," Rumsie declared.

Rumsie, Gaelyss, Ulysses, Blanchard, Debby, and Morganne soon arrived. Beaux, Klunkus, Coweta, Hamilton, Joe, Frank, Reynolds, Clarke, Tomayo, and Glinne watched the field. Thousands of Drolls and Kiennites chaotically ran about.

Noting the wyvern's wounds, Morganne asked, "The beast is seriously wounded. What can we do?"

"I know nothing of healing wyverns. I've primarily avoided becoming a snack for such a beast. Have you read anything of them in the *Gifts of Andreas to the People of the Forest*, Gaelyss?" the elder Ulysses asked.

"It's an animal. It eats, sleeps, breathes, and...well, you know. Give the critter some enhancing root stew and aloe juice. A Healing Spell might work. Wyverns are Magick and Nature. I...I can't do a heal spell at this moment," Gaelyss answered and slumped beside Edkim on the thick moss.

Rigorous spell casting again sapped his energies.

"Try placing healing balm on the beast's wounds. We owe it. Bring enhancing stew," the Teacher struggled to advise.

Blanchard and Debby, elders of Alms Glen, and Morin from Meadowsweet brought enhancing stew and thick amber balm. Tentatively, the elders placed the balm on the wyvern's wounds. Kirrie offered the fragrant stew and the beast wolfed it down. The great beast sat on its haunches, snorted, and covered the elder Blanchard with purplish mucous. Blanchard grumbled something about a filthy beast. The wyvern glanced at Debby and licked its chops. Kirrie glowered and stopped the beast's philandering.

The Kiennish warren leaders, Woodrow, Wilson, Calvin, Coolidge, Theodore, Delano, and Roosevelt shamefacedly returned from the road leading to the north.

Delano spoke, "Lord Saligia. We thought you were dead. We thought it best we return to Aulgmoor and organize defenses against a counterattack."

Saligia rubbed his frostbitten fingers together briskly and fumed, "You are a chicken ****, Delano. You ran to save your sorry ***. You deserted my warriors and me. We have killed four Spellweavers. Now we must kill a fifth. The machines I designed have paved the way to the heart of their precious forest. Now we must drive a stake through their exposed heart. Warren leaders, organize our warriors into seven sections. I expect you to be at the head of the columns in full battle regalia. Do any Drollen commanders remain on the field?"

A large Droll ignored an arrow imbedded in his right shoulder and growled, "I stand with you, Lord Saligia. My warriors await your command."

"Organize your warriors in three columns. Send one directly into the gap created in the trees by the war wolves. Tell me your name," Saligia asked.

"My name is Fargo, Lord Saligia. I'm from the Dakota clan. A wyvern killed my sister Hannah. I'll serve you as best I can," the Droll answered.

A Drelve named Lightfoot ran breathlessly to the area where the Drelve leaders aided the Teacher Edkim, the wyvern Dallas, and Gaelyss.

"Sergeant Major Rumsie, the Drolls and Kiennites are regrouping. The banners of Aulgmoor fly in the wind. Clarke says an attack is imminent. He asks that you return," Lightfoot panted.

"Morganne, stay with the Teacher and Gaelyss. Kirrie, attend the wyvern. The rest of you come with me," Rumsie commanded.

Morganne placed her hand on Gaelyss's shoulder. Kirrie frowned but turned her attention to the injured wyvern. Dallas gulped down more fruits.

"I know you'd prefer meat, but the fruits of the forest will give you strength," Kirrie said aloud.

The wyvern made a low guttural sound, which resembled the purr of a large cat.

Edkim struggled to his feet.

"Teacher, you must rest! Please!" Morganne insisted.

Edkim straightened his tattered raiment, passed the Cold Stone to Gaelyss, and asked, "What can you make of this stone, Spellweaver?"

Gaelyss opened his tired eyes, took the spherical rock, and studied the gray stone. The spherical gray maintained its shape and feel. The rock emitted no lights, sounds, or smells. Its coldness only equaled other stones. Spellweavers innately detected Magick. The effort required no conjuration.

Gaelyss spoke, "As near as I can tell, Teacher, it's just a rock."

"Please keep it, Gaelyss. I feel it may regain some value," Edkim said. He continued, "Morganne stay by Gaelyss. Keep vigilant and guard well the stone you possess."

"Where are you going Teacher," Morganne asked with concern.

"Kirrie and I have a task. Kirrie, will you please ask your friend Dallas to assist us once more?" the Teacher asked.

Kirrie rubbed the wyvern's hard snout and murmured softly. The beast snorted. This time Ulysses was quicker on his feet and avoided the mucous.

"He's ready," Kirrie said.

On the field, Fargo organized the Drollen warriors into three groups, and the seven warren leaders gathered the Kiennites into seven groups. General Saligia ordered the Kiennites to carry bows. The General commanded the first wave of Drolls attack in force at the breach in the forest's defenses with swords, axes, and halberds. Seven groups of Kiennites were to follow the first wave, move into bowshot range, and fire volleys of arrows into the forest in support of the Drolls. The second and third groups of Drolls were to attack at the right and left flanks of the primary assault and hack away at the underbrush and any Drelves they might encounter.

Rumsie reached the forward area quickly and saw the banners of Aulgmoor flying in the center of the field. The Drolls and Kiennites were doubtlessly massing for an assault. Sergeant Major Rumsie hustled to the edge of the woods, charged to the front, and called the rangers to him.

"Listen up! Now's the time for swords! The war machines have destroyed our cover. Stand here until the enemies charge. Allow them to chase us to the pathway to Alms Glen. Gaelyss has cast Walls of Thorns and Entangle Spells along the pathway. Walkabout bushes and triffids have moved into gaps in the trees. Being so slow, our friends the orange triffids can't effectively fight, unless the enemies are dumb enough to come within the reach of a swinging bough. Where we stand, the gap between trees is several hundred paces. Two hundred paces behind us the opening narrows to twenty paces. At that point the Walls of Thorns Spells will funnel the enemy into the narrow passage. The narrow passage will allow only 10 to 12 Drolls to battle abreast and reduce the impact of their superior numbers. As you fight, step back and allow them to move forward. If we can draw a narrow column of the enemies into the pathway, we'll stand a better chance. Now we wait," Rumsie commanded.

The veteran Clarke stood by Rumsie. Young Loganne stood by Clarke. Three young Drelves named Vera, Chuck, and Dave stood by Loganne. The three youths hailed from Redberry Fields, a small community far to the southeast. Morin the elder of Meadowsweet was Vera, Chuck, and Dave's grandfather.

"Are you scared?" Loganne asked Clarke.

The burly older Drelve looked at his young companion and answered, "Yes."

"I'm scared too," Loganne confessed.

"Remember your training. Though horrific, the Drolls' halberds and spears are unwieldy and slow. You and I complement each other well. I fight with my left hand and you fight with your right. Keep concentrating, move fast, and jab them with your sword. We'll let them know they've been in a fight," Clarke said.

Loganne gripped her well-made short sword, pulled her shield to her body, and waited.

With a shout, Fargo ordered his warriors forward, and the Drolls charged. Many Drolls funneled to the area where the war machines had denuded the Drelve forest. Kiennites armed with bows fanned out behind the Drolls. When the Drolls and Kiennites came into range, the Drelvish archers repeatedly volleyed arrows, but sheer numbers supported the Drolls. Saligia brazenly approached the line, staying barely beyond bow shot range. The enemies neared the Drelves' lines.

"Take your positions! Form ranks! Establish the battle formation Clarke taught you. Make ready! In the trees, fire as long as you can," Sergeant Major Rumsie ordered.

The wolf-faced Drolls rumbled toward the waiting Drelves. When the Drolls closed to fifty paces, the Drelves broke and ran toward the deeper woods. Drelvish archers fired another volley over the head of Rumsie's retreating fighters and dropped several charging Drolls. Quicker afoot, Rumsie's rangers reached the area where the pathway to Alms Glen had been widened to twenty paces. Created by Gaelyss's Magick, Walls of Thorns occupied the spaces on both sides of the pathway.

When the Drelves passed 10 paces beyond the Walls of Thorns, Rumsie yelled, "Stop, turn, fight!"

The Drelves formed four ranks and stood twenty abreast and shield to shield. Archers stood behind the infantry.

As the Drolls closed Rumsie shouted "Now!"

Abruptly, the four ranks of Drelves knelt. Archers behind them sent a volley of arrows into the front ranks of the charging Drolls, then turned, and ran fifty paces down the pathway.

"Backward!" Rumsie shouted.

The four ranks of fighters followed the archers and retreated fifty paces further along the trail.

"Stop, turn!" the Sergeant Major ordered.

The disciplined Drelves reformed into ranks ready to fight. Some canopy now covered them as they had retreated into the forest that was beyond the range of the trebuchets. The trees afforded archers more vantage points.

When the Drelve commander yelled "To the ground!" archers fired over them and from the trees as well. The short-range bowshots felled more of the enemies.

Again Rumsie ordered, "Fall back!"

The Drelves retreated another fifty paces. Triffids and walkabouts extended root structures into the pathway after the Drelves passed and tripped the charging Drollen warriors. More Drolls floundered and fell over their comrades in the ground. This slowed the advance of the enemies and enabled Rumsie's troops to reform and prepare for the enemies. More arrows slammed into the Drolls. Unfortunately for the Drelvish defenders, the Drolls continued to reach the path in numbers, climbed over their fallen brethren, and approached the Drelves' positions. The width of the path narrowed to about fifteen paces. Still twenty Drelves stood side by side and outnumbered the Drolls in the front rank. Once again Rumsie ordered his ranks to kneel and the archers' arrows flew over the kneeling Drelves into the beleaguered attackers. While the surviving Drolls reorganized, the Drelves retreated another fifty paces. Loganne saw the towering Old Orange Spruce, the Teacher's traditional home as she retreated along the path.

"These Drolls are persistent," Clarke grumbled.

Standing in the second rank behind Rumsie, the veteran Tomayo added, "They'd rather knuckle our heads than eat when hungry."

"Nowhere to run. Nowhere to hide. Time to fight! Die well, my friends!" Rumsie shouted.

The battle became hand-to-hand. The Drolls closed, and their halberds and spears clanged against the Drelves' shields. A direct hit oft splintered the shield. Reacting as they had been taught, the Drelves counterattacked and attempted to maintain their formation. To avoid fatigue, Drelves fought and then rotated to the rear of the formation. Archers dropped their bows, drew short swords, and created two additional ranks. The battle formation worked well, but the powerful stronger wolf-faced enemies oft times knocked the smaller defenders backward and off their feet. Casualties mounted.

Bravely, Drelves maneuvered through the trees to pick off Drollen warriors on the ground. Kiennish archers returned fire and actually hit more of their allies than Drelves. Frustrated Drolls kept from the front line hurled spears. The projectiles injured and smote Drelves.

As Dallas carried them above the field, Kirrie looked down and said, "Teacher, the Drolls have reached our outermost lines. Per Rumsie's plan, our rangers lead the enemies down the widened pathway to Alms Glen. This takes them near the Spellweaver. All will be lost if they breach Rumsie's ranks of rangers."

"I see...I see. Kiennites spread out across the field. An ornately dressed leader accompanies each group, but I see the Kiennite who carried the dragon shield in the rear. Kirrie, direct Dallas to the Kiennites' leader's position. Hold tightly to the reins. I must be steady," Edkim declared.

The wyvern circled and brought the Drelves to within a hundred paces of the Kiennites' leader. Arrows and spears sailed around them. Several struck Dallas, but the wyvern stayed focused. Kirrie controlled and consoled the beast.

Edkim directed both hands toward the Kiennite and sent a purplish force toward him. Saligia anticipated the attack and raised his shield to protect his chest and head. The unerring Magick Missile opened a grievous wound in the General's left leg. Writhing in pain, Saligia dropped his reins, lost his hold on the shield, and fell from the saber-toothed mare. Frightened of the approaching wyvern, the ice mare ran away. Seeing the General fall, the Drolls to the left flank of the primary attack broke and ran from the field, deserting their fellows who pursued the Drelves into the woods.

Kirrie guided the wyvern into the air. Kiennish arrows zipped around the wyvern. Several arrows struck Dallas. The wyvern's wings created a large target. Horrific pain told Kirrie an arrow had found her right leg. Still she guided the wyvern upward and avoided further injury to herself and the beast.

Upon the wyvern, Kirrie gleefully said, "Good shot, Teacher! Can you finish him?"

Edkim silently slumped against Kirrie's back. The little she-Drelve urged Dallas back toward Alms Glen. Drolls and Kiennites saw Saligia fall and fled the field. The Kiennish warren leader Delano saw Saligia's plight, took the reins of his stone pony, and rode toward the General. While many Drolls and Kiennites ran past, Delano dismounted and applied a field dressing to the General's grievously injured leg. Mounted on warhorses and also wounded, three Drolls saw General Saligia's predicament. The Drolls stopped and helped Delano lift the wounded general, carefully place Saligia on a warhorse, and secure their leader with strong ropes. Delano remounted his stone pony, led the warhorse bearing Saligia from the battlefield, and followed the road to the north. The wounded Drolls followed as best they could.

Oblivious to the events on the meadow, Rumsie's rangers battled hand to hand. Slowly the Drolls pressed inexorably forward toward the Spellweaver's location. The Sergeant Major saw Vera, Chuck, and then Dave fall. Loganne struggled against a huge Droll. Then Rumsie heard the wyvern's wings overhead. Gaining strength, he managed to thrust his sword into the broad chest of the wolf-faced warrior in front of him. This freed him to land a glancing blow against the shoulder of the Droll fighting Loganne and at least temporarily save the young she-Drelve. Immediately two Drolls replaced their fallen fellows and engaged Rumsie and Kirrie. To Rumsie's left a Drelve named Karlheinz fell to a Droll's ax. Led by BJ Aires, Drelvish archers sent volleys toward the Kiennites and the rear of the Drolls' column. Suddenly the archers in the trees broke into cheers. Rumsie concentrated on the snarling Droll directly in front of him. The big beast ripped his halberd through the air and narrowly missed the Sergeant Major's head. Loganne parried three blows from the Droll attacking her. Taking its toll, fatigue prevented her mounting an offense. Old Clarke battled gamely to Rumsie's right. Experience triumphed over strength as the old ranger fended off Droll after Droll. Banderas from Lost Sons gamely battled the Drolls. Unable to help Loganne, the exhausted Rumsie barely parried the Droll's next attack. Loganne fell to the ground but managed to roll away from the Droll's downwardly directed blow. His heavy axe dug into the soil, and the forest's floor became Loganne's ally. She stabbed the Droll's calf and he howled in pain. Loganne left her blade in the Droll's flesh, rolled over twice, and narrowly avoided another Droll's lance. Suddenly the Droll in front of Rumsie grunted and lurched forward. Rumsie saw BJ's arrow had passed through the big Droll's neck. Buoyed by BJ's shot, Rumsie found strength, stabbed the Droll harassing Loganne, and enabled the she-Drelve to get back on her tired feet. Rumsie, Clarke, and Loganne braced for another foe, but none came.

Abruptly the Drolls turned, tucked tail, and fled.

Drelvish archers fired into the retreating Drolls and felled another twenty. Rumsie ordered his rangers to stand their ground and resist pursuing the enemies. BJ instructed the archers to hold their fire. Enemies abandoned their weapons and chaotically retreated from all areas of the ravaged Lone Oak Meadow.

But for Delano, the warren leaders of the Council of Aulgmoor abandoned their folk. Surviving Kiennites sought their individual warrens. Drolls fled haphazardly northward.

Fortunately for the injured and unconscious General Saligia, Delano encountered a minstrel. The minstrel possessed various and sundry unguents and potions, including a small jar of Menders' Panacea. The Kiennish warren leader placed General Saligia on the back of the wagon and applied the thick gooey purple salve to his leader's wound. Hoping to keep the General alive long enough to reach Aulgmoor, Delano conscripted the minstrel's wagon and raced toward the Kiennites' stronghold. The Mender Fisher served the Council of Aulgmoor. Fisher might save Saligia.

Kirrie guided Dallas to the clearing near the Old Orange Spruce. Morganne stood by Gaelyss with her sword drawn. Morin, Ulysses, and Carinne helped Kirrie remove the unconscious Teacher from the wyvern. The Drelves carried Edkim into the Old Orange Spruce and placed him on his bed.

Rumsie remained wary. Two thousand Drolls and Kiennites remained in the propinquity of Alms Glen. When the enemies left the field, the Sergeant Major ordered Beaux, Klunkus, and Banderas to follow the Drolls and Kiennites. Clarke and Tomayo supervised the destruction of the remaining war machines.

Fighting fatigue, Rumsie and Loganne and rushed toward the Old Orange Spruce and Alms Glen. When they reached the Teacher's home, they saw Kirrie leaning against the massive wyvern. Morganne stood by the Old Orange Spruce.

"Kirrie, where is the Teacher?" Rumsie panted.

"He's...he's in the tree with the elders. He fainted after casting the Magick Missile Spell that felled the Kiennites' leader. He didn't speak after casting the spell," Kirrie sobbed.

The elder Morin of Meadowsweet walked through the tree's thick red-orange bark and said, "The Teacher has regained consciousness. Gaelyss and Ulysses work with him, but..."

"How is he?" Rumsie asked.

"We've done what we can. Magick places great demands on its casters. Though intelligent and learned, Edkim was not a Spellweaver," Morin reported.

"May we enter?" Rumsie asked.

"I suggest you not delay," Morin said and looked downward.

Morganne, Kirrie, Rumsie, and Loganne entered the tree. The elders Ulysses, Blanchard, and Debby labored with Edkim. The pale Teacher gasped for breath. Gaelyss sat dejectedly by the bed and held the Teacher's hand.

"How goes the battle?" the Teacher asked feebly.

"We've won the field. The Drolls and Kiennites are in full retreat. Clarke supervises the burning of the war machines and the log-walled hideaway. Scouts followed them a ways into the woods toward the Doombringers. There are a few stragglers, but no organized threats," Rumsie reported.

"And the leader?" Edkim continued.

"Dragged from the field by an underling. Witnesses say he was badly wounded. I doubt the Kiennite survived," Rumsie answered.

The Teacher sighed and spoke softly, "Our people, the forest, and the world have suffered the loss of the great Lone Oak. We've lost the tree herder Old Yellow and so many of our people. The Drolls and Kiennites lost so many. I entrust the protection of our people to Gaelyss and Sergeant Major Rumsie. I entrust the teaching of the youth to one who is well qualified. Soon you'll understand of whom I speak."

"Rest, old friend. We still have many trips to make to the Green Vale," Rumsie argued.

"Not for me, old friend. I have loved every day I've lived in these forests; save times of war and the day young Yannuvia left us. I …I did not teach him…them…you, Gaelyss, well enough…" Edkim struggled.

"Rest, Teacher. I've had the best Teacher. *You*. Save your words," Gaelyss pleaded.

"Thank you, Gaelyss. I…leave you now," Edkim sighed, smiled weakly, and breathed no more.

A faint buzz came from Morganne's raiment. Gray light filled the room, and then concentrated on the she-Drelve.

Morganne clearly whispered, "I am the Teacher."

"What do you mean?" Blanchard asked.

"The stone Edkim touched and returned to me is a Stone of Knowledge. With his death, the gray rock imparted the Teacher's knowledge to me. He knew… he also knew casting the last spell would kill him. Still he did it," Morganne sobbed.

"But for his efforts…but for…we'd all be dead," Rumsie said tearfully.

Grief overwhelmed the Drelves in the Old Orange Spruce.

Outside the wyvern Dallas bled profusely from many wounds. The beast stared hopefully toward the Old Orange Spruce and waited for Kirrie. The grief stricken she-Drelve remained within the tree.

Dallas died alone.

CHAPTER 47
Aftermath

The veteran Clarke watched flames engulf the war machines and the log-walled hideaway the Drolls and Kiennites had constructed. Battle weary Drelves changed their short swords and bows for rope and spades. Some respectfully placed many bodies of fallen Drolls and Kiennites into the deep pits in the burned out meadow. Cherry bombs thrown by the fallen Drelves Zack and Bryce created the deep craters. Others carried oil to cover the corpses. Funeral pyres burned throughout the next amber period.

Clarke again sent runners northward up the road leading away from the erstwhile red meadow to look for signs of the enemies' return. Scouting parties checked the wild woods, but found few signs of life within five thousand paces of the burned, frozen, bloodstained, dying, erstwhile red meadow. Clarke went to the site of the carnage of the Lone Oak and scanned the ground for evidence of leaves or other remnants of the tree, but the enemies had totally destroyed the ages old icon of the forest. Old Clarke scooped up ashes from the ground and kept them. Did they come from the Lone Oak or the Tree Herder Old Yellow?

Tomayo supervised the heartrending task of gathering the Drelves' dead and returning them to Alms Glen. Drelves from Lost Sons arrived and helped out the clean up and recovery effort. Carinne and Glinne assisted the wounded.

"Tomayo, please take command of the field. I must report to Rumsie and the elders. I sense I don't yet know the full extent of our losses," Clarke wearily asked.

The old Drelve's dark brown hair matted against his forehead. Clarke suffered numerous nicks and bruises. The battle left few Drelves unscathed.

Tomayo wiped sweat from his brow and nodded affirmatively.

Clarke gathered the ashes he had taken from the ground in the middle of the field. He saw rows of his brethren lying unmoving on the ground. Drelves had meticulously covered the bodies with large leaves and stood by the fallen to keep away vermin. Clarke hurled his bow and bloodied sword to the ground, muttered something about futility, and walked away from the field. Flames crackled and smoke billowed into the air.

No animals or birds called.

Death ruled the day.

Inside the Old Orange Spruce tears flowed from all eyes gathered around the Teacher Edkim. Morganne held the gray Stone of Knowledge. Now spherical, the artifact was indistinguishable from the Cold Stone, which Edkim had given Gaelyss. Neither gray stone produced lights, sounds, or auras. For all intents and purposes, both were only very smooth spherical gray rocks.

The elder Debby entered the Teacher's home and said, "Our losses grow. The wyvern has died."

Kirrie sighed and turned toward Gaelyss. The young Spellweaver stood bewildered and speechless.

Morganne abandoned her inexperienced youthful voice and instead spoke confidently with a scholarly tone, "My people, we are bereft of a great Drelve, the Teacher Edkim. Deep are the wounds of our spirits, bodies, and the forests we love. I dread hearing the final tally from the frontline. The stone I hold now has no exceptional qualities. When Edkim touched the stones together, they gave him this familiarity. The Stone of Knowledge has but one Magick, passing on the knowledge of its possessor at the time of his or her death. When Edkim died, I received the Teacher's awareness. The reason is unbeknownst to me. Perhaps Edkim chose me to be his successor. Did my possession of the Stone of Knowledge dictate my succeeding him? Why did I receive the gray stone? I certainly *was* not qualified. But now the role of Teacher is my task, and mine alone. I will educate our young to the best of my ability and supervise the harvest of the enhancing root tubers when the time is right. I cannot teach Magick, but I'll support Gaelyss in *any* way I can. I'll look to Gray Andreas for guidance. Hopefully we'll see an Approximation soon. The Gray Sun Andreas eases our pain. Studying the gray stones in the gray light may bear fruit. Sergeant Major Rumsie, what are your immediate plans for defense?"

Rumsie wiped a tear and answered, "We won't again have the perimeter we enjoyed at the red meadow. The Lone Oak stood as a beacon to our lands. These are the first cycles of Meries that I've lived without the presence of the great tree and the tree herder Old Yellow. The trees at the forest's edge are evermore ruined. The land is as forlorn as my spirit. Our brethren from Lost Sons have arrived and relieve our exhausted rangers. The battle did not spare Lost Sons. Drolls constantly probed the area around the hamlet and kept the elders Dienas and Yiuryna busy defending their trees. Banderas arrived before the battle's end and stood by us against the Drolls. His daughters Joulie and Jonna assist in the clean up. Our scouts find no sign of the enemies. For now, all is quiet on the dead meadow. We will maintain vigilance."

Kirrie looked to Morganne and said defiantly, "*You* are too young to be the Teacher!"

Morganne quickly and forcefully answered, "I *am* the Teacher. Many facts fill my mind. I'm not the person I was a few hundred heartbeats ago."

Rumsie sniffed and added, "You have my support. No one is more expert at tending the enhancing plant and harvesting the tubers. No one served more bravely on the field of battle. I suppose no one is more qualified to be Teacher. You…we have plenty of work to do. I must return to the field to assess the situation and check our wounded."

Morganne said, "My first task as Teacher is to honor the fallen. Please gather the names for me. Elders Blanchard, Debby, and Morin please attend the body of Edkim and arrange for a eulogy for those we have lost. Gaelyss, you are exhausted. I'd suggest you rest here in *my* home. Kirrie, will you attend the wyvern? The beast deserves a pyre. I appreciate all you have done. I am going to the field to render what aid I can to Sergeant Major Rumsie and his gallant wards."

The elders summoned assistance from the common area of Alms Glen, and a number of Drelves carried the body of Edkim from the Old Orange Spruce. Morganne bent forward and gently kissed Gaelyss's forehead. The *Teacher* took a robe from the armoire in the foyer and walked through the thick trunk of the great tree.

The Teacher Morganne walked to the new edge of the forest. Purplish clouds blessed the careworn Drelves and the beleaguered forest with refreshing drizzling rain. The Teacher passed Drelves carrying dead and assisting wounded as she approached the ravaged meadow. Rumsie stood with his arms folded before him and stared blankly across the field. The new Teacher approached the veteran Sergeant Major.

"What were our losses?" Morganne asked.

"In terms of lives, Teacher, the final assault of the Drolls cost us 64 lives, including Vera, Chuck, and Dave, the elder Morin's grandchildren. In terms of damage to the woods and land, immeasurable," Rumsie stoically replied.

"How many Drolls and Kiennites lost their lives?" Morganne asked.

"I'm…I'm not sure. Many. Our people have placed their dead within the craters. Clarke supervised and insured me the enemies' remains were treated with respect. Their pyres burn now," Rumsie answered.

"Thank you, Sergeant Major Rumsie. Will you please join me in Alms Glen for the ceremony to honor those lost?" the Teacher Morganne asked.

"Yes, Teacher," Rumsie answered.

The Dark Period arrived as Morganne reached the common area of Alms Glen, which was now much closer to the forest's edge. A small fire crackled in the center of the common area. Drelves from all the surrounding villages gathered. Beaux and Klunkus volunteered to monitor the field, but nothing had stirred since the Drolls and Kiennites had fled.

Morganne began, "I first want to honor those who gave their lives in the final assault by the Drolls. Sergeant Major Rumsie has given me 64 names of our lost brethren. They hailed from all villages. Our heartfelt sympathy goes to the elder Morin who lost three grandchildren Vera, Chuck, and Dave. In addition, we honor Magill, Lil, Nancy, Julia, Molly, Anna, Sally, Lizzy, Michelle, Eleanor, Lucy, Rita, Madonna, Joan, Rose, Valerie, Pam, Maggie May, Mary Jane, Clarabella, Carol, Bonnie, Lucille, Martha, Penny, Lane, Georgia, Rigby, Queenie, Jude, Prudence, Sadie, JoJo, Mary, Loretta, Martin, Pepper, Teddy, Rocky, Sinclair, Abbey, Marlene, Gustav, W.C., Diana, Bob, Marilyn, Aldous, Karlheinz, Sigmund, Aleister, Edgar, Karl, Monroe, Oscar, William, Marlin, Stan, Dylan, Oliver, and Lenny. Please grant one heartbeat of silence for each of our brothers and sisters."

Silence enveloped the common area.

After sixty-four seconds of silence, Kirrie stood, walked over to the fire, and solemnly addressed the gathered Drelves, saying, "I ask consideration for the wyvern Dallas. Magick took the beast's freedom, and he died serving us. Kiennites slaughter young wyverns to make shields and armor from their hide and scales. At least Dallas gained a measure of vengeance for his lost fellows. I…I attended his remains."

Morganne followed, "Thank you, Kirrie. Let's pause another moment to remember the beast."

Everyone remained silent for a heartbeat's time.

Then Morganne continued, "Edkim eulogized those lost before the final battle. I only knew the Teacher briefly in life, but I know him with great depth now. He cared deeply for the forest and his people. I've never met your lost Spellweaver, Yannuvia. Having touched Edkim's memories, I understand his fondness for the missing young Spellweaver. But he is missing! Time and recent events tell us he is unlikely to return. Gaelyss tempered the enemies' attacks. The Kiennish war machines decimated our defenses. Gaelyss's spells prevented the enemies' walking into Alms Glen. Like the lost Spellweaver, our beloved Edkim has left us. I will carry on his work to the best of my abilities. I ask for your support."

Gaelyss cast a Dancing Lights Spell. Brilliant auras glittered all around the red oaks. The Drelves strummed lutes, played toot and see scrolls, and sang mournful laments. After the ceremonies honoring the fallen,

Morganne talked with the elders Blanchard, Debby, Morin, Ulysses, Dienas, and Yiuryna. The Teacher arranged a meeting in the common area on the morrow and left for her new residence in the Old Orange Spruce. Exhausted from days of spell casting, Gaelyss went to his tree.

Rumsie went back to the dying meadow and confirmed the enemies had not returned. Only then did the Drelves' commander take his rest. Loganne assumed the watch assisted by young Drelves from Lost Sons and Fox Vale named Jonna, Joulie, Megyn, Lauren, Gretchen, Ainsley, Brett, Beck, Laura, and Jamie.

The veteran Clarke climbed to the observation point relieved Loganne. Young Ainsley sat with the old ranger.

"Did you know the lost Spellweaver?" Ainsley asked.

"Yannuvia was talented but a bit rebellious. He wanted to experience the world and learn of Nature and Magick. I loved him," Clarke answered.

"Please tell me more about him," Ainsley requested.

"Young Kirrie knew him well. She and Yannuvia shared many adventures. She'd be able to tell you more than I," Clarke answered.

"Kirrie never leaves the Spellweaver Gaelyss's side. Tell me of Yannuvia, Clarke," Ainsley pleaded.

Old Clarke relayed stories of Yannuvia's youth.

Morganne reached the Old Orange Spruce. She muttered three old Drelvish phrases, walked through the tree's thick orange bark, and stood uncomfortably in the foyer of the dwelling long occupied by the Drelves' Teachers. The title "Teacher" overwhelmed the young she-Drelve.

"I am the spiritual and educational leader of my people the Drelves," Morganne somberly muttered aloud.

How did the gray stone bestow the knowledge of Edkim upon her?

Why did the Teacher choose her as his successor?

Did Edkim choose her?

Hundreds of more experienced Drelves lived in Alms Glen, and she was an outsider of sorts. Morganne attended the enhancing plants at Green Vale and met many Drelves from Alms Glen, including Gaelyss, Edkim, Kirrie, Rumsie, Beaux, Klunkus, Meryt, Bryce, Zack, and Debery. The battle of Lone Oak meadow had made all Drelves brothers and sisters, and the people of Alms Glen had accepted Morganne even before she had become Edkim's successor. Morganne inherited Edkim's knowledge and some insight into the late Teacher's feelings and emotions. Briefly her thoughts returned to her brief interludes with Gaelyss. To actually touch, feel, and kiss him…Morganne managed a smile. She'd already risked her life several times and would willingly again to protect Gaelyss.

The Spellweaver intimidated Morganne. *Spellweavers intimidated everyone!* Working with a Spellweaver was every Teacher's dream. She was five years older than Gaelyss. Perhaps she intimidated him! Morganne again smiled.

Then fatigue overwhelmed her. On the morrow she had much to discuss with the elders, Rumsie, and Gaelyss.

Rest....

Rest was imperative.

Drelvedom had witnessed tragedy. She must visit the outlying hamlets, support all Drelves, and then prepare for the harvest of the enhancing root. The she-Drelve sighed deeply, removed her cloak, and momentarily sat on the couch. The *Teacher* then ascended the spiral stair to the master bedroom, fell onto the soft bed, and fell asleep immediately.

Dreams came. Then redness...

Wisps...

Threads...

Threads of Magick...

Threads of fate...

Threads of time...

Threads connecting worlds ...

Dreams connecting worlds ...

Dreams of Magick...

The Magick of Dreams...

Magick connecting dreams...

Magick connecting worlds...

Dream raiders...

Elf pressure...

Albtraum...

Albträume, elf dreams, nightmares...

Dreams...

...

Ó ∞ Ó

LaVergne, TN USA
12 October 2009
160651LV00002B/5/P